"You make me realize how small my life is at the moment."

He raised a brow.

Becky shook her head as she pressed the button inside the car to close the side door. How could she explain the tumult of emotions racing through her? "We've had dinner twice now."

"Enjoyable both times," he said quickly.

"The first time, you had to hear about my late husband. Tonight we covered all my insecurities about motherhood. Not exactly scintillating conversation on either count."

"It is to me." He took her hand and drew her forward so that they were standing a few paces away from the car door, out of the line of sight of the twins in their car seats. "I can't quite explain it, but everything about you fascinates me."

She laughed. "I might be the least fascinating person in Rambling Rose."

"You are brave, strong, independent, determined, loyal, loving."

"You make me sound better than I am." His words rolled around her brain. Could she actually see herself the way Callum did? She loved the idea of it.

"That is who you are."

The Trouble with Twins

USA TODAY BESTSELLING AUTHOR
MICHELLE MAJOR

&

NEW YORK TIMES BESTSELLING AUTHOR
TINA LEONARD

Previously published as *Fortune's Fresh Start*
and *Her Callahan Family Man*

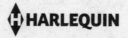

ISBN-13: 978-1-335-41880-7

The Trouble with Twins

Copyright © 2021 by Harlequin Books S.A.

Fortune's Fresh Start
First published in 2019. This edition published in 2021.
Copyright © 2019 by Harlequin Books S.A.

Special thanks and acknowledgment are
given to Michelle Major for her contribution to
The Fortunes of Texas: Rambling Rose continuity.

Her Callahan Family Man
First published in 2014. This edition published in 2021.
Copyright © 2014 by Tina Leonard

**Recycling programs
for this product may
not exist in your area.**

For questions and comments about the quality of this book,
please contact us at CustomerService@Harlequin.com.

Harlequin Enterprises ULC
22 Adelaide St. West, 40th Floor
Toronto, Ontario M5H 4E3, Canada
www.Harlequin.com

Printed in U.S.A.

CONTENTS

Michelle Major grew up in Ohio but dreamed of living in the mountains. Soon after graduating with a degree in journalism, she pointed her car west and settled in Colorado. Her life and house are filled with one great husband, two beautiful kids, a few furry pets and several well-behaved reptiles. She's grateful to have found her passion writing stories with happy endings. Michelle loves to hear from her readers at michellemajor.com.

Books by Michelle Major

Harlequin Special Edition

Crimson, Colorado

Anything for His Baby
A Baby and a Betrothal
Always the Best Man
Christmas on Crimson Mountain
Romancing the Wallflower
Sleigh Bells in Crimson
Coming Home to Crimson

HQN

The Magnolia Sisters

A Magnolia Reunion
The Magnolia Sisters
The Road to Magnolia
The Merriest Magnolia

Visit the Author Profile page at Harlequin.com for more titles.

Fortune's Fresh Start

MICHELLE MAJOR

To Jennie.
Thanks for all the fun times and morning chats.
I treasure our friendship.

Chapter 1

"You're going to be late to your own party."

Callum Fortune turned at the sound of his sister's teasing voice. "It's a ribbon-cutting ceremony, Squeak. Not a cocktail gala."

Stephanie Fortune, younger than Callum by three years but the oldest of David and Marci Fortune's four daughters, approached Callum's shiny silver truck. Her pale red hair was pulled back in a braid and she wore dark jeans and a gray sweater that could have benefited from a lint roller. As a vet tech and all-around animal lover, Stephanie was often covered in dog and cat fur. Or whatever breed of animal she was caring for that day. Her heart was as big as her personality and one of the things Callum loved most about her.

"It's past time you stop calling me that," she told him with an exaggerated eye roll. "What if someone in Rambling Rose hears you and the nickname catches on? I'd be mortified."

"It's our secret," he promised with a wink. "But you'll always be my Pipsqueak no matter where life takes either of us."

"I'm home," Stephanie said, her tone definitive. "There's no other place I'd rather be."

"Then I'm glad you came along on this adventure."

Callum agreed there was something special about Rambling Rose, Texas. The small town sat equidistant between the larger metropolitan areas of Houston and Austin. Callum had first learned about it through a documentary, *The Faded Rose*, he'd watched late one night when he'd had trouble sleeping. Shortly after, he'd traveled to Paseo, Texas, with his father for the wedding of David's brother, Gerald Robinson—or Jerome Fortune as he was once known. On a whim, Callum had driven to Rambling Rose and within a week he'd made offers on a ranch in a gated community outside town as well as a half-dozen commercial properties.

Real estate development was Callum's passion, and he'd made a name for himself in his home state of Florida and a good portion of the Southeast as someone who could revitalize small-town communities by working together with residents, local businesses and government agencies. He loved the challenge of breathing new life into spaces that had seen better days.

From that perspective, Rambling Rose was a perfect next step in Callum's career. The town had a long history in Texas but was sorely in need of a face-lift and someone to invest in the local economy. Callum's father, David, had his doubts. The entire Fortune family, both new and established members, had been shaken by the kidnapping that had almost ruined Gerald's wedding to his first love, Deborah, six months ago. David was a huge success in his own right thanks to his wildly profitable video game empire and had reservations about claiming his place in the extended Fortune brood even before that shocking turn of events. Even though the day had turned out happily in the end, David's protective instincts had kicked into high gear. He'd encouraged his eight children to stay far removed from any sort of involvement with the Texas Fortunes.

He and Marci, Callum's beloved stepmother, had been understandably concerned at Callum's rash decision to move to the small town, especially when his older stepbrother, Steven, younger brother, Dillon, and half sister, Stephanie, came with him. But Callum trusted his instincts when it came to real estate. He had no doubt Rambling Rose was the right decision, and his siblings' joining him was an added bonus.

He stood with Stephanie in the parking lot of the new Rambling Rose Pediatric Center, which was due to officially open its doors in two days. Callum was proud of everything his crew and the subcontractors he'd hired had accomplished in the past few months.

The building, which was situated about ten minutes north of Rambling Rose's quaint downtown area, had been almost completely gutted and rebuilt to house a state-of-the-art health facility where local children would receive primary medical, dental and behavioral health care at a facility designed just for them.

"We should go in," he said before Stephanie asked the inevitable question of whether he saw himself staying in Rambling Rose long-term. She wouldn't have wanted to hear his answer, but the thought of committing to the town longer than it would take to finish their projects made his skin itch.

Since he'd started his construction company, his modus operandi had always been to go with the work. He focused his efforts on small-town revitalizations but once he'd met his goals in a community, Callum moved on.

He wasn't a forever type of guy, at least not anymore.

"How are things at the vet clinic?" Stephanie asked as she fell into step next to him.

"On schedule to open next month," he answered, giving her a gentle nudge. "Don't worry, Squeak. We'll make sure you're still gainfully employed."

She gave him a playful nudge. "What do I have to do to get you to stop calling me that?"

"The dishes and my laundry for a week."

"Done."

He chuckled. "I should have held out for a month."

"Don't push your luck. I know how much you hate folding clothes."

"Been there, done that," he told her. He'd been three and his brother Dillon two when their father had married Marci. She'd had two boys of her own that she brought to the marriage: Steven, who was two years older than Callum, and Wiley, who was Callum's age. They'd had Stephanie right away and the triplets had followed five years after that. Marci was a great mother and treated all the kids with the same love and kindness. But the pregnancies had taken a toll on her health.

As a young boy, Callum had found himself responsible for the girls and running much of the household while his father focused on the explosive success of his first video game launch. The role had come naturally to Callum, but the added responsibility had robbed him of much of his childhood. He'd managed laundry for a household of ten from the time he was in elementary school until Marci's health had improved.

He didn't regret the time he'd dedicated to his siblings, but it definitely made him less inclined to take on more domestic tasks than were necessary to function as an adult.

"You still can't fold a fitted sheet the right way," Stephanie said in the flippant tone she'd perfected as an adorable but annoying little sister.

"No one can," he countered.

"Martha Stewart has a tutorial on it."

He shook his head as they approached the entrance of the pediatric center, where a small crowd had gathered. "I'm not watching Martha Stewart."

A flash of color caught his eye, and he noticed a woman pushing a double stroller toward the entrance. Two toddlers sat in the side-by-side seats, and one girl's blanket had slipped off her lap. The corner of the fabric was tangled in the wheel and the girls' frazzled-looking mother struggled to free it.

"There are Mom and Dad, with Steven and Dillon," Stephanie told him, taking a step toward their family, who stood near the swath of ceremonial ribbon that stretched in front of the center's entrance.

"Be there in a sec."

Without waiting for an answer, Callum jogged toward the woman and her two charges.

"Can I help?" he asked, offering a smile to the toddlers, who were mirror images of each other. Twins. No wonder their mom seemed stressed. He remembered what a handful his triplet sisters had been at that age.

The woman, who knelt on the pavement in a bright

blue dress, looked up at him. Callum promptly forgot his own name.

She was beyond beautiful…at least to him.

A lock of whiskey-hued hair fell across her cheek, and she tucked it behind her ear with a careless motion. Her features were conventional by most standards—a heart-shaped face, large brown eyes with thick lashes and creamy skin that turned an enchanting shade of pink as she met his gaze. Her mouth was full and her nose pert, but somehow everything came together to make her stunning. The sparkle in her gaze and the way her lips parted just a bit had him feeling like he'd been knocked in the head.

"It's caught in the wheel," she said, and it took him a moment to snap back to reality.

"Mama," one of the girls whined, tugging on the other end of the blanket.

"We'll get your blankie, Luna." The woman patted her daughter's leg. "This nice man is going to help."

Nice man. Callum wasn't sure he'd ever heard anyone describe him as "nice" but he'd take the compliment. He tried to remember the definition of the word while forcing himself to ignore the spark of attraction to a stranger who was probably some equally nice man's wife.

He crouched down next to the twins' mom and carefully extricated the fabric from the spokes of the wheel. It took only a minute and he heard an audible sigh of relief next to him once the blanket was free.

"Bankie," the girl shouted as she tugged the pink-and-yellow-checked blanket into her lap.

"Mama," her sister yelled like she wanted to be in on the action and then popped a pacifier into her mouth.

"Thank you," the woman said as they both straightened.

Callum was about to introduce himself when she stumbled a step. Without thinking, he reached out a hand to steady her.

"Are you okay?"

She flashed a sheepish smile. "Sorry. I stood up too fast. I didn't have time for breakfast today but managed two cups of coffee. Low blood sugar."

Callum had to bite back an invitation to go get breakfast with him even as he surreptitiously glanced at her left hand. No wedding ring, which didn't necessarily mean anything. Still, he could—

"Callum!"

He turned at the sound of his name. Steven waved at him from across the clusters of people gathered for the ceremony. Right. He was here for business, not to lose his head over a pretty woman.

His turn for an apologetic smile. "I have to go," he said.

She nodded. "Thanks again."

"You should eat something," he told her, then forced himself to wave at the girls and turn away after his brother called to him again.

Odd how difficult it was to walk away from a perfect stranger.

"The pediatric center would just be a dream for this community without the work of Callum, Steven and Dillon Fortune and everyone at Fortune Brothers Construction."

Becky Averill watched as Rambling Rose's effervescent mayor, Ellie Hernandez, motioned for the brothers to join her in front of the blue ribbon. How was it possible that Becky's stroller catastrophe hero was also the man she had to thank for her new job?

When the pediatric center officially opened a few days from now, she'd be the head nurse in the primary care department, reporting directly to Dr. Parker Green, who was heading up the entire center.

It was such a huge step up from her last position working part-time for an older family practice doctor who saw patients only a few days a week. In fact, it was Becky's dream job, one that would provide a livable wage, great health benefits for her and her girls as well as on-site day care. She couldn't believe how far she'd come from that horrible moment two years ago when a police officer had knocked on her door to relay the news that her husband had died in a car accident.

Becky had been only nine weeks pregnant when Rick died. They hadn't even learned she was expecting twins yet. Everything about her pregnancy had become a blur after that, as if she'd been living in some kind of hazy fog that never lifted.

Of course, things had become crystal clear the moment she heard her baby's first cry. Luna had been born two minutes before Sasha, but both babies filled Becky's heart with a new kind of hope for a future.

Her parents had wanted her to move back to the suburbs of Houston, but she refused. She and Rick had chosen Rambling Rose together, and despite being essentially alone in the small community, she never doubted that she belonged there.

Her girls were sixteen months old now, and life as a single mother hadn't exactly been a cakewalk. Rick's small life insurance policy had covered funeral expenses and allowed her to make her mortgage payments each month, but there hadn't been much left once she covered the essentials.

Not that she needed much for herself, but she wanted to give her daughters a good life. This job would go a long way toward her goal, but not if she messed it up by making a fool of herself before the center even opened.

Which was what she'd almost done with Callum Fortune. She hadn't been lying about missing breakfast, but her light-headedness had more to do with her reaction to the handsome stranger who'd come to her rescue.

Between work and caring for her girls, Becky hadn't even realized her heart could still flutter the way it did when Callum's dark gaze met hers. Butterflies had danced across her stomach and she'd had a difficult time pulling air into her lungs. Most women probably had the same inclination toward Callum. He would have been a standout in a big city like Dallas or Houston, but in the tiny town of Rambling Rose he was like a Greek god come to life.

Even now, her heart stuttered as she watched him smile at Ellie. Then his gaze tracked to hers, as if he could feel her eyes on him. His expression didn't change but there was something about the way he looked at her that made awareness prick along her skin. Dropping her gaze, she shoved a hand in the diaper bag that hung off the back of the stroller and pulled out a plastic container of dried cereal. The girls immediately perked up and she sprinkled a few oat bits into the stroller's tray before shoving a handful into her mouth. She really did need to remember breakfast.

Certainly an empty stomach was to blame for her dizziness, not the way Callum made her feel.

They cut the ribbon and the crowd, made up mostly of new employees of the center, cheered.

Luna clapped her hands at the noise while Sasha's chin trembled.

"It's okay, sweetie." Becky bent down and dropped a soothing kiss on her shy girl's cheek. "It's happy noise."

Sasha's big eyes widened farther as she looked around but after a moment she let out a sigh and settled back against the seat.

Meltdown averted. At least for now.

With twins, Becky rarely went for any long period without some sort of minor toddler crisis, but she wouldn't change a thing about either of her girls.

Callum and the rest of the pediatric center's VIPs had disappeared into the main lobby by the time Becky straightened.

"I hear they have cupcakes inside," a woman said as she passed Becky. "Your girls might like one."

"They're a little young for cupcakes," Becky answered with a laugh. "But I could use a treat."

"Those Fortune men are a treat for the eyes," the older woman said, giving Becky a quick wink. "If I were twenty years younger and not married…"

Becky was plenty young but also far too exhausted to consider dating. At least the fact that she could appreciate Callum's movie-star good looks proved motherhood hadn't destroyed her girlie parts completely.

As they approached the entrance, the woman asked, "You're the one who lost her husband a couple of years ago, right?"

She nodded, considering the joys and pitfalls of living in a small town.

"It's good you stayed in Rambling Rose. We take care

of our own. I'm Sarah. My husband, Grant, is the building manager for the pediatric center." The automatic doors whooshed open, and they walked into the lobby together. "Our kids are grown and moved away, so I've got more time on my hands than I can fill right now. If you ever need help—"

"Thank you," Becky said, forcing a smile. "I appreciate the offer, but I've got things under control."

Sarah gave her a funny look but nodded. "I understand. If you change your mind, Grant can get you my number."

Becky kept the smile fixed on her face until the woman walked away, then pressed two fingers to her forehead and drew in a steadying breath. She'd received at least a dozen similar offers since the twins' birth and had rejected every one. She hadn't really lied to Sarah. At this exact moment, she did have things under control. The girls were both sitting contentedly in the stroller watching the crowd.

Of course, things could go south at any moment. She'd handle that, too, on her own. She took the girls to a day care center when she worked, but otherwise didn't like to accept help. It had been her choice to stay in this town where she had no family. She didn't want people to think she was some kind of over-her-head charity case, even though most days she felt like she was treading water in the middle of the ocean.

But she didn't focus on that. She just kept her legs and arms moving so that she wouldn't go under. Her girls deserved the best she had to give, and she wouldn't settle for offering them anything less.

She was pushing the stroller toward the refreshment table when someone stepped in front of her path.

"Cupcake?" Callum Fortune asked.

Becky's mouth went suddenly dry, but she took the iced pastry from him. "Thanks," she whispered, then cleared her throat. "You did a great job with the building."

He shrugged but looked pleased by the compliment. "I love rehabbing old spaces, and this one is special."

"Ellie mentioned in her speech that the building used to house an orphanage." Becky took a small bite of cupcake and failed to smother a sigh of pleasure. It tasted so good.

Callum grinned. "Breakfast of champions," he told her with a wink. "And, yes. It was called Fortune's Foundling Hospital and dated back to the founding of Rambling Rose."

"Your family's ties to the town go back that far?"

"Apparently. I'll admit I'm still getting caught up on all the different branches of the Fortunes spread across Texas."

"You're royalty here," she told him, but he shook his head.

"Not me. I'm just a guy who loves construction."

"I think you're more than that." As soon as the words were out of her mouth, she regretted them. Somehow they sounded too familiar. People surrounded them, but for Becky the thread of connection pulsing between her and Callum gave the moment an air of intimacy that shocked and intrigued her.

His mouth quirked into a sexy half grin. "I appreciate—"

Suddenly, a woman burst into the lobby, clutching her very round belly. "Help me!" she cried. "I think I'm in labor."

"Get a gurney," Dr. Green shouted, elbowing his way through the crowd.

Becky took an instinctive step forward. Panic was clear on the woman's delicate features, and Becky understood that panic could accompany childbirth. But she couldn't leave her girls unattended.

Dr. Green straightened, his gaze searching the crowd until it alighted on her. "Becky, I need you," he called across the lobby.

She nodded and turned to Callum.

"I've got the girls," he told her without missing a beat. "Go."

She worked to calm her racing heart as adrenaline pumped through her. "Are you sure?"

She gave each of the girls a quick kiss and the assurance that Mommy would be back soon, then hurried toward the first patient in her new job.

"They're safe with me," he assured her, and although she'd just met Callum Fortune, she didn't doubt him for a moment.

Chapter 2

"Who knew Callum was such a spectacular nanny?" Steven asked an hour later, chuckling at his own joke.

Callum fought the urge to give his older stepbrother and business partner the one-fingered salute. Two adorable toddlers watched him from where they sat on a blanket he'd spread out in the pediatric center's lobby, so he wasn't about to model that kind of behavior.

The ribbon-cutting attendees had long since departed, the celebration cut short by the arrival of the pregnant stranger. Neither Parker Green nor the girls' mother had made an appearance again, and he wondered at the fate of the soon-to-be mom and her baby.

"We all know Callum is amazing with babies and children," Marci told Steven. "I'm not sure what I would have done without him when you all were little."

Steven was one of Marci's two sons from her first

marriage, but Callum's father had adopted both boys shortly after marrying his mother. The blended family had felt strange at first, but Stephanie's birth had solidified the bond they all shared. When Callum's construction business started to grow, Steven had joined him as a business partner, with Dillon coming on board soon after that. He'd changed the company name to more aptly describe their partnership, and Fortune Brothers Construction was still going strong.

"He'll be a great father one day," Callum's dad added with a knowing nod, prompting Steven and Callum to share an equally exasperated look. It was no secret their parents were intent on seeing both siblings happily married and starting families of their own.

Callum hadn't discussed future plans with his brother but got the impression Steven was as reluctant to settle down as Callum.

Stephanie walked through the doors that led to the center's small cafeteria. "I found plastic cups and spoons," she said. Callum had sent her in search of items to entertain the twins.

He took the makeshift toys and began stacking cups. The more confident of the girls, Luna, clapped her hands as if encouraging him to continue. He handed her a plastic spoon, which she waved in the air like a magic wand. One of the other nurses had told him the twins' names and that their mother was Becky Averill.

He'd asked about calling a husband and had been shocked to learn that Becky was a widow and single mom. It made him feel like even more of a heel for chastising her about breakfast. Becky was clearly an amazing woman, raising two children on her own while balancing a demanding career. No wonder she forgot to eat.

The shy twin, Sasha, scooted toward him. He held out a spoon to her, his chest tightening when her bottom lip trembled.

"Don't cry, darlin'," he told her softly and then scooped her into his arms. It had been an instinctual move. Callum had held plenty of babies when his sisters were younger. Sasha went rigid in his arms. Had he made a huge mistake? Then she relaxed against him with a quiet sigh, smelling like baby shampoo and oat cereal.

The front doors opened and two paramedics strode in. A moment later, Becky appeared from the medical clinic wing of the center. She and Dr. Green were wheeling out the pregnant stranger. The woman, a pretty brunette with big blue eyes, kept her worried gaze fixed on Becky, who appeared to be talking the patient through whatever was happening now.

There was no baby, and the woman seemed stable, so Callum could only assume things were good. Glancing over, Becky's expression softened as she caught sight of her twins. She said something to the pregnant patient, offered a quick hug and then walked toward Callum.

"How is she?" Stephanie asked immediately.

"We've given her something to slow her labor," Becky explained. "The baby's vitals are good, but Dr. Green thinks it will be better for her to give birth at a facility with a NICU. The paramedics are going to take her to San Antonio."

Callum's father nodded. "So she and the baby will be okay?"

"They should both come out of this healthy," Becky told them.

"Thank heavens," Marci added.

Callum stood, still holding Sasha in his arms. "It's

a good thing you and Parker were here for the ribbon cutting."

"Dr. Green was essential," Becky clarified. "Anyone could have done what I did." She held out her hands, and Sasha reached for her, leaving Callum with an unfamiliar sense of emptiness.

"I doubt that's true," he answered. "You stepped in to help that woman without hesitation."

"I also foisted my kids off on you, and I appreciate you volunteering to watch them." She glanced down at Luna, who was still happily occupied with the spoon and cups, and then gave him a hesitant smile. "I'm Becky, by the way."

"One of the nurses told me," he said, that small smile doing funny things to his insides.

"You volunteered?" Marci stepped forward, patting Callum's shoulders. "I'm so proud."

"It wasn't a big deal," he mumbled.

"Your daughters are adorable," she said to Becky. "I'm Marci Fortune." She gestured to Callum's father and siblings. "My husband, David, and our daughter, Stephanie." Her smiled widened. "You know Callum, obviously. These are two of our other sons, Dillon and Steven."

Becky's caramel-colored eyes widened a fraction. "How many kids do you have?"

"Eight," Marci said proudly and without hesitation. Callum had always appreciated that his stepmother never differentiated between the children who were hers biologically and the two boys she'd taken on after marrying David.

"Wow," Becky murmured. "You must have been really busy."

"It's how we liked it," Marci assured her. She put a hand on Callum's arm. "Callum was such a help with his younger sisters. We also have triplets—Ashley, Megan and Nicole."

Dillon stepped forward. "Callum's nickname was Mary Poppins," he said in a not-so-quiet whisper.

Stephanie laughed while Becky tried to smother her smile.

"No one called me that," Callum told his brother with an eye roll. "Don't you all have somewhere to be?"

"You'd think with eight children," Marci said to Becky, ignoring Callum's question, "that we'd have a few grandchildren already."

"Gotta go," Dillon announced in response.

"Me, too," Steven added.

Stephanie grabbed her eldest brother's elbow. "I'll walk out with you."

Callum silently cursed his siblings as each of them gave Marci a peck on the cheek, told Becky it was nice to meet her and then quickly made their escape.

"You know how to clear a room, dear," David said, wrapping an arm around his wife's slim shoulders.

Marci only laughed. "I'd be an amazing grammy."

"Someday," her husband promised. "But we should go, too. We have a long drive to the airport."

Luna had lost interest in the makeshift toys and pulled herself up, then toddled over to Becky, who lifted her without missing a beat. "You aren't from Texas?" she asked Callum's parents.

David shook his head. "Fort Lauderdale, Florida. We flew in to see Callum's latest success. It's been quite an adjustment having four of our children move halfway across the country."

"The pediatric center is amazing," Becky said, glancing at Callum from beneath thick lashes. "It's lovely that you came all this way."

"Are you close to your parents?" Marci asked her.

Callum gave his father a look over the top of his stepmother's head. As much as he loved his big family, their friendly exuberance could be overwhelming. He didn't want to scare off Becky before he'd even had a chance for a proper conversation with her.

Before Becky could answer, David reiterated the need to get to the airport.

"I'll walk you out," Callum told them, then reached out and touched a hand to one of Luna's wispy curls. "Becky, I'll be right back."

She gave a quick nod, then seemed shocked when Marci leaned in and enveloped both her and the twins in a hug.

Marci turned to Callum at the entrance of the pediatric center. "She seems like a lovely girl," she said, her tone purposefully light.

"She's a single mother of twins," Callum felt obliged to point out. "And a widow."

"Tragic," Marci agreed as they walked into the cool January day. "I feel for those babies and for her. She deserves to find happiness again."

"It's not with me," Callum said. "I've committed to staying in Rambling Rose until the final project wraps up. Who knows what will happen beyond then?"

"I like this town more than I expected to," his father interjected. "Of course, we'd love to see you back in Florida or somewhere closer, but if Texas makes you happy, that's most important."

"What about your mandate that we stay away from the Fortunes?"

David quirked a brow. "The only Fortunes in Rambling Rose are you and your siblings. I can live with that."

Callum walked them to the black sedan his father had rented. "Thank you both for coming to the opening." He hugged Marci first and then his father. "I'm proud of what we've accomplished here in such a short time."

"You should be," his father said.

"We're proud of you, as well," Marci added. "We always have been. But you work too much, Callum. Don't forget to take some time for yourself."

He didn't bother to argue. They wouldn't understand that his career fulfilled him in a way nothing else had. He knew people considered him a workaholic. Hell, that had been the main cause of his divorce. His ex-wife, Doralee, couldn't accept his hours or his dedication to the projects he managed.

But nothing made him happier than revitalizing older and historic commercial districts.

They said another round of goodbyes, and his parents climbed into their car and drove out of the parking lot.

As he walked back toward the entrance, Becky emerged, pushing the stroller.

"Thank you again," she said as he caught up to her. "I'd really like to repay you for your help today."

"No need." He held up his hands. "Thanks for stepping in with that woman. She seemed so terrified when she walked into the center."

A shadow seemed to darken Becky's delicate features. "She was scared and alone," she said, almost to herself. "And about to take on the greatest responsibility of her life."

"She didn't have a boyfriend or husband somewhere?" he couldn't help but ask. He fell in step next to Becky as she walked toward a nondescript minivan at the edge of the parking lot.

"Not that she'd tell us." She once again tucked her hair behind an ear and glanced over at him. "No family, either. I know how it feels to be alone, but there was something different about her. It was as if she was a speck of dandelion fluff floating in a breeze with no place to land." She let out a soft laugh. "I'm sure that sounds silly, but the woman—Laurel was her name—seemed like she really wanted to find a place to land."

"It sounds insightful," Callum murmured. In a single instant, his attraction to Becky Averill had gone from a physical spark to something more, something deeper.

"Sleep deprivation has robbed me of too many brain cells to be considered insightful." She pulled a key fob out of her bag and used it to open the minivan's side doors and cargo hold. "But I do feel for Laurel. I hope she and her baby flourish wherever she ends up."

Callum wanted to offer to do something to help with the twins and their stroller, but he felt like he needed to keep his distance. He'd been totally astounded by this woman today, but he had no place in her life and nothing to offer her. If his ex-wife had accused him of working too much, what would a single mother think of his crazy hours?

It didn't matter, he reminded himself as Becky turned to him with a tentative smile. "Are you sure there's no way I can thank you for today?" she asked. "I'm a pretty good cook and—"

"It's fine," he said, realizing how harsh he sounded only when her brows furrowed. "It was nice to meet you, Becky." He made his tone friendly but neutral. "You have cute kids." Without waiting for a response, he turned and walked away.

Becky finished with her final patient of the day, a three-year-old with double ear infections, and glanced at her watch as she walked toward the nursing station.

"Girl, you've been holding out on us." Sharla, one of the medical assistants in the primary care wing of the pediatric center, wagged a finger in Becky's direction. "We just heard Callum Fortune was your babysitter when that pregnant lady came in during the ribbon-cutting shindig."

Becky willed her face not to heat, but felt a blush rising to her cheeks anyway. This was her third shift at the center, and so far she'd loved every minute of it. Dr. Green, or Parker, as he insisted she call him when they weren't with patients, was an intelligent and caring physician. He had a rapport with both children and their parents, and Becky could see he took the utmost care with every patient.

Sharla and the other two nurses, Kristen and Samantha, were friendly and easy to talk to, and they all had good things to say about the doctors at the center. Becky had worked in enough different offices to appreciate the setup here.

"He offered to help," she said with what she hoped was a casual shrug. "It wasn't a big deal."

"Are you blind?" Kristen asked. "That man is ten kinds of a big deal."

"His brothers are just as hot," Samantha added.

"They aren't as handsome as Callum." Becky couldn't help the comment. Yes, the Fortune family had won the genetic lottery, but only Callum made her heart race. Every time she thought of the intensity of his dark gaze, her body seemed to heat from the inside out.

Sharla let out a peal of laughter. "I knew you had to notice."

"I'm a single mom," Becky muttered. "Not dead."

"So what are you going to do about it?" Kristen asked.

"There's nothing to be done." Becky placed the digital device she used for electronically entering patient data on the charging station. She wasn't going to admit to these three women that she'd offered to repay him for his kindness and he'd all but bolted from her.

Maybe it had been the minivan or her silly musings about the pregnant stranger or the reality of a woman with two toddlers in tow. Any one of those would have been a turnoff to a man. Add to that her reputation in town as the grieving widow and it was no wonder Callum had made a quick exit.

She'd obviously mistaken the intriguing thread of attraction between them or it had been all one-sided. No one would blame her for harboring a few harmless fantasies about a man like Callum, but that's all they were.

"My brother's insulation company is working on all of the Fortune Brothers Construction projects." Kristen tapped a finger to her chin, her green eyes sparkling. "I could get him to tell me when Callum is at one of the job sites and you could make an appearance there. He said all three Fortune brothers are really hands-on."

Sharla laughed again. "I'd like some Fortune hands on me."

Becky shook her head while the other two women

joined in the joke. "I can't just show up at some construction site. What am I going to say? Remember me and will you hold one of my babies while I change the other one's dirty diaper?"

"Not the best pickup line I've heard," Samantha admitted.

Becky hadn't ever used a line on a man. Rick had been her first boyfriend. They'd met at freshmen orientation and dated through college, waiting to get married until after graduation because that's what her family wanted. He'd been an only child and not really close to his parents, who lived on the East Coast. Her mom and dad had expected her to hold off on marriage even longer, and their constant reminder that she and Rick had their whole lives to settle down had irritated Becky from the start. If she knew then what she did now, she would have married him right away so that they could have had more time together as a family.

No one could have predicted the car accident that had killed him, and Becky would always be grateful for the years he'd been a part of her life. But often she stayed busy, gave everything she had and more, because she was afraid if she ever stopped moving it might be too difficult to get up again.

"I'm not interested anyway," Becky lied. "I have too much going on to think about—"

"He's here," Sharla whispered.

All three of Becky's coworkers glanced at a place directly behind her, then quickly busied themselves.

As the fine hairs along the back of her neck stood on end, Becky turned around and came face-to-face with Callum Fortune.

"Hello," he said, running a hand through his thick

mane of wavy dark hair. "I hope I'm not interrupting." He was dressed more casually today in a blue button-down shirt, dark jeans and cowboy boots. Callum looked perfect and she was painfully aware of her messy bun and the shapeless scrubs that were her work uniform. She glanced down to see some sort of crusty stain—probably baby spit-up—on her shoulder. Great. He looked like he owned the place, which he sort of did, and she was a scattered mess.

"Nope." Becky cleared her throat when the word came out a squeak. "I'm just finishing my shift and about to pick up the girls from day care."

She gave herself a mental head slap. Like he needed a reminder that she was a single mom with two young daughters.

"I'll walk with you," he offered.

"Oh." She stood there for a moment, trying to remember how to pull air in and out of her lungs.

"You remember where the day care's located, Becky?" Sharla asked from behind her. "Far end of the building and to the right."

She narrowed her eyes as she glanced at the other woman. "I remember. Thanks."

Callum offered a friendly smile as they started down the hall. "How's work going?"

"It's great," she said. "The facility is really great. The staff has been—"

"Great?" he asked with a wink.

"Sorry," she said automatically. "I'm always a little brain dead at the end of the day."

"Understandable. I can't imagine balancing everything you handle."

"It's not a big deal." She hated drawing attention to

her situation. Becky found that the best way to stave off being overwhelmed was not to think about it. "I like to stay busy. What brings you to the center?"

She frowned as Callum seemed to stiffen next to her. Had she said the wrong thing again?

"Um... I needed to check on...some stuff."

"Sounds technical."

That drew a smile from him, and she felt inexorably proud that she'd amused him, even in a small way.

"I didn't mean to rush off the other day after the ribbon cutting," he told her as they approached the door that led to the child care center. "I think I interrupted a potential invitation for dinner, and I've been regretting it ever since."

Becky blinked. In truth, she would have never had the guts to invite Callum for dinner. She'd been planning to offer to cook or bake for him and drop it off to his office as a thank-you. The idea of having him to her small house did funny things to her insides.

"Oh," she said again.

"Maybe I misinterpreted," Callum said quickly, looking as flummoxed as she felt. "Or imagined the whole thing. You meant to thank me with a bottle of wine or some cookies or—"

"Dinner." She grinned at him. Somehow his discomposure gave her the confidence to say the word. He appeared so perfect and out of her league, but at the moment he simply seemed like a normal, nervous guy not sure what to say next.

She decided to make it easy for him. For both of them. "Would you come for dinner tomorrow night? The girls go to bed early so if you could be there around seven, we could have a more leisurely meal and a chance to talk."

His shoulders visibly relaxed. "I'd like that. Dinner with a friend. Can I bring anything?"

"Just yourself," she told him.

He pulled his cell phone from his pocket and handed it to her so she could enter her contact information. It took a few tries to get it right because her fingers trembled slightly.

He grinned at her as he took the phone again. "I'm looking forward to tomorrow, Becky."

"Me, too," she breathed, then gave a little wave as he said goodbye. She took a few steadying breaths before heading in to pick up the twins. *Don't turn it into something more than it is*, she cautioned herself.

It was a thank-you, not a date. Her babies would be asleep in the next room. Definitely not a date.

But her stammering heart didn't seem to get the message.

Chapter 3

Callum stood outside the soon-to-open veterinary clinic the following afternoon, frowning at the open back of the delivery truck.

"It's all pink," Stephanie reported.

"I see that," he answered, then turned to the driver. "We ordered modular cabinets in a pine finish."

"I just deliver what they give me," the man responded, scratching his belly. "Where do you want 'em?"

"Not here." Callum looked toward Steven, who was on his phone, pacing back and forth in front of the building's entrance.

His brother held up a finger and then returned to the phone call.

"This is a vet clinic." Stephanie gave a humorless laugh. "Not an ice cream parlor."

The cabinetry for the exam rooms and clinical areas

had been ordered more than a month earlier. They needed it installed soon in order to keep the project on time and within budget. Callum and his brothers were sharing the responsibility of the vet clinic renovation, working with the staff of the local practice to design the space.

A moment later, Steven joined the group. "Take it back," he told the delivery driver before turning to Callum and Stephanie. "It was a clerical error. They typed in the wrong color code."

"Whatever you say, boss," the driver answered and pulled shut the overhead door of the delivery truck.

"It would have been my dream come true when I was eight," Stephanie said as the driver climbed into the vehicle and pulled away. "Working in a pink vet clinic."

"Where does that put us as far as the schedule?" Callum asked.

Steven's mouth tightened into a thin line. "I can get it done."

"I know that." Callum nodded, understanding that his older brother didn't appreciate being doubted. "I'm asking because if you need me to shift resources from other projects or change subcontractor timelines, we can make it work."

Steven's shoulders relaxed under his Western-style button-down shirt. "It's going to be tight. The supplier is putting a rush on the order so the cabinets should be here in two weeks. I can have the crew work on the flooring and finish the exterior. It's not ideal, but we'll make sure nothing falls behind."

"Let me know if we need to change our move-in date." Stephanie addressed them both. She not only worked at the current location of the vet center, but also acted as the liaison with the construction crew. "It's going to be all hands on deck at Paws and Claws to make it a smooth transition for our patients."

"Got it." Steven chuckled, then muttered, "Pink cabinets. We've had some strange setbacks, but that one might be the most colorful."

"If that's the worst unforeseen stumbling block in this whole process," Callum said, "I'll take it."

"The pediatric center opened without a hitch." Stephanie scrunched up her nose. "Other than a woman almost giving birth in the lobby."

Callum nodded. "I stopped by today, and the facility is already busy. Clearly there was a need for a children's health clinic in Rambling Rose."

"It feels like the town grows every day," Stephanie observed. "Have you noticed the new houses being built down the road from the ranch?"

Steven rubbed his thumb and fingers together. "Lots of money coming into the community. Hopefully that will mean plenty of business for each of our new ventures."

"Who needs a margarita?" Stephanie asked. "The pink cabinet fiasco made my head hurt, but it's nothing a salted rim along with a big plate of enchiladas won't cure."

"I'm in," Steven said.

Callum pulled out his phone and checked the time on the home screen. "I'll have to take a rain check. I have dinner plans tonight." He responded to a text from his foreman, then glanced up to find his brother and sister staring at him with equally curious expressions.

"Spill it," Stephanie said.

Callum feigned confusion. "What are you talking about?"

"He's evading answering." Steven elbowed their sister. "My money's on the cute nurse from the other day."

"He bombed out with her before he even got a chance," Stephanie said. "Tell me it's not that barista at the coffee shop in town who always flirts with you. She has crazy eyes."

"Enough with the inquisition." This was the issue with coming from such a close-knit family. Since they'd moved to Rambling Rose, he and his siblings had mostly hung out together. Sure, each of them had made a few casual friends. But they stuck together. The ranch they'd purchased just outside town had a sprawling main house as well as several guesthouses on the multiacre property.

He figured if his brothers and sister ever wanted more privacy in Rambling Rose, he'd buy out their portion of the ranch. But none of them seemed inclined to move out on their own anytime soon. It worked for Callum. He'd needed space after going to school at a local college in Florida. That was part of the reason he'd started looking for projects to take on in other areas of the Southeast. Coming from such a big family and growing up with so much responsibility for Stephanie and the triplets on his shoulders, he'd needed a break.

But after the wreck of his short marriage and subsequent divorce, life had become too quiet. Now he liked being close to his siblings. It had made the move to Texas not so daunting and gave him a sense of confidence, which was probably why he'd taken on a slate of so many ambitious projects.

"Then tell us," Stephanie prodded. "Don't think I won't follow you. Remember when I was in eighth grade and crashed your date with Ava Martin after you snuck out to meet her?"

"How could I forget?" he replied, trying and failing to hide his smile. "I got grounded for a month."

"You were already grounded, which is why you got in even more trouble."

"No one is going to ground me now," he told her.

"Come on, Callum. Just spill it."

"I'm having dinner with Becky from the pediatric center."

"Called it." Steven did an enthusiastic fist pump. "You were so obvious the other day."

"I wasn't obvious," Callum said through clenched teeth. "I was helpful, and she's thanking me with dinner."

"How romantic," Stephanie said in a singsong voice.

"Her twins will be sleeping in their bedroom. It's hardly romantic."

"Mom and Dad had four boys under the age of five when they were first married," Steven reminded them. "They still managed to find some time for romance."

"This isn't anywhere near the same thing, and you both know it. You're just trying to get under my skin."

Stephanie wiggled her eyebrows. "It's working, too. I can tell." She leaned closer. "I can also tell you like her. You were pretty obvious at the ribbon cutting."

"Go back to Florida," he told her, deadpan.

"I'm like a rash," she countered. "You can't get rid of me."

Steven laughed. "You do realize you just compared yourself to a bad skin condition."

"Fitting," Callum said.

Stephanie only rolled her eyes at their gentle ribbing. "What are you bringing?"

Callum shrugged. "Nothing. She said she'd handle it all."

She groaned. "Don't be an idiot right out of the gate. What about flowers or wine or chocolate?"

"You sound like Marci," Callum told her. "Enough with the matchmaking."

"Li'l sis is right," Steven said. "Step up, Callum. Your pretty nurse has been through a lot. Even if it's just a thank-you, make her feel special."

"She's not 'my' anything," he protested, although his heart seemed to pinch at the thought of a woman like Becky belonging to him. He should listen to that subtle sharpening and not get any more involved with her when it could only end badly. "But she is special."

"Then show her," Steven urged, laughing when Stephanie gave him a playful slap. "Hey, what was that for? It's good advice."

"I'm just shocked it came from you."

"Remember, I'm the oldest." Steven pointed a finger at each of them. "That also means I'm the wisest."

"Hardly," Callum said on a half laugh, half cough. But his brother had a point. He didn't know much about Becky Averill, but it was obvious she worked hard, both at her job and taking care of her girls. She deserved to have someone treat her special. Despite knowing he could never be that man, he couldn't help wanting to ignore the truth—even for one night.

The doorbell rang at exactly seven o'clock that night.

Becky stifled a groan as she finished fastening the snaps on Luna's pajamas. "Of all the nights for things to go off the rails," she said to her girls as she lifted them into her arms and hurried toward the front of the small house.

She opened the door to Callum, who stood on the other side holding the most beautiful bouquet of colorful flowers she'd ever seen. "Am I early?" he asked, his dark gaze taking in the twins as well as Becky's bedraggled appearance.

"Bedtime is running late," she answered.

Luna babbled at him and swiped a chubby hand at the flowers while Sasha snuggled more deeply against Becky's shoulder.

"What can I do?"

Her heart did that melty thing she couldn't seem to stop around this man. "Give me five minutes," she told him as she backed into the house. "This night is to thank you for helping the first time, not to force you into another round of child care duties."

"I don't mind," he assured her, grinning at the girls.

"The flowers are beautiful," she said.

"They're for you." He looked down at the bouquet, then up at her again. "You probably guessed that."

Despite her nerves and the craziness of the evening, Becky grinned. "I have a bottle of wine on the counter. Would you open it while I put them down?"

"Sure."

It felt a bit strange to leave him alone in her house when he'd just arrived, but she didn't have a choice.

She began to sing softly to the girls as she made her way back to their bedroom. As if on cue, both Luna and Sasha yawned when Becky turned off the overhead light in the room, leaving the space bathed in only the soft glow from the butterfly night-light plugged in next to the rocking chair in the corner.

She placed them in their cribs, smiling as they babbled to each other in that secret language they seemed to share. She finished the song, gave each one a last kiss and said good-night. After checking the monitor that sat on the dresser, she quietly closed the door to their room.

Once in the hallway, she glanced down at herself and cringed. The twins were normally asleep by six thirty so Becky had thought she'd have a few minutes to freshen up before Callum arrived. She'd changed from her scrubs into a faded T-shirt and black leggings, both of which were wet thanks to the dual tantrums she'd dealt with during bath time.

Hurrying to her bedroom, she changed into a chunky sweater and dark jeans, cursing the fact that she hadn't been shopping for new clothes since before the girls were born. She hadn't done anything for herself in far too long, which was why this night felt so special.

She dabbed a bit of gloss on her lips, fluffed her hair and headed for the kitchen and Callum. Her heartbeat fluttered in her chest once again.

Her reaction to his presence felt silly. He'd helped with her daughters and agreed to come for dinner. Nothing more. He probably regretted it already and was counting the minutes until he could make his escape.

But the warmth in his gaze when he looked up from his phone as she walked into the kitchen told a different story. One that made sparks tingle along her spine.

"You arranged the flowers," she murmured, taking in the bouquet that had been placed in a vase on the table.

"I found a vase in the cabinet." He offered a sheepish smile. "I hope you don't mind. It was one less thing you'd have to deal with tonight."

"They're perfect," she told him, then breathed out a soft laugh. "You can manage multiple construction projects and excel at the art of floral arranging. Quite the Renaissance man, Callum."

Her silly comment seemed to relax them both. She could hardly believe he had nerves in the same way she did, but the thought made her feel more confident.

"Something smells really great," he told her.

"I almost forgot about dinner," she admitted, pulling a face. "It's not fancy, but I hope you like chicken potpie."

"I like everything."

And didn't those words just whisper across her skin like a promise? Becky gave herself a little head shake. He was talking about food and she stood there staring at him like he was the main course.

"My grandma used to make it when we went to her house for Sunday dinner. I make some modifications so the recipe doesn't take so long, but the crust is homemade."

"I'm impressed." He handed her a glass of wine. "To new friends and new beginnings."

She clinked her glass against his and took a drink of the bright pinot grigio. It was only a sip but she would have sworn the tangy liquid went right to her veins, making her feel almost drunk with pleasure.

More likely the man standing in her kitchen caused that. The first man who'd been there with her since her husband's death.

"New beginnings," she repeated softly, then busied herself with dinner preparations.

She'd done most of the work when she got home earlier. The pie was warm in the oven, and the scent of chicken and savory dough filled the air when she took it out and set it on the trivet she'd placed on the kitchen table.

She took a salad from the refrigerator, then frowned at the simple supper. Surely a man like Callum was used to fancier fare.

"I haven't cooked for ages," she admitted as she joined him at the table. "I'm out of practice at entertaining."

As if understanding there was an apology implicit in her words, Callum shook his head. "This looks amazing, and I appreciate you going to the trouble for me."

"It was no trouble." She dished out a huge helping of the classic comfort food onto his plate. "I hope you're hungry."

As he took a first bite, he closed his eyes and groaned in pleasure. "I could eat this every night."

"I used to make things that were more gourmet, but with the girls' bedtime routine I figured I'd have better luck with a recipe I know by heart."

"I'm not much for gourmet."

"That surprises me." She forked up a small piece of crust, pleased that it tasted as good as she remembered. "I figured anyone with the last name of Fortune would be accustomed to the finer things in life."

"Nothing finer than a home-cooked meal," he said, helping himself to another portion.

She chuckled. "Do you always eat so fast?"

"Only when it's this good." He shrugged. "My branch of the family is relatively new to the notoriety of the Texas Fortunes."

"Really? Is that why you moved here? To get your moment in the spotlight?" She mentally kicked herself when he grimaced. He'd helped her and now her nerves had her babbling so much she was going to offend him. "I'm sorry. That came out sounding rude."

"Rambling Rose appealed to me because I'm here in Texas, which gives me a sense of connection with the Fortune legacy, but it also feels like I'm blazing my own path."

"That's important to you?" She stabbed a few pieces of lettuce with her fork.

"Very important. You met my dad and stepmom and three of my siblings. Imagine four more added to the mix. There wasn't much time for individuality growing up. I could hardly do my own thing when I constantly had a brother or younger sister trailing me."

"Are you the oldest?"

He studied his plate for a long second, as if unsure how to answer. "No. Dillon, who was at the ribbon cutting ceremony, is a year younger than me. Our parents divorced when I was a toddler, and Dad met Marci shortly after. They married almost immediately. She also had two boys from her first marriage. Steven is two years older and Wiley is my age, although he has a couple of months on me. It felt like I went from being the oldest to the little brother overnight."

"That's a lot of blending," Becky murmured, not quite able to imagine how that would have felt for a young boy.

He nodded. "We were a handful, especially at the beginning. I think each of us had something to prove. Unfortunately that meant we pushed every one of Marci's buttons any chance we got."

"How did she handle it?"

"Like a champ," Callum confirmed. "I didn't see my real mom much after the divorce, but Marci always made

Dillon and me feel like we were her sons as much as Steven and Wiley. If we were testing her, she passed with flying colors."

"And things got easier?"

"Stephanie was a turning point for the family. She was the most precious thing I'd ever seen. Suddenly, these four rowdy boys had something in common—our sister. She brought us together."

"It's obvious you're close with her."

"Yeah." The softening of his features gave her that fizzy feeling again. "Mom…" He cleared his throat. "Marci became mom to me pretty quickly. She loved having a big family, but had a couple of pregnancies that ended in miscarriage after that. It took a toll on her."

"I can imagine."

Fine lines bracketed his mouth, as if the thought of the woman who'd become a mother to him hurting caused him physical pain, as well.

"Then the triplets were born. They were miracle babies, really."

"Multiples are special," Becky couldn't help but add, thinking of her sweet girls.

"It took Marci some time to recover. There were complications and she wasn't herself for a while after."

"From how she made it sound, you were a huge help."

His big shoulders shifted and an adorable flush of color stained his cheeks. "I kind of had a way with the ladies, even back then."

Laughter burst from Becky's mouth, and the excitement bubbling up in her felt like she'd gulped down a flute of champagne. Was there anything more attractive to a mother than a man who was good with children?

"You certainly worked your charms on Luna and

Sasha," she told him. "They aren't accustomed to having men in their lives."

"Someone told me your husband died while you were pregnant," Callum said quietly. "I'm sorry."

The pleasure rippling through her popped in an instant. Grief had been a sort of companion to her after Rick's death, and she knew the facets of it like the back of her hand.

"It was a car accident," she said. "I'd just taken a home pregnancy test but we didn't know I was carrying twins." She bit down on the inside of her cheek. "I wish I could have shared that with him. I wish I could have shared a lot of things."

She held up a hand when he would have said more because she knew another apology was coming. Not that he had any responsibility, obviously, but people didn't know how to talk to her about the loss she'd suffered. Some things were too unfathomable for words.

"We're okay," she said, which was her pat line even when it wasn't true. Sometimes she struggled, but she was dealing with it and making the best of things for her daughters. She blinked away the tears that stung the backs of her eyes.

"In some ways Rick is still with us," she told Callum. "There's a park outside of town where he and I used to go on walks after work. Now I take Luna and Sasha there when I want to feel close to him. I sit on the bench near the pond and talk to him, and I feel him with us. I know how much he would have loved his girls and he's their guardian angel. Some people don't get that or they think I'm just trying to see the silver lining in a tragedy that has none. But it's what I know."

His cleared his throat as if unsure how to respond.

Becky mentally kicked herself. No guy wanted to spend an evening talking about a woman's dead husband, even for a homecooked meal. This was the reason she could never hope to date, especially not someone like Callum Fortune. She had enough emotional baggage to fill a freight train.

"Can I ask why you stayed in Rambling Rose?" Callum asked after several awkward moments.

She opened her mouth to give him a pat answer, but was somehow unable to tell this man anything but the complete truth. "This was the home Rick and I chose together." She glanced around the small kitchen. "And we picked this town because we wanted to be a part of a close-knit community. Neither of us was tight with our families growing up."

"Do you have brothers and sisters?"

She shook her head. "Only child. Rick was, too." She lifted the wineglass to her lips, watching Callum from beneath her lashes. Maybe it was inappropriate to talk about her late husband with a man she felt attracted to, but Callum's steady presence made her feel like she could share anything with him.

She appreciated that more than she could say. Yes, she'd loved her husband deeply and would give anything to change the tragedy that had stolen their future.

That loss was woven into the fiber of her being. It had formed her into the woman she was today, resilient and fiercely protective of her daughters. She understood the only way to celebrate Rick's life was by honoring what had brought her to this point.

Callum helped her clean up the dishes after they finished dinner, another point in his favor. They said goodbye, and Becky watched him drive away as she tried to tamp down the disappointment at the night ending so soon. Seriously, she needed to get out more. One simple thank-you dinner and she felt like a silly girl with a crush on the most popular boy at school.

Callum had called her a friend and that was how she should think of him, as well. Too bad her body wouldn't cooperate.

Chapter 4

"What's your next move?" Stephanie asked as she joined Callum in the main house's expansive kitchen later that week.

The morning had just begun to dawn, with the sky outside the window turning the Fame and Fortune Ranch a dozen shades of pink and orange.

"I don't have one," he said, keeping his gaze trained on his laptop. He took another drink of coffee as he perused the article on trends in the food and hospitality industry. "What would you think about an upscale restaurant in Rambling Rose?"

"I think it won't compete with the local Mexican food," she said, dropping into a chair across from him at the table.

"The idea isn't to compete," he explained. "I want to expand the options for folks around here. What if you wanted to go on a special date?"

"At this point," Stephanie said with a slightly sad smile that tugged at his heart, "my favorite men have four legs and fur."

Callum hated that his sister seemed to have given up on her chance at love. Unlike him, Stephanie had so much to give. "Hypothetically," he clarified.

"Are *you* looking for a setting for a special date?" Stephanie kicked his shin under the table. "You still haven't said anything about your dinner with Becky the other night. I'm tired of waiting for details."

"She's a great cook," he said.

"I don't care what you ate." Stephanie pushed his laptop closed. "You like her, right?"

"She's nice." Callum reached for his coffee, ignoring his sister's raised brow. Of course, *nice* was a wholly inadequate way to describe Becky. He'd never met anyone like her. She'd suffered a devastating tragedy yet still seemed to be filled with a bright light that wouldn't be dimmed.

He didn't understand the connection he felt with her and knew it could go nowhere even if he wanted it to. Which he didn't because he'd learned his lesson about commitment and getting hurt the hard way. Things were better all around when Callum focused on the parts of his life he could control. Matters of the heart definitely didn't fall into that category.

"What did you talk about?"

"Stuff."

"You know how persistent I can be," she said. "I'll follow you around all day until you spill it." Stephanie grinned when he narrowed his eyes. "Might as well just tell me now."

"We talked about a lot of things." He shrugged. "My family, her family. Her late husband."

She made a soft sound of distress. "Was that awkward?"

"No," he answered simply. Maybe it should have been. Although the way she'd described Rick made the man sound just about perfect. Callum knew he was bound to pale in comparison. There was no use pretending that he'd gone to dinner at Becky's just to be kind. He couldn't stop thinking about her.

He wasn't just attracted to her physically. He wanted to know as much as he could about her, which included her past. Losing a husband so young had obviously played a large part in shaping the person she was today.

"I haven't seen you like this since Doralee." Stephanie tapped a finger on the tabletop, and Callum focused his attention on that instead of meeting her insightful gaze.

"It isn't the same," he muttered.

"I can tell." She leaned forward until he lifted his gaze to hers. "Your divorce doesn't define you, Callum. At least it shouldn't."

"I know," he agreed, although the wreck of his marriage had changed him. All the things he'd thought he wanted from life shifted in the wake of his pain and the blame his ex-wife placed squarely on his shoulders.

He deserved every bit of it. Growing up in a large family had led him to assume the path of marriage and kids was the one that made the most sense for him. But he'd been dedicated to his business and not able to give Doralee the attention she'd wanted. They'd had a whirlwind courtship of only six weeks before getting married, both of them enamored by the heady feeling of new love.

Once the novelty wore off, it had become clear they

weren't compatible in most of the ways that counted. She had unrealistic expectations and he seemed doomed to fail at meeting them. It was a blessing for both of them that she'd had the guts to end things. He hadn't wanted to hurt her but couldn't seem to do anything right. He'd believed he was building a future for the two of them, laying the groundwork for their life together. Turned out to be a foundation built on sand, shifting and crumbling under the pressures of life.

Of course his failings had shaped him, but in a different way from how Becky's had her. She'd had tragedy befall her and risen above it, while he'd been the cause of his own pain. He might be infatuated with her, but he wasn't about to open himself up to that kind of hurt again. Becky's life was complicated and he remained determined to keep his as simple as he could manage.

"You can find love again," Stephanie continued.

"I'm not looking for love." He pushed back from the table and walked toward the counter to refill his coffee. "It was one dinner. You're making too much of it."

"I know you, Callum. All I'm saying is don't shut the door on a possibility before you've given it a chance."

He paused with his hand on the coffeepot's handle. His sister was right, of course. He'd decided after his divorce that he valued his independence too much to make a committed relationship work. The decision hadn't been a problem because no one he'd met had made him question it.

Until Becky.

"When did you get too smart for your own good?" he asked.

Stephanie grinned. "I've always been brilliant. You're just realizing it."

"I'll keep that in mind," he said with a laugh. They talked some more about possibilities for an upscale restaurant in Rambling Rose, and then Callum headed out to start his morning.

He appreciated the pace of life in Texas. He could move quickly, but things also seemed to adjust to fit the wide-open spaces and the sense of community pride that felt uniquely Texan. This was a setting that made a man earn his place. The residents of Rambling Rose might be curious about his ties to the famous Fortune family, but people seemed more concerned with his dedication to the town.

Callum felt at home here in a way he hadn't during any of the other projects he'd taken on over the years. It made his desire to succeed burn even brighter and caused the future to beckon in ways he hadn't anticipated.

Later that week, Becky looked up from the lunch she'd packed to see Callum walking toward her across the pediatric center's sunny courtyard. A slow smile spread across her lips as awareness tingled along her spine. This was the third day Callum had appeared during her lunch break.

Maybe she shouldn't read too much into it. He'd explained he had business at the pediatric center. She had no reason not to believe him.

"What's on the menu today?" he asked as he slid into the seat across from her. Becky always took her lunch early since most mornings she didn't have time for breakfast.

"Turkey and cheese," she said, then pulled out the

extra sandwich she'd made. "I have one for you if you're hungry."

He stared at the plastic baggie for so long she wasn't sure if he was going to take it or get up from the table and run the other direction. When he finally reached for the sandwich, it embarrassed her that she'd even made the effort to bring something extra for him. "Thank you," he said. "That's thoughtful."

Electricity zipped along her skin as his fingers brushed hers. Her reaction to Callum continued to surprise her. She couldn't remember a time when anticipation had played such a huge part in her life. Despite her busy work schedule and how much effort she put into mothering her girls, Becky felt like she had energy for days. Just the idea of seeing Callum at some point during the day had excitement zinging through her veins like a jolt of caffeine.

"Are you here checking on the mechanical systems again?" she asked.

"Um…yes."

"Will they have it fixed soon?" She pulled a container of apple slices from her lunch sack.

"Probably." He took a bite of sandwich. "Although I may need to stop by for a while longer to make sure it's all going well."

"That has to be frustrating. I'm sure you're ready to move on to your other projects."

"I like seeing how well things are going here," he told her, then leaned in close. "Talking with you is an added bonus."

"Oh." Heat bloomed in her cheeks. "That's nice."

She gave herself a mental head slap. A man said something sweet and her reply was completely boring.

She imagined men like Callum came out of the womb knowing how to flirt, and Becky reminded herself that it didn't mean anything. That she didn't *want* it to mean anything.

"How are the girls?" he asked, grinning at her like she wasn't making an absolute hash of flirting with him.

"They're enjoying the new day care." She tugged her lower lip between her teeth. "I'd like to visit them during the day but the director told me it's too disruptive for their schedule."

"You're a dedicated mom," he murmured.

"Sasha and Luna are my whole world," she told him. That was probably the wrong thing to say, as well. What single man wanted to hear a woman gush over her children? But she couldn't deny it.

"Maybe I could take the three of you to dinner?" His smile turned almost bashful. "If you have a free night sometime?"

She clasped a hand over her mouth when a hysterical laugh bubbled up in her throat.

"What's so funny?"

"All of my nights with the girls are free. Unless you include dinner, bath time and reading board books as a busy schedule."

"So dinner would work?"

"Sure." She felt a frown crease her forehead. "Why would you want to subject yourself to a meal with two toddlers?"

He inclined his head as if pondering a response. "Um…we all need to eat and as great as my brothers and sister are, I sometimes need a little break from the family togetherness."

"I'm not sure dinner with the twins constitutes a break, but I won't say no to an evening out."

"How about tomorrow night?"

"Yes," she breathed, then cleared her throat. "Tomorrow would be great. I get off work at five, which I understand is early for dinner. But with the girls' bedtime…"

"Do you like the Mexican restaurant in town?"

"I haven't been there in ages," she told him with a smile, then gave a nervous laugh. "Not because I don't like it. I do. It's great. I haven't been anywhere, really." She covered her face with her hands, then spread her fingers to look at him. "I'm babbling."

"It's cute," he said, his tone soft like velvet. "You're cute, Becky."

"You're cute, too."

He chuckled. "No one has ever called me that."

She lowered her hands and arched a brow. "I bet you were an adorable baby. A handful, but adorable."

"Definitely a little terror," he agreed.

She sighed. "You have a way of making me jittery, then calming my nerves in the next instant."

"I'm glad."

"I'm glad you asked me to dinner," she said honestly.

"Me, too."

They sat in a charged silence for a long moment. His full lips quirked into a smile, and she wondered what it would be like to feel that mouth against hers. The desire zipping through her was a thrill. She longed to see where it might take her.

Nowhere fast, a voice inside her head warned. Not with this man. She hushed that voice and offered Callum a wide smile. "I need to get back to work. I'll see you at the restaurant tomorrow?"

He stood as she did, leaning close to whisper in her ear. "I can't wait."

Her nerve endings buzzed with the pleasure of his breath tickling the fine hairs along her neck.

Not trusting herself to speak, she simply nodded, then grabbed her lunch sack and hurried toward the primary care wing.

She had a date with Callum Fortune.

Tomorrow couldn't come soon enough.

Later that evening, Callum stared at the familiar name on his cell phone's screen for a few seconds before accepting the call.

"Hey, Doralee," he said as he put the phone to his ear. "This is a surprise."

"Hello, Callum," his ex-wife said, her voice the same rasp he remembered. It seemed like a lifetime ago that they'd flown to Vegas and gotten married on a whim. He'd been young and in love, not exactly sure he was doing the right thing but willing to take a chance because he knew it would make her happy.

In the end, their rash decision had achieved the opposite effect. He'd always regret hurting her, even though it had never been his intention.

"It's good to hear from you," he lied, not sure how this conversation was supposed to go.

She laughed. "I don't believe you for a minute, but I still appreciate hearing it. How's Texas?"

"Big."

"Are the projects going well?"

"So far they are. There have been a few hiccups, but we're on schedule."

"No doubt thanks to your time and dedication."

He gripped the phone more tightly. "I can't tell if that's a compliment or a veiled criticism."

"You're the best at what you do," she answered without hesitation. "The rest of your life might take a hit because of it, but I'm sure you'll have as much success in that tiny town as you did back here."

"Thanks," he murmured. He didn't exactly appreciate her willingness to point out what he'd sacrificed for the sake of his career but he also couldn't deny it. "How are things?"

"Great." He heard her blow out a slow breath. "That's actually why I'm calling, Callum. I have some news that I wanted you to hear from me first."

His stomach pitched like he'd just raced down the first big drop on a roller coaster. "What news?" he asked, although he had a feeling he knew what she was going to say.

"I'm engaged."

"Congratulations," he said, forcing his tone to stay neutral. "I'm happy for you." That part wasn't a lie. He wanted the best for his ex-wife. Just because things hadn't worked out for the two of them didn't mean he'd stopped caring about her.

"I appreciate that," she said. "John is a great guy. He wants to start a family right away, and you know I wanted children."

"Yes," he managed before his throat constricted. Her desire to have children and his unwillingness to start a family had been one of their biggest ongoing arguments during their short marriage.

"It seems like we're both getting the lives we wanted," she continued. "You have a thriving business and I'm going to have a family."

When he didn't respond right away, she continued, "We're planning a spring wedding. Not that you care but like I said, I just wanted you to know."

He swallowed and tried to keep his regret over the past in check. "Please tell your fiancé I said congratulations."

"I will. Are you dating anyone?" she asked, but continued before he could answer. "Never mind. I already know the answer. Even if you're dating it isn't serious. The business is your first love and no one can compete with that."

He mumbled something about wishing her luck, and they ended the call. A thin sheen of sweat covered Callum's forehead.

Up until the moment of hearing Doralee's news, he would have also claimed his life was happy. But her comments about his devotion to his career, whether well-meaning observations or insidious slights, made his gut twist.

He didn't disagree with her assessment of his dedication to the company, but suddenly that seemed like a paltry excuse for the choices he'd made to avoid serious relationships since the divorce.

His ex-wife had moved on with someone who would probably make her far happier than Callum ever had. It was an unwanted but necessary reminder of what he was unwilling to give in a relationship, in large part due to the responsibilities he'd taken on as a child. He couldn't make that kind of commitment and the thought that he might be giving Becky the wrong signals made him doubt everything.

Should he cancel the date with Becky?

He couldn't play around with the emotions of a single

mother, especially one who had survived the tragedy of losing her husband. In truth, it didn't feel like he was toying with her. Becky was like a Fourth of July sparkler come to life. Through everything she'd endured in life and how hard she worked to support her daughters, she practically sparkled with energy. She made him feel alive in a way that even his work hadn't for a long time.

Doralee had reminded him of how little he had to give, but thoughts of Becky inspired him to be more. To give more. To want more. If only he could be that man.

Chapter 5

Becky parked the minivan around the corner from Las Delicias, the Mexican restaurant situated on Rambling Rose's quaint main street. She remembered the first time she and Rick had made the trip to visit the town. She'd been charmed by the rustic beauty of the town, a little worn down and in need of some love but with so much potential and the feeling of home.

Now the man she'd agreed to meet for dinner was the one breathing new life into the community. It wasn't just the pediatric center. She knew Callum was working on a new vet clinic, an upscale shopping mall, a spa and even had plans for a boutique hotel. Up until his investment in the town, most of the money had been limited to the outskirts of the community. He lived in a wealthy enclave, but many of those residents kept to themselves, as if they didn't want to tarnish their fancy image by rubbing shoulders with the true locals.

Becky wasn't exactly a local, but she was raising two daughters who'd been born in the town. She appreciated that Callum didn't seem to care about the differences between them and that he wasn't intimidated by her situation.

Part of why she hadn't thought about dating in the past two years was her fear that a man would assume her twins were simply complications. Becky wasn't sure her heart could stand that.

She quickly checked her makeup in the visor's small mirror. Normally she didn't bother, but tonight she'd actually put some effort into her appearance. It had felt good, like she was some kind of single mom butterfly emerging from her chrysalis. With the help of a dab of concealer and a few subtle swipes of shadow, she looked more like the Becky she remembered and less like an exhausted, overworked mom.

The change made her smile.

"Mama," Luna shouted from the back seat. "Go."

"Go," Sasha repeated softly.

Her girls were learning new words every day, and Becky loved this time in their development. They were little sponges, soaking up everything and making even the most mundane parts of life an adventure.

But she couldn't deny that kids complicated dating, especially two squirming toddlers. Becky unstrapped the girls from their car seats, scooped them up and then slung the diaper bag over her shoulder. She hit the fob to close and lock the car just as Luna dived for her ring of keys. They fell from Becky's grasp and landed on the pavement, skittering underneath the vehicle.

"Uh-oh," Sasha said, her voice grave.

"Mommy will get them," Becky promised, cursing the pale yellow jeans she'd chosen for the evening. They'd seemed so fresh at her house, but this latest small catastrophe was the exact reason she normally didn't wear anything but jeans, scrubs or sweatpants.

"I've got it," Callum said, appearing at her side like some kind of superhero. He deftly crouched down to retrieve the keys, the fabric of his striped shirt stretching across the lean muscles of his back.

"Thanks," Becky said when he straightened again, wishing she could control the blush that seemed to appear every time he looked at her.

"My pleasure," he answered. "You ladies look lovely this evening." He held out his hands, and to Becky's surprise, Sasha reached for him.

"She usually doesn't let other people hold her." Becky's mouth went slack as Callum grinned at her shy daughter, then tucked an arm around her like it was the most natural thing in the world.

"Sasha and I have an understanding." He winked at Becky. "She's helping me win points with her mom."

"Very true." Becky returned his smile. "You have a way with babies." They started toward the restaurant. The evening was particularly mild for this time of year, and the fresh air helped to cool her heated cheeks.

"I had way too much experience in my own family."

The words were spoken lightly, but somehow she could sense that they meant more to him than he was letting on. If that was how he felt about children, what was he doing there with her and the twins?

"There were four brothers all around the same age, right?"

Callum nodded.

"I'm wondering why you were designated your stepmother's helper."

"It started with Stephanie," he said. "I had a connection with her from the start. I didn't even realize what I was taking on until it happened. There were things that Marci needed done with the baby, so I did them. Even if Stephanie was crying like crazy, she'd settle down once I played with her."

"I bet your parents appreciated that." Becky knew she would love that kind of baby whisperer.

"Yeah," he agreed. "They also came to rely on it in a way that none of us realized was too much for a kid my age to handle. The same thing happened when the triplets were born."

They'd reached the restaurant and he held open the door for her. The interior was a homey homage to south-of-the-border decor. Strands of lights hung against warm yellow walls, with colorful flags and sombreros rounding out the decorations. The place was more than half-full, which Becky thought was good for so early on a weeknight.

A stocky man with a pencil-thin mustache strode forward to greet them. "Mr. Fortune," he said, pumping Callum's free hand. "We have your table ready. What a beautiful group of women you have with you tonight."

"I'm a lucky man," Callum answered easily.

Becky felt the eyes of a pretty hostess behind the podium assessing her. Like Becky, the young woman probably wondered what Callum was doing out with a mom and two toddlers. Rambling Rose was a quiet town, but there were enough available women that he could have enjoyed an evening without a baby's sticky hands patting his cheeks, the way Sasha did to him now.

The man, who introduced himself as the restaurant's owner, led them to a table in a quiet corner, already set up with two high chairs. The girls, unaccustomed to dining out, looked around at their new surroundings with wide-eyed curiosity. She and Callum strapped each of them into a high chair, and she took out the travel toys she'd brought to entertain them. A waitress quickly brought water and took their drink orders before hurrying off again.

Becky smothered a giggle as she took a seat next to Luna. "I've never been treated like this at a restaurant," she admitted, glancing around to make sure no one could hear. "Even before I had the twins. Now on the few occasions I've tried to go out to eat with them it feels like the waitstaff resents every moment I'm taking up space. Must be nice to be a true VIP."

Callum blinked as if he'd never considered his elevated status or the perks that came with it. "Why would anyone mind if you had the girls with you?"

As if on cue, Luna chucked a wooden block across the table. Callum reached up and caught it without missing a beat.

"You just intercepted the first reason," Becky told him with another laugh. "There's also the distinct possibility of a meltdown by one or both of them. Not to mention more food falls on the ground than makes it into their mouths."

"People go out to eat with kids all the time," he countered. "It's no big deal."

She shrugged and glanced down at the menu. "Maybe I feel it more because I'm on my own. I don't get to tag out or divide the responsibility. I wouldn't change having twins, but it can be a lot. I'm sure that's why your stepmom ended up depending on you so much with the triplets."

The waitress returned to the table with a beer for Callum and a margarita for Becky. They ordered, and then Callum lifted his glass in a toast when they were on their own again.

"Tonight's toast is to you being the VIP for the night," he told her, the warmth in his gaze setting off an answering heat low in her belly. Luna lifted her sippy cup, and Callum gamely clinked his beer against her plastic cup and then Sasha's. "And a toast to me being with three very important ladies tonight," he said, making funny faces that had the girls squealing in delight.

Becky tried to shush them, but he seemed to enjoy the noise. She couldn't figure out Callum's contradictions. Although he clearly loved his family, it was just as obvious that he still harbored some resentment over the position he'd been put in as caregiver to his younger sisters. Why would he willingly get involved with her when he knew her situation?

She took a breath and put those thoughts aside.

It didn't matter why. She needed to just enjoy the evening.

They talked and laughed, and Callum continued to entertain her girls. When Sasha began to fuss, Becky pulled out a binky and the girl popped it in her mouth and sucked contentedly. Luna wasn't so easy to pacify, so Becky was grateful that the toddler appeared completely enamored of Callum.

Like mother like daughter.

Just as their food arrived, Luna decided she'd had enough of the high chair. Becky lifted the girl into her arms, a pro at eating one-handed.

"I forgot how good food tastes when you don't have to cook," she told Callum around a bite of chicken enchilada. "It's the closest I've had to gourmet in ages."

"What would you think of going out sometime, just the two of us?" he asked as he deftly caught the pacifier Sasha tossed at him. The girl offered a wide grin and put it back in her mouth when he returned it to her.

Becky tried not to react, but the words turned the yummy food she'd eaten into a lead balloon in her stomach.

"I'm sorry," she said automatically, still bouncing Luna on her knee. "This was a terrible idea." She pushed away her half-eaten plate of food and began gathering the girls' things into the diaper bag. "If you see the waitress, I'll take care of the check… It's the least I can do."

Callum covered her hand with his. "What's wrong? Did I say something?"

She shook her head as she stared at the back of his tanned hand and the smattering of fine hair covering it. His body was so different from hers, and just the thought of it made her heart swoop and dance.

But it didn't matter if he couldn't accept the reality of her life. "It's not you. It's me." She made a face. "That sounds like a line, but I mean it. This is why I haven't dated. The girls and I are a package deal. I get we're a lot, and I don't expect you to be okay with it. I just thought—"

"I know how dedicated you are to your daughters," he told her, squeezing her fingers gently. "Your unconditional love for them is one of the things I admire about you. I've never felt that way about anything or anyone. I'm not sure I have it in me."

"Then why are you suggesting I leave them behind?"

She hated the catch in her voice and the tears that pricked the back of her eyes. The problem with loving her girls so darn much was that everything about them made her emotional. Or perhaps that was due to exhaustion or loneliness or the silly hope she'd allowed herself to have that Callum might not care about the tragedy that defined her life and her responsibilities as a mom.

"I'm not. I promise." He laced their fingers together, and the heat of his hand spread into all the cold, lonely places deep within her. "Of course I want to spend time with them. I just thought a night off would be good for you. Give you a little break."

"I don't need a break."

He traced tiny circles on the inside of her palm with his thumb. "Every mother I've ever known needs a break at some point. I'm not saying that because of how much I helped Marci growing up. You work full-time and dedicate every other waking minute to your daughters."

"They're my life."

He stared at her, and she found herself fidgeting under his perceptive gaze. "After Rick died," she said softly, "my parents pressured me to move back to Houston. When I refused, my mom told me I'd regret staying here on my own. She said if I didn't return home they wouldn't help me. I'd have to do everything on my own."

"I'm sure she was just angry and worried," he said.

"They haven't seen the twins since they were six months old."

"What about their first birthday?"

"I took them to the park on my own."

His thumb stopped moving.

"I don't understand," he told her. "These are their granddaughters."

Becky shrugged. "Maybe they'll come around eventually. It's not a big deal. The girls are too young to realize anything." She tugged her hand away from his when the waitress came to clear the plates. Luna's head drooped against her chest. "But I guess it's left me with something to prove. If I admit that I need time off from being a mom…" Her breath hitched, and she swallowed back the emotion that formed a ball in her throat. "That feels like failure."

Sasha gave a tiny cry, and Callum reached for her without hesitation. Becky tried and failed to stay unaffected by his easy way with the girls.

"You must know you're an amazing mother. Your girls are clearly happy and thriving."

She sniffed and busied herself loading the diaper bag while he managed to take out his wallet and then his credit card with one hand.

"I can take her," she offered, shifting Luna in her lap.

"All good." Callum waited until the waitress had taken his credit card to continue. "Tell me you know I wasn't trying to avoid being with Luna and Sasha."

"I know," she said with a nod. "I'm sensitive about them. About my status as a single mom."

"Your status is safe with me," he said in a tone that produced the desired result of making her laugh.

It had been so long since she'd laughed at anything but the antics of her toddlers. "I overreacted," she admitted. "Force of habit." She figured she didn't need to explain to him that at this point her life consisted of one spiral of exhaustion after another. It would be the height of foolishness not to want a night off, especially if it meant spending an evening alone with Callum.

"I don't have any babysitters I trust," she said honestly. "I guess I could ask one of the women from the pediatric center day care. The girls adore them." The waitress returned with Callum's card. He signed the slip and they both stood. "Would you like me to take Sasha?" she offered.

"I've got her," he said, snagging the diaper bag from the table and slinging it over his empty arm.

"Thank you," she said.

He gave her a slow half smile that she felt all the way to her toes. For a moment it was difficult to remember they were in a public place, each of them holding one of her daughters. The urge to lean in and brush her lips across his was almost too much to resist.

His grin widened as if he could read her mind and liked the path of her thoughts.

She spun on her heel and hurried out of the restaurant.

"You move quick for a woman holding a baby," he said lightly when they were on the sidewalk.

"I can do almost anything holding a baby." She cringed at how strange the comment sounded. "I mean—"

"I remember that from when my sisters were babies." He fell in step beside her as she started toward her car. "Stephanie was four when the triplets were born. All three of them loved being carried. We used to joke that for the first two years of their lives, their feet never touched the floor."

"My upper body is super strong," she said with a smile. "Although they're getting big enough that I won't be able to carry them both at the same time for long. Someone is going to have to learn to like walking since they're stuck with just me."

"They aren't stuck," Callum reminded her gently.

They'd reached the minivan. Becky hit a button on the key fob, and the side door slid open. She strapped the girls into their car seats, and the two of them immediately began babbling softly to each other.

"Spending time with you makes me feel like the lamest person in the world," she told Callum as she straightened from the car.

He blew out a disbelieving laugh. "I make you feel lame?"

"That didn't come out right." She pressed two fingers to her chest as her heart beat at a manic pace. "You make me realize how small my life is at the moment."

"Small and lame." He raised a brow. "The hits just keep on coming."

She shook her head as she pressed the button inside the car to close the side door. How could she explain the tumult of emotions racing through her? "We've had dinner twice now."

"Enjoyable both times," he said quickly.

"The first time, you had to hear about my late husband." She flicked a glance toward the car. "Tonight we covered all my insecurities about motherhood. Not exactly scintillating conversation on either count."

"It is to me." He took her hand and drew her forward a few steps so that they were standing a few paces away from the car door, out of the line of sight of the twins in their car seats. "I can't quite explain it, but everything about you fascinates me."

She laughed. "This isn't selling myself short, but I might be the least fascinating person in Rambling Rose."

"You are brave, strong, independent, determined, loyal, loving."

"You make me sound better than I am." His words

rolled around her brain, searching for a place to fit. She'd always thought of herself as a survivalist. She did what she needed to in the moment. Could she actually see herself the way Callum did? She loved the idea of it.

"That is who you are."

His voice rumbled over her, and she realized she'd swayed closer to him, lured by the promise of someone seeing her in the way Callum did.

The longing to kiss him that she'd felt in the restaurant pulsed through her again. Even in the dim glow of the streetlight, she could see the gold flecks in his dark eyes. They'd appeared solid brown at first glance but they were more distinct than that. Much like Callum, the nearer she got the more detail she could appreciate. There were so many facets to this man underneath the polished facade. She wanted to know them all.

She felt the hitch in his breath and then his mouth brushed over hers, light as a touch of a butterfly's wings. Awareness zinged along her skin like his touch was electric. Or maybe it was the energy inside her that had been waiting to be set free.

When he would have pulled back, Becky leaned in, unwilling to let the moment go so soon. Her enthusiasm was rewarded by Callum's soft groan of pleasure. He fitted his mouth to hers more thoroughly and his fingers gripped the back of her shirt like he was trying to root them both in place. Desire raced through her, a cresting wave she wanted to ride forever.

As lost as she was in his embrace, a soft squeak from inside the car had her jerking away. She peered in the window to see Luna and Sasha holding hands. It wasn't clear which one of them had made the noise, but they appeared content for the moment.

"I should go," she whispered, pressing her fingers to her kiss-swollen lips. It was a wonder she didn't feel a sizzle even now, like a drop of water on a hot pan. "The girls need to get to sleep. Thanks again for dinner."

"It was the highlight of my week," Callum said.

"Me, too," she told him, hoping her knees didn't give out. She didn't want the night to end but climbed into her car as Callum watched, her heart full and her body alive in the most intoxicating way.

Chapter 6

The next morning, Callum found his sister unloading supplies into a storage closet at the vet clinic. "Can you do me a favor?" he asked.

Stephanie looked over her shoulder. "As long as it doesn't involve patching the drywall or installing flooring in the front lobby."

"No manual labor," he confirmed. "I need you to babysit."

She turned. "That's cute, Callum, but you're a big boy now. I'll make you a snack, but I don't think you need a babysitter."

"Funny, Steph." He massaged a hand over the back of his neck. Asking for help of any kind didn't come easy to him. But he needed this. "Would you babysit Becky's twins for a night?"

His sister's eyes lit up. "Are you serious? I'd love to get my hands on those babies."

"Maybe take the enthusiasm down a notch. You sound a little scary right now."

"Do you want my help or not?" She gave him a playful nudge. "Those twins are adorable. I'm not scary, but I'm surprised Becky is willing to leave them for an evening. Obviously they go to day care, but she seems like the type of mom who'd have trouble taking any time for herself."

He sighed. "That's why I need your help," he admitted. "Luna and Sasha are adorable and sweet, but I'd like to treat Becky to a night out. She's worried about leaving them with a sitter."

"It's understandable," Stephanie said, her tone turning wistful in a way he didn't understand. "Being a mother is a big responsibility, especially on your own."

Callum studied his sister, trying to figure out where this contemplative mood had come from. He'd been in the role of big brother for so long that sometimes he forgot his younger sisters were adults with aspects of their lives he knew nothing about. "You'll find someone," he told her gently.

"I'm not looking for a man," she said, almost defiantly. "I don't need to fall in love to have a full life."

He held up his hands, palms out. "I understand that. I'm just saying I want to see you happy."

"Goes both ways. Becky makes you happy, doesn't she?"

How could he put into words all the things Becky made him feel? Excited. Nervous. Distracted. Enamored. Beside himself with desire. "We're friends," he said simply.

"Just because your marriage ended the way it did doesn't mean you're trash at relationships."

Callum chuckled. Leave it to Stephanie to cut right to the heart of his issue. Yes, he had a feeling he was garbage at commitment, to say the least. Too much responsibility on his shoulders so young in life had left him with a fierce streak of independence. He didn't like to be tied down by anything except his work because that was the only piece of his life he could truly control.

"I appreciate the vote of confidence."

"It's true."

"Maybe. But who knows how long I'll stay in Rambling Rose? All of our projects are on schedule. Once everything is up and running, it might be time for me to move on. I've been looking at a couple of locations around Texas—communities with potential."

"What about the potential for you to stick around?" Stephanie grabbed another box of supplies. "You can't keep hopping from one location to the next. We all need roots."

Sometimes those roots can feel like they're choking you, Callum thought, although he wouldn't say the words out loud. The topic of his role in the family and how that had impacted the man he'd become was a sensitive one.

He never wanted his sisters to feel as if he resented the role he'd played in their lives but he couldn't deny its effect on him.

"I'm happy with the life I have," he said, earning an eye roll from Stephanie.

"One of these days you're going to want more," she told him as if she were far older and wiser than her twenty-seven years. "For now, let's leave it that I'd be happy to babysit for Becky's girls. Most of my evenings are free so just let me know what night."

"Thanks." He pulled her close for a quick hug. "Steven texted that the new order of cabinets is almost ready. That should keep things on schedule."

"I never doubted either of you," she said.

After checking in with the on-site foreman, Callum drove over to the future site of The Shoppes at Rambling Rose, which was scheduled to open after the veterinary clinic, and then checked out progress at the spa. He thought about what could happen if he decided to make Rambling Rose his permanent home. His stomach pitched in response. A benefit to keeping his connections to the communities where he worked casual was he had no fear of being forced to put down roots or disappointing anyone when he couldn't. He was like a revitalization fairy godfather, swooping in to make changes, then moving on to the next big thing before anyone expected too much of him.

Callum wasn't sure if he had the capacity to change who he was now, even if he tried.

"Thank you so much for agreeing to stay with them." Becky offered Callum's sister a grateful smile. "They can be a handful."

"I'm used to multiple energy thanks to the triplets," Stephanie answered. Her shiny hair was pulled back into a loose bun and she wore a casual sweater and faded jeans, the epitome of effortless beauty. "And I love babies at this age." She grinned as Sasha started a game of peekaboo. Never wanting to relinquish the spotlight to her sister, Luna also began hiding her face behind her blanket, then popping back out. "The three of us are going to have a great evening." She met Becky's gaze, understanding darkening her blue eyes. "Don't worry. I'll text with updates and call if we need anything."

Becky gave a jerky nod. "I left instructions on the counter."

"We should go." Callum put a gentle hand on her elbow. "I'm not sure they'll hold the reservation if we're late."

Nervous energy fluttering in her chest, Becky kissed both girls goodbye. Often one or the other of them made a fuss when she tried to walk out of the day care center in the morning, but tonight they seemed more than ready to stay with Stephanie.

"Your sister is really good with kids," she told Callum as she shut the door behind them. Tonight he wore dark slacks and a white button-down shirt that seemed to accentuate his tanned complexion. His hair skimmed the collar, and the top button of the shirt was open. Becky had the almost uncontrollable urge to kiss that soft spot at the base of his neck.

"She was excited to babysit," he confirmed.

Becky scanned the street in front of her house. "Where's your truck?"

He grinned. "I thought we could take something a little sportier tonight since we don't have car seats to contend with."

He pointed to a sleek, two-seater Audi parked at the curb.

"How did I not notice that car?" Becky stifled a giggle. "It's so out of place in this neighborhood." She tugged on the sleeve of the dress she'd chosen for the evening, a floral-patterned wrap dress that just skimmed her knees.

Although she'd had it for a few years, she hadn't had the opportunity to wear it since before her pregnancy. Slipping into it tonight, she was shocked to discover that it fit her differently from how it used to. She thought she'd lost her pregnancy weight, but the dress clung to her breasts and hips more tightly than she remembered. "Is this too casual for where we're going?"

"You look beautiful," he said as he took her hand. "Your skin is like ivory satin."

"Callum Fortune, are you a secret poet?" she asked with a grin.

"Just trying to live up to my reputation as a Renaissance man." He opened the door of the Audi for her, and she slid into the passenger side, unable to resist running her palm across the car's leather interior.

She'd never been in such a luxurious vehicle, and the reminder of how different their lives were had anxiety flitting through her like caffeine pumping in her veins.

"It's just a car," Callum said as he got in next to her. "It doesn't mean anything."

She barked out a laugh, then rolled her eyes at him. "Only a person who could afford a car like this would think that. You're rich."

He pulled away from the curb, shooting her a genuinely confused glance. "Is that a bad thing?"

"Would you believe I've never known any really rich people?" She scrunched up her nose. "Doctors around here make a good living, but not like your family."

"The car was a stupid idea," he muttered, and she instantly felt guilty.

"No. Of course not." She shook her head. "The car is fun." She placed a hand on his arm. "I just want you to understand that you don't need to try to impress me with your money or your connections or anything material. I like you, Callum. Who you are as a person means more than anything else. Even if you drove some kind of a beater car and didn't live in a huge mansion in a gated community, I'd want to spend time with you. I like you because of you."

They'd stopped at a red light just before turning onto the highway that led out of town. Callum looked toward her with so much intensity in his gaze, heat flamed her cheeks. "You're staring," she told him softly.

"You calling me out as a rich boy might have been the nicest thing anyone has ever said to me." He leaned over the console and quickly kissed her before the light turned green.

She laughed. "I meant it as a compliment. I know you work hard, and I'm not judging you for having money. But it isn't why I like you."

"I'm glad."

She blew out a breath and settled back against the seat as he drove. She was glad he hadn't been offended by what she'd told him. Saying the words out loud made her relax in a way she hadn't expected. There wasn't a true explanation for why the disparities in their backgrounds affected her. Becky had a feeling she was looking for any excuse as to why things couldn't work out between them.

She was falling for Callum, which gave him the power to hurt her. She normally kept her emotions on lockdown for the sake of her girls. There were certain things she didn't allow herself to feel—pity or regret for the life she'd lost when Rick died or bitterness at having to manage all the things on her own. Callum made her want to throw the shackles off her heart and claim a second chance at love.

Biting down on the inside of her cheek, Becky reminded herself that this couldn't be love. She'd known the man for just a week. He was handsome and kind. End of story. At least for her.

"This is why Rambling Rose needs more dining options," Callum said as the sun dipped below the horizon. "I don't want to have to drive almost an hour to take my girl out on a date."

His girl. Warmth bloomed inside her at the thought of being claimed by Callum. Could she trust what was happening between them? Was she even on the right page about it?

"A more upscale restaurant would be a nice addition to the community," she agreed. "Probably some of the people who live out by you would like that better."

He threw her a sidelong glance. "You make it sound as if we're the Texas version of *Downton Abbey*."

She groaned. "Do I sound like I have a chip on my shoulders? I don't mean to. My parents always made it really clear that I should know my place, so I guess that advice stuck."

"Know your place," he murmured. "What does that mean exactly?"

"Not to reach for things above my station."

"Seriously?"

"They meant it in a helpful way." She shook her head. "I think. When I say it out loud, it sounds terrible. I'd never want my girls to believe they shouldn't try for the moon. Whatever they want to accomplish, I'll support them, even if they fail."

"Everyone fails at something," Callum said, and his voice held a note of regret she didn't understand.

"What is your biggest failure?" she asked, curiosity and trepidation warring inside her.

His knuckles turned white as his fingers tightened on

the steering wheel. He was silent so long Becky thought he might not answer. "Marriage," he said finally.

Becky tried to hide her gasp. "You were married?"

"And divorced after a year," he continued.

"What happened?" she blurted before thinking about it. Maybe he didn't want to share that part of himself with her. They'd had two dinners and a handful of lunches together and he hadn't mentioned having an ex-wife.

"I was a terrible husband." He pulled into the parking lot of a fancy-looking restaurant housed in a historic mansion on the outskirts of Austin.

"Callum."

He turned off the car, then faced her, regret shining in his eyes. "I shouldn't have brought this up tonight, Becky. I'm sorry. I've been wanting to tell you but now isn't the right time."

She reached for his hand. "I've talked to you about far too many details of my life. I'm glad you shared that bit of yourself with me. If it makes you uncomfortable, I understand. But I want to hear about it. I want to know you."

Lifting her hand to his mouth, he brushed a gentle kiss across her knuckles. "You really are amazing."

"Hardly." She laughed and dropped her gaze to her lap.

"Let's get our table and have a drink." He gave her a pleading look. "Then I promise I'll tell you anything you want to know about my past."

She tried not to let nerves settle over her as they entered the restaurant. It had a modern farmhouse vibe but still held true to the era of the house with rich textures and beautiful artwork. A stone fireplace dominated the far wall, and she wondered if she'd ever been in such a gorgeous establishment.

"What made you choose this place?" she asked as they approached the hostess's stand.

He shrugged. "It's been written up in several regional papers to rave reviews. Apparently, people come from all over to eat here. When I think about opening an upscale restaurant in Rambling Rose, I want to know what is already working in the area."

The hostess took his name and led them to a cozy table near the fireplace.

"So it's a date *and* a research trip?" Becky asked with a wink.

"Ninety-nine percent date," he assured her.

The waiter, an older gentleman with a shock of white hair, brought each of them a menu and explained the evening's specials, which included a scallop sashimi appetizer and Kobe beef tenderloin medallions with braised leeks for a main course. Becky was certain she'd never eaten anything as fancy as the dishes he described.

Callum ordered a bottle of wine, and she saw the waiter's eyes widen a fraction. When he left, she leaned in over the table. "What's so special about the wine you ordered?"

His thick brows drew together. "Nothing really. It's simply a good vintage."

"Does that translate as pricey?"

"Will you let me spoil you tonight?" he asked softly, reaching across the table to lace their fingers together. "Please?"

The *please* got her.

"If you insist. We'll enjoy this evening and you can make me feel like a princess." She leaned closer to him.

"Although I'll let you in on a little secret in case you haven't picked up on it. I always feel special with you."

His chest rose and fell as if her words made it difficult for him to catch his breath. She liked the idea of affecting him in that way. She didn't want to be the only one caught up in the spell of whatever was happening between them.

Chapter 7

Callum was grateful that the wine steward approached their table at that moment. He'd been half tempted to tug Becky right out of her seat and into his lap. Or better yet to skip dinner altogether and find a nearby hotel where he could spend the next several hours making her feel special from head to toe.

The sommelier held up the bottle for his inspection and, at Callum's subtle nod, began to uncork it while praising the vintage and offering bland small talk about the wine industry. Callum was used to this routine in the restaurants he frequented, especially after ordering a five-hundred-dollar bottle. Of course, he wouldn't share the price with Becky. Part of him worried she'd be too nervous to actually take a drink if she knew how much it cost.

He hadn't been lying when he told her he wanted to

treat her this evening. If he'd been more on the ball, he would have chartered a helicopter and flown them to Houston or Dallas for a true five-star meal. Next time— if she gave him a next time.

As he took the cork from the sommelier, Callum felt a light pressure on his leg. He went to take the requisite sniff and ended up almost shoving the cork up his own nose when he realized it was Becky playing an innocent game of footsy with him under the table. Every nerve ending tensed and it took a herculean amount of effort to keep his features neutral.

One corner of her mouth curved up into a mischievous smile, but she kept her gaze trained on the wine steward.

"Perhaps the lovely lady would like a taste," Callum suggested as he handed the cork back to the man.

With an agreeable nod, the sommelier poured a finger of the deep burgundy liquid into a glass and gave it to Becky. She didn't bother to swirl the glass, and Callum noticed the man's mouth furrow into a disapproving scowl.

Instead, she took a dainty sip. "Tastes like red wine," she reported after a moment.

There was an indignant mew of distress from the sommelier. "It's not just ordinary wine," he explained, and Callum could tell the man was doing his best not to sound horrified. "That is a perfectly balanced vintage that's both bold and complex. It's like a symphony in your mouth."

"Which is a complicated way of saying 'great red wine,'" Callum explained, earning a slightly wider smile from Becky. What would it take to coax a full-fledged grin from her?

He desperately wanted to know.

"It's lovely," she told the sommelier, taking pity on the wine expert's obvious distress.

"I'm glad you're enjoying it," the man answered as he poured more wine into her glass. He filled Callum's glass as well and then left the table. The waiter returned to take their dinner orders, and then they were blessedly alone. Or as alone as they could be in a quiet corner of the restaurant.

"You distracted me," Callum accused playfully.

Becky held up her wineglass. "To distractions."

"You can distract me anytime," he told her as they clinked glasses, then frowned as he took a sip. "I'm missing something."

"What's that?"

"Your foot under the table."

She giggled, then flashed the exuberant grin he'd been waiting for all night. "I should probably apologize, except I'm not sorry. That man was far too serious for his own good."

"But you like the wine?"

"I understand very little about what makes it so special, but even I can tell that it is."

Callum opened his mouth to reply, then shut it again. He felt the exact same way about Becky. Yes, she was beautiful. He'd dated beautiful women before. Women who were ambitious and accomplished. But he couldn't remember ever having been so affected by any of them.

"Do you still want to know about my past?" he asked almost reluctantly.

"Of course."

He gave a gruff nod and took another drink. As much as he didn't want to speak about it, he knew they couldn't go further unless she understood his shortcomings. He liked and respected Becky, and was crazy attracted to her, but none of those things changed who he was on the inside. What he could and couldn't offer her. Best to have it all out now so she wouldn't hope for more.

"Doralee and I met at a bar in Nashville. It was a fast courtship, and we married within a couple of months."

"Like Rick and me," she murmured.

He hadn't realized the similarity in the time frame of their previous marriages. "I'm not sure I'd compare the two. I thought we were on the same page as far as the paths we wanted our lives to travel. Turns out we weren't even reading from the same playbook." He shook his head. "My business was starting to take off, and I had people coming to me about real estate deals in several smaller towns throughout Tennessee and the surrounding area. Steven and Dillon had joined me at that point, and I spent a lot of time working."

"You're dedicated."

"I should have been more dedicated to my marriage," he admitted, shifting in his seat. "She resented everything about Fortune Brothers Construction. In turn, I felt restricted, like she wanted to control me. The whole thing was a mess, and the entirety of it was my fault."

Becky inclined her head as she studied him, her gaze gentle. If she argued with him or offered false platitudes to assuage his guilt, Callum might lose his mind. He couldn't go back and fix the pain he'd caused his ex-wife, so the regret he carried with him like his own version of Sisyphus's boulder was all he had.

"Do you ever speak to her?" Becky asked, one slender finger circling the rim of her glass.

The breath he hadn't realized he was holding escaped

his lips on a sudden hiss. "She called me this week, actually." Something flashed in Becky's dark eyes. He couldn't name the emotion, but it warmed him just the same.

"Just to catch up?" she asked, a little too evenly.

"To tell me she's engaged." He drained the rest of his wine, then waived away the server who moved to refill his glass. "She's been dating a guy since shortly after our divorce was finalized."

"How does that make you feel?"

"Like more of a failure than I already did."

"Callum, no."

"I'm joking." He gave what he hoped was a convincing laugh. "Sort of. I'm happy for her. She deserves a good man and a great life. I wish I could have been the one to give it to her. I'm sorry she had to go through our wreck of a marriage to find her happily-ever-after or whatever you want to call it."

"Sometimes it takes going through a difficult period to truly appreciate the happiness on the other side."

They were pretty words, but he didn't know if he could allow himself to trust them.

"Do you really believe that?"

The smile she gave him was filled with yearning. "I have to."

Right. Because this woman had been through something so much worse than the breakdown of a marriage.

Their food arrived, and he loved the way her eyes lit up at the sight of the mouthwatering dish the server set on the table in front of her. Becky had ordered some complicated chicken dish while he got steak.

She moaned in pleasure after her first bite. "I might not know a lot about fancy wine, but this is the most amazing dinner I've ever had." She pointed her fork at Callum. "You should definitely take notes on this restaurant and recreate its goodness in Rambling Rose. Steal away the chef if you have to. I'll spend a month eating peanut butter sandwiches for every meal just to save money to go out to a place like this."

He wanted to assure her that she didn't have to worry about money because he'd take care of her, but he couldn't make that promise. Even if he could commit to it, he had a feeling he'd just offend her by offering. Even if they didn't say so out loud, most of the women Callum dated liked his wealth. The fact that Becky made a point of being genuinely not impressed felt refreshing.

"That's a ringing endorsement."

She nodded around another bite, then lifted up her hand to obstruct his view of her face. "Sorry," she said after a moment. "Eating quickly is a habit with me now. I can't remember the last time I ate at a leisurely pace."

"Have more wine," he suggested.

She flashed him a look of mock horror. "Are you trying to get me tipsy?"

"Not at all," he answered without hesitation. "But I do plan to kiss you tonight. A lot. And I want no question in either of our minds that we're both willing participants."

"I'm willing," she whispered, her eyes sparkling.

He smothered a groan. "When you look at me that way I want to skip dessert and ask for the check right now."

"When we're together," she said, leaning closer, "you make me want to be the dessert."

Color flooded her cheeks as she made the flirty statement, but the effect on him was the same as if she'd been a seasoned seductress.

As perfectly prepared as the meal was, Callum barely tasted it. He couldn't wait to be alone with Becky, even for a few moments.

"I'm so embarrassed," she murmured. "I don't say things like that."

"Then I'm not sure whether I'm more honored or turned on," he told her with a laugh.

They finished eating, the air around them charged with an electric current of desire. She left the table to call and check in with Stephanie as he paid the check. He found her just outside the restaurant's entrance, staring up at a clear night sky filled with stars.

"Everything okay?" he asked as he moved toward her.

"Yes," she reported with a relieved sigh. "Your sister said the girls went to bed without a fuss and have been sleeping soundly ever since." She dipped her chin, looking up at him through her lashes, and added, "She said to take our time."

"I intend to," he said, his voice rough even to his own ears. He took her hand and led her around the side of the building, then turned his back to the cool brick, drawing her closer. Need rushed through him as their lips met, and there was no holding back the flood of desire. She seemed as frenzied as he felt, opening for him as soon as he drew his tongue across the seam of her lips. The kiss deepened, need exploding through him like a wildfire.

Her body formed to his, soft where his was hard, and he spread his hands across her back, wanting more from her than she could possibly give out in the open, even sheltered as they were by the darkness and shadows.

He forced himself to bank his yearning, to slow the pace to where he could savor her. They kissed until he couldn't tell where he left off and she began. The flare of desire almost overwhelmed him with its intensity, his body hot and ready.

She broke away from the embrace when a horn sounded in a parking lot, glancing around in shock before offering a tentative smile. "I was afraid we were going to get caught making out like teenagers."

"Wouldn't have been the worst thing that's happened."

"But mortifying just the same." She straightened her dress. "I'm a mother of twins. Moms don't kiss like that."

He reached out and cupped her jaw, unable to stop himself from touching her. "Who told you that?"

She arched a brow. "Chapter three in *The New Mom Handbook*."

"There's a handbook?"

"I'm joking." She leaned into his touch, like a cat begging to be petted. He flicked the tip of her earlobe with his thumb, and she bit down on her lip. "We should go. I don't want to take advantage of your sister's generosity."

He wasn't ready for the night to end, but didn't want to push too far. This had been a big step for Becky, trusting her daughters with a babysitter and allowing herself a rare evening out.

"I've had the best time," he said as he took her hand.

"You really spoiled me," she told him. "I almost feel like a princess."

There was so much more he wanted to give her, to show her. If only she'd let him.

The thought pinged through his brain that maybe he should pump the brakes on their connection. Hell, he couldn't even commit to the restaurant idea, as strong as it was, because that would mean more time in Rambling Rose. His original plan had been to move on after the last of his initial slate of projects opened. That was his sweet spot as far as staying in one place. Enough time to make a difference in the community but not so long that he'd be tempted to stay.

Becky was a temptation he hadn't expected, and he had no clue what to do about it.

The next week was a blur for Becky. The pediatric center continued to be busy, and her days sped by in a whir of patient care and paperwork. Of course, that didn't count the moments she spent fantasizing about Callum.

She couldn't deny that her feelings had intensified since their special evening out. He was so much more than she'd expected him to be. Handsome as sin was hard enough to resist. Callum was the whole package—smart, successful, generous and kind.

As great as the fancy restaurant had been, she had just as much fun with him on casual nights at her house. He came over almost every evening after she got off work. They took turns grocery shopping and would cook together while the twins watched from the high chairs or played nearby. She would have thought he'd get bored with her daily routine, but he didn't seem to mind the monotony of life with toddlers.

After the girls went to bed, Becky and Callum would spend hours each evening talking and then even more time kissing. She came alive in his embrace. It became more difficult each night to let him go. He seemed as reluctant to leave her as she was to watch him drive away through the flutter of curtains at her front window.

Which was how she found herself on an ordinary Tuesday night, standing in the open doorway of her small house trying to force her arms to unwind from around Callum's broad shoulders.

"I have to go," he said, then claimed her mouth with his.

"It's late," she agreed when they finally came up for air. "You should go."

It took another several minutes before she finally lowered her hands to her sides and backed up a step.

"I had an amazing time," he told her.

"We ate spaghetti with sauce from a jar and watched reruns," she pointed out with a laugh.

"It doesn't matter." He dropped a kiss on the tip of her nose. "With you, it's always amazing."

Stay, she wanted to tell him. Surely he would understand what that one word meant. She wanted more from Callum. As much as he could give her.

Right now she simply wanted him to stay.

But she didn't speak the word out loud.

Instead, she watched as he shoved his hands into the pockets of his jeans and backed away down her front walk.

"Good night, Becky," he called and then turned and jogged to his car. Almost as if he couldn't wait to get away.

She hoped he was moving quickly so that he wouldn't turn around and invite himself back into her house.

She slammed the front door shut like she might chase him down the street without the barrier between them. She moved to the window because it hurt her heart—not to mention the rest of her body—to know he was driving away. His taillights glowed red against the midnight darkness as he pulled away from the curb.

He'd driven only a few feet when his brake lights

went on. Becky's breath hitched as the truck reversed back into its former spot against the curb in front of her house. For several long minutes nothing happened. No movement. No lights. No Callum.

Then the truck's interior lit up for a few seconds as he climbed out of the cab. He walked around the front of the vehicle and up her walk. Back to her house. To her.

Becky didn't give fear or doubt a chance to take hold in her brain. She dropped the curtain and rushed to the front door, throwing it open and dashing toward Callum. He grinned as she hurtled herself into his arms.

"I want you to stay," she whispered into his ear.

"Exactly what I hoped you'd say," he said as he carried her into the house.

Chapter 8

As soon as Callum kicked the door shut behind them, Becky's doubts returned in full force. She wanted him more than she could have imagined, but her husband was the only man she'd ever been with in that way. And while she wasn't anywhere near over the hill, motherhood had changed her body.

She also had to deal with the issue of how much of her heart she could to give Callum. For her, sex meant more than just the physical act. Although she had no doubt he would be attentive and thoughtful, what if for him it was just a release? Scratching an itch between two people untethered to anyone else.

"Does it hurt?" he asked as he took a step away from her.

She blinked. "What?"

His mouth curved into that sexy hint of a smile that

never failed to drive her crazy. "You look like you're thinking way too hard. Typically, my brain hurts when I try that."

"You should *try* being less perceptive," she told him with an eye roll. "It's kind of annoying."

He chuckled, the low sound rippling across her already taut nerve endings. "Nothing has to happen tonight, Becky. You're in control."

Her breath caught in her throat. When was the last time she'd felt truly in control? Before tragedy had turned her into a widow and a single mother of two unborn babies. Since that moment, she'd been furiously treading water with the waves constantly lapping over her head.

"We can talk," he continued. "You can tell me to go."

"But I told you to stay," she reminded him.

He tucked a loose strand of hair behind her ear. "You're allowed to change your mind."

"I haven't," she blurted. "I'm just nervous. It's been a while and…" She shook her head.

"And…"

"Carrying twins pretty much wrecked my body," she said on a long exhale.

It was now, apparently, Callum's turn to blink. Poor guy. She had no doubt any man would struggle with a good response to that kind of statement. It had been stupid to put the silly doubt into words but…

"You're beautiful," he told her gently. His finger traced a path from the side of her jaw down her throat and along the edge of the neckline of the dress she wore. "Sometimes when you blush, it flushes all the way to your chest. I'm dying to know if I can make your whole body blush."

Her mouth went dry.

"I love how you're soft in all the places where I'm hard." He stepped closer, his warmth heating her like a fire on a cold winter night. "It's as if you're formed in the exact right way to fit me. If this is too soon, we don't have to—"

"I want to," she admitted, unable to offer any other response. She knew she had to stay in the moment. She had a feeling this was uncharted territory for both of them.

"Are you sure?" he asked, and she appreciated that he was giving her so many chances to decide. The feeling of being in control was a revelation in her current life where every day she felt strapped into an exhilarating and exhausting roller coaster with no safety harness.

She took his hand and led him through the quiet house to her bedroom. It had been the one space she'd changed after her husband's death, when sorrow had been her late-night companion. She'd thought her grief might engulf her, even knowing she carried a legacy of love inside her. Then she'd felt the first flutter of movement. A quiver of butterfly wings signaling the lives growing in her belly. At that moment she'd understood that she needed to make peace with her sorrow and try to find some measure of happiness again. For her babies.

She'd cleaned out the room, not just of Rick's belongings, but everything. She'd spent a portion of her meager savings to buy new furniture and hired a local handyman to repaint the walls from nondescript beige to a soft yellow. The color felt like hope, and now she realized she had been preparing for this new chapter in her life without even realizing it.

Moonlight slanted through the window, alighting on Callum's strong features. Slowly, she stepped closer and wound her arms around his neck. She didn't move deliberately because of fear. Somehow his allowing her to choose had chased away her doubts, at least for the moment. Instead, she wanted to enjoy each second they had together. Unwrap this experience like a precious gift.

He kissed her like he felt the same, molding his lips to hers until soft sounds of aching hunger escaped her throat. His hands moved along her back, over the dress's fine fabric, sending shivers along her skin. As good as his touch felt, it wasn't enough. She broke the kiss and began to unbutton his shirt, her fingers shaky with need.

"Let me," he told her as he took over. Within seconds he'd made quick work of the buttons and was shrugging out of the crisp fabric.

Becky did her best not to whimper. It had been no secret that Callum had an amazing body, his muscular physique evident even under his clothes. His bare chest and perfectly toned muscles made her forget her own name.

"Do you go to a tanning bed?" she asked, taking in all that golden skin and needing to regain some self-control.

He chuckled. "Uh, never."

She put her hands on her hips. "I just can't get over how naturally bronze you are."

"Do you want me to prove I have no tan lines?" He winked as he unhooked his belt.

"Yes, please," she whispered, and he laughed again.

"I think you need to catch up," he told her. "I'm feeling slightly underdressed at the moment."

"Don't let it bother you," she assured him. "It's working for me."

He arched a brow in response.

She hitched up the hem of her dress. The soft fabric pulled on over her head, no zipper or buttons to fuss with. But it also meant that in the disrobing, she'd bare her body to him without being able to see his split-second initial reaction. Becky couldn't decide if that was a blessing or a curse.

"Here goes everything," she whispered and lifted the dress up and off in one fluid movement. It fell to the floor in a whisper of sound, leaving her standing in front of Callum in her bra and panties. She didn't even own a matching set since motherhood had changed her breasts.

He didn't seem to mind. A shiver rippled through him as he stared at her. Her heart leaped in her chest at the intensity in his brown eyes.

His throat bobbed as he swallowed. "You take my breath away."

Confidence building in step with the desire pooling low in her belly, she reached behind her back and flicked open her bra. The straps dropped from her shoulders and then the lace fell to the floor.

Callum muttered a strained curse, his eyes going darker than she thought possible.

He closed the distance between them in two quick steps, claiming her mouth for a rough and ravishing kiss. She met his need with her own, thrilled when his big hands cradled her breasts, thumbs skimming over the sensitive peaks of her nipples.

Just as her knees gave way, he caught her and moved toward the bed, yanking back the covers and lowering her gently onto the sheets. They continued to kiss as he explored her body. It felt as if he was trying to memorize every curve and dip. She barely recognized herself in the way she responded, her desire greedy and sharp.

Becky was at her heart a people pleaser, always wanting to accommodate others without taking anything for herself. So the soft demands she spoke startled her, but Callum had no problem following every one. It was clear he wanted to learn how she liked to be touched. In the process, his inventive hands and mouth offered new insight into pleasure.

He was both gentle and demanding as he explored her. She easily opened for him as his fingers skimmed below the waistband of her panties, delving into her hot center in a way that made her arch into him. Blood roared in her ears, and pressure built inside her, more intense than she'd ever experienced. Her skin fairly crackled with the pleasure of the way he touched her.

She cried out his name when her release roared through her with all the force of a cannonball. Callum whispered sweet words into her ear as her body recovered, but still she wanted more.

"I need you," she said against his skin, delighted by the subtle tremor that threaded through him.

"The best three words I've ever heard." He kissed her swiftly, then climbed off the bed and reached for his discarded pants. He took a condom packet from the wallet, then turned to face her. Anticipation flooded her once again as he shucked out of his boxers, appearing not self-conscious in the least about standing naked in front of her.

Why should he? His body was perfection. He sheathed himself as he returned to the bed, his weight giving her a feeling of safety.

"Every night," she said, leaning up to kiss the base of his throat, "I've watched you drive away, and a part of me has wanted to call you back."

He settled between her legs but didn't move to enter her. "Which part?"

"All of them, really." She offered a slow smile. "All of me."

With his elbows resting on either side of her, he cradled her face in his hands. "Those are the parts I want," he confirmed. "All of you."

"I'm yours," she whispered as he filled her in one sure thrust.

She'd been made for this moment, and it was everything and more. Her fingers trailed along the muscles of his shoulders and back, reveling in his strength and power. He continued to rain kisses along her face as they found a rhythm unique to the two of them. Time seemed to stand still as they remained suspended in this moment.

Her nerve endings shuddered when the pressure built again, different from what had happened to her minutes earlier. This time she and Callum climbed the high peak together, and then suddenly fireworks exploded throughout her body. She felt Callum go taut and he said her name like it was the most beautiful word he'd ever spoken.

"Amazing," he said into her hair moments later, dropping kisses like feathers on the top of her head.

She didn't know how to respond, what to say to explain how much this moment meant to her. She couldn't even admit it to herself, because she knew she loved this man. Not just because of great sex, although that was a bonus. She'd fallen for him for so many reasons, and being with him in this way had only served to crash through the last of her defenses.

Instead, she kissed him again, hoping to convey what she wanted him to know without giving away too much of herself. She let out a little groan of protest when he left her to go to the bathroom, only to return a few minutes later and gather her close.

"I'll be gone before morning," he promised, the comfort of his warm body making her blissfully drowsy. "But let me hold you awhile longer."

As an answer, she snuggled closer, falling asleep with his arms around her.

"Please don't say you're going to try to become a farmer now, too?"

Callum turned with a grin as Dillon and Steven walked into the abandoned feed house situated two blocks off the main drag of Rambling Rose's downtown.

He held out his hands, palms up. "Not exactly, although right now I don't think there's anything Fortune Brothers Construction can't accomplish in this town."

Dillon shook his head, a lock of sandy-blond hair falling across his forehead. "You shouldn't say that to anyone," his younger brother warned. "I've already heard rumblings about the locals not liking how much property we've bought in town. People think we're catering to the new millionaires—the gated community crowd."

"Not true," Steven argued before Callum could speak. "The pediatric center serves everyone, as will the vet clinic."

"What about the spa and the upscale shopping center and hotel?" Dillon kicked a toe at the dirty concrete floor. "Those aren't exactly meant for the average resident."

Callum stepped forward. "But they'll generate revenue and tax dollars that will help the town." He put a hand on Dillon's muscled shoulder. Dillon had always been the peacemaker of the family and the worrier within their business partnership, his cautious nature balancing the ambition that Callum and Steven shared.

"So if you aren't reopening the feed store," Dillon said, spinning in a slow circle to take in the dilapidated space, "why are we here?"

"Because I wanted the two of you to be the first to see the site of our next project."

Both of his brothers blinked.

"We're developing an upscale restaurant," he explained.

"In a feed store?" Dillon barked out a laugh. "I like the irony. Feed store as a restaurant, although it doesn't actually lend itself to upscale."

"You just need to see the vision," Callum assured his brother. He walked a few paces away from them and pointed to an open stretch of wall. "Imagine a long bar there, serving hand-mixed cocktails." He gestured to the far side of the space. "A kitchen with state-of-the-art equipment. We'll source local and regional ingredients along with the craft beer and liquor."

"My mouth is watering already," Steven said.

Dillon shook his head. "Do I need to point out that none of us has experience running a restaurant? We're contractors."

"But Ashley, Megan and Nicole do," Callum reminded him. "I talked to the three of them last night and they are interested in investing and heading up the design and menu."

"They want to come to Rambling Rose to run a restaurant?" Dillon scratched his chin.

"Their own restaurant," Callum clarified.

"The triplets are a force of nature." Steven shook his head. "You realize that, right?"

Callum smiled. "We've got plenty of room at Fame and Fortune." It might drive him crazy sometimes to balance all the intricacies of such a large family, but he and his siblings were undeniably tight. The thought of having the triplets in Texas felt right at a soul level.

Dillon paced halfway across the open space and then back again. "It has potential, but don't you think we've got enough on our plates?"

"If we don't seize the opportunity," Callum said, "someone else will. Ashley wants to target a late-spring opening. They can get things up and running plus work out any kinks before the summer tourist season swings into high gear."

Steven pulled his phone from his back pocket. "A guy over in Brenham emailed me about a barn that's being torn down. He's got almost a dozen pallets of reclaimed wood." He passed the device to Dillon, who then handed it to Callum.

"That would be perfect for the bar and an accent wall," Callum said, glancing from the photos on the phone to his brother. "I bet the girls would love it."

"I was thinking the same thing," Steven agreed.

Dillon had taken a few steps away, his back to them. Frustration pricked along Callum's spine. He didn't want to move forward without having both his brothers on board. The company was busier than ever since he'd moved operations to Rambling Rose. The pace of business would take all three of them working together in order for it to be a success. Failure wasn't an option.

If Dillon shot down the idea for their sisters to open a restaurant, Callum would respect that. He might be the company's founder, but it was a partnership now.

His younger brother spun around, meeting Callum's

worried gaze with an unreadable expression. They stood like that for several seconds until Dillon gave a barely perceptible nod. "If we keep the pipes and ventilation ducts exposed, that will cut costs and make installation simpler. The concrete floor needs to be cleaned and polished, so insulation, electrical and plumbing are going to be the biggest hurdles, assuming there's no structural damage."

Callum and Steven exchanged a fist bump.

"What's that about?" Dillon demanded, eyes narrowed.

"I'm all about the big picture," Callum explained. "Steven goes right to design. You're the detail guy. If you're already working out the HVAC systems, that means you think the project is a go."

Dillon rolled his eyes. "Of course it's a go. What the triplets want, they get. Besides, once the 'big picture' guy is set on something, the rest of us make it happen. How do you think we ended up in this tiny speck of a town in the first place?"

"Not so tiny once we're through," Callum pointed out. "The Fortune brothers are putting Rambling Rose on the map."

"Does that mean you're going to stay?" Steven asked, his tone casual. "After all the current projects are up and running?"

Callum shrugged, irritation making him twitch. Of course he wasn't going to stay in Rambling Rose. He'd made certain that long-term ties weren't part of the equation since the end of his marriage. He wouldn't take the chance of hurting someone the way he had his ex-wife or opening himself to that kind of pain. But ever since his night with Becky, it felt like his priorities had been turned upside down.

He'd spent so long making his career the most important thing in his life because that kept him safe and in control. His growing feeling for Becky and her girls scared the hell out of him, and moving on would be the quickest way to keep them in check.

"I'm scheduled to drive over to a little town on the eastern edge of San Antonio next week," he said by way of an answer. "It's long past its heyday, but has great bones and easy access to the interstate. The place has potential."

One of Steven's thick brows lifted. "We were under the impression your relationship with Becky had potential, as well."

Dillon cleared his throat. "Couldn't help but notice your headlights coming down the driveway in the wee hours most nights. And a few early mornings."

"Are you a vampire now?" Callum asked.

"Light sleeper," Dillon said with a chuckle.

"You need to move into one of the guesthouses," Callum suggested, not bothering to hide his annoyance.

"Who would have coffee ready for you in the morning?" Dillon shot back.

"Manny," both Steven and Callum said at once, referring to the older caretaker who had come with the property. Manuel Salazar had worked at the ranch for decades. He had a gift with horses and happened to be a decent cook, as well. Callum and his siblings had come to rely on Manny to manage the property and their lives.

Dillon sniffed. "His coffee tastes like tar."

"But he serves it with the best huevos rancheros I've ever had," Steven countered.

"I won't argue that," Dillon admitted. "And no one better tell him I dissed his coffee. I've almost got him convinced to share his green chile recipe with me."

"Becky loves green chile," Callum murmured, remembering how excited she'd been when he'd brought a taco casserole to her house two nights earlier. He'd felt like a bit of a slouch admitting that an employee had actually done the cooking, but she hadn't seemed to care.

"Come on."

Callum stumbled a step as Steven brought him back to the present moment with a shove. "What?" he demanded.

"You like this woman," Steven said.

"Maybe even more than like," Dillon added, doing an annoying shimmy across the dirty floor.

"Shut up," Callum told both his brothers. "We're hanging out. She's nice. It's nothing more."

"Oh, look at that." Dillon pointed at him. "Your pants are on fire."

"Because you're a liar," Steven said helpfully.

"I get the reference." Callum felt a muscle start to tick in his jaw. "You both need to mind your own business."

"Our business is you," Steven said. "That's the way it works with family. Don't act surprised. Especially after you decided to buy a building for the express purpose of helping the triplets."

Callum blew out a breath, his annoyance disappearing. It would be great to have his younger sisters living in Rambling Rose.

"No more talk about my love life," he told them. "Let's discuss restaurant plans. I'm less likely to punch you that way."

Both his brothers laughed. "We'll let you off the hook," Dillon said.

Steven nudged him again. "For now."

Callum would take whatever kind of reprieve he could get.

Chapter 9

"I'm not sure about this," Becky whispered, more to herself than anyone else.

"My sister's the best hairstylist in Rambling Rose," Sarah Martensen told Becky the following evening. "Brandi is an expert at color."

That vote of confidence did little to ease Becky's nerves, but she smiled. At this point, she sat in a stranger's basement hair studio, with the twins being entertained by Brandi's teenage daughter in the adjacent space. She'd wanted to update her look and remembered Sarah offering to babysit during the pediatric center's opening.

Becky had gotten to know Sarah's husband, Grant, well over the past couple of weeks. The building manager for the pediatric center, he was the kind, paternal type of man she would have wished her girls to have for a grandfather.

With few other options, she'd asked him for his wife's number and called Sarah to see if she would be willing to babysit while Becky got her hair cut and colored. She hadn't sported a real style since the girls had been born.

Sarah had immediately suggested that Becky make an appointment with Brandi, her younger sister, who'd recently opened a hair salon out of her home. It was a simple room in her basement but had all the essentials as far as equipment and supplies.

A benefit was that she'd been able to bring her daughters with her. Sarah had planned to watch them, but Brandi's sweet teenager, a senior at Rambling Rose High School, had captivated the twins.

"I'm going to make you so beautiful," Brandi promised with a wink, "that the handsome Fortune is going to fall at your feet."

"Brandi, hush," Sarah told her sister on a rush of breath.

Becky felt her eyes go wide. "How did you know I was doing this for Callum?"

Sarah shrugged, looking ten kinds of self-conscious. "Grant mentioned that the boy has been stopping by to visit you on the regular."

"He has business at the pediatric center," Becky protested weakly. It wasn't as if she and Callum were trying to keep their relationship—or whatever they'd call it—a secret. But it still felt odd to know people were discussing her personal business. The perils of small-town life, she supposed.

"My husband says Callum Fortune is quite taken with you." Sarah giggled like a schoolgirl. "To be honest, I don't know how you get any work done. I'd spend my days waiting for him."

"I love my job," Becky told them. She didn't bother to mention that she also loved Callum. Hair salon small talk was one thing. Revealing her biggest secret was quite another. "It's nice that he visits, but we're just having fun."

"A woman could have a lot of fun with a man like that." Brandi gave a throaty chuckle as she gestured for Becky to stand so she could move the salon chair in front of the sink attached to the wall. As Brandi turned on the water, Becky sat again, leaning back to rest her neck on the basin.

It felt strangely indulgent to have another person rinsing her hair. Brandi tugged at the thin strips of foil, then used a shampoo that smelled like lavender on Becky's hair. She closed her eyes and let out a blissful sigh.

Would Callum notice the change? In a way it didn't matter. She appreciated this small bit of pampering. It had been too long, she realized, since she'd taken care of herself. She hadn't even taken a vitamin since her jar of prenatal gummies had run out just after the girls were born. Luna and Sasha would continue to be her priority, but it was past time she started taking care of herself as well as them.

Not just with Callum as a motivator, but because she wanted her girls to see that joy and fun were an important part of life.

All too soon, Brandi turned off the water and tapped Becky's shoulder to indicate she could sit up.

"That was the most luxurious thing I've done in ages," Becky told the sisters, prompting them to share an incredulous look.

"Maybe Callum Fortune isn't as much fun as he looks," Sarah said, both women dissolving into fits of laughter.

Color rushed to Becky's cheeks. "Not counting Callum," she muttered.

"Atta girl," Brandi said as she toweled off Becky's hair.

The next half hour rushed by in a blur of snipping scissors and small talk. Every few minutes, Sarah peeked out of the salon to confirm Brandi's daughter was still entertaining the girls. In this makeshift cocoon of feminine camaraderie, Becky suddenly felt connected to the Rambling Rose community in a way she hadn't since making her home in the small town.

Her status as a widow and single mother had defined her, and she'd allowed it to keep her from truly becoming close to people. A part of her expected everyone to judge her in the same way her parents had. Her mom and dad had never believed she could make a life for herself on her own. She'd wanted to prove them wrong, but in her quest for self-reliance, she'd cut herself off from making real friends in the process.

Brandi and Sarah were decades older than Becky, but the women made her feel like part of their tribe.

Becky was so lost in thought it took her a few seconds to really focus on her reflection in the mirror when Brandi finally spun her around to see her finished hair.

"It's gorgeous," she whispered, reaching up a careful hand to touch the soft strands. Instead of the one-dimensional brown she'd known her whole life, now her hair was subtly highlighted with strands of gold and auburn. The cut was layered around her face, but still hung over her shoulders in a way that looked both effortless and stylish. "You really are a genius with hair."

Brandi gave her a quick hug from behind. "Sweetie, my job is easy when I have someone as pretty as you in the chair." She undid the black smock covering Becky and gave her a hand mirror to inspect the back.

Becky swallowed down the emotion that welled up in her throat. She felt beautiful for the first time in ages, like she was still a woman and not just a mommy.

She paid Brandi, then walked out of the tidy hair salon room. The twins were curled into Brandi's daughter's lap, while the girl read them one of the board books Becky had brought over in the diaper bag.

"Mama," Luna called, scrambling up to toddle over to Becky.

She crouched down to hug her daughter, then glanced at Sasha, who studied her with a wary expression. "It's still Mommy, sweetheart," she said gently.

Sasha's features relaxed and she held up her arms. "Mama."

"Your girls are adorable," Sarah said as they walked up the stairs. "But I didn't get much of a chance to watch them."

"They're so sweet," Lilly, Brandi's daughter, murmured. "I hope I have twins someday."

"Shush your mouth," Brandi told her daughter in an exasperated tone. "I don't want you thinking about babies for another decade."

The girl groaned. "Duh, Mom. I'm just saying—"

"Don't say another word." At the top of the stairs, Brandi wrapped Lilly in a tight hug. "You're going to give me a heart attack otherwise."

Becky laughed at the obvious affection between mother and daughter. She hoped she'd have that kind of open relationship with her girls one day.

She said goodbye with a promise to call Sarah if she needed a babysitter and headed home. Callum had invited her and the twins to dinner at his family's ranch tonight. She felt both nervous and excited about being around the Fortune siblings en masse. While Callum made it easy to forget about the differences in their backgrounds, she wasn't certain things would be the same with the rest of the family. But she wanted to know the people who were important to him and see for herself how they interacted. The role he'd played as a caregiver in his family clearly had shaped the man he was today.

He seemed to believe he was a failure at commitment, yet somehow also remained a steadfast rock for his siblings. Who was the real Callum Fortune? The man who was attentive with her girls and so tender and sweet that Becky couldn't help but fall for him? Or the shrewd businessman who'd move onto the next challenge and town instead of putting down roots?

Becky had to figure out the puzzle of Callum before her heart was truly at risk.

"Stop pacing," Stephanie said, dipping a tortilla chip into the guacamole Manny had prepared before heading to his bunkhouse for the night. "You're like a nervous schoolboy."

Callum ran a hand through his hair as he stared out the window above the kitchen sink that offered a view of the long driveway leading away from the ranch. "I *am* nervous," he admitted. "It's weird. I've never really considered our family name or what it means to have money. I don't want Becky to think I'm some kind of rich snob living out here in this gated community."

Stephanie sniffed. "That's right. Women are so turned off by men with money."

He gave her a narrow-eyed glare over his shoulder. "You know what I mean."

"I do," she agreed after a moment. "I always hated girls fawning over my brothers because of our last name. And that was before we landed in Texas where the Fortunes are something of a dynasty."

"She doesn't care about any of that, which is refreshing."

"You really like her." Stephanie stepped closer.

"Is that such a surprise?" he demanded quietly. If his sister wanted to lecture him on getting involved with a single mother or a woman who'd experienced more than her share of tragedy, Callum would put up one hell of a fight.

"No," Stephanie answered without hesitation. "Becky seems great and her daughters are precious. I just can't figure out if this means you're planning to stay in Rambling Rose long term." She put a hand on his arm. "You convinced us to come to Texas, and now it looks like the triplets will be here, too. This town feels like home, Callum. But you've never been one to put down roots."

"Why does everyone keep harping on the future?" He blew out a long breath as dust whirled up at the edge of the horizon and Becky's minivan crested the hill and made its way toward the house. "She and I are enjoying the moments we have together. It doesn't matter to either of us what comes next."

When Stephanie didn't respond, he turned to find her staring at him, arms crossed over her chest and one foot tapping on the floor in apparent exasperation. "You know nothing, Callum Fortune."

He rolled his eyes. "Just be nice tonight. Make her feel welcome."

"You say that as if I'm normally a social ogre. Remember, brother, I'm a proud rescue animal mom. Between the dogs, the cats and the bunny, those twins are going to love me."

With a chuckle of assent, Callum moved past his sister toward the front door. The property was perfect for him and his siblings. It allowed them to be close but still have their own space. He wouldn't have traded it for another home in the area and hoped Becky wasn't overwhelmed by its size.

He jogged down the steps and came around the front of her vehicle just as she climbed out. The afternoon was clear, with only a few puffy clouds floating along the wide expanse of Texas sky. The temperature hovered in the low fifties, cool enough for long sleeves, but still comfortable. He couldn't wait to take the twins to the barn and see their reaction to the horses.

"Wow." He stopped in his tracks as Becky turned to face him.

She tugged self-consciously on the ends of her hair, which had been transformed since the last time he'd seen her. Her chestnut hair now gleamed with gold highlights that gave it a cohesively warm look.

"I got my hair done," she said as if he needed clarification.

"You look beautiful."

"You tell me that every time we're together," she said with a laugh.

"It's always true." He closed the distance between them and kissed her, threading his fingers through her soft locks. "I like the new do."

"Thanks." She grinned up at him. "It was time for a change."

The style might be a subtle update but the shift in Becky's confidence felt massive. Of course, he liked her no matter what, but was thrilled to see the light in her eyes that made him know she liked her new look.

"Do you two like Mommy's hair?" He took a step toward the open door of the minivan and Luna and Sasha. His chest pinched as both girls kicked and squirmed at the sight of him.

"Cawl," Sasha shouted in her high-pitched voice.

"Up," Luna demanded.

"They're so excited to see you." Becky leaned into the minivan to unstrap the girls. She wore a simple yellow sweater and a pair of snug jeans tucked into cowboy boots.

"The feeling is mutual," he assured her, ignoring the fast thumping of his heart as his sister's words played on repeat in his head. Was he considering staying in Rambling Rose? He couldn't think about the future without sweaty palms and a nagging feeling that he was bound to mess things up with Becky. That's what he did.

He might want to commit, but he knew there was something broken inside him that prevented him from giving himself fully. Too deep of an independent streak perhaps or he lacked the gene for commitment. Either way, he didn't want to consider the idea that he could hurt or disappoint Becky and her daughters. They meant too much to him.

"Are you okay?" Becky asked softly.

He squeezed shut his eyes for a quick moment, then grinned at her. "Sorry," he said automatically. "It's been a long week with the finishing touches on the Paws and Claws clinic and the triplets' constant barrage of texts and calls with ideas for the restaurant."

"If you want to reschedule dinner…" She bit down on her lower lip, and he cursed himself for the doubt that flashed in her dark eyes.

"Not at all." He lifted his arms, gratified when Sasha reached for him. "I've been looking forward to showing the three of you my home."

Becky took Luna from her car seat, then hit the button on the vehicle's interior to shut the side door. "It's really great." She cleared her throat. "I actually don't think I've ever been in a house this big."

"The footprint makes it seem larger than it is," he assured her, earning a laugh.

"I don't care that you're rich," she told him, going up on her toes to kiss his cheek. "I like you despite the gobs of money, not because of it."

"I wouldn't describe it as *gobs*," he said, looping his free arm around her shoulder.

"Massive piles?" she suggested playfully.

"You're funny."

She giggled. "I try."

"What would you like to see first? The house or the barn?"

"I think the twins would love to visit the animals, if that's possible."

"Anything is possible for you." He dropped another kiss on the top of her head and led the way to the barn that sat adjacent to the main house.

His sister was waiting inside the wide row of stalls that connected to a spacious arena. The previous owner had been a show jumping enthusiast, and although the arena went largely unused by the Fortunes, Callum appreciated having it available. Unbidden, an image of Sasha and Luna a few years from now popped into his

brain. They had the same dark hair as their mother a
wore matching riding costumes as they trotted pon
around the arena.

He felt a muscle tick in his jaw as he forced away
mental picture. By the time the girls were old enough
riding, he'd be a distant memory to them and their moth

"I hope you don't mind me crashing your date," Step
anie said, shooting him a curious glance. "I couldn't p
up the opportunity to get my hands on these little cutie

"It's nice to see you again," Becky said as Luna wav
Sasha, always the more cautious twin, snuggled agai
the soft fabric of his chambray shirt, but smiled sh
when his sister tickled her leg.

Luna was happy for Stephanie to hold her, and
look of delight on his sister's face gave him a bit c
start. He knew Stephanie liked babies and young ch
dren, but the mix of happiness and yearning in her b
gaze as Becky's daughter relaxed into her arms seen
oddly intense. Stephanie wasn't dating anyone seriou:
at least as far as Callum knew, but she certainly look
like a woman ready to become a mother.

"Your hair is so great," Stephanie told Becky. "I n
a reference for your stylist."

"She's a local," Becky explained quickly, "who wo
out of her house. I'm not sure she'd be—"

"Perfect." Stephanie grinned. "I'd love to give
a call."

At the sound of a soft whinny, Luna squealed a
Sasha sat upright, her eyes widening. "Do you hear
horsey?" Callum asked.

"That's Buttercup," Stephanie told the girls a
Becky. "He likes visitors." She reached into the fr

pocket of her jeans and pulled out a handful of baby carrots. "And treats."

They walked forward to where the sleek bay had popped his head over the wall of the stall.

"Sweet boy," Becky murmured. "Isn't he a beauty, girls?"

She stepped forward and held out her hand, palm out. The horse snuffled and rubbed against it. The twins watched in obvious awe as their mother loved on the large animal.

"Do you want to pet him?" Stephanie asked Luna gently. "He loves little girls."

"Uh-huh," Luna murmured, spellbound.

Callum stayed back with Sasha, who seemed less willing to investigate the big horse close up. She watched with fascination as Stephanie helped her sister reach out a hand to touch the animal's soft nose.

Buttercup blew out a contended breath, reveling in the attention. Stephanie placed a carrot in Luna's chubby hand and uncurled the girl's fingers so that the horse could snuffle it up.

"I've never seen her look so happy," Becky said with a wide grin.

"She's horse crazy already." Stephanie dropped a gentle kiss on top of the girl's head, then turned to Callum and Sasha. "What about you, sweet girl? Do you want to give Buttercup a treat?"

Sasha looked less confident than her sister but nodded nonetheless and reached for Stephanie.

"I'll trade you," Callum said with a laugh as he and his sister switched twins.

Becky pulled out her phone and snapped photos of the girls taking turns petting and giving carrots to all the horses housed in the barn. When they'd visited with each of them, Stephanie introduced them to her personal menagerie, which included two cats, Violet and Daisy, plus two dogs, Mack and Tallulah, not to mention a bunny named Orville who charmed both her daughters.

By the time they were finished, the girls were sticky, sweaty and covered with a fine coat of dust. Becky beamed from ear to ear, and Callum's heart felt full to bursting.

The rest of the evening was just as perfect. He'd purchased two high chairs in town, which seemed to make Becky inordinately grateful. She slayed him with her low expectations. If he had his choice, he'd give her anything in his power. Except the one thing that deep inside he feared she wanted the most—his heart.

It was getting more difficult by the moment to ignore his inability to commit to making Rambling Rose his permanent home.

Once again, he focused on the present. They ate the chicken fajitas Manny had prepared, and Becky seemed to be entertained by Steven and Dillon. His brothers flirted with her and the twins, and it was obvious she was both delighted and embarrassed by their attention.

They stayed later than the girls' normal bedtime, and Luna and Sasha had already dozed off by the time they loaded them into the car seats. "I'll see you tomorrow," he told Becky as he kissed her under the sliver of moonlight.

She shivered when a breeze kicked up, and he pulled her closer.

"I'm working tomorrow," she told him.

"It's Sunday. You don't work on Sundays." He wasn't fazed at having her schedule memorized. The moments he spent with Becky, even on her lunch break, were always the best of his day.

She laughed. "I know, but one of the other nurses needed the day off for her son's birthday. The girls like going to the day care center, and it shouldn't be busy."

"How about lunch?" he asked.

"You don't have to—"

"Please." He brushed his mouth over hers. "Let me see you again."

"You see me all the time."

"I can't get enough."

She bit down on her lower lip. "That makes me happy."

"You make me happy."

"Lunch tomorrow," she promised. "I should be able to take a break around noon. Does that work?"

"I look forward to it." He smoothed his hands over her cheeks. How could she be so precious to him after such a short time? There was no explaining the deep connection he felt, but no denying it, either. He'd take her to lunch, to dinner. Hell, he'd drive her to the gas station to fill up her minivan if that's what she needed from him.

He watched her drive away, then turned to walk back up the porch steps. Funny how one evening with Becky and her girls had made his big house finally feel like a home.

Chapter 10

As she and Callum drove toward the pediatric center the following afternoon, Becky stole glances at her fingers entwined with Callum's larger, tanned hand, her heart hammering in her chest. They'd had lunch at the diner in town and then Callum had taken her to see the feed and grain building he'd just bought with a plan for his younger sisters to convert into a restaurant.

More Fortunes were coming to Rambling Rose, causing nerves to bubble up inside her. She wanted to meet Callum's younger sisters, both because he talked so fondly of the triplets and also due to her curiosity about the bond of adult multiples. Would her girls always be as close as they seemed now? She hoped so, and from what Callum had told her, Ashley, Nicole and Megan might provide great insight.

But each time her ties with the Fortune family deep-

ened, she worried about what that would mean when and
if Callum decided to leave Rambling Rose.

Although her love for him seemed so sure and strong,
she still had no idea how he felt about her. Certainly she
knew he cared for her and her daughters. But that was
different from being in love. She thought about broach-
ing the subject even though the doubtful part of her heart
worried about what answer she might get.

"Looks like trouble at the center," Callum said, his
tone laced with concern.

She looked up from their joined hands to the pediatric center's entrance. Two police cars, lights flashing,
were parked in front of the building.

Becky's first thought went to her daughters, although
she knew Luna and Sasha were safe in the building's secure day care center.

"Will you drop me off in front?" Adrenaline pumped
through her.

As soon as Callum pulled to a stop, she bolted from
the truck, flashing her employee badge to the officer
who stood just inside the sliding doors when it looked
like he might stop her.

Grant Martensen stood near the information desk
with another officer. Shannon Goering, the young ad-
missions attendant, stood next to him, wiping at her
cheeks.

"What's going on?" Becky's instinct was to rush to
check on her girls, but she forced a deep breath. Nothing good would come of her panicking. She placed a
hand on the woman's arm, wanting to offer comfort for
whatever was so upsetting.

"I didn't know," Shannon said miserably, shaking
her head. "She wanted to leave the baby and we learned

about the Safe Haven law in training. If I thought the mom might be a danger to herself, I would have tried to keep her here."

Becky looked from Shannon to the thin-lipped police officer to Grant.

"The baby's with Dr. Green," the older man said. "He can give you the details."

Relief and worry battled inside Becky as she headed toward the primary care wing. Relief that the crisis was limited to a single child, but concern about the details of that baby's situation. Parker Green leaned against the high counter of the nurse's station as she entered, holding a phone to his ear. He gave her a swift nod and crooked a finger, beckoning her forward.

"Tell me about the baby," she said when he put down the phone, her eyes darting to the exam room with the closed door.

"He's stable." Parker massaged a hand along the back of his neck. "Vitals are good and no signs of neglect."

"How old?" She was already moving past him. "What's the story?"

"Becky, wait." He placed a gentle hand on her shoulder. "It's the little guy from the ribbon cutting."

She blinked, trying to follow his words. There had been no patients at the opening ceremony except…

"The woman in labor," she said, absently rubbing her arms. "Laurel?"

The young doctor nodded, lines of tension bracketing his mouth. "She left a note tucked into the blanket she'd wrapped the baby in. She said he's better off here for a while and she'll be back as soon as she can."

"Where is she now?" Becky's heart broke for a mother who felt so desperate to relinquish her baby. Thanks to

Callum watching the twins, Becky had been the one to stay with Laurel. The woman had been a heartbreaking mix of strength and fragility. She'd seemed terrified about becoming a mother but determined to take care of her baby.

Becky had empathized with her plight on so many levels. It was exactly how she'd felt the moment her water broke with Luna and Sasha. As much as she'd tried to prepare during her pregnancy, panic had fluttered through her chest like a bird caught without shelter in a rainstorm. She hadn't known how she would handle the reality of motherhood, but she had managed due to a deep sense of devotion to her babies.

She didn't for one instant doubt Laurel's love, but Becky also understood that there were so many factors that went into successful parenting. If Laurel was experiencing some form of postpartum depression and had no support system, it could force her into an act of desperation.

Like giving up her child.

"The authorities are reaching out to the hospital where she delivered the baby," Parker said, as if reading her mind. "The law provides for anonymity, but they want to make sure she's not a danger to herself. Shannon said Laurel seemed to be coherent, but the note mentions the history of the Fortune's Foundling Hospital. It's as if she believes she was leaving the baby at a modern-day orphanage."

A sick feeling spread through Becky's stomach, but she forced herself to focus on what she could do to help. "Can I see the baby?"

"Of course," Parker answered immediately. His phone rang at the same moment. "I've got to take this. I'm trying to coordinate a plan with the Department of Human Services."

Foster care. Becky drew in a sharp breath at the thought of the tiny infant going to a stranger. Then she reminded herself there were amazing families involved in the foster care system in Texas. If Laurel felt she needed to relinquish her baby, she must have had a good reason, and the welfare of the child was critical at this stage.

She pushed open the exam room door, surprised to find the space empty other than a portable bassinet situated at one end. Her rational side understood. The child's arrival on a low-staffed Sunday afternoon had thrown the pediatric center into crisis mode.

But the mother in her roared in silent disapproval. This baby had been abandoned. He needed someone with him. On instinct, she dimmed the lights, knowing that a baby born only a few weeks ago needed the calmest environment she could provide.

A soft coo from the bassinet had her hurrying forward. She paused long enough to wash her hands in the exam room's small utility sink. One of the other nurses had swaddled him in a hospital blanket and placed a tiny blue cap on his head. He looked like a squirming burrito.

"Hello, big guy," Becky said gently, reaching out to stroke a finger across the boy's cheek.

He immediately turned toward the touch, his rooting reflex kicking in, and she realized he was hungry.

The door to the exam room opened, and Sharla entered, holding a bottle. "Poor little dude." She frowned. "He doesn't have any idea what's going on."

"I'll feed him," Becky offered immediately. "There has to be some explanation. I talked to the mom during her labor. She seemed overwhelmed, but it was clear she loved her baby even then."

"Who knows," the other woman murmured, handing the bottle to Becky. "My hormones got all out of whack after Thomas was born. It took months of me crying on the bathroom floor before my husband insisted I talk to the doctor. She helped me, but this munchkin's mom was totally alone. Maybe she didn't have anyone to tell her she'd be okay."

"I wish I would have been here when she came in today." Becky lifted the baby into her arms, then took a seat on the bench meant for family members waiting with a young patient. "Maybe I could have helped. Did the note give any details about his care?"

Sharla shook her head. "We don't even know if he was breast- or bottle-fed. All we can do now is try to keep him healthy and hope they track down the mom or find an amazing foster care placement for him."

The baby sucked greedily from the bottle, his tiny fingers grasped on to the front of Becky's scrub shirt. "Does he have a name?" she whispered, tears pricking the back of her eyes at his vulnerability and resilience.

"There wasn't anything in the note about a name." Sharla sighed. "We know Laurel is the mom, so he started out as Baby L. I'm calling him Linus on account of the blue blanket he was wrapped in when he got there."

Becky fingered the soft white fabric that swaddled him now. "Where is that blanket?"

"We got him a fresh one. Figured the blue one might be in need of a good washing."

"Don't do that. It probably smells familiar."

"Do you think she'll come back?" Sharla asked so[...] "His mama?"

"I hope so, but more than anything I hope she's ok[...] Becky maneuvered baby Linus onto her shoulder [...] gently patted his back until he let out a robust burp. "[...] eating like a champ."

The door to the room opened again, and Cal[...] peeked in. "Parker filled me in on the situation,[...] said gravely.

"You can keep the two of them company," Sh[...] told him, moving toward the door. "I need to chec[...] another patient."

Callum washed his hands without being asked, [...] came to sit next to Becky.

"Can you take him for a minute?" she asked. [...] that it was just her and Parker, she was having tro[...] holding back tears.

"Sure." Parker easily transferred the baby to his a[...] then took the half-full bottle and offered it to Linu[...]

"I don't understand how this happened," Becky w[...] pered, wiping at her eyes. "I know Laurel loves hi[...]

Parker's mouth thinned. "She obviously felt like[...] couldn't care for him the way he needed."

"She should have asked for help."

"That's not easy for some people," Callum remi[...] her.

Becky knew that all too well. Sometimes it felt [...] she'd muscled through those first few months of m[...] ering twins on willpower alone. Like Sharla, she'd [...] almost every day from sheer exhaustion, but ha[...] wanted to admit to anyone how she was strugglin[...] fear they'd judge her or deem her unfit to care fo[...]

girls. Looking back, she understood all three of them would have been better off if she'd asked for help.

Even now, she struggled to reach out even though the friends she had in the Rambling Rose community seemed happy to rally around her.

"What's going to happen to him?" Callum asked as the baby finished the bottle. Becky was amazed at how naturally he handled the infant. He'd told her how much responsibility he'd taken on with his younger sisters. Obviously, those skills were deeply ingrained in him. He didn't miss a beat with burping Linus, even thinking to pull a towel off the counter to flip over his shoulder.

Becky glanced down at her own shoulder and cringed at the wet spot of spit-up. She'd never been great at re-membering a burp cloth. "Do you mind sitting with him for a few minutes while I get an update from Dr. Green?" She used the edge of her sleeve to dab at the corner of one eye. "I'd also like to take a look at the note Laurel left. I'm hoping something helps me make sense of this whole thing."

She took a step toward the door without waiting for an answer, shock making her feel fragile.

"Becky." At the sound of her name in his deep voice, she stilled.

He came up behind her and pressed a kiss to the top of her head. "It's not your fault."

How did he know what she was thinking?

Drawing in a steadying breath, she turned and glanced down at Linus in Callum's strong arms. The baby had fallen back asleep, lulled by a full stomach and the feeling of security he no doubt had being held by Callum.

"What if I had done more?" she asked, realizing she

sounded as miserable as she felt. "I could have offered to go along with her in the ambulance…"

"You had the twins with you that day," Callum pointed out gently. "I have mad babysitting skills and an insanely trustworthy face, but I doubt you would have just left them with me indefinitely."

"Mad skills," she repeated with a soft laugh. "In so many areas."

When he wrapped his free arm around her, she rested her head against his chest, the steady beat of his heart calming her slightly.

"I could have followed up with her," she said against his shirtfront. "I've thought about her so many times since that day. I saw a lot of myself in Laurel and her situation. What if I'd intervened and given her the support she needed to not give up on herself?"

"You still could," he told her. "There's no telling what will happen next. Hopefully, they find her quickly and get her the help she obviously needs. If that happens, Laurel and Linus will benefit from any support we can give them. Until then, this little guy is most important."

"You're smart, ridiculously handsome and have mad skills as a baby whisperer. Remind me again why you haven't been scooped up by some lucky lady?"

She meant the question as a joke to lighten the mood but knew she'd miscalculated when his body went rigid.

"I'm a bad bet in the commitment department," he said without emotion, taking a step away from her, his gaze shuttered.

She wanted to argue. To tell him that he just needed to believe in himself and to find a woman willing to take a chance on love with him. She could be that woman if he'd let her.

But Callum was right. Linus had to be the priority at the moment, the way Luna and Sasha were always first in Becky's heart and mind. If Laurel couldn't give her baby what he needed, Becky would make sure the community stepped in to help until the situation could be resolved.

"I think you're the perfect bet," she murmured, then quickly left the room, not wanting to gauge his response to her comment.

Dr. Green—or Parker, as he'd told her on multiple occasions to call him—was still at the nurses' station. He ended another call as she approached.

"How is he?"

"He just took down two ounces like a champ." She gave what she hoped was a reassuring smile. "We're going to take care of him."

"That boy will need our care." Parker spoke absently, almost more to himself than her. "It could be a rough road for such an innocent baby."

Becky couldn't allow herself to consider that possibility. She needed to stay focused on resolving the situation. "Any leads on tracking down Laurel?"

Parker's jaw tightened. "She relinquished the baby," he said quietly.

"Temporarily," Becky clarified. "Her note specified that. It's what she told Shannon, as well. She needed a temporary reprieve."

"I understand. But the point of the law is to offer a safe option for the baby that also protects the parent who can't care for him."

"Temporarily," Becky repeated, enunciating each syllable. "You were here when she came in the first time, Parker. You know as well as I do that she loves her baby.

I don't know what Laurel is going through at the ment, but she needs our help and support as muc Linus does."

"Unless the hospital in San Antonio doesn't bel she's a threat to herself, the authorities won't aid in search for her," he explained, his voice tight. " isn't how it works when someone voluntarily give a child."

"She left him at what she believed was a decades- orphanage." Becky threw up her hands. "She's conf and she could even be suffering from postpartum pression. We can't just abandon her."

Parker drew in a deep breath, closing his eyes a moment as if he were deep in concentration. He turned his strained gaze to hers. "We're on the s side, Becky. I want to find and help Laurel and reu her with Linus if that's what's best for the child."

She opened her mouth to argue that of course b with the mother was best, but she'd worked in pec rics long enough to know that wasn't always the c Still, nothing could shake her belief that Laurel w be a good mother if given the chance and the sup she needed.

"Where does that leave us?" She pressed a tremb hand to her chest and forced herself to ask the ques that had been burning a hole in her gut for the past minutes. "What happens to Linus now?"

"I've talked to a half-dozen people from social vices already." Parker looked past her toward the e: room where she'd left the baby with Callum. "He'll to be placed with a foster family, and we'll make it's someone who will give him the right kind of c: He thumped a hand on the top of the counter, cle frustrated at not being able to come up with an easy fix for the situation. "Let's go take another look at Baby L."

"We're calling him Linus." Becky fell in step with him. "Callum is with him now."

Parker gave her a funny look. "I wouldn't have expected Callum Fortune to be so comfortable with a baby."

"He took care of his triplet sisters when he was younger." Becky couldn't help the pride that swelled in her tone. "He's really great with kids."

She opened the exam room door to find Callum just finishing up a diaper change for the baby.

"He does diaper duty, too," Parker murmured behind her, chuckling softly. "This one might be a keeper, Beck."

Tension gathered between her shoulder blades at the way Parker's teasing words made her heart leap. She should know better than to allow herself to daydream about the future, but with Callum she couldn't help it. In the weeks and months after her husband's death, Becky had resigned herself to a life with Luna and Sasha as her only focus. She had to be both mom and dad for them, and she'd become accustomed to the loneliness that sometimes found her in the rare quiet moments.

Callum filled that void, but she had to keep reminding herself their relationship was only temporary. He knew how to make her feel special and was a natural with her girls, but when his work in Rambling Rose was finished, he'd move on. If she wasn't careful, he'd take her heart with him when he left.

"All systems are a go for this little trouper," Callum reported, cradling Linus in his arms once again. "What's the plan?"

Parker shook his head. "Social services can't arrange a foster placement until tomorrow morning, so I think he's going to be a guest of the pediatric center tonight."

"I could take him home," Callum said.

Becky felt her mouth drop open, shocked at his willingness to step in. By the way color tinged his cheeks, she had a feeling he was just as surprised at his offer.

"I know I'm probably not the first choice to be responsible for a baby," he clarified, his tone almost self-deprecating in its casualness. "But we might as well take advantage of all that training I had with my younger siblings."

"Callum would take good care of him," she told Parker, hoping Callum knew how much his actions meant to her. Linus was a precious boy but not a child with whom Callum had a personal connection. It was just the kind of man he was to take on a virtual stranger's baby because it was the right thing to do.

"I'm sure you're right," Parker said, giving Callum a tight smile. "Unfortunately, that's flaunting protocol a bit too flagrantly, even for a small-town medical center." He stepped closer to peer down at the sleeping baby. "It's not ideal, but baby Linus will be spending the night with us. I'll make sure the nurses on duty take good care of him."

"Then I'll stay." Callum's hold on the baby tightened ever so slightly. "If it's okay with you? That way we'll know someone is with him at all times."

Parker appeared marginally affronted by that. "You can stay if you'd like, but rest assured my staff does an exemplary job of caring for our patients."

"I have full confidence in your staff," Callum said, his gaze darting to Becky. "I'll still stay."

"Your choice." The men shared a silent look that

Becky couldn't interpret but somehow eased the tension crackling between them. It was as if they'd come to an understanding, and Becky felt her heart go soft at the sight of these two strong men bonding over the care of an abandoned infant.

"I'll have our largest room made up with a bed for you," Parker said before leaving them alone again. "Thanks, Callum. We all appreciate it."

As the door shut behind the doctor, Becky checked her watch, then let out a frustrated sigh. "I have a short shift today because the day care center closes early on Sunday." She offered a wan smile. "I'd rather not bring the girls to see him since he seems to have settled in so peacefully. The last thing this baby needs is more unfamiliar stimulation at this point."

"It's fine." Callum pressed a swift kiss to her mouth. "I'm going to text my brothers and Stephanie and let them know I won't be home tonight. The nurses will take care of both Linus and me tonight."

"I know," she said softly. "It's an amazing thing you're doing."

He chuckled. "I'm sleeping on a hospital bed for the night. Not quite hero material."

"You are to me," she blurted, then felt her cheeks heat as a look of panic passed over his face. "I'll check in later," she said quickly, careful not to meet his gaze. The emotions churning inside her from the baby's plight were making her speak without thinking. She'd been careful not to push Callum more on his future plans. She had to believe that his willingness to become involved with Linus meant he was ready to commit to Rambling Rose. He cared about this town, and she hoped he cared about her, as well.

Chapter 11

Callum woke the next morning to the sound of his sister's soft singing and the smell of fresh coffee. Stephanie stood in front of the bassinet, blocking his view of the sleeping infant.

He scrubbed a hand over his eyes and they focused on Becky entering the room. She walked over to him and gently swept her fingers along his jaw, then kissed the top of his head. Her touch was comforting in a way that pricked along his nerve endings. Last night had made him far too vulnerable, more than he'd expected or felt equipped to handle.

He'd told her yesterday he wasn't a hero. He'd simply gone with his natural instinct to protect little Linus, whose young life had changed irreparably in an instant. Coupled with his need to ease the tension he saw in Becky, he'd had no choice but to get involved.

It wasn't the man he knew himself to be, and his greatest fear at this point was that she would expect from him something he wasn't capable of giving.

"Why aren't you in the bed?" Becky frowned as he stretched his neck and sat up straighter in the chair where he'd spent most of the night.

"I was afraid of falling asleep too deeply and not hearing him," he admitted. "What time is it?"

"Almost seven." Becky handed him a cup of coffee. "Stephanie and I arrived at the same time. You look like you could use this."

"Intravenously," he said with a laugh.

"Did Linus wake a lot?" Stephanie asked over her shoulder as she leaned down to pick up the baby.

"Every three hours like clockwork," Callum said, marveling at the care with which his sister held the small baby. Once again, he was struck by the maternal side he hadn't realized was part of Stephanie's makeup. "Bottle, diaper change and some deep conversations about life. The little man and I covered all the bases."

He took Becky's hand, brushing a kiss across her knuckles. "Where are the twins? I thought it was your day off so they wouldn't be coming to day care."

"A friend is watching them." At his raised brow, she added, "It's Sarah, the building manager's wife. She's really good with them, and I wanted to check in on you and Linus."

"I took a personal day," Stephanie said, finally turning toward them. "I couldn't stay away."

"Since when has your biological clock been ticking like a gong?" Callum asked his sister.

"She cares about Linus and Laurel." Becky pushed a

brown paper bag toward him with more force than
necessary. "She's got a big heart."

"Yeah," Stephanie agreed, her eyes narrowing. "
ten to your girlfriend, Callum. She's obviously the br
between the two of you."

He tried to hide the agitation that rose to the surfa
Stephanie referring to Becky as his girlfriend. Of co
she was his girlfriend. What else would he call a wo
with whom he spent almost every night?

But something about the word gave their relation
a gravity that made his flight instinct kick into high ;
Or maybe it was just his lack of sleep. Either way
busied himself with opening the bag and pulling (
foil-wrapped burrito.

"It's from the food truck out near Mariana's," B
told him, her voice unusually light. "Best breakfa
town."

Callum wasn't familiar with Mariana's but didn't
unsure how to handle the strange current of tension
ning between them. If Stephanie noticed the awkw
ness, she didn't mention it, all of her attention foc
on the baby.

The door opened and Parker walked in, his ;
tracking between the three of them. "Then you've h
the news," he said to Becky and Callum before tur
to Stephanie. "You're doing a wonderful thing."

"Holding a baby?" Callum scoffed in the way o
brothers everywhere. "She's not that impressive.
until she deals with her first blowout diaper."

"There'll be plenty of time for that," Parker said.
soon as the social worker gets here, we'll finaliz(
paperwork."

Callum finally glanced up at Becky, who looked as confused as him. "What paperwork?" he asked.

"I haven't told them," Stephanie said, biting down on her lower lip.

"What's going on?" Callum rose from the chair, placing the coffee and breakfast on the counter. He didn't like the way Dr. Green was looking at his sister, like they shared some kind of secret.

"It's not really my news to tell," Parker said carefully. "I'll give you all some time. Stephanie, come to my office when you're ready and we'll go over a few items."

"Ready for what?" Callum demanded as the doctor closed the door behind him.

"Hush," Stephanie whispered when the baby stirred in her arms. "You're going to wake him."

"I should go, too." Becky took a step toward the door, but Callum instinctively reached out and enclosed her thin wrist with his fingers. He might bristle about putting a label on what was between them, but that didn't change the fact that he wanted her at his side.

"You're overreacting for nothing," Stephanie said, then transferred her gaze from Callum to Linus. "I've been approved as this sweetheart's foster mom."

Callum felt his mouth drop open. He looked to Becky, who seemed as bewildered as him. "Since last night?" He shook his head. "That's impossible. It takes—"

"Months," Stephanie finished. "I put in my application right when we moved. I've gotten background checks, gone through interviews." She looked up at him and cringed. "I even did a home visit that weekend in November when you, Steven and Dillon went camping."

"I don't understand." Callum prided himself on knowing every intricacy of his siblings' lives, especially Stephanie and the triplets. They'd always been close. How could she have undertaken something so monumental without telling him about it? "Do Mom and Dad know?"

"I called them this morning," his sister answered, her tone thick with emotion. How had their parents reacted to the news?

He ran a hand through his hair, fatigue and frustration threatening to engulf him. "You shouldn't have done this without running it by the family first."

Stephanie's shoulders went rigid. She carefully placed Linus into the bassinet, then took the few steps across the room to stand in front of Callum. At the same time, he felt Becky shift closer and was profoundly grateful for her sweet protectiveness, even if it was unnecessary.

As one of eight kids, Callum was well versed in sibling squabbles. He loved his family beyond measure and knew they could disagree and still maintain their closeness. But he'd never seen a fire like the one that glowed in his sister's eyes at the moment.

"I'm an adult," Stephanie said, her hands on her hips, her voice like a laser cutting through him. "Don't forget, I'm only a few years younger than you. So as much as I appreciate the big-brother-knows-all routine, you don't know everything about me. I make decisions for my life based on what is right for me." She tapped her chest with two fingers. "I'm going to be that baby's foster mom, and I will care for him like he's my own as long as he needs me."

"This will change everything," he said, although he wasn't sure whether he spoke the words for her benefit or his own. "Paws and Claws is about to open. You'll be busy with that. There's so much going on. Fostering Linus is going to—"

"Give my life more meaning," she interrupted, a gentle catch in her voice. "It will make me happy and challenge me in ways I probably can't imagine." Stephanie laughed softly. "I know what I'm getting into, Callum. You might not be ready to settle down and build a life and home in Rambling Rose, but I am."

Becky let out a startled gasp next to him, but he couldn't take his eyes off his sister. It was like seeing her for the first time, or at least seeing her in a different light. Only a few years separated them in age, but he'd taken on a protective role toward her as much as he'd had with the triplets. Now they'd all grown up.

Ashley, Megan and Nicole were going to open their restaurant in Rambling Rose, linking three more members of his family to this community. And Stephanie was becoming a foster parent to a sweet, innocent baby who needed her. Linus would be living under their roof until his future was settled. Was that odd pain in his gut the uneasy feeling of his siblings passing him by?

He'd thought he knew what he wanted from life, but now questions and doubts swirled through him like a cold gust of wind. He didn't know how to buffer his heart from the potential damage other than to close it off.

All he could control was his reaction to the present moment, and right now he understood he needed to change his attitude. He might not understand Stephanie's reasons for choosing this path, but his only job was to support her on it.

"I'm sorry," he said gently. "Blame it on sleep deprivation or—"

"Your typical high-handedness," she added, but one side of her mouth curved into a smile.

"That, too," he admitted. "You will be the most amazing foster parent. All of us, and especially Linus, are lucky you made that decision." He ran a hand through his hair. "It's one of the most selfless things I can imagine, and I'm actually in awe of you right now."

Stephanie sniffled and dabbed at the corner of her eye. "It's about time."

"It really is a gift you're giving baby Linus," Becky added. "If there's anything I can do to help you with the transition, please let me know."

For the first time since she'd revealed her plans, Stephanie looked the tiniest bit panicked. "I'll take you up on that," she told Becky. "I have the best of intentions, but very little experience with infants. And virtually no supplies."

Becky wrapped his sister in a quick hug. "That I can take care of for you."

He could see Stephanie relax and understood that response. Becky's generous spirit and quiet confidence had that effect on him, as well, easing any of the sharp edges of his life and allowing him to enjoy the small moments that meant the most.

"I'd appreciate it so much." Stephanie offered Becky a wide smile. "I'm trying to appear like I know what I'm doing, but inside I'm terrified."

If Callum hadn't felt like a jerk before, that admission sealed the deal. His sister needed his support, not judgment or doubt.

"You'll do great," Becky assured Stephanie. "While you meet with Parker and the social worker, I'll head home and gather up supplies. I didn't find out the sex of the twins during the pregnancy, so I still have tons of neutral baby clothes. I'll meet you at the ranch and get Linus settled in with you."

Stephanie nodded. "Thank you. I just realized I don't even have a car seat for him." She shook her head. "What kind of foster parent doesn't have a car seat?"

"The kind who wanted to meet her tiny charge right away." Becky squeezed Stephanie's arms, then took a step toward the door. "We keep a couple of infant seats stored in the utility closet next to the day care center in case patients need them."

"I'll go get it," Callum offered, needing to feel useful in some way. "Then I'll call Steven and Dillon to explain what's going on." He flashed a wry smile at his sister. "I can at least save you from having to deal with them the way you did me."

"It's probably good that your initial reaction was so lame." Stephanie winked. "Now you'll feel guilty about it for weeks and will happily do diaper duty or late-night feedings to make it up to me. Right?"

He wrapped her in a tight hug. "Whatever it takes, li'l sister."

Becky tried to focus on the twins' happy babbling from the back seat as she drove toward the ranch and not on the disappointed beating of her own heart.

All those silly fantasies she'd had of Callum had evaporated like dew on the grass in the morning sun. Listening to him speak to his sister about losing her freedom made Becky know that he wasn't thinking of staying. At least not now.

She had no idea how he felt about her and her girls. Sure, he liked spending time with them. And the way he touched her body in the quiet hours of night made her feel cherished. But was it all just a temporary arrangement for him?

The Fortunes were doing so much for Rambling Rose. She hated to think that he could easily move on after all the work they'd put into revitalizing the town. She'd heard rumblings that some of the locals weren't happy with all the changes. People were afraid that their community was falling prey to a sort of cowboy gentrification, and that longtime residents would be pushed aside for businesses that catered to the wealthy people moving into areas like the Rambling Rose Estates.

She knew that wasn't the intent of Callum or his brothers. They wanted to add to the community, but if his plan didn't include staying long-term, how much would Callum care about his impact?

And what about the impact he'd already had on her heart, she thought as she pulled up to the gatehouse at the entrance of the gated subdivision.

She offered a smile to the uniformed attendant, who frowned in response, giving her dusty minivan a dismissive once-over.

Acid seeped into Becky's veins. Callum and his family had never made her feel like less because of their differences in social and financial status. The man staring at her now, with his cropped cut and ice-blue gaze, managed to do just that without saying a word. The older gentleman who'd been working the first night she'd come to the ranch was nowhere in sight.

"I'm visiting the Fortunes," she said, forcing a cheerful tone.

"You aren't on the list," he said flatly.

"It's been a whirlwind kind of morning." Becky

hitched a thumb toward the cargo area of her vehicle. "I'm bringing supplies for Stephanie and her new baby. Maybe you heard about the baby relinquished at the pediatric center yesterday? The Fortunes have stepped in to care for him, and I'm helping with that."

She drew in a breath and tried to calm her beating heart. Nerves made her babble, and the way this man looked at her as if she were dirt on the bottom of his boot gave her a feeling of indignity she didn't appreciate.

Sasha began to whimper from the back seat, as if she could sense her mama's tension and wanted to offer her own kind of toddler empathy. Unfortunately, the last thing Becky needed was a meltdown on top of everything else.

"I'm Callum Fortune's girlfriend," she said, changing tactic. "He's expecting me."

"Not on the list," the man repeated. He pointed to a few open parking spaces. "You can turn around over there."

Becky almost did what he told her. That was how she was raised. Listen to authority. Don't make waves. Know your place.

This surly man was a literal gatekeeper. She was tempted to drive home and ask Callum to come and pick up the baby supplies from her house. It would be much easier that way.

If motherhood had taught her one lesson, though, it was that she possessed enough strength that she didn't have to take the easy way out. She understood how to win a battle of wills. If this dude thought he had anything on a pair of grumpy toddlers, he was sorely mistaken.

"I'm not leaving," she said, moving her sunglasses to the top of her head so she could return the gatekeeper's glare. "You can choose to trust me or you can call Callum." When the guy opened his mouth to argue, she held up a hand. "But just so we're clear, he's going to be very angry that you doubted me."

The guard's already pinched mouth thinned even further. After several long moments of staring at the clipboard in his hands, he thrust it at her. "Write down your name, address and phone number. If there are any questions, we'll know how to contact you."

"Okay," she answered and scrawled the information with trembling fingers. It had worked. She'd held her ground and gotten her way. Forcing herself not to cheer or break out in song, she returned the clipboard to him. "You made the right decision today. Thank you."

He gave a brief nod, then went into the gatehouse and hit the button to open the wrought-iron gate.

Becky drove through with a wide grin on her face. "Did you see how Mommy stood up to the rude man?" she asked her daughters, glancing at each of them in the rearview mirror. Sasha stared at her solemnly, binky shoved in her mouth, while Luna stared out the window at the rolling hills. "You girls are going to understand your worth a lot earlier than I did. I'm going to make sure you know that you deserve to be treated well all the time. No exceptions."

She blew out a shaky breath, adrenaline pumping through her at the small stand she'd taken. "We will respect authority, but also know that we should be respected, as well. I'm going to become a strong woman so I can raise strong women." She laughed at the depth of conversation she was having with her daughters. They couldn't understand the meaning of her message but she continued to speak about their value as she drove down the winding drive that led to the Fortune ranch, needing to say the words out loud for herself as much as for them.

Callum and Steven walked down the porch steps as she pulled to a stop in front of the large house.

"How are Stephanie and Linus?" she asked as she came around the front of the car.

Steven grimaced. "Who knew our sister had the heart of a drill sergeant? She's been barking orders in a weird singsong voice since they got here."

"I don't think she wants the baby to realize that he's being cared for by a foster mom dictator," Callum added with a snort.

The brothers shared a pained look that made Becky stifle a giggle. The combined handsomeness of the two of them almost took her breath away. She knew they were stepbrothers, but the similar way they held themselves showed their family connection. She glanced up as the front door opened and the third of the Rambling Rose Fortune men appeared.

She knew from Callum that Dillon was his full-blood brother. He had sandy-blond hair and was more thickly muscled than the other two, but his features resembled Callum's. She'd met their father only on that one occasion, but both boys looked like David Fortune. She could only imagine the string of broken hearts they'd left in their collective wake and hoped to never be among that group.

"Linus is a lucky boy," Becky said, wanting to show solidarity with Stephanie.

Callum laughed softly. "Good answer."

"She sent us out here to unload the haul," Dillon told her.

Becky hit the button on the key fob to unlatch the

back cargo door and then opened the side door to reveal the twins. Both girls looked with wide-eyed curiosity at the trio of handsome men staring at them.

The Fortune brothers could even dazzle ladies still in diapers. Impressive.

Luna clapped her hands as her gaze fell on Callum.

"Cawl," she shouted happily.

Sasha pulled her binky from her mouth and squealed his name, as well.

"Nice fan club," Steven told Callum and then followed Dillon to the back of the vehicle.

Becky leaned in to unfasten the girls' car seats, but Callum quickly grabbed her from behind, pulling her close and reaching around to plant a gentle kiss on her throat. "Hi," he whispered against her hair.

"Your brothers will see," she protested, wiggling out of his grasp.

"I'm pretty sure they know I kiss you." He chuckled at his own joke, but released her. "Did you have any problems at the gate?"

She stilled. "Why do you ask?" She threw the questioning glance over her shoulder.

"The new guy is a real piece of work," Dillon said, reappearing with a bouncer seat. "He actually made me show him my driver's license the other night. As if I don't live here."

"I didn't have any trouble," Becky lied. It was easier to let them believe she'd made it through without incident.

"He probably took one look at you," Steven told her as he hefted a big box of clothes, "and thought he better not mess with a boss mom."

Color rose to her cheeks. "That's me," she confirmed with a grin.

As she spoke to his brothers, Callum had reached around her to get the twins. He lifted Luna out of her car seat and handed her to Becky, then undid Sasha's car seat strap and straightened with the girl in his arms.

"Do you think Stephanie's up for visitors?" she asked, pausing at the base of the porch steps. "If you think she'd rather get settled in peace, I can come back another time."

"I know she'd love to see you," Callum told her with a smile. "She's already started a list of baby care questions for you. I think she's hoping you'll be her expert resource."

"Anything I can do to help." Becky followed him up the steps and he paused to let her enter the house before him.

"I really appreciate—"

When his words cut off, Becky glanced up at him.

"I appreciate you," he said, the intensity of his tone sending shivers down her spine.

She drew in a breath. Maybe she hadn't misinterpreted how he felt. Maybe her heart was safe with Callum after all. Could she dare to believe that?

Chapter 12

Callum sat in his truck, finger hovering above the send button on his phone. It was nearly midnight, and he should be home and in bed. The problem was he didn't want to be in his bed, not without the woman whose house he'd been parked outside for the past fifteen minutes.

He'd driven to Becky's on a whim, without a plan for what to do once he arrived. If he texted her, would it look like a booty call? He didn't mean it that way and certainly wanted to avoid giving her that message. Not that holding Becky in his arms wasn't as damn near close to perfection as he could imagine.

But after the unexpected events of the last twenty-four hours, he craved something more. The comfort he found in her arms.

Linus's arrival and the thought of the baby's mother

out there in the world, so desperate that giving up her son felt like the best option, had rocked him to his core. Despite the unrest in his early years from his parents' contentious divorce, Callum had always known love growing up. Marci had come into their lives and immediately taken him and Dillon into her heart.

Even when her health suffered during those years of trying to conceive again and after the triplets' birth, she'd never wavered in her maternal devotion. He'd had two parents who loved him and a gaggle of siblings who made him crazy but also helped him to never feel truly alone.

The baby his sister had taken on had been abandoned in the world. At least for now. He knew Stephanie would do everything in her power to love and protect little Linus. His sister had shown a depth of spirit and service that humbled Callum. He couldn't force himself to commit to staying in Rambling Rose long-term because of the risk of being hurt, or causing pain to someone who loved him, the way he had with Doralee.

He'd never thought of himself as a coward. He'd established his company and grown the business to the point where he could cherry-pick the most appealing projects. His brothers had found a place with him, and he'd naively assumed that his success as a real estate developer and contractor was enough for a fulfilling life.

A couple of hours ago he'd understood how far he truly had to go, and it had terrified him.

A part of him had wanted to cut and run. He'd gotten in his car after an hour of restless tossing and turning, not sure whether to head out of town or just drive until exhaustion sent him home again. Almost unaware of where he was going, he'd ended up at Becky's.

He startled as his phone vibrated now, the tone alerting him to an incoming message.

Are you going to sit in your truck all night or come in?

A text from Becky.

He glanced through his windshield toward the house to see Becky standing at the family room window, the lamp behind her bathing her in light.

His fingers trembled as he typed in a two-letter response.

In.

He climbed out of the truck and headed for the front door, heart pounding.

Becky met him at the door, her honey-colored eyes unreadable. She wore a thin cotton nightgown with two kittens curled together on the front and the words *snooze squad* scrawled beneath them. He must have it bad when he found kittens sexy as hell.

"I know it's late," he said, offering an apologetic smile. "If I woke you I'm—"

His words were cut off when she launched herself at him, wrapping her arms around his neck as she fused her mouth to his.

He lifted her off the ground as he stepped into the house, kicking the door shut behind him. She seemed as frenzied with need as he felt, like she couldn't get enough of him. Her tongue delved into his mouth, and he groaned out loud, almost stumbling at the power of the desire pulsing through him.

Instead of moving toward the bedroom, he detoured

into the nearby family room and lowered her to the couch. "I need you so badly," he whispered, shocked by the intensity of his own voice.

"Yes," she answered, smoothing her soft hands across his face. "Please, Callum."

It was as if he'd devolved into some kind of inexperienced schoolboy overwhelmed at the possibility of a night with his biggest crush.

In such a short time, Becky had come to mean so much to him. He still couldn't allow himself to acknowledge the depth of his feelings in his heart or mind, but his body seemed to have no such constraints.

It took only a few seconds to pull the sweatshirt he wore over his head and unfasten the button on his jeans. He paused then because Becky had sat up on the sofa and taken off her nightgown. She sat before him in only a pair of lacy blue panties, the perfection of her body making his mouth go dry.

"You never cease to blow me away with your beauty."

"You should close the curtains," she told him with a slight smile. "Before you give my neighbors a glimpse of a full Fortune moon."

He yanked the ends of the linen drapes together, then kicked off his shoes and pushed his jeans and boxers down over his hips. He grabbed his wallet from his pocket before stepping out of them, taking out the condom packet as he turned back to her.

"It goes both ways," she said as he moved toward her. "The way you look takes my breath away." She bit down on her full lower lip. "And the way you look at me makes me want you more than I thought was possible."

He closed the distance between them and lowered himself over her, taking her mouth in a kiss that he hoped communicated everything he wasn't able to say out loud. As the kisses deepened, he moved his hand down her body, loving the feel of her soft skin and the way she arched into his touch. He cupped one full breast in his palm, skimming his thumb over the sensitive peak.

She moaned, and he caught the sweet sound in his mouth. Then he moved lower, snagging the waistband of her panties with his fingers. Trailing kisses down her throat and chest, he continued to move lower, pushing the scrap of cotton over her hips and lower until she was completely naked under him.

He gently spread her legs and pressed a kiss to the most intimate part of her. She gasped and reflexively stiffened, but he murmured words of encouragement and praise, feeling like he'd won some kind of lottery when she relaxed again.

"Let me have all of you," he told her, glancing up to meet her desire-hazed gaze.

She gave a shaky nod, and he turned all of his attention to pleasing her. With his tongue and lips and fingers he explored her, gratified at the sensual noises she made.

Soon her whispered words became a chorus of *yes* and *please* and his name. When the release broke over her, it was almost his undoing. Her body seemed to come apart with pleasure.

He plucked up the condom packet he'd dropped to the floor, ripped it open with his teeth and then sheathed himself. As he positioned himself above her, she gave him a smile that just about melted his heart. This was how he wanted to make her feel all the time—languid and blissfully content.

She reached for him, opening again and taking the length of him as if they'd been made to fit together. They moved as one and he lost track of where she started and he began. As pressure built inside him, he tried to tamp it down. His needs didn't matter until she was fully satisfied.

Her nails skimmed lightly across his back, sending quivers of need swirling through him. He lost track of time and place, lost in the moment and the joy of sharing it with Becky.

When she finally cried out his name and her body clenched around him, his breath caught in his throat. The release roared through him like a runaway train, pounding euphoria through every cell in his body.

He'd never experienced something so intense, and the force of it caught him off guard. His body tightened for several long seconds as he was suspended in a maelstrom of emotion. As the shockwaves subsided, he lowered his head, nuzzling the side of her neck.

She smelled of citrus and woman, a combination that he would forever associate with Becky.

He almost laughed at the thought that he'd never be able to smell the scent of lemons without thinking of this moment.

She pushed her fingers into his hair, and he lifted his head to drop a kiss on her forehead. "Sorry I ruined your good night's sleep."

She flashed a slow smile. "I'll forgive you this time." Her eyes darkened. "What brought you here tonight, Callum?"

"I wanted you." He didn't dare try to express to her all the emotions tumbling through him. The level of need he felt. At this point, it was easier if she believed their physical connection had led him to her. Anything more would reveal too much.

She continued to smile but for an instant he w
have sworn a shadow passed over her gaze. "I'm g
she answered, although he got the feeling she wa
to say more.

He didn't want the moment to end but forced hir
to get up, grabbing his boxers from the floor. "I'
right back," he told her, hoping he was imagining
awkwardness suddenly radiating between them.

It took him only a few minutes in the bathroom
he figured she might have moved to her bedroom i
meantime. Instead, he saw the glow of a light co
from the kitchen.

As he entered the room, Becky gave him a tight s
"Thanks again for stopping by." She held out his j
and T-shirt, which she'd folded into a neat pile a
with his socks and shoes. "You'll probably want t
dressed before heading out."

"Um…" He frowned but took the clothes from
"Yeah. Is everything okay?"

"Fine." Another stiff smile. "I have an early da
morrow, though, so I should get to sleep."

"Sure." He realized he sounded like an idiot
all of his one-word responses, but her actions left
rattled. They'd just shared mind-blowing intimacy
best of his life. Now she was basically kicking him

What the hell?

Instead of arguing or asking for an explanatio
quickly donned his clothes and shoved his feet int
boots. As far as she knew, he'd gotten what he cam
and if he wasn't willing to reveal the depth of his
ings for her, he didn't deserve any more.

She stood leaning against the cabinets on the fa
of the room, her expression guarded. The adorabl

tens on the front of her nightgown seemed to taunt him. They had a place here, and he had a big pile of nothing.

Because he had nothing to offer. And apparently Becky knew it.

"Thanks again for…" What exactly should he say?

Her chest rose and fell on a quick inhalation of breath.

"Everything," he finished softly.

The smile that curved her lips looked forced, but he didn't ask about it. Not when his own emotions felt too jumbled and unsure.

"I'll talk to you tomorrow," she told him as she walked him to the front door. "Or I guess I should say later today."

He sighed. "I'm sorry I woke you tonight." He had to offer something.

"You didn't. I got up to check on the girls and saw your truck out the window. I'm glad I saw you." She shook her head and huffed out a faint laugh. "Otherwise, you could still be sitting at the curb."

Why did he feel like he was being kicked there now?

She gave him a quick kiss after opening the front door. "Good night, Callum."

He said good-night and a moment later stood alone in the darkness of an empty January night.

"I'm the one who's sleep deprived," Stephanie told Callum later that week as they stood in the front lobby of the veterinary clinic. "Why are you so grumpy?"

"I'm not grumpy," he answered through clenched teeth, earning a laugh from his sister.

When he didn't respond, she sucked in a quick breath. "Tell me there's not another delay for the clinic." She gestured to the men carrying in the new cabinets for installation. "You and Steven managed to avoid one potential disaster. My nerves can't take another one at this point, not with the opening coming up so quickly."

He pulled out his phone and glanced at it for what felt like the hundredth time that morning, then lifted his gaze to Stephanie's. "Everything's on track. The crew will be putting in some long hours, but the facility is going to open on time and be fully functioning." He flicked another look at the annoyingly dark phone screen and then added, "It's all good."

"Something isn't right with you." Stephanie reached out a finger and tapped it on the edge of his phone case. "Are you angry about Linus?"

Callum blinked. "What are you talking about?"

"I get that you had your fill of kids underfoot when we were growing up." She flashed a weak smile. "Even though he's still tiny, it's kind of shocking how much stuff comes along with having a baby. The peacefulness of the house has been disrupted, and I'd understand if you resent the intrusion."

"I don't," he told her, shocked and a bit chagrinned that he'd given off that impression. "Linus is adorable and I meant it when I said you're doing an amazing thing for that baby."

"Yes," she agreed slowly. "But I'm beginning to wonder about Laurel returning. No one has heard from her." Stephanie crossed her arms over her chest. "Of course I'm happy to keep him for as long as needed, but I guess I thought it would be a short-term placement. What if his mama doesn't return to claim him?"

Callum looped an arm around his sister's shoulder.

"Then he'll be lucky he's got you as a foster mom. I'm sorry I made you question whether I'm okay with having Linus in the house. Make no mistake, Stephanie. He's where he needs to be, and I support you 100 percent." He squeezed her arm. "The baby routine is an adjustment for all us, but I wouldn't have it any other way." He frowned. "I like babies. Hell, I helped take care of the triplets for years. And Becky's girls love me. Why do people think I'm antibaby?"

She patted a hand against his chest. "That's funny. No one believes that, but you've made it pretty clear that domesticity isn't your cup of tea at this point. I don't necessarily agree with that and would offer Becky and the twins up as evidence to the contrary, but—"

"Do you think that's why she's avoiding me?" he blurted.

Stephanie took a step away from him, inclining her head. "I didn't realize she was, but it certainly explains your mood."

"My mood is fine," he growled.

"Uh-huh. Tell me more about being ghosted."

He ran a hand through his hair, glancing around to make sure no one could overhear them. From Callum's experience, construction workers liked to gossip as much as a posse of teenage girls. The last thing he needed was to be the topic of conversation for his crew.

"I wouldn't call it ghosting. We had lunch once this week and I took her and the girls to dinner last night. She's not ignoring me completely, but there's a distance between us, even when we're together. I can't figure out why or what's causing it."

His sister frowned. "When did it start?"

"After Linus arrived at the pediatric center," he said

after thinking on it for a few seconds. "But that doesn't make sense. Becky has a clear attachment to his welfare. I think she bonded with Laurel on that first day."

"Becky has been an amazing support for me," Stephanie said with a nod. "She checks in several times a day and answers every tiny question I have right away. Since he started going to the day care at the center at the beginning of the week, she's made a point of stopping by and sends me updates on how he's doing. I don't get any strange vibes from her."

"Then what could it be?" Callum shook his head, frustrated that he couldn't figure this out. Part of why he was so successful in the renovation business was his love of solving complex problems. With a historic building or old property in need of revitalization, there were always unique challenges that didn't present themselves with new construction. He thrived on managing those kinds of issues. The fact that he couldn't seem to decipher the actions of one woman made him want to shout in frustration.

The toe of Stephanie's boot tapped on the newly installed floor. "Have you been an idiot?"

"What kind of question is that?"

"A valid one based on your defensive tone."

He shook his head. "I don't know. I don't think so. I like her. She likes me. Her girls like me."

"Are you sure *like* is the *L* word you're looking for at the moment?"

"Stop." He held up a hand. "It's been a few weeks. You know what a bad bet I am, Stephanie. We can't rush into anything when I don't even know if I'm staying in Rambling Rose."

She shook her head. "That's your past talking, Callum. Not your future. You know Dad always says it only took him a moment to know Mom was the one. If he'd let his divorce from your mother define him, our family wouldn't be what it is today."

Callum swallowed. How could he explain to the sister who looked up to him that their father was a better man in so many ways?

"Maybe she's just changed her mind about things," he forced himself to say. "I know she was wary of getting involved in the first place because of the twins. They're her priority and I respect that. It could be as simple as Becky not wanting her life complicated."

"You sound pathetic," his sister told him.

He rolled his eyes. "Not at all helpful."

"Could be the kind of help you need is a swift kick in the pants."

"Forget I mentioned anything."

"I want you to be happy," Stephanie said, her tone gentler. "Tell me if there's anything I can do. Maybe I could talk to Becky for you?"

"No." He shook his head. "This isn't junior high where I need you to pass her a note and have her check the box whether or not she likes me."

"I hated those notes," his sister murmured. "So much pressure."

"Yeah." Feeling pressured was exactly his problem at the moment. But he didn't want to push Becky until he felt certain about what he could offer her. If only he could work out the puzzle of his heart, maybe everything else would fall into place.

Chapter 13

Becky sat in front of the computer at the nurses' station entering stats on a recent patient when she felt someone watching her. She looked up to find Sharla and Kristen staring at her from the other side of the counter.

"I didn't eat the last doughnut," she lied without hesitation, wiping a finger across her bottom lip in case any leftover crumbs might give her away.

"We're not here about doughnuts," Sharla said, crossing her arms over her ample chest.

Kristen nodded in agreement. "We just saw Callum Fortune walking out of the building looking like someone stole his new puppy."

"He doesn't have a puppy," Becky muttered, refocusing on the computer.

"What's going on with the two of you?" Sharla demanded. "Don't tell us you're going to waste your chance with a man who is hot, rich and clearly way into you."

Dragging in a slow breath, Becky pushed back from the desk and stood. "I'm not telling you anything. There's nothing to tell."

"We haven't seen the two of you together as much lately," Kristen pointed out, none too helpfully.

"Things are busy around here," Becky countered. "As you'd know if you stopped trying to pump me for information."

Sharla arched a superbly penciled brow. "Defensive much?"

Becky set her jaw and returned the other woman's steely stare. "I'm not..." She paused, concentrating on the air that seemed caught in her lungs like a moth in a spider's web. "I don't know what's going on." She glanced around to make sure no one could overhear their conversation. "I did a really stupid thing."

"You're pregnant again," Sharla guessed, her eyes widening.

"No." Becky shook her head. "I fell in love with him."

Kristen reached out a hand and squeezed Becky's trembling hand. "Oh, honey. You're only human."

Becky laughed. "Right?" she agreed. "The problem is I don't know how he feels about me. I'm not even certain he's planning to stay in Rambling Rose long term. What if I give him my heart and he breaks it?"

Sharla started to answer, then snapped her mouth shut when one of the exam rooms opened and Parker walked out. "We're just waiting on a lab report and then they'll need a follow-up appointment." He approached the desk. "Everything okay here?" he asked, concern in his tone.

"Peachy keen, Dr. Green," Kristen answered.

He must have heard something in her voice that made him wary because he stopped in his tracks and immediately pulled his phone out of the pocket of his white lab coat. "Look at that. I need to return this call. I'm going to just… I need to go my office." He flashed a tight smile. "And close the door."

"We'll hold down the fort out here," Sharla told him.

"I'm going to go check on the family waiting for labs," Kristen said, then pointed a finger at Becky. "Whatever Sharla tells you, that's what you're going to do. No questions asked."

Becky gave a small shake of her head. "I don't know about—"

"No questions," the redheaded nurse repeated.

"Okay," Becky whispered, watching Kristen disappear into the exam room.

Sharla propped her elbows on the desk and leaned in. "Have you told him you love him?"

"Of course not."

"Do you think you might want to start there?"

"What if it freaks him out and he breaks up with me?"

"What if he feels the same way and doesn't know how to tell you because you're acting so strange?"

"I'm not acting…" She clasped a hand over her mouth when a sob tried to break free. "It wasn't supposed to happen like this," she said, more to herself than Sharla. "I already had my love story. Rick was the love of my life. If I tell Callum I love him, am I being disloyal to my late husband? Am I a terrible person?"

"For wanting to be truly happy again after overcoming a tragedy no one should have to face?" Sharla offered a tender smile. "Of course not. You're a good person, Beck, and an amazing mother. I didn't know your late husband, but I can only imagine he'd be proud of the life you'd made for your girls. You deserve happiness."

"Thank you," Becky whispered. She hadn't realized how badly she needed someone to give her that permission until her friend did. "I don't just want to blurt out the words while we're taking turns feeding the twins. I know Callum cares about the girls and they will always be my priority, but I'd like to do something special for him." She shrugged. "Romantic gestures aren't exactly my forte. Any ideas?"

"Oh, girl." Sharla swiped at her eyes, then grinned like the cat that ate the canary. "I've got you covered on romance."

"You need to come with us."

Callum turned from where he was meeting with the foreman at The Shoppes to find Steven and Dillon striding toward him.

"What happened? Is it Linus? Stephanie?" He threw up his hands. "What's going on?"

"Bro, chill. Everything's fine." Dillon gave him a strange look. "You're wound as tight as a top."

"We've got a lot of work going on," he told his brother, gesturing to several dozen pallets of lumber lined against the far wall. "In case you haven't noticed."

"I've noticed," Dillon told him. "And we've got it all covered."

"At least for the next twenty-four hours," Steven added with a smug smile.

"You two aren't making any sense." Callum narrowed his eyes. "Are you drunk?"

"Give us a couple of minutes, Dan," Steven told the

older foreman when he chuckled at Callum's accusatory question.

"Sure thing, bosses." The wiry man with a shaggy beard walked toward the space where the electricians were roughing in recessed lighting.

"Seriously, you need to loosen up." Dillon walked behind Callum and half guided, half pushed him toward the door.

"You still haven't explained what's going on," Callum said through clenched teeth. His patience was at an all-time low. He hadn't seen Becky since he'd stopped by the pediatric center yesterday, and she'd done little more than give him a swift kiss before turning her attention back to whatever she was doing on her large desktop monitor.

Not that he expected her to drop her work for him, but he missed her. He missed the closeness they'd had and hated the tension he couldn't quite put his finger on that seemed to pulse between them.

He'd texted her earlier in the morning, but hadn't received a response. And no, he told himself, he definitely wasn't compulsively checking his phone in case he'd missed the tone or vibration of an incoming message.

"Do you trust me?" Dillon asked as he continued to herd him like a farm animal.

"Normally, yes." Callum shrugged off his brother's grasp but continued walking to the building's entrance. "Right now I trust you about as far as I can throw you." He pointed a finger at Steven, who stood holding open the front door.

"You'll be sorry you doubted us in about ten seconds," his brother warned with a Cheshire cat smile. "What do you think of that Corvette over there?" He gestured toward a vintage sports car parked in the shopping mall's empty lot.

"It's a beauty." Callum squinted at the cherry-red vehicle, shading his eyes from the bright winter sunlight. "Did you buy a…" His voice trailed off as Becky appeared from the driver's side. Her hair tumbled over her shoulders and she offered a tentative wave.

"Waiting for the apology," Steven said with a nudge.

"What's going on?" Callum whispered. "Why is she here?"

"Your girlfriend has more appreciation for romance in her pinkie finger," Dillon said, thrusting a duffel bag into Callum's arms, "than you do in your entire lunkheaded body."

"Becky arranged an overnight getaway for the two of you," Steven explained. "We're covering you for the next twenty-four hours. A smart man would stop asking questions, mute his phone and go kiss the beautiful woman waiting for him."

Callum's mind might be spinning in a thousand different directions, but he wasn't a total idiot. "You two are the greatest brothers in the history of the world. If you tell Wiley I said that, I'll deny it. But thank you."

"Have fun," Steven told him with a grin.

"Don't do anything I wouldn't do," Dillon added.

When Callum shot him a look, his younger brother laughed. "I'm giving you a wide berth of options."

"I think I can handle it," he murmured, flipping his phone to silent mode. He slung the duffel over his shoulder and headed toward Becky.

She watched him approach, looking almost as wary as she did excited. "I hope you don't mind a little kidnapping," she said.

He cupped her cheeks between his palms and kissed her by way of an answer, ignoring the cheers and wolf whistles from his brothers.

"Are you sure about this?" he asked when they finally broke apart several minutes later. He smoothed the pads of his thumbs over her cheeks. "What about the girls?"

"Sarah and Grant are staying with them for the night," she answered, and he couldn't help but hear the catch in her voice.

"You don't have to leave them," he assured her. "I don't need a getaway, Becky. Any time we have together is special."

"I want this night," she said, her gaze sure and steady as she looked into his eyes. "If you do?"

"More than anything," he said and kissed her again.

They climbed into the car, and Becky pulled out onto the road that led to the highway.

"New ride?" Callum asked, grinning as she giggled at the Corvette's rapid acceleration.

"It's Grant's weekend car," she explained. "He inherited it from an uncle who lived in Florida. I guess he and Sarah don't drive it much around Rambling Rose, but he thought it would be more of a statement than picking you up in the minivan. I know it's not as fancy as the Audi, but—"

"You could pick me up on a bicycle, and I'd be happy."

"This is way more fun than a bike ride," she said with a wink.

He laughed. "That's true. Can I ask where we're headed?"

"Austin. We have reservations for dinner at a farm-to-table restaurant that has great reviews, and then a room at the Driskill. Your sister recommended the hotel, and the photos online look amazing."

"Everything about this is amazing," he told her without reservation.

After the doubts and worry that had been weighing on Callum's mind the past few days, being swept away for a romantic night in the city was the last thing he would have expected. Excitement zipped through him. He and Becky talked and laughed as she drove, and a heavy weight slowly lifted off his chest, replaced with an almost giddy lightness.

He could imagine how much it took for her to leave Sasha and Luna for the night, even with friends she trusted. It humbled him that she'd made that choice in order to spend more time with him.

The day was clear with the winter sun shining down on them like a bright omen. They arrived in Austin in the late afternoon and checked into the hotel located in the heart of downtown. Becky seemed enchanted by the Driskill's opulent lobby and the old-world charm of the decor. She insisted on giving her credit card to the front desk, and while Callum appreciated the gesture, he hoped he could convince her to allow him to pay for both dinner and the room. Just the fact that she'd arranged this evening meant the world to him.

He carried his duffel and her overnight bag to the room and watched with delight as Becky marveled over every understated but luxurious detail of the hotel. He liked seeing the world through her eyes. Despite all she'd been through, Becky still seemed able to appreciate the small joys.

"Oh, my gosh."

He was taking in the view from the room's wide window when she rushed out of the bathroom.

"There are three shower heads in one shower. I've only seen that on fancy home improvement shows."

Tenderness radiated through his heart and he pressed two fingers to his chest, unable to identify the feeling. Unwilling was more like it. He understood on some level that if he acknowledged the depth of his emotions toward this woman, they would change him in ways he couldn't handle at the moment.

So Callum did what he seemed to do best where Becky was concerned. He shoved down all the unfathomable feelings and concentrated on what was simple.

His need for her.

"We have some time before the dinner reservation." He made a show of looking at his watch as he walked toward her. "Just enough time by my calculations."

She bit down on her lower lip, sending a wave of lust rushing through him. "Enough time for what?"

"For the best shower of your life."

Her eyes went even darker. "You sound pretty confident about that."

"One thing I'm not lacking—" he nipped at the edge of her mouth "—is confidence in my ability to please you."

"That makes two of us," she said and led him into the hotel room's oversize bathroom.

"Can you zip me?" Becky asked, walking out of the bathroom later that evening.

Callum gave her an exaggerated ogle. "If I say no, can we get naked again and order room service for dinner?"

She rolled her eyes. "We've been naked pretty much since arriving in Austin," she reminded him.

"Best trip ever," he agreed.

The look in his dark eyes made her heart flutter. She never wanted that feeling to end, and somehow she knew with Callum it would last forever. Or at least as long as they had together. They'd had a magical afternoon, first in the shower and then moving to the bed. Part of her wanted to take him up on his half-joking offer. To spend the entire night wrapped in his arms.

But she gave a playful shake of her head and turned her back to him. "I've never been to Austin. We're hitting the town before we hit the sheets again."

"Whatever you want," he whispered, placing a gentle kiss on her exposed back before zipping up the dress. "You look beautiful tonight."

Becky drew in a deep breath as she glanced in the mirror that hung above the hotel room's cherry dresser. She felt beautiful. She'd bought the dress she wore, a silk sheath in a gorgeous blue, just before she found out she was pregnant. Only a few weeks prior to the accident that had claimed her husband's life.

When she went to pack for the trip early this morning, she'd found it shoved in the back of her closet, tags still intact.

Tears had pricked her eyes at the memory of those dark days after Rick's death. She'd been desperate and overwhelmed, unsure of how she was supposed to manage her world without him. At that time, she hadn't even been able to imagine a moment when she'd feel as happy as she did right now.

Things weren't settled between her and Callum.

She hadn't yet told him the three little words that could change everything. *I love you.* She wanted to wait for the right moment, but the longer she put it off the more significance the declaration seemed to take on in her mind and heart.

Still, the past few hours had bolstered her confidence. Callum seemed relaxed in a way that felt like a positive sign for the future. She couldn't imagine that he wouldn't return her feelings. Even if he wasn't ready to say the words back to her, she knew in her heart that he cared. Every thoughtful touch, every intense look made her know that she mattered to him.

As long as they were both willing to work at it, she believed they could overcome the pain of their individual pasts to build a shared future that would last a lifetime.

Chapter 14

As they walked back to the Driskill later that night, Becky felt like she was floating on air, her feet barely touching the sidewalk.

"This night has been wonderful." They held hands, and his thumb grazing the pulse on her wrist made shivers track along her spine. "Austin is such a great city." She glanced up to the historic buildings they passed on their way to the hotel. "I can't believe how much of Texas I haven't seen when I've lived here all my life."

"Your parents didn't take you on many vacations?"

She shrugged, the mix of bitterness and affection she always felt when thinking of her parents settling over her like a blanket. At the moment, affection for them won out. It was difficult to feel anything but happy with her heart so full.

"My parents are simple people. They didn't feel like

they needed to travel, and money was always tight. My grandma and grandpa lived down on the coast, so I spent most summers with them. Even though I didn't go any-where special, I never felt the lack of it growing up. I loved spending long days exploring the woods near their house and taking trips to the beach. Those memories are part of why we moved to Rambling Rose. I didn't want to raise my family in the city. Wide-open spaces are important."

"What about after you were married?" he asked qui-etly.

They were almost to the hotel, and she paused to enjoy the lights of the city. One day when they were older, she'd bring the girls here for a long weekend. They'd go to the zoo and the children's museum. She wanted to give them every experience she could so they'd under-stand life was an adventure. Hope burned in her like a flame that she and Callum might share that adventure.

It was strange to be thinking of that after he'd asked a question about her late husband. She wanted to believe Rick would be happy for her finding love again. He was that kind of man, and she knew he'd approve of Callum.

She glanced up at Callum, then straight ahead again. It was too difficult to share these deeply personal parts of herself while looking into his dark eyes. "Rick didn't talk about it, but he supported his mom financially from the time he graduated high school. His parents had divorced and his mom was an alcoholic, in and out of rehab. They weren't exactly close, but he loved her and wanted to take care of her." She took comfort in the steady pres-sure of Callum's hand holding hers.

"She was diagnosed with ovarian cancer after two years of sobriety. Rick and I had just gotten married. We decided to postpone the honeymoon so that he could be with her through the surgery and treatments."

"He sounds like a wonderful son."

"He was a good man," she agreed. "His mom didn't have much in the way of health insurance, so there were a lot of doctor and hospital bills. We took care of as many of them as we could, but that meant there wasn't much money left over." That period ran through her mind like a movie. It had been stressful on Rick and on their marriage, but she would have never argued with his need to take care of his mother. "I guess my whole point is I haven't had a lot of opportunity for traveling."

"You can change that," he told her, lifting his free hand to tuck a lock of hair behind her ear.

"Oh, yes." She laughed. "One-year-old twins are really portable. There will be time for adventures. And I plan to take the girls on as many of them as I can manage."

With you at my side, she added silently. She should just say the words. Put them out there so that he knew how she felt.

But something held her back.

Callum wrapped his arms around her and pulled her close. "The more I learn about you, Becky, the more impressed I am at what a spectacular person you are."

"Anyone would do the same in my situation," she said automatically.

"I don't know about that." He kissed the top of her head. "I think you're special."

"Thanks," she whispered.

"Your late husband was a lucky man."

"I was the lucky one," she corrected, then pulled away to look at him. "I still am."

His jaw tensed for a split second before he flashed a smile. "We should get back to the hotel. It's late, and I have plans for you."

"For us." She lifted a hand to his face, smoothing her fingers over his stubbled jaw. "We're in this together."

"Together," he repeated softly.

Now, she told herself. *Tell him now.*

Her breath hitched and her mouth went dry. Why was saying she loved him so darn difficult? Was she truly so afraid of his reaction, or could it have more to do with the feeling of being disloyal to her late husband?

That thought made her stomach clench. She took Callum's hand and continued toward the hotel, hoping her sudden silence didn't tip him off to her emotions.

As difficult as it was to express how she felt, Becky had no trouble telling him everything she wanted to say with her body. Every time they came together, she learned more about both Callum and herself. And when she drifted off to sleep in his warm embrace, Becky couldn't help but believe everything would work out for the best.

The next morning, Becky and Callum checked out of the hotel and then walked to a popular breakfast spot a few blocks away. After filling up on omelets and stuffed French toast, they headed for a path near Lady Bird Lake. The temperatures hovered in the high fifties with low clouds on the horizon that meant they might be driving back to Rambling Rose in the rain.

A mother jogging behind a double stroller on the trail made her miss her girls. As lovely as the evening had been, she couldn't wait to get home and hug her babies. Sarah had FaceTimed her earlier, and the twins had smiled and blown kisses, bringing happy tears to Becky's eyes.

She felt refreshed but also anxious. She'd promised herself that before they left Austin to return to Rambling Rose, she'd talk to him about their future together.

"I hate for our getaway to end," Callum said with a charming grin. "I appreciate all the work you put into making last night special. It's going to be hard to top that as far as romance goes." He leaned in closer. "But I've got a few tricks up my sleeve."

She stopped walking and turned to fully face him. "I love you," she blurted.

He blinked and then blinked some more.

Becky opened her mouth, an apology ready to slip from her tongue. But no. She wasn't sorry. Even though Callum looked at her as if she'd just sprouted a second head, she didn't regret telling him how she felt. Maybe she could have done it with a bit more eloquence, but already she felt less nervous than she'd been since she'd decided she had to tell him.

"It's okay if you can't say it back to me." She offered what she hoped passed for an encouraging smile. "I don't want to rush things, but I needed to share that. You're an amazing man and these past few weeks have made me happier than I've been in a long time. I want it to continue. I want us to continue." The anxiety that had melted away for a moment began to reform, congealing in her belly like curdled milk. Something was wrong with Callum, and she couldn't bear to consider the reason for his reaction.

He continued to stare at her, then turned on his heel and stalked several steps away. His shoulders went rigid with tension as he raked a stiff hand through his hair.

Something was very wrong.

"Callum." She moved toward him, reaching out a hand.

The moment she touched him, he recoiled, spinning to face her again.

"I'm leaving, Becky."

"Excuse me?" Her mind reeled. "I get it. We're both leaving this morning but—"

"Rambling Rose." He shook his head as if trying to shake his thoughts into some order. "Not for a while, at least not until the first round of projects opens. But after that…" He gave her an apologetic shrug. "I have to go."

"Why?" She breathed out the word on a ragged puff of air. "You love it in Rambling Rose." *I thought you loved me*, her heart screamed.

"I'm sorry," he said, sounding as miserable as she felt. "My business takes me all over the place. It's how things have always been."

"But they don't have to continue that way," she insisted. It wasn't like Becky to push. Normally she accepted whatever someone told her as fact and didn't argue or put up a fight. Her love for Callum made her a fighter. "I don't care if you travel. We can find a way to make it work. You and me together, Callum. I want—"

"That's just it." He started walking toward the street that led to the hotel, and she fell in step beside him, trying to make sense of what he was saying. "This isn't only about you and me. You have the girls to consider."

"They love you, too." As soon as the words were out of her mouth, she realized they were wrong. For a man clearly terrified of commitment, hearing that a pair of toddler twins cared about him might send him running even faster in the opposite direction.

"I don't want to hurt the girls or you."

"You already are," she told him, forcing herself to be honest. "I think you're hurting yourself the most. By believing the worst or that you're incapable of commitment or whatever bogus line you're telling yourself in your head and your heart. You're hurting all of us."

His step faltered as he glanced down on her, a pain so raw etched across his features it took her breath away. They'd come to the hotel's entrance, and she watched as couples, families and the hotel's efficient valet staff moved about. She thought she might have finally gotten through to Callum. Made it past whatever defenses he'd erected to avoid risking his heart.

But instead of uttering the words she longed to hear, he opened his mouth, then closed it again, shaking his head. "I'll get the car from the valet. I can drive home if you want."

"Sure," she whispered. *Home.* The word ricocheted around her mind like a bullet tearing through flesh. Callum had come to mean so much to her. He'd made her lonely little house feel like a home. But it had all been an illusion. No wonder she hadn't been able to express her feelings before now. Apparently, she should have trusted her preservation instincts.

Now she wanted to run and hide.

Instead, she wiped the emotion from her features and thanked the valet who opened the Corvette's passenger door for her. Everything about the past twenty-four hours seemed to mock her. The time she'd taken to set it up. Borrowing the car and making reservations. The fact that she thought last night was a turning point in their relationship.

Turning it all to hell.

Callum climbed in behind the wheel and pulled out onto the downtown street. "Becky, I know—"

"You don't know anything," she said, working to keep her heartache in check. "I'm done talking for a while, Callum. I just want to go home and see my girls."

He gave a sharp nod, and a strained silence fell between them. Becky closed her eyes and let the sound of the engine lull her to sleep. As broken and rejected as she felt, somehow her body knew she needed a respite from the pain. It felt like only minutes passed, but the next time she opened her eyes they were pulling off the highway toward Rambling Rose.

"I guess I owe you an apology for keeping you awake most of last night," Callum said, flashing a sheepish smile. "You needed some extra sleep."

"I'm a single mother," she answered stonily, swiping a finger across the side of her mouth in case she'd drooled during her nap. "I always need sleep."

His smile faded. "I handled things badly this morning. I'm sorry. It's a huge honor to hear your feelings for me. I wish I could be the man to deserve your love."

"Seriously?" She took a deep breath. "Are you really going to give me the line about how 'it isn't you, it's me'? You're a good man, Callum. Everyone except you seems to realize it."

"I don't think I'm a bad guy," he said slowly as he pulled to a stop in the parking lot at The Shoppes, where the Fortune brothers had their modular office. "But I know I can't give you what you need."

Becky unbuckled her seat belt. "*Can't* and *won't* are two different things."

His eyes widened slightly.

She still wasn't ready to play nice when so much was

on the line. She'd loved and lost once before. The tragedy and sorrow of her husband's accident had brought her to her knees, literally and figuratively. It had taken a long time for her to manage to get up on her feet again. As much as her heart hurt, she wouldn't let herself fall back down again.

"I'm sorry," he repeated. "This doesn't mean things have to end between us right now. I'm leaving tomorrow on a scouting trip to San Antonio for a couple of days but when I get back—"

"San Antonio?" She turned to face him. "So you already have a plan for where you're moving next?"

"Not exactly a plan, but Fortune Brothers Construction has a few irons in the fire."

She swallowed against the bile rising in her throat. He'd known all this time he was leaving. She shouldn't be surprised. Callum hadn't made promises to her. Yet how could she have misread the situation so completely?

"It would be better if we ended this now," she managed, not bothering to worry that a tiny sob slipped out along with the words. She dabbed at the corners of her eyes. "I need to think about the future for myself and my girls. If you aren't going to be a part of it, there's no point in continuing."

"I care about you, Becky."

"It's not enough." Before he could answer, she got out of the car and slammed shut the passenger door. She was too close to losing it to continue this conversation. Besides, what was left to say?

She couldn't stand for him to try to convince her they could continue until he finally left Rambling Rose. Her daughters already had a special connection with him.

A few more months would only make it harder when he left for good. Not to mention what it would do to Becky.

A clean break now was the right decision even though her heart screamed in protest.

He got out of the car as she walked around the front.

"Things don't have to end this way," he said, moving to stand in front of her.

She forced herself to look up at him. "Things don't have to end at all, but you're too afraid of being hurt to commit to anything." She drew in a ragged breath. "You're too much of coward to even try."

He seemed to freeze at her words, and she elbowed her way past him and into the car. With shaking fingers, she gripped the steering wheel with one hand and the gearshift in the other. She put the car into Drive and roared out of the parking lot, leaving a cloud of dust and Callum Fortune behind.

Chapter 15

Callum threw himself into work for the next several days, refusing to discuss Becky or their breakup with Stephanie or either of his brothers.

He told himself the situation was his personal business, but in truth he didn't want or need his siblings to point out how he'd behaved like an idiot. Not when he was handling that so effectively on his own.

How could he have been so happy and then ruin it on purpose? He barely understood why he'd made the choice to tell her he planned to leave Rambling Rose.

Up until that instant, he hadn't decided anything for certain. Hell, he hadn't actually scheduled a visit to potential investment properties near San Antonio, although he needed to come up with a plan for where his company could do the most good.

Too bad that the thought of leaving held no appeal.

He'd dropped that little bomb in the aftermath of those three tiny words she'd shared with him. Any man would be lucky to be loved by a woman like Becky. Callum knew that without a doubt.

Unfortunately, he also believed that eventually— whether he meant to or not—he'd hurt her. His short-lived marriage had taught him that he simply didn't have the capacity for love a man needed to keep a woman happy. He was a man who needed independence. He'd already given everything he could and had nothing left.

Becky might want to believe he was worthy of her, but Callum knew better. He rolled his shoulders as he stared at his computer monitor, trying to shrug off some of the tension that had rooted there like one of the ranch's decades-old oak trees.

Whenever he wasn't on-site, he was, like today, at his desk in the Fortune Brothers Construction office near The Shoppes. There were so many aspects of the business to manage, especially now that the triplets had jumped headfirst into designing the restaurant. Ashley, Megan and Nicole were planning to visit Rambling Rose at the end of the month, and Callum wanted to make their trip a productive one. The breadth of projects they'd taken on in this town were the most expansive of his career.

He'd also never felt so connected to a place as he did to this small town. His father had worried about them moving to Texas and the possible influence of the extended Fortune family. The kidnapping that had occurred at last year's wedding of Callum's uncle Gerald had shaken David, making him wary of deepening his branch's ties to the rest of the Fortunes. Callum hadn't given it much thought. Before now, the locations he'd chosen for his projects had been based solely on the historic value and financial prospects.

Rambling Rose was proving to be different, and not just because of Becky. Maybe it was the history the Fortune family played in the town. It still gave Callum goose bumps to think about the pediatric center, their first major project, being built on the site of the Fortune's Foundling Hospital. Linus also had a link to that piece of history, given that his mother had purposely left him at the site of the former Fortune orphanage.

If he didn't know better, he'd swear he could feel the spirit of this community trickling into him, changing who he was at a cellular level. It was a ridiculous thought, of course, brought on by the lack of sleep and missing Becky.

A million times since that drive home from Austin, he'd wanted to call her. He hated how they'd left things, what she must think of him. He hated that he couldn't be the man she wanted.

"Is this an okay time for a break?"

A smile broke over his face as his stepmom walked into the office. For the first time since Becky drove away in her red Corvette, he took a full breath. Marci wore beige slacks and a cashmere sweater, not a hair out of place as she grinned at him.

"This is the best surprise I could imagine," he told her, standing and walking around the desk to wrap her in a tight hug.

Marci smelled like lilacs and vanilla, two scents he'd always associate with home. "Stephanie said she didn't need help," his stepmom explained, placing a quick kiss on his cheek. "But that baby is such a cute little guy. I couldn't resist an opportunity to love on him."

"We're all so proud of her. Everyone is still holding out hope that Linus's mother returns, but there's no better place for him than with Stephanie."

Marci's smile turned wistful. "You were such troupers when the triplets were born. I know you took on the lion's share of the responsibility for them when I needed help."

"It wasn't a big deal." He didn't like discussing that time with anyone in his family because the lingering resentment he harbored made him feel like a jerk. He loved the triplets and the rest of his family. It had been his choice to step up when Marci needed help. No one had forced him. He'd simply done what he had to for his family.

"All that responsibility took a toll on you," she said softly.

There was no point bothering to deny it. Not with his perceptive stepmom. "Would you like to see some of the projects we're working on?" he asked instead. "We can start right here at The Shoppes."

She studied him for a moment, clearly understanding a distraction when one was shoved at her. "I'd love that."

Callum breathed a sigh of relief as he led her from the office. "Have you seen Steven and Dillon?"

"Not yet. I flew into Houston last night and drove over to Rambling Rose this morning. I called Stephanie on my way into town and met her at the pediatric center so that I could visit Linus at day care. Then I came here."

"Steven had a meeting about the hotel, but then he was due back here so we could go over some paint samples with the designer. Dillon is probably at the spa or the vet clinic."

"It feels like you're so busy," Marci said, and he heard

the pride in her voice. "I can't believe how much you've taken on in such a short time."

"I like to be busy." Callum laughed softly. "But we both know Fortune Brothers Construction wouldn't be half as successful without Steven and Dillon in the mix. The three of us together bring the magic."

"You've always had a soft spot for your brothers and sisters." Marci reached across the console and patted his arm. "I can't help but worry about what that's cost you."

They walked from the modular office toward the entrance of The Shoppes at Rambling Rose. The building had housed an old five-and-dime, but they'd taken it nearly down to the studs to rebuild it into an upscale set of shops that ultimately would include fashion, jewelry and a designer home accessory store. Their neighbors in Rambling Rose Estates seemed especially excited about this upcoming addition to the community, although Dillon still worried locals weren't totally on board with the plan.

He didn't give much credence to that. Every one of his projects had received a bit of pushback in the initial stages. He believed beyond a doubt they were improving this town for everyone, and Callum hoped that as the longtime residents began to patronize the new businesses they'd realize the changes benefited everyone.

"I have a great life that's even better because of how close we all are. Although it's going to be interesting when the triplets arrive. I'm not sure Rambling Rose has ever seen anything like the three of them on a mission."

"If anyone can help ease the transition for the girls, it's you." Marci stopped and shook her head. "I'm sorry, Callum. That's the problem. We all assume you'll help with whatever someone in the family needs."

"I will," he answered without hesitation.

"But you shouldn't have to," she told him gently. "It's past time we allow you to put your life first. The family you create for yourself with your own—"

"No." He held up a hand. "I tried going down that path and failed. I'm not going to have a family of my own. My independence means too much to me."

"You and Doralee weren't a good match. That doesn't mean you have to give up on love completely. What about that nurse and her adorable twins from the ribbon-cutting ceremony? Stephanie told me you've been spending a lot of time with her."

"Stephanie shares too much," he said and started walking toward the building again. He waved to a few guys on the crew as Marci caught up to him.

"Don't get snippy. Your sister wouldn't have to keep me apprised of what's going on in your life if you'd tell me yourself."

"Becky and I are over," he said simply. "She doesn't want to waste time on a guy who's a bad bet for the future."

"You are not a bad bet," his stepmom insisted, sounding affronted that he'd dare utter those words.

"I love you," he said, giving her shoulder a quick squeeze. "But I'm not ready to talk about it."

"I'm here when you are," she answered.

Steven caught sight of them at that moment and strode over with a wide grin, catching Marci in a big bear hug.

The pain in Callum's chest eased slightly as he spent the rest of the workday with his brothers and stepmom. After a quick tour of the progress on The Shoppes, they caught up with Dillon at the planned spa location. Like the devoted mother she was, Marci oohed and aahed at all the improvements they were making in town.

They took her to lunch at the Mexican restaurant where he'd eaten with Becky and the girls, and then they headed toward the old feed and grain building that would be the triplets' restaurant.

"The three of them have been able to talk about little else since you put the wheels in motion on this project," Marci confided as she spun in a slow circle to take in the space. "It's really exciting."

"We're staging a Texas takeover," Dillon said with a laugh.

Marci arched a brow. "You're a few decades behind the curve on that. Fortunes have been making their mark in Texas forever, it seems."

"But this place is ours," Steven clarified. "I know the Fortunes have longstanding ties here as well, and maybe that's why Rambling Rose feels like home."

Callum's chest ached at his brother's words. A significant part of why the town felt like home to him was Becky. Even though not speaking to her over the past few days had been horrible, he could still feel their connection. She might hate him at the moment, but just knowing she was nearby gave him some comfort.

Of course, it also motivated him to ensure the current slate of projects stayed on schedule so there'd be nothing to prevent him from moving on. Surely some other man would swoop in and capture Becky's heart. Though it might actually kill Callum to see her with someone else.

"You look so sad," Marci told him quietly as Dillon and Steve launched into a discussion about how many treatment rooms they'd need.

"I wish Dad wanted to spend more time in Texas,"

he told his stepmom when her perceptive gaze landed on him. Let Marci think his inner turmoil centered on that and not Becky.

"He worries about all of you and wants you to be safe."

"We are."

"I know." She offered a gentle smile. "He'll come around. He was so proud of you at the opening of the pediatric center, and he's excited to see the vet clinic, especially since Stephanie will be working there." Marci checked her watch. "Which reminds me, she's picking up Linus in a few minutes and I promised I'd be at the ranch when they arrived."

"We can head back to the office to get your car."

They said goodbye to Dillon and Steven, both of whom would be joining them for a big family dinner at the house later. If Becky hadn't ended things, she and her girls would have been invited, too. He knew Marci would have been thrilled to have three babies to love on.

He didn't mention it, but he missed Becky more than he could say. How many times would he have to remind himself the breakup was for the best before he believed it?

Becky drove out to the ranch the following afternoon, her stomach fluttering with nerves.

To her surprise, the surly young man who'd given her so much trouble when she'd approached the gate the last time waved her through with a smile on this occasion.

She should feel vindicated, but it had been difficult to muster any kind of happiness ever since she'd said goodbye to Callum.

Stephanie had texted and asked her to visit baby

Linus. Callum's sister hadn't directly referenced the breakup, but she'd made a point in the text of telling Becky that Callum wouldn't be home.

Maybe Becky should have said no. Cutting off ties with anyone named Fortune was probably best. But she wanted to see the baby and considered Stephanie a friend. She hadn't just lost a boyfriend when she ended things with Callum. The Fortunes had made her feel so welcome, and she'd soaked up their generosity and friendship like she was a sponge left out in the rain.

"Cawl," Luna shouted as they pulled up to the house. How had she remembered?

Sasha popped the binky out of her mouth. "Cawl."

Blinking away tears, Becky unbuckled her seat belt and turned to face her daughters. "Callum's not here right now, but we're going to see baby Linus and Miss Stephanie."

"Gog," Sasha whispered.

"Yes." Becky smiled at her sweet girl. "I'm sure we'll get to see the animals, too."

She got the girls out of the minivan and carried them toward the front door. Before she could knock, it opened to reveal Marci Fortune, Callum's elegant stepmother.

"Hi," Becky breathed, her hold on the twins tightening.

"Hello, Becky." Marci gave her a disarmingly friendly smile. "It's nice to see you again. Please come in. May I hold one of your sweet girls?"

"Sure."

As soon as Marci held out her hands, Luna reached for her. Sasha rested her head on Becky's shoulder, watching her sister as she sucked on her beloved binky.

"Stephanie didn't mention you were visiting," Becky

said, then blushed at the thought that Marci must know about her breakup with Callum. He'd told her that Marci was protective of her children, even as adults, and wondered what the older woman thought.

Probably that Becky was the biggest idiot alive to reject her handsome, wealthy, charming stepson.

"My daughter appreciates all the help you've given her with the baby," Marci said as she led Becky through the house toward the wing that Stephanie occupied. "She tells me you've been invaluable sharing your expertise and offering support."

"It's a wonderful thing she's doing with Linus," Becky answered honestly. "Obviously she had a great role model because her maternal instincts are spot-on." She cleared her throat, then added, "I'm still holding out hope that Laurel returns to claim her baby. We talked a bit that first day she came to the pediatric center. Who knows how much she remembers of the things she told me, but it was clear she had a lot of love to give. I don't know what happened to push her to the point of relinquishing Linus."

"Becoming a mother isn't always as easy as people want you to believe," Marci said with a sigh. "I struggled with my health, both physical and mental, after the triplets. Even before when we were trying for more children." Her eyes gleamed with unshed tears. "I'm sure Callum shared with you how much responsibility he took on during that time."

"I know he loves you and his sisters very much."

"That's kind of you to say, but it took a toll on him. I didn't realize how large of one until recently. He cares about you, Becky. You and your girls." She bounced Luna gently in her arms.

Becky nodded. "But he's planning to leave Rambling Rose. My life is here, and I can't have someone become close to the girls who isn't going to be a part of their lives long-term. It's not fair to them."

"I understand." Marci reached out to stroke a finger across Sasha's cheek. "They're precious. My hope would be that he changes his mind and you give him another chance."

Becky closed her eyes as she considered that possibility. Would she give him another chance? She almost laughed at the absurdity of the question. Callum could have a thousand chances if that's what it took.

"Mom." Stephanie appeared in the doorway, the baby wrapped in a blue blanket and cradled in her arms. "Stop hogging Becky. I want her to see Linus before he falls asleep again."

"I think he's gotten bigger already," Becky exclaimed as she walked to her friend, and Stephanie beamed in response. "Hey, buddy."

Her girls babbled at little Linus and they all headed for the sitting room Stephanie had set up with a play mat, bounce seat and motorized swing.

They visited while her girls played with the baby's toys, largely entertained by Marci. Stephanie had a list of questions about the infant's care and specific milestones that Becky was happy to answer.

Neither Stephanie nor her mom brought up Callum again, which was both a relief and a disappointment. She wasn't sure she could handle talking about him, but wanted so badly to ask how he was doing.

Was he as miserable as she?

After almost an hour of wakefulness, Linus fell asleep

in Stephanie's arms. She transferred him to her mother and walked Becky and the twins to the front door.

"Thanks for coming over," she said. "I hope it wasn't too weird with how things stand between you and Callum."

"Actually, it wasn't," Becky said, surprised to find the statement to be true. She buckled Sasha and Luna into their car seats and then turned to Stephanie. "Even though things ended with your brother, I hope we can still be friends."

"Me, too," Stephanie said. "You might be the first real friend I've made in Rambling Rose. At least the only one who doesn't think I'm crazy for becoming a foster parent."

"They must not realize how big of a heart you have."

Stephanie leaned forward and gave Becky a hug. "Thank you," she whispered, then added, "I'm sorry my brother's a big dummy."

A laugh popped out of Becky's mouth. "He's a good man," she corrected. "He just needs to realize it."

After another squeeze, Stephanie released her and Becky climbed into the minivan and headed home. The sun had started to set across the western sky, leaving trails of pink and orange in its wake. A glance in the rearview mirror showed that her girls were staring out at the beauty of the sky, and their wide-eyed wonder made Becky smile.

She didn't know if it was possible that she and Callum might get another chance, but the conversation with his sister had given her a bit of hope.

Hope that turned to dust in her throat as she approached the entrance gatehouse. A large silver truck, which she immediately recognized as Callum's, pulled through the gate.

Becky's heart hammered in her chest as their gazes met. Then she realized he wasn't alone. In the passenger seat sat a beautiful blonde. It was difficult to get a good look at the woman as she drove past, but Becky could tell she was young and strikingly gorgeous.

Swallowing hard, she turned her attention back to the road and tried not to cry. The moment was over in seconds, but the meaning of it lashed her like the sting of a whip.

Callum had moved on. His sister and stepmom might claim he still cared about Becky, but how much could she have meant to him if he was already on a date and bringing the woman home?

Becky hadn't realized it was possible for her heart to break any more until it splintered into a million pieces.

Chapter 16

"I thought you were going to try to get home early last night."

"Good morning to you, too," Callum told his step-mom as she walked into the kitchen early the next morning. He'd expected to be gone by the time anyone else in the family woke, but should have known Marci wouldn't let him off the hook so easily.

"Good morning," she said with a smile. She joined him at the counter. He handed her a mug from the cabinet and then watched as she filled it with the coffee he'd just brewed. "Did I misunderstand the plan?"

Frustration wove its way through his veins like a needle and thread. He'd planned to return home before Becky left, hoping he'd get a chance to talk to her. He missed her so badly it felt like he'd lost part of his heart without her in his life. "I got sidetracked by a neighbor's daughter. She's home from college for the weekend and her car broke down in town. I helped her get it to the mechanic, then gave her a ride home." He rolled his shoulders. "Becky was just pulling through the main gate when I drove in."

"She's lovely, Callum. Not just her looks, either, although she's quite pretty."

"Beautiful," he countered softly.

Marci inclined her head. "Beautiful. Yes. But I got a sense of her kindness and strength yesterday. Her daughters adore her and she patiently answers every one of Stephanie's questions and seems so interested in Linus's welfare, even after a full day at work. I could tell she's a truly good person."

"Is this supposed to make me feel better?" He pushed out a laugh to soften the question when his tone came out harsher than he'd meant it. "I know I messed up with a one-in-a-million woman. But there's nothing—"

"You can fight for her," his stepmother interrupted.

"I've texted to check in with her every day since she ended things. She never replies."

"Your generation and those infernal devices." Marci sniffed. "You don't win a woman back with a text. Be bold, Callum. Give her a reason to try again."

"I'm afraid I don't have one," he admitted, pressing the heels of his palms to his closed eyes. "I'm not willing to risk my heart. She was right about me."

"What makes you think that?" Marci asked. "Your divorce?"

He dropped his hands to his sides and forced himself to meet his stepmother's concerned gaze. "I failed at marriage once, and it about killed me to hurt Doralee that way."

"She wasn't right for you from the start."

Both he and Marci turned as Stephanie joined them in the kitchen, a sleeping Linus cradled in her arms.

"I'm not sure I can take being double-teamed by the two of you," he told his sister.

Stephanie rolled her eyes. "Be an awesome brother and pour me a cup of coffee. This little guy was up more than normal last night. I'm dragging right now."

"I'll take him," Marci offered, setting down her coffee. "While you talk some sense into your brother." She smiled when Callum narrowed his eyes. "I'm stepping back so you don't feel like we're ganging up on you. But know I agree with everything Stephanie says."

His sister handed the baby to Marci, then faced Callum. "You're an idiot," she said simply.

Callum snorted. "What happened to the family rule of no name-calling in front of Mom?"

"It's not exactly how I would have put it," Marci admitted, "but she has a point."

"You know it, too." Stephanie accepted the cup of coffee he offered, sighing as she took a long drink. "You love Becky Averill and her daughters and you want to make a life with them." She pointed a finger toward him. "In Rambling Rose."

He shook his head. "I don't—"

"This is your home," Stephanie interrupted. "And Becky is your person. Stop trying to deny it."

"She broke up with me," he pointed out, his heart twisting painfully in his chest.

"From what I gather, you left her no choice." She leaned in closer. "I tried to get her to talk bad about you last night. I really did. And she wouldn't do it. She loves you and if you'd just get out of your own way, you could have the life we all know you want."

Marci joined her daughter. "I told you I'd agree with everything she said. We all know how much you sacrificed for this family and how the divorce made you question things. But you're a family man at heart, Callum. You always have been."

He opened his mouth to argue, then paused and drew in a deep breath instead. He'd spent a lot of years convincing himself he didn't want the responsibility of that kind of commitment.

Now he couldn't imagine his life without Becky and the girls in it. He hadn't expected his life to take this turn, but his sister was right, as usual. He'd be an idiot not to risk his heart when he had this chance at real happiness. And yet...

"I can't compete with her late husband," he said quietly, finally voicing his greatest fear when it came to Becky. "From all accounts, he was damn near a saint. The perfect husband who would have been a perfect father."

"Callum." Stephanie squeezed his arm. "I promise you that Becky isn't looking for perfect. Her girls don't need that, either. They just need someone to love them."

"I do," he whispered. "I will if she'll let me." Allowing himself to acknowledge that undeniable fact lifted the weight that had been crushing his chest.

His stepmom and sister shared a smile. "Then don't you think it's time you shared that with Becky?"

He gave them each a quick hug, dropped a kiss on the top of baby Linus's downy head and quickly headed for his truck.

Becky would be at work by now, so he drove straight

to the pediatric center, trying to work out a plan in his mind for how to win her back.

The best he could think of past his racing heart and sweaty palms was throwing himself to his knees and begging her for another chance.

Surely something better would present itself in the moment, but either way Callum wasn't going to let anything stop him.

He rushed through the lobby and down the hall that housed the primary care wing.

Becky's friend Sharla sat at the nurses' station, giving him a look that could freeze the sun as he approached.

"I need to speak with Becky," he said, forcing a calm tone.

"She's not here."

He glanced around as if he could will her to appear. "When will she be back?"

"Dunno."

Okay, this wasn't going the way he'd planned, but if his bid for another chance with Becky needed to include groveling to her coworker, he'd do that.

"I've been an idiot," he told the surly medical assistant. He figured if his sister had been willing to tell him that out loud, most people in Becky's life must agree.

"Go on," Sharla said slowly, proving him right.

"She's the best thing that ever happened to me, and I'm sorry I hurt her."

"You hurt her badly."

He sucked in a breath. "I want to make it up to her and the twins. I can't lose them. They're my world."

The woman studied him for several long moments before nodding. "I actually believe you… But she still isn't here."

He sighed. Damn. "When will she be back?"

"Two days." Sharla tapped a finger against her chin. "Maybe three. If she doesn't decide—"

"Decide what?" Callum's mind reeled. "Where did she go? She left Rambling Rose? That's impossible. This is her home."

"Slow down, cowboy." Sharla stood and placed her palms on the desk. "I believe you love our Becky, but that doesn't mean I'm convinced you're what's best for her. Especially after she saw you bringing home another woman."

Callum felt his mouth go slack. "What woma—" He muttered a curse. "Last night when I passed her at the gatehouse? I wasn't on a date or bringing anyone home. I'd wanted to get to the ranch before Becky left, but I had to give my neighbor's daughter a lift home when her car broke down in town."

Sharla's pink-glossed lips formed a small O.

"Please don't tell me Becky left town thinking I was already dating someone else."

"I won't tell you." Sharla made a face. "Which doesn't make it any less of a fact."

"I have to talk to her."

A patient came out of one of the exam rooms with Parker, who lifted a questioning brow in Callum's direction.

"I might have fibbed about her return date," Sharla said quickly. "I need to get back to work, but she went to see her parents in Houston. She's planning on coming home tomorrow night. Talk to her then and you better make it good. Becky deserves the best you've got, Mr. Fortune."

"She deserves the best of everything," he agreed. He just hoped he could convince her a second chance was best for both of them.

Becky blinked away tears as she watched her mother place a kiss on Sasha's chubby cheek. The quieter twin sat in her mom's lap while Luna grinned and banged a wooden spoon on the colorful xylophone that had been Becky's as a child.

"I can't believe you saved all these toys," she told her mom.

Ann Averill shrugged. "They were your favorites, so I figured if you had kids one day they'd like them, too."

"The girls are in heaven."

It wasn't just the twins, either. A sense of peace had descended over Becky as she'd relaxed in her childhood home. Despite how they'd acted toward her in the past, she wished she hadn't waited so long to reach out.

A twinge of sorrow pinched her chest as memories of the weeks after Rick's death filled her mind. She'd been overwhelmed by grief, which had quickly morphed into anger when her parents tried to convince her to move home to Houston.

She'd felt their lack of confidence that she could make it on her own in Rambling Rose like a slap in the face. Her pain had made her even more determined to manage life on her own without asking for help. They'd never been a particularly close family, and the rift had seemed to widen on its own until it had been easier not to speak to them at all than to listen to her mother's subtle digs or her father's outright condemnation.

Spending time with the Fortunes had reminded her of the importance of family. Her relationship with her parents might not be perfect, but she wanted her daughters to know their grandma and grandpa.

"They look like your grandmother," her mom said, her gaze wistful as she snuggled Sasha and smiled at Luna. "I thought the same about you when you were a baby."

Becky nodded. "And they have Rick's smile," she whispered.

"You're a good mom, Beck." Becky glanced up to where her father stood in the doorway, a spatula in hand. Her dad grilled all year round and had started prepping the steaks almost as soon as Becky and the twins had arrived that morning.

Tom Averill was a gruff man, quiet and solid, and he'd always communicated his affection through action rather than words. Some of the best memories Becky had from her childhood were of her father flipping pancakes while Becky watched Saturday morning cartoons at the kitchen counter.

"Thanks, Dad." Becky managed the words without crying, which she knew would embarrass her stoic father.

He gave a curt nod and disappeared again.

"He's proud of you," her mother said. "We both are."

"Really?" Becky laughed. "I had the impression you thought I was in over my head."

"Perhaps at the time of Rick's death," her mother admitted. "We were so worried about you recovering from that kind of tragedy. Then when you found out you were carrying twins…" Ann shook her head. "I didn't believe in you as much as I should. You're much stronger than either your father or I realized."

"You raised me," Becky said softly, "so you can take some of the credit."

Her mother chuckled. "No. You get it all." Her expression sobered. "I still worry about you and wish you'd move home. The girls need—"

"Rambling Rose is our home, Mom." Becky smiled and clapped along with Luna's enthusiastic banging. "We're part of the community." Her breath hitched as she realized how true that statement was. She owed a large debt to Callum for helping her finally muster the courage to come out of her shell. Because of the way she was raised, she'd thought of asking for help as a weakness.

Rick had been equally independent and their relationship had been the two of them against the world. It worked until his death, and then she was lost at sea with not even a paddle to aid her in getting to dry land.

From the first moment Callum had volunteered to watch the twins while she helped Laurel, he'd made it easy to lean on him. She'd gotten close to the people at work in a way she hadn't before and begun to expand her circle of friends, enriching both her life and the twins'.

Would she have been willing to make that happen without Callum's innate support? Hard to say, but Becky would remain forever grateful to him.

Her feelings about Callum must have shown on her face because her mother's expression became suddenly assessing.

"Have you met someone new?" Ann asked as she smoothed a hand over Sasha's back.

"I went on a few dates with a guy, but it didn't work out."

"Why?"

"We wanted different things, I guess." Becky picked

an invisible piece of lint from her pant leg. "He's not sure if he's going to stay in Rambling Rose long-term, and my life is there."

"Is it?" Her mother sounded more curious than judgmental. "You're a nurse, Beck. You can have a career anywhere. The girls are so young that a move wouldn't really impact them. There's something about how you look right now that makes me think this man was special to you."

Becky drew in a sharp breath, and her mother sighed. "We might not have the closest relationship," Ann said, "but I'm still your mom. I know you, sweetheart."

"I can't leave my home," Becky said, her voice cracking on the last word. She cleared her throat. "Rick and I chose Rambling Rose. Even if I wanted to relocate, I don't know how I could. It would feel like I was being disloyal to his memory. Like I was moving on."

"No," her mother answered immediately. "That isn't true."

Sasha climbed off her grandma's lap, as if sensing Becky's distress, and toddled toward her, Luna quickly following suit.

Becky opened her arms and cradled her twins. "People tell me that," she said to Ann. "They tell me it's okay to move on. But I don't want to *move on*. Rick will always be a part of me. He's a part of our beautiful daughters. His death made me who I am today."

"I understand." Her mother nodded. "Which is why I don't believe you have to stay in Rambling Rose. It's fine if you want to. I'm not trying to convince you to leave. But if you meet someone who makes you and the girls happy, that's important. Rick would want you to be happy again. You can honor him by living life to the fullest."

Was she doing the opposite now? Yes, she felt a connection to Rambling Rose. The town was her home. But it didn't compare with how happy she'd been with Callum. She didn't know if he'd even consider the option of Becky and the girls going with him when he left. But she knew his fear of staying in one place wasn't about her. They could make a life together wherever the work took him if that's what he needed. She understood his fear about settling down, but she could show him that the home they both craved wasn't simply a matter of four walls. It was in their connection to each other. Had she given up too easily? Had her doubts and fears about what she had to offer led her to make the biggest mistake of her life?

Callum's heart beat double time as he drove past the park on the edge of town and saw Becky's minivan parked in the gravel lot.

Sharla had texted him that Becky was definitely coming to work the following morning so his plan had been to talk to her after her shift tomorrow night.

He could still do that, he thought, as nerves thrummed through his veins. Chances were she'd gotten back recently and probably wanted some time to decompress after the visit with her parents.

Excuses. He had a million of them.

None could mask the fact that he was afraid Becky wouldn't give him a second chance. That he'd put his heart on the line and have it well and truly broken. His ex-wife hadn't been the only one hurt when their marriage ended. It had taken a while for Callum to admit it, but he still carried the scars from his divorce.

He'd been a less than perfect husband and didn't want to ever fail in that way again. But now he realized if he continued to guard his heart so tightly that there wasn't room for anyone inside it, he might protect himself from pain but he'd also prevent himself from finding true happiness.

The kind he knew he'd have with Becky.

Before he changed his mind, Callum pulled into the parking lot and stopped next to her vehicle, refusing to waste one more minute on doubt and regret. It was close to sundown, but the air was calm and the lingering scent of an earlier rain shower made everything earthy and fresh.

He passed a few people walking dogs or jogging on the path as he walked toward the bench overlooking a small pond where he knew he'd find Becky and the girls.

His hand strayed to the side pocket of his cargo pants and the outline of the black velvet box he'd carried around with him since that morning.

She seemed lost in thought as he approached, her lips moving as if she were talking to her daughters or maybe to her late husband. She'd shared that this was the place she felt closest to Rick, and suddenly Callum felt like an interloper, intruding in a moment where he didn't belong.

Then Luna, who was leaning forward in the double stroller, spotted him.

"Cawl," she cried, then shoved a piece of oat cereal into her mouth and lifted her arms toward him.

Sasha pulled the binky out of her mouth to call out to him as well, and Becky met his gaze with a gasp.

"I hope you don't mind company," he said as he got closer.

"No," she whispered and offered a tentative smile.

The girls bounced and clapped and reached for him, like two little baby birds in the nest. "Is it okay if I pick them up?"

"Of course." Her fingers clasped and released the hem of her faded sweatshirt over and over. Apparently, he wasn't the only one with a case of nerves.

He unbuckled the girls, lifted them into his arms and then sat next to Becky on the bench.

"I heard you went to visit your parents," he said as Sasha snuggled into him and Luna patted his cheek. He'd missed not only Becky this week, but her girls, as well. His heart stammered at the thought of getting another chance to be in their lives, hopefully on a permanent basis.

"Just for a night," she confirmed, then frowned. "How did you hear?"

"I stopped by the pediatric center yesterday."

"Oh."

"To see you."

"I gathered that," she said with a slight smile.

"You haven't returned my texts."

Her gaze softened. "I thought a clean break between us would be easier."

"Right," he muttered. "And now here I am intruding on your evening walk."

"It's okay, Callum. I'm glad to see you."

Hope had never played a huge role in his life, but now he grabbed on to the kernel of it, holding it close to his heart like a lifeline. "Were you visiting with Rick?" he forced himself to ask.

"I know it seems silly, but yes. I wanted to talk to him after being with my parents and this is the spot where I come for that."

"Is anything the matter with your folks?"

She shook her head. "It had been too long since I've seen them. I want the twins to know their family." She reached out a hand and squeezed his arm. "The Fortunes have inspired me, actually. It's great how close all of you are, even when you live halfway across the country from each other."

"Family is a gift." He kissed the top of Sasha's head. "Until they drive you crazy."

"Yeah." She laughed and lifted Luna from his arms. "It was good to see the girls with their grandparents. Hard to tell if we'll be able to put everything in the past behind us, but I'm glad I made the effort. My mom actually had some great advice about my future."

A momentary flicker of panic gripped his gut. "Tell me you aren't moving away from Rambling Rose."

"No plans for that at the moment." She adjusted her hold on Luna. "Although Mom doesn't understand my devotion to this town, and what she said made a lot of sense."

"It's your home," he argued, not wanting Becky to compromise her commitment for anyone. "Rambling Rose is the place you and Rick chose to build a life. Of course you're dedicated to this town."

She studied him for a moment. "Believe it or not," she said, "she wasn't judging me. That's what I'd always thought about my parents. I think they're glad that I'm happy here, but they also want me to know I could make a home anywhere. Rick will always be with me."

"And with your girls. His love is a part of all three of you."

"Exactly." She swiped at her cheek. "You understand."

"I hope *you* understand that I'd never try to take his place." Callum swallowed. Hard. "But I love you, Becky. I should have told you before now, and I'm sorry I hurt you. You were right to call me a coward. You make me want to be brave. I'd do anything for another chance. I promise I won't mess it up again."

"I love you, too," she whispered. "I never want you to think that this town—that anyplace—is more important to me than you."

He lifted a finger to her lips. "It's your home, and it's my home, too. I want to build a life here with you." He hugged Sasha closer. "With the girls. They will never forget their father, but it would be my great honor to raise them and be as much of a dad as I can be."

"Do you mean that?" She sniffed and the tenderness in her gaze made his heart melt all over again. "I know you've had enough of a burden with taking care of little ones and that—"

"It would never be a burden," he corrected. "Being a part of the twins' lives would be the best thing that I could imagine."

He fished in his pocket for the velvet box. "In fact..."

Becky's dark eyes widened.

"I hope you'll excuse me if I don't get down on one knee," he said with a chuckle. "Sasha seems to have fallen asleep on my shoulder and I don't want to disturb her."

"No knee necessary," she whispered.

"Becky Averill." He flipped open the box to reveal the

ring he'd chosen at the jeweler's that morning. It was a round diamond set in a platinum band with two smaller stones flanking the one in the center. "Would you be my wife? I promise to never give up on our love and to spend the rest of my life making you happy."

Luna cooed out her approval of the ring as she grabbed at it. Becky held her daughter out of reach, then met Callum's gaze. "Yes," she told him and it felt like a symphony swelled in his chest.

"There's something else." He set the box on the bench and reached in his opposite pocket, taking out a small velvet pouch and handing it to Becky. "I got these for the girls."

She pulled out the two gold bracelets he'd also chosen at the jewelers. "I love you, Becky," he repeated. "And I love your daughters. This is my way of telling you that my heart belongs to all three of you." He shook his head. "You're crying. Don't cry."

"They're happy tears," she promised, her voice catching on the last word. "But you better put that ring onto my finger now. I'm not sure I can wait any longer."

"Then let's not wait," he said, plucking the ring from the box and slipping it onto her left hand. "I want us to be a family."

She leaned in and brushed a kiss across his lips. "Don't you know we already are?"

For the first time in forever, Callum felt truly at home. He knew in his heart that the joy of this moment would last forever.

Epilogue

"I like seeing you smile."

Becky turned toward Callum as he parked the truck in front of the Paws and Claws Animal Clinic, so much happiness filling her heart she could almost feel it beating against her rib cage. It was another Texas blue-sky day, the brightness of the sunshine reflecting the glow in her heart.

"You make me smile, Mr. Fortune," she told him.

"For the rest of our lives, Mrs. Fortune," he answered.

She glanced down at her left hand and the eternity band that had joined the engagement ring on her finger.

It had been a little less than a week since Callum proposed, and they'd driven to the county courthouse with the twins earlier that morning to exchange their wedding vows.

Some people might question a whirlwind courtship

and wedding, but Becky didn't worry any longer about raising eyebrows. The moment Callum had sat down on the park bench with her, any doubts and fears she'd had fled like night shadows chased away by the light of dawn.

She'd felt her late husband's spirit surrounding them, a quiet whisper of approval that she could move forward and truly love again.

They were a family and had both wanted to make it official as soon as possible. With Callum's busy schedule, her dedication to the pediatric center and the continuing saga of baby Linus's future, a simple ceremony felt right.

Callum's stepmom got them to agree to celebrate with a larger reception once their lives calmed down a bit, although Becky wondered if that would ever happen. She didn't care. Becoming Callum's wife, even with no fanfare, fulfilled her in ways she couldn't have imagined.

They'd driven straight to the vet clinic so they could attend the afternoon's grand opening celebration and would begin the process of moving Becky and the girls to the ranch later that night.

As Becky opened the passenger door, Marci and David greeted her. Her new mother-in-law enveloped her in a tight hug, whispering words of congratulations into her ear.

"Welcome to the family," David told her when it was his turn for a hug.

"It makes me so happy to be a Fortune," she said, and the older man kissed both of her cheeks.

"I'm a grandma," Marci murmured as Callum put Luna into her arms.

"Gigi," the girl said with a toothy grin, staring into Marci's eyes.

"That's perfect," the older woman said, blinking back tears. "I'm your Gigi."

"And you can call me Papa." David held out his hands for Sasha, who automatically reached for him. Once again, the Fortune charm had worked its magic on Becky's cautious daughter.

"Papa," Sasha repeated.

"Uh-oh." Callum shut the door and placed an arm around Becky's shoulders, pulling her close. "I have a feeling our girls are going to be spoiled rotten by their Gigi and Papa."

"Nothing rotten about spoiling our granddaughters." Marci looked between Becky and Callum. "You've made us so very happy."

Becky nodded, unable to speak around the emotion clogging her throat. The sense of contentment she felt at being a part of the Fortune family almost overwhelmed her.

Callum squeezed her arm. "Let's go check out the new vet clinic. I'm sure the rest of the family will be champing at the bit to give you a proper welcome."

"It feels like they already have," Becky told him. The triplets had arrived yesterday and they'd had a big family dinner at the ranch. It amazed her how warm and gracious every member of Callum's family seemed to be. They made her feel as if she belonged with them, and she knew that whatever life brought, she could handle it surrounded by that depth of love.

As much as Becky loved Rambling Rose, she'd found her true home with Callum. Gratitude bubbled up inside her along with an abiding joy. Tragedy had marked her but not defined the whole of who she was.

She linked her arm with her husband's as they headed toward the new building, thrilled to walk toward their future together.

* * * * *

Tina Leonard is a *New York Times* bestselling and award-winning author of more than fifty projects, including several popular miniseries for Harlequin. Known for bad-boy heroes and smart, adventurous heroines, her books have made the *USA TODAY*, Waldenbooks, Ingram and Nielsen BookScan bestseller lists. Born on a military base, Tina lived in many states before eventually marrying the boy who did her crayon printing for her in the first grade. You can visit her at tinaleonard.com and follow her on Facebook and Twitter.

Books by Tina Leonard

Harlequin American Romance

Bridesmaids Creek

The Rebel Cowboy's Quadruplets
The SEAL's Holiday Babies
The Twins' Rodeo Rider

Callahan Cowboys

A Callahan Wedding
The Renegade Cowboy Returns
The Cowboy Soldier's Sons
Christmas in Texas
A Callahan Outlaw's Twins
His Callahan Bride's Baby
Branded by a Callahan
Callahan Cowboy Triplets

Visit the Author Profile page at Harlequin.com for more titles.

Her Callahan Family Man

TINA LEONARD

Many thanks to the wonderful readers who have taken the Callahan family into their hearts— your enthusiasm has made their stories possible.

"The Callahans fight to win. They'd rather die than give an inch. And there's not an inch of quit in them."

—Neighboring ranch owner Bode Jenkins, when asked by a reporter why the Callahans simply didn't move away from Rancho Diablo

Chapter 1

Jace Chacon Callahan stared back at the petite fireball glaring at him. Sawyer Cash was his nemesis, his nightmare, the one woman that could keep him awake at night, racked by desire. Her killer body and haunting smile stayed lodged in his never-at-rest brain. And now here she was, red hair aflame and blue eyes focused, oblivious to the fact that his mind was never quite free of her. "*You're* the bidder who won me at the Christmas ball?" Jace demanded.

Sawyer shrugged. "Don't freak out about it. Someone had to bid on you. I was just trying to contribute to your aunt Fiona's charity. Are we going to do this thing or not?"

He seemed to be locked in place, thunderstruck. For starters, Sawyer was telling a whopper of a fib. There'd been plenty of ladies bidding a few weeks ago for the chance of winning a dinner date with a Callahan bachelor, which happened to be him.

But what had him completely poleaxed was that the little darling who had such spunk—and whatever else you wanted to call the sass that made her an excellent bodyguard and a torture to his soul—was that Sawyer was quite clearly, this fine February day, as pregnant as a busy bunny in spring.

In a curve-hugging, hot pink dress with long sleeves and a high waist, she made no effort to hide it. Taupe boots adorned her feet, and she looked sexy as a goddess, but for the glare she wore just for him.

A pregnant Sawyer Cash was a thorny issue, especially since she was the niece of their Rancho Diablo neighbor Storm Cash. The Chacon Callahans didn't quite trust Storm, yet in spite of that fact they'd hired Sawyer to guard the Callahan kinder.

But then Sawyer had simply vanished off the face of the earth, leaving only a note of resignation behind. No forwarding address, a slight he'd known was directed at him.

Jace knew this because for the past year he and Sawyer had had "a thing," a secret they'd worked hard to keep completely concealed from everyone.

He'd missed sleeping with her these past months. Standing here looking at her brought all the familiar desire back like a screaming banshee.

Yet clearly they had a problem. Best to face facts right up front. "Is that why you went away from Rancho Diablo?" he asked, pointing to her tummy.

She raised her chin. "Are we going on this date or not? Although it won't surprise me if you back out, Jace. You were never one for commitment."

Commitment, his boot. Of his six siblings, which consisted of a sister and five brothers, he'd been the one who'd most wanted to settle down, maybe even return to his roots in the tribe. By now he'd been fighting the good fight for Rancho Diablo for such a long time he never thought about living anywhere but here, or at least no farther away than the land across the canyons, which his brother Galen had shocked them all by acquiring, in a direct assault on Aunt Fiona's marriage raffle for the property.

The siblings thought Galen had cheated, or at least "rigged" the ranch deal in his favor. Jace and Ash hadn't had a chance to marry and have babies, all prerequisites for Fiona's ranch raffle. Ash was still steamed as heck with her big brother, Galen, whom she adored—although not when it came to acquiring the ranch she'd already named Sister Wind Ranch, which was actually called Loco Diablo by him and his brothers.

Jace wanted the land for himself, but he'd never pushed hard enough to find a lady with whom he could settle down and start a family, a necessary component of the marriage raffle. He'd been too busy chasing Sawyer night and day—or, to be more precise, letting himself get caught by her.

He gazed at her stomach again, impressed by the righteous size to which she'd grown in the short months since he'd last seen her—and slept with her.

He wished he could drag her to his bed right now.

"I'm your prize, beautiful," he said. "No worries about that. But before we go, you're going to admit whether that child you're carrying is mine or not." He wouldn't be able to eat a bite, thinking about another man finding his way into Sawyer's sweet bed. Jace broke into an uncomfortable sweat just imagining someone else with his adorable darling.

"I'm hungry, and in no mood to chat." Sawyer turned to walk away, and he caught her hand to stop her, pulling her toward him. That she was avoiding the topic told him everything he needed to know.

"It's my baby," he stated quietly, his gaze pinning hers. "Don't deny it."

"I'm not."

Her perfume wrapped around him; her heart-shaped lips were close enough to kiss. His ears rang with her admission, and Jace struggled to take in that he'd awakened this frosty February morning in Diablo, New Mexico, a free man—and would go to bed a caught man, and a father. "You're having my baby?"

She gazed at him with those blue eyes that had long intoxicated him, even though he knew she was sexy trouble. "I'm having your *babies*."

If he hadn't been such a strong person, a man of steel forged by fire, as he frequently told himself, he'd have raised an eyebrow with surprise. *"Babies?"*

"Twins. One boy, one girl, if the doctor's correct."

Stunned was too gentle a word for the emotion searing him. The vixen who'd avoided him these past four months, not even letting him know where she was—who'd made him believe he was never going to hold her in his arms again—was the sin to which he was now tied.

His family was going to razz him a good one—and they weren't going to toss confetti in congratulations. They'd say he'd gone over to the dark side, had slept with the enemy's niece.

Hell, yeah, I did. And she's having my children.
I'm on top of the world, even if I'm going to Hell.

* * *

Sawyer Cash grew wary as the handsome cowboy she'd spent months dreaming about steered her toward his truck. She didn't like the sudden glint in his eye when he'd realized she was pregnant with his children—and she knew the Callahans well enough to know that a glint in the eye meant their wild side was kicking in. "Where are we going?"

"On the date you bid for and won, darling. Be a lamb and hop in my truck," Jace said, opening the door for her.

She'd always love the wild in Jace Chacon Callahan. His eyes were that navy color all the Callahan men had, but his were both a little distant and a little crazy. His hair was always tousled, dark strands going haywire except when tamed by a cowboy hat. Even his laugh was a bit wild, tinged with the devil-may-care attitude that most of the Callahan men possessed.

She'd always been attracted to Jace—but right now he made her nervous.

"Since I won you, I get to pick the date parameters, right? I mean, I paid for something."

He smiled, slow and sexy, heating her with memories of snatched passion they should never have shared. "Whatever you want, little darling. Now slide in so I can buckle you up good and tight."

Warnings howled in her psyche. She didn't like anything about his sudden determined mood. "There's a cute little restaurant in Tempest we could check out."

"Tempest." He buckled her in with care and stared into her eyes, just inches from her face. "It's a funny thing, but the night of the Christmas ball, all I learned about the woman who won me was that she was from Tempest."

"At the time I bid, I was working for your brother Galen in Tempest," she said, a little breathless at the devilish look in Jace's eyes. "At Sheriff Carstairs's place. You know about what happened there."

He had to have heard about the night Sawyer and her cousin Somer had taken shots at each other, quite by accident. Hired by Galen, Sawyer had been doing her job—and Jace hadn't had any idea she was only a short truck ride away in Tempest, which was how she'd wanted it.

All the same, it had been hard not to drive "home" to Rancho Diablo to see him. But she'd known that to see Jace meant falling under his spell and into his arms.

She'd done far too much of that. Obviously.

"You covered your tracks real well." He checked her seat belt again and she smacked his hand away, making him laugh in a throaty, teasing growl. He was just itching to get on her nerves in every way, and he was certainly succeeding. "Disappeared for months, then took a job with Galen, which I consider a bit traitorlike on your part. Then deliberately won me at Aunt Fiona's auction. As I recall, the bidding went sky-high that night. I, the last Chacon Callahan bachelor to be on the block, fetched the highest price ever. Which you paid, and no one twisted your arm at all."

She couldn't look away from the knowing laughter in his eyes. "You're a bit of an ass, Jace."

"Yes, ma'am." He closed the door, went around to the driver's side. She could hear him guffawing with delight at her admission that she wanted him.

Well, she *had* wanted him, and she *had* paid a record amount for him at the Christmas ball, determined that no other woman should win him that night, not when she'd just learned she was pregnant. Five thousand dollars had gone to Fiona's favorite charity, thanks to her sexy nephew. Jace's aunt had no idea how many times Sawyer had fallen under Jace's spell, seduced by the hot cowboy with a wicked penchant for frequent, enthusiastic lovemaking.

She couldn't even comfort herself with the thought that he was a dud of a lover, or lacked the skills or attributes a female adored. No, he was pretty much perfect as a lover. And darn well aware of it, too. "So, we'll head to Tempest for dinner?"

He started the truck, pulled out from the driveway at Rancho Diablo, where she'd agreed to meet him as his mystery date. "Sure, we can eat there. But not tonight. Tonight, we're going to take a romantic drive." He glanced over at her. "You cute little thing, trying to sneak up on me with this surprise pregnancy. You didn't have to win me at the auction just to tell me about the babies. I would've married you even if you hadn't bid for me. You could have had me for free."

He was so arrogant! "I did not want, and do not want, to marry you. Put that right out of your insane mind."

Apparently Jace thought her words were a real thigh-slapper. Sawyer's brows drew together in a frown as he laughed. "Something funny?" she asked.

"Reverse psychology is an excellent tool." He glanced over and stroked her cheek. "You didn't pay five grand just to have dinner with me, doll face."

He was insufferable. Why had she bothered to try to keep another woman from getting her manicured hands on him?

Sawyer should have thrown him to the wolves with a smile on her face.

"Jace, tonight is about dinner only. I've lived without you just fine for the first several months of this pregnancy, and I can continue to do well on my own. I suggest you try to grasp that. While you and I may have some parenting details to work out, there'll be no resumption of our former relationship."

"Could you classify that former relationship for me?"

He was definitely digging down to find his deepest layer of smart-ass. "Working professionals with benefits. You know that as well as I."

"And now that you're pregnant, those benefits are no longer beneficial?"

She could hear the smirk in his voice. "That's right."

He hit the main road, but they weren't heading for Tempest. "I believe you went the wrong way," Sawyer stated.

"I'm going the only way we need to go," Jace said. "You and I are taking a side trip to Vegas. We're going to give my children my name. Then if you want to sleep alone, that's your choice. I won't fight you about that. But being a father to my children, Sawyer, I will fight for." He glanced at her, his smile slightly amused. "I'm a pretty good fighter."

She knew that. All the Callahans were stubborn, steeped in loyalty to family and land. It was one of the reasons she'd fallen in love with Jace. Now he wanted to marry her, have a quickie wedding to seal the torrid love affair they'd shared under the family radar. She was a Cash and he was a Callahan, and the two were never supposed to meet on more than a professional basis.

"We can do this without marriage," Sawyer said a bit desperately as he sped toward Vegas. "We can divide custody with the use of legal instruments instead of a marriage ceremony."

"We've come this far, we may as well go all out. My family's going to flip out when they find out I've…" He hesitated, then glanced at her with a grin. "That I'm having children."

"That you've impregnated the enemy?" She glared at him. "I can't think of a worse reason to get married."

"I can't, either, but we're apparently past needing a reason and are moving swiftly on to cause. Those children deserve a proper start in life. That's all there is to this, Sawyer Cash. Don't feel guilty because you've worked your wiles on me, and are finally getting what you wanted all along, when you made your way into my bed."

"*Not* your bed." Not with the furtive lovemaking they'd enjoyed. There'd been nothing traditional about their stolen moments together.

"Doesn't matter if it was truck bed, front seat, barn, canyon or Rancho Diablo roof. We misused ye olde condom somehow, and now the piper must be paid."

She rolled her eyes. "About that time on the roof…"

"You said you wanted to see the stars. I believe we achieved your goal."

He really was an insufferable jackass, quite confident that his lovemaking was the end-all to a woman's dreams, the gold buckle of mind-blowing sex.

She couldn't argue the point. She'd left Rancho Diablo when she'd realized she'd fallen head over heels in love with him, and that he had zero desire for a serious romance between them. He'd never said it in so many words, but she knew the difficulty of their relationship as well as anyone.

She'd thought she was in the clear, had made her escape with her pride intact. And then the morning sickness had begun.

"I don't want to get married, Jace."

"It's not about you. It's about our children. Now try to get some rest. There's a blanket in the backseat if you want it. When you awaken, it'll be time for us to find the fastest house of I do in Vegas."

Great. That sounded like a wedding she could always look back on with a fond smile. No magic wedding dress for her, no marriage at the beautiful seven-chimneyed mansion at Rancho Diablo like all the other Callahan brides.

Drat. I had to fall for the one Callahan for whom a quickie, no-strings-attached marriage is just ducky.

Sawyer pulled the blanket over herself and closed her eyes so she wouldn't think about what she'd done, blowing her entire bank account on the wildest, wooliest Callahan of all. When she'd known quite well that the Callahans and the Cashs were never, ever going to trust each other.

Babies notwithstanding.

Chapter 2

"It does trouble me that you felt like you had to win me to have this conversation," Jace told Sawyer an hour later, as he sped toward Las Vegas. "I'm flattered you spent several months of your Rancho Diablo salary keeping me from another woman, but I would have withdrawn myself from Aunt Fiona's bachelor raffle if I'd known I was a father."

He looked over at Sawyer, noting that the spicy red-head looked as if she wanted to give him a piece of her mind, and probably would in a moment. He remembered the first time he'd ever laid eyes on her. Galen and he had played backup to Dante when he went over to see Storm Cash, and Sawyer had opened the door instead of her uncle, catching all of them off guard. Jace had seen a big smile, a slender, athletic body, cute freckles across a tiny nose, big blue eyes twinkling at him, and felt himself fall into deep, fiery lust—lust so strong that every time he saw her, he wanted her.

Of course, he'd known better. There were some lines one could cross, but sleeping with the enemy was a mistake only a man with his mind anywhere but on his job would make. But then she'd been hired on at Rancho Diablo by his brother Sloan and Sloan's wife, Kendall—and suddenly the red-hot neighbor sex-bomb was in Jace's sights like a tornado he couldn't avoid.

It hadn't taken him long to respond to the magnet pulling him toward Sawyer—only to discover that she seemed to feel the same desire. They'd made love as often as possible, as discreetly as possible, keeping their affair completely locked away. Sawyer didn't want to jeopardize her job, knowing that she still had to earn Callahan trust—and Jace hadn't wanted his family harping on his lack of loyalty.

His family was in for a big shock, but right now, he had to make certain his little firecracker mama got to the altar.

One thing about the Callahans: they were deadly serious about their ladies once they found them. But rare was the Callahan bride who'd made her way to the altar quietly.

He intended to avoid that unnecessary heartburn.

"I did not," Sawyer said with annoyance, "want you to withdraw from Fiona's event. You'd been advertised on barn roofs and billboards for months as Diablo's prize of the century. It wouldn't have been right to tell you at Christmas that you were going to be a father, and make you withdraw. That would have devastated Fiona, taken all the fun out of the Christmas ball and denied the charities that she funds much needed revenue, which comes from the purses of women who are hoping to win the dream man lottery."

Jace perked up at the idea that Sawyer might think he was a dream man, suddenly hopeful that shoehorning her into marrying him would be simpler than it had first seemed. She didn't appear all that anxious to say I do.

Unaware of his hopeful state, Sawyer took a deep breath and stated, "I took care of the obvious problem of my children's father hanging out with another woman simply by winning you. It wasn't that big of a deal, Jace."

"You cute little thing." He smiled at her, impressed by the starch in her attitude. "I'm not going to lie and say that I'm not thrilled to find out you're my mystery girl. I'll be happy to put a ring on your finger tonight, Sawyer." And then, if good fortune smiled on him, maybe after the I dos were said, he'd finally get his little darling into a real bed, in a room with a closed door that locked, so he could enjoy her for hours on end.

"It's going to feel great not to rush things anymore," he said, not really aware he was speaking out loud, and Sawyer said, "I feel pretty certain we're rushing marriage. Marriage is the one thing in life that shouldn't be rushed at all."

"Well, that cow is long out of the barn, so we won't worry about that. Let's move on to big decision number two."

"I'm not even sure I want to be a Callahan," Sawyer said. "I think I'll keep my maiden name."

He nearly stomped on the brakes. "That's not going to happen, sweet cheeks. You and I are going to be Mr. and Mrs. Callahan, just like all my brothers and their wives. We share the children, we share the last name."

She sent him a frown. "I'm not persuaded."

"You will be. That's my gift, persuasion." He hoped she bought that corny line, and plowed on, "The second most important decision we make in life is where to live. I think the babies should be at the ranch, but everything's hot around there right now, as you know." They'd hired Sawyer in the first place because they'd needed bodyguards for the Callahan children. But later, they'd brought in more personnel to help keep Fiona and any other weaker links safe.

Of course, his redoubtable aunt would bean him a good one if she ever heard him refer to her as a weak link. But whether she liked it or not, she and Burke were getting up there in years.

"I can take care of myself. And the babies," Sawyer said. "It won't be much different from when I took care of Kendall's twins."

"I don't like it," Jace murmured, thinking out loud.

"No one asked you to like it."

"The problem is, bodyguards are supposed to be unemotional about their assignment. You can't be unemotional about your own children. No, I'll have to look into hiring someone for you and the babies."

"No, you won't," Sawyer said, and it sounded as if she spoke through tightly clenched teeth. "I don't want a bodyguard. I'm not planning on living with you."

He checked her expression. Yep, she had that serious look on her face, and he recognized yet another hurdle in his relationship with the saucy redhead.

She didn't want him in her bed. That's what this was all about.

His wooing would have to be played very smoothly, because he absolutely would be in a real bed with Sawyer, undressing her, with a ceiling overhead and not the sky. He wanted to hold her in his arms and make her cry his name, without having to quietly rush through each and every encounter.

Sooner rather than later he intended to have his way with the beautiful bodyguard, sharing lovemaking that would be record-breaking in length and very, very satisfying. That was the plan for tonight—if he could figure out the key to the tight lock she was trying to keep on her heart.

Lucky for him, he was really good at picking locks.

They were halfway across Arizona, halfway to Las Vegas and the Little Wedding Chapel, when Sawyer hit him with a bombshell.

"Several members of your family are on the way to witness our wedding."

To say his jaw dropped nearly to his lap would be putting it mildly. "My family?"

"Yes, and my uncle Storm, and his wife, Lulu Feinstrom." Sawyer beamed at Jace. "I know how your family loves a wedding, so I texted them. They'll be on the family plane soon and on their way, ready for wedding cake. At least that's what your sister said. Ash also mentioned she ordered us a whopper of a cake, because everyone in your family has had a sweet tooth since they were born. Her comment, not mine." Sawyer smiled, delighted that she'd outplayed him.

He'd seen her busily working on her phone, but he'd assumed she was looking up places to wed. Her decisive strategy meant Aunt Fiona and maybe even Uncle Burke were on their way. Jace knew he'd never get Sawyer into a bed for hours tonight, not with his partying family there. They'd want to kick up their heels and spend the evening giving him grief about how he'd surprised them with this sudden dash to the altar, blah, blah, blah, and they'd talk him to death, when he should be concentrating on undressing the redhead next to him.

It was really all he had on his mind.

Instead, he was going to get a whopper of a wedding cake.

"I don't have much of a sweet tooth," he said, casting a longing glance at her body in her hot pink dress. "I prefer spicier fare."

"I'll try not to feed you too big of a bite, then." She went back to texting, and he wondered if it was too late to text his family and explain that, while he loved them, he really wanted to handle this momentous occasion alone, because he was going to have a devil of a challenge getting his wife into a bed with him. He didn't have time for celebrating and family hijinks. Every second of his life until these babies were born had to be spent romancing his wife. After they arrived, he'd have precious little time alone with her, and he hadn't yet enjoyed his woman the way he wanted to.

He felt like a man who'd starved a long while in plain view of the most delicious meal he'd ever seen.

"It was nice of you to invite my relatives," he said, even though family was the last thing he wanted around.

"And mine," she said, her voice bright. "No bride wants to be married without someone to give her away."

There was the problem. His family and hers didn't get along, making the situation ripe for discomfort and fireworks.

"Anyway, I knew your family wouldn't want to miss the last Callahan bachelor getting married." Sawyer smiled at him, her big blue eyes completely innocent, when he knew that she was trying to put as much distance between them as possible.

"If we're going to marry, I want us to start out on the right foot with the in-laws and the outlaws," Sawyer said. "I wouldn't dream of leaving them out."

"Where are they booking rooms?" Jace asked.

"I don't know. But I'm booking us rooms at a bed-and-breakfast nearby."

He swallowed. "Rooms?"

She glanced up from the sudden storm of texts she was sending. "I meant room."

No, she hadn't. Jace could tell he was going to have to keep a very close eye on his little woman. No drinking too much and finding out she'd shuttled him into a room with his family. No visiting too much, or he'd probably find her headed back to Diablo without him. "Sex is what got us into this, darling."

"That's how it works," Sawyer said.

"Yet I have the strangest feeling you don't want to be alone with me."

"Callahans are known to have a lot of strange qualities. I wouldn't let it bother me now, if I were you."

"We'll stop and get you a ring," he said, giving up on sex for the moment.

"I don't need a ring. The vows are more than I want."

He grunted. "The ring is part of the ceremony. You'll have a ring."

"Are you going to wear one?"

He hadn't planned on it, but he sensed this was treacherous water. "Why wouldn't I?"

"I don't know." She ran a considering eye over him. "But if you are, I will."

"Back to our discussion of our domicile," he said.

"I'm planning on going to Rancho Diablo," Sawyer stated.

He blinked, hearing the thing he'd been sensing, the trouble at the end of the supposedly peaceful road. "Like, as soon as the 'I do' leaves your mouth?"

"Well, not until we've cut the cake." She looked at him, puzzled. "Of course I plan to stay for the cake your sister ordered. It would be rude to leave!"

Great. Nothing said love like worrying about the sister's cake purchase. "I was thinking we'd live together."

"This morning, you didn't even know you were a father. So we don't have plans," Sawyer pointed out. "Spur-of-the-moment decisions are rarely a good idea."

"As in getting married in Vegas?"

"As in getting married in Vegas." She nodded. "I liked our relationship just the way it was."

He shook his head. "We didn't have a relationship. We had sex, but not a relationship."

She met his gaze. "Was there a problem?"

The problem had come when she'd left, and he realized he'd been parked at the gates of heaven for too long. Now he was hoping to crash through those gates and land in the paradise waiting for him—if he could just figure out how to explain that to Sawyer. How could a man tell his woman that, while frequent, horny sex had been fun, and fired by the forbidden, he sensed the next phase of their relationship could be that much sweeter?

Especially since she didn't seem inclined to recognize the possibility for an ongoing, more meaningful relationship between them.

"Not a problem, exactly," he said carefully. "But it seems that we should be open to the idea of a new phase in our friendship."

She didn't reply. "I know this pregnancy changes your life significantly," he added.

"Yes. It does." Sawyer turned her head to gaze out the window.

He had one reluctant little mama on his hands.

"Yours, too," she said. "I know the Callahans have a pattern. You find out you're expecting, and immediately want to get married. Then the wife gets shuttled off to a safe location." Sawyer finally looked his way. "I'll expect you to treat our pregnancy differently."

"How differently?"

"By not trying to send me off to your family in Hell's Colony, or Tempest."

He swallowed. That had been the next plan. "The reason my brothers have been so determined for their wives and children to be in another location is because Rancho Diablo isn't safe. You know as well as anyone that my uncle Wolf has made things very difficult at the ranch. It's even worse now. Which is why your uncle Storm sold us his ranch and moved into town with Lulu Feinstrom."

"I'll be fine. I've already rented out a room from Fiona. Didn't she tell you? I called and asked her about renting a room before I came back to Rancho Diablo for our date. I do need a place to live now that my job in Tempest is completed."

"*You rented* a room?"

Sawyer nodded. "A marriage license won't mean I want to be a wife in anything other than name."

Well, there was nothing he could say to that. She'd ridden all over his poor flailing heart. It beat wildly in his chest, stressed and unhappy with his current circumstances.

There was only one thing to do.

He pulled over at the next rest stop and parked the truck. Then he pulled Sawyer close and laid a kiss to end all kisses on her. He didn't let her go, either, making certain she knew how much he desired her, kissing her long and thoroughly, communicating in a different way what he couldn't say out loud. And searching for that answer he wanted so badly: that she did, in fact, still want him.

It was a risky move, but when he felt her lips mold against his, Jace knew his belief in high risk, high reward had paid off.

His little darling still had the hots for him big-time— no matter how tightly she was trying to close those sweet, pearly gates.

Sawyer was so annoyed with herself for giving in to Jace's charm that she sat stiffly staring out at the landscape rushing past. He'd caught her off guard, that was all. If she'd had a second's notice of his intention, she could have controlled her reaction better.

Jace drove down the road with a sexy, confident, "I win" curve to his lips, a true cat that ate the canary. Sharing that kiss was a huge setback to her plan, and devastating to her heart.

I promised myself that wouldn't happen. No more falling under his spell. Not one woman who married a Callahan kept her independence. It was as if they got their wedding ring and poof! instant Callahan copy. Babies and bliss.

Babies and bliss in every corner.

"I'm renting a room from Fiona because I'll be in Diablo only until the babies are born. Four months after that I'll be living in New York," Sawyer said.

That wiped the smirk off his face. "New York?"

"Yes. I've taken a job with a firm that provides security for high-profile clients."

"You're going to be a bodyguard while you should be staying at home with my children?" Jace shook his head. "I can see two big problems with your plan, doll face. One, my children aren't going anywhere without me. Two, it's going to be terribly hard for you to be a homeroom mother and a bake sale coordinator while you're working. My children need you more than high-profile clients do."

She stiffened. "I'm sure you're hoping I'll thank you for your opinion. However, I'm fully capable of making my own decisions."

"Yes, you are. And I trust you'll make decisions that are in the best interest of our family, not harebrained ones that are purely designed to keep you and me from sharing a bed."

He'd gotten pretty close to the truth. "That's not the reason I took the job, Jace. I'm a very good bodyguard, and there's still a lot I want to do and learn."

"Yes, but your days of living on the edge are over. You can get your fill of that at Rancho Diablo."

"So you'd be all right with me and the children living at Rancho Diablo?"

He hesitated. "I didn't exactly say that."

"Then we have nothing to discuss."

"We have plenty to discuss. And now that we've just passed the Nevada state line, we're getting closer to our destination, so I won't hesitate to mention that this is the happiest day of my life."

She gave him a curious glance. "Why?"

"It's not every day a man finds out he's going to be

married and a father." He glanced at her. "Even better, that the woman who's providing all this excitement wanted him badly enough to pay five grand for him, thereby scuttling all other females' chances. Just so very cute of you." He laughed out loud, pleased with himself. "You put up stop signs, but there's lots of green lights flashing all over you, Sawyer Cash."

He was angling for a good hard takedown to his ego. Sawyer told herself Jace had always been a goofball, and ignored him.

"Have you asked Galen to hire you on again at Rancho Diablo?" Jace asked, stunning her.

"No." Out of the corner of her eye, she saw him shrug.

"We're always looking for staff we can trust."

"Are you saying you trust me?" Sawyer asked.

"Are you insinuating I can't? Or shouldn't?"

His gaze met hers, and she found herself drawn in, the way he'd always drawn her in. With the memory of his hot kiss still warm on her lips, she'd be lying to herself if she tried to pretend she didn't want to experience once again what he could do with those wandering hands of his. Experience the sweet satisfaction of what miracles he worked with a mouth that never ceased talking smack, and the to-die-for sexy things he whispered to her during lovemaking.

But she couldn't allow herself to get caught in the snare of sex. The goal was far more important than the pleasure.

"I'm not insinuating anything. I don't want you and your family to give me busywork." Sawyer knew how this story would play out. The moon would be promised—and she'd wind up with nothing but a crash to earth. "I'm not the kind of woman who'll be happy staying home to wash your socks, Jace."

He laughed, and Sawyer favored him with a frown.

"My socks?" Jace chuckled again. "You have a problem with my socks?"

"I don't want to be a Callahan housewife. I intend to keep doing what I do."

"You're jumping the mark, sister. No one ever said you can't work. I encourage it."

"You do?"

"Sure thing." He grinned. "In fact, I'll stay home with the babies. How's that for a compromise?"

She blinked, not certain where he was going with that. While all the Callahan men stayed close to home once married, she didn't think Jace would be happy as a Mr. Mom while she earned the family bread. "You'll do diapers and bath time?"

"Sure." He shrugged, not fazed at all. "The babies will have organic food I prepare myself, too—none of that jar stuff. Baths with lavender oil, and a nightly de-stress rubdown. I'll sing lullabies and tell them stories I heard when I was a child in the tribe." He looked satisfied with that plan. "I'll have to see if Grandfather Running Bear can add to my collection."

"I don't believe a word you're saying."

He picked her hand up, brushed it against his lips. "Believe it. You work, and I'll be the best stay-at-home dad you ever saw."

"You're too much of a chauvinist, Jace."

"I resent that remark, darling. Don't you worry about a thing. This is going to work out so well, you'll wonder how you ever lived without me. Be the best five grand you ever spent."

She raised a brow. "That really wound your ego up, didn't it? Me spending that kind of money for a date with you?"

"Oh, angel." He kissed her hand again. "You paid that kind of cash for exactly what you're getting—a husband."

She sucked in a breath. "Jace, honestly, I don't know how you fit in this truck with your ego."

He laughed. "I bought the biggest truck I could."

There was nothing else to say to such enthusiastic patting of his own back. Anyway, she'd already gotten two concessions out of him: she could live at Rancho Diablo and she could keep her job.

His ego could take a flying leap.

Jace's phone buzzed. "Excuse me," he told Sawyer. "I have to take this." His gaze slid over to her as he pulled off the road so he could talk on the phone. "Hello, Grandfather."

Whenever Chief Running Bear spoke, everybody listened. The man said almost nothing unless it was important. Sawyer couldn't tell much of what was being communicated, but it was clear Jace's attention was clearly engaged.

"That's interesting news. I'll see what I can do."

He hung up, then steered the truck back onto the highway again. "Running Bear suggests we go into hiding immediately."

Sawyer gasped. "Hiding! Why?"

"Apparently Wolf's right-hand man, Rhein, was arrested today on suspicion of smuggling. This means the Feds have decided to clamp down on the illegal operations that are being run across the canyons. Running Bear says this will have the effect of ramping up Wolf's goal of taking over Rancho Diablo. He says that because of your pregnancy, it would probably be best. Wolf will post bail for Rhein soon enough, and no doubt the sheep will hit the fauna."

Sawyer shook her head at his attempt to be light-hearted about something that wasn't funny at all. "I'm not going into hiding."

"I thought you'd feel that way," Jace said. "We have another option."

She didn't smile at the devilish wink he sent her. "What option?"

"I'll guard you."

"You mean *I* would be assigned to you as a body-guard," Sawyer said. "You have no experience."

He grinned. "However you want to play it, babe. I'd let you guard my body any day."

"It won't work. You wouldn't take it seriously." She shook her head. "Once I'm on bed rest, you'd drive me insane. The two of us working together would be an unfocused assignment." She thought about the babies, and what she would do once they were born. They'd be targets; they'd need special protection. She'd worked for the Callahans long enough to know that Running Bear's words were worth heeding. If he said that Rhein's arrest would add to the heat at Rancho Diablo, it couldn't be ignored. "If that was your only option, it wasn't a serious one."

"We're either on the road in hiding, or we stick together like glue. I guess it's going to depend on how you feel. When will the babies be born?"

"I'm five and a half months pregnant. I'm hoping to make it at least as far as April. But I know your sisters-in-law didn't carry their twins and trips quite as long as they would have liked. I'm in good shape, and the doctor says I'm on track for a normal pregnancy. So we'll see what happens."

"Okay. The goal is keeping you stress-free and resting. Hard to rest if you're on the run."

"Are we seriously talking about this?" She looked at him. "It's not in me to be afraid."

"I'll do it for both of us." He glanced at the rearview mirror. "In fact, we're being followed, and it's not by a Callahan. Aren't you glad you won me now, beautiful?"

Chapter 3

Jace didn't want to scare Sawyer, but she'd been around Rancho Diablo long enough to know the odds against them were long. There wasn't time to coddle her into seeing things his way. He was going to have to give her a push; Sawyer and the babies were his number one priority right now. "How are you for train travel?"

"I'm not," Sawyer said, "going into hiding. I'm not running."

"We are going into hiding. Take your pick. It's either a sunny locale or the mountains. What's your preference?"

"My preference is that you take me home right now. I'll stay in the house my uncle is selling your family, so I'll be close enough for you to keep an eye on."

"This isn't a game," Jace said quietly. "You know that, Sawyer. You know what Wolf is capable of. He means business. I'm not going to risk anything happening to you and the children."

The thought filled him with dread. There was good reason to worry. Taylor, his brother Falcon's wife, had been kidnapped and taken to Montana for months during her pregnancy. Aunt Fiona had been kidnapped, and she'd burned down Wolf's hideout during her rescue. The memory made him smile—but it was also a compelling reason to treat this newest threat seriously. Wolf had a long memory.

"Okay, here's what we'll do. We're driving to Texas," Jace said. "We'll get married, and we'll call our long road trip a honeymoon."

"You're not going to whitewash us going into hiding by calling it a honeymoon."

He had one unhappy lady on his hands. But what else could he do?

In Texas he had family. He couldn't go to Hell's Colony—it was too hot right now with the Wolf situation, and there was no reason to bring the heat to his Callahan cousins. But they could find a nice, out-of-the-way cabin deep in the piney woods of East Texas that would be really hard for Wolf to find.

If Jace had learned anything from the past few years of being hounded by Wolf, it was that caution was as important as bravery.

His mind made up, Jace sped toward Vegas and, hopefully, a slew of Wedding Elvises eager to say wedding vows as quickly as possible.

"I absolutely am not going to marry him," Sawyer told Ashlyn Callahan when they met at the chapel in Vegas.

The place was white, but that was its only concession to being a wedding stop.

Ash glanced at the pastor and his doughy little wife. The man had on a tall top hat and wore a white satin suit. His wife was arrayed in a vintage period gown, purple with red feathers. "Maybe it wouldn't be my first choice, either. But it's a good first start."

"First start?" Sawyer stared at Jace's silver-blond-haired sister. Ash had always seemed like an ethereal fairy to her—and yet it was said that of all the Callahans, she was the most dangerous. "A marriage only gets started once, doesn't it?"

Ash shrugged. "Where you say the words isn't important. Getting you and my niece and nephew safe is."

A chill swept Sawyer. How did Ash have so much information about her pregnancy, so soon? Callahan gossip always spread like wildfire.

"I just figure it'd be like Jace to split the deck. No commitment." Ash looked at her. "Except to you, it seems."

Sawyer shook her head. "Jace isn't committed to anything except his children. And Rancho Diablo."

"Don't go on what he says, is my advice. My brother never really was much of a talker, not about anything that made much sense." Ash smiled, looking pleased with herself when she realized Jace had caught her jibe. He came over to ruffle her hair.

"Jace, if you mess up my hair, you'll have a scary sister in your wedding photos," she complained. "Your bride thinks you have commitment issues."

He looked at Sawyer and grinned. "I do. But not to the degree that Sawyer does."

She met his gaze. "I'm not marrying you here."

"Well, you have to," Ash said. "At least, you have to try on the magic wedding dress. Fiona sent it with me, said you should try it on. I always think my aunt's advice should be heeded," she said, tugging Sawyer away from Jace's suddenly interested gaze.

Sawyer made herself follow Ash down the hall and into a private room. "I don't want to try on a dress."

"This one you do," Sawyer said. "It's magic."

"That's a myth, a fairy tale." She'd heard about the dress's supposedly supernatural qualities and didn't believe it. "There's nothing wrong with the dress I have on."

Ash glanced back at her before opening a closet where a long, white bag hung. "If you're going to be a runaway bride, at least do it in style. This dress," she said, pointing to the bag, "exudes style. High fashion, even."

"No, it doesn't," Sawyer said. She wasn't getting near it, wouldn't be enticed to even take a peek. "I saw the dress on Rose when she and Galen were married. It's beautiful and traditional, but not high fashion."

Ash stared at the bag. "I thought a gown that made every woman beautiful would be considered high fashion."

"No. It would be considered lucky."

"Oh," Ash said, recoiling. "We don't do lucky in our family. Mysticism and respect and ancient lore, and perhaps a little supernatural wonder, but never luck."

Sawyer shook her head. "I'm fine wearing what I have on."

"Aren't you afraid you'll regret it?" Ash asked. "You've been rendezvousing with my brother secretly for a long time. You might as well admit you're in love with him. And when a woman's in love, she wants to be beautiful on her wedding day."

Sawyer didn't know what to say to that outrageous statement. Down the hall, a wedding march played—probably for the couple who'd been waiting in the hall nervously when she and Jace had walked into the chapel.

"I'll leave you alone," Ash said. "Give you a chance to collect your thoughts. I won't be far if you want to do some more sisterly bonding. Feel free to call me if you do."

She went out, closing the door behind her. Sawyer glared at the garment bag. It wasn't going to work. She wasn't going to try on the gown, which was exactly what Ash wanted. Temptation—the Callahans were very good at temptation.

"It may be mission failure," Ash said, coming to stand next to Jace as he waited anxiously for whatever his bride and sister decided. He was well aware that Sawyer would need to be coaxed into marrying him. He'd seen some reluctant brides in his time, but she seemed to take reticence to a new level. He shook his head as his sister patted his back in sympathy.

"It's not mission failure. She wants to marry me." He refused to believe that after all they'd shared, Sawyer didn't want him. She had to know it wasn't just sex for him—and yet he was pretty certain that's what she'd say if he asked her what she thought it was the two of them had going.

He wasn't about to ask how she defined their relationship.

"She probably thinks you were sowing your wild

oats, brother," Ash said cheerfully. "After all, you never stepped up to the plate meaningfully."

"Thank you," he said, "I think I had that much figured out. Now if you can wave your magic wand and tell me how to fix it, I'd be happy to listen to that advice."

She fluffed her silvery hair, glancing in a mirror that was hanging in the foyer. "You and I may be doomed to never ease our wild hearts."

He refused to accept that. Sawyer and he had been seeing each other a long time. It had been wild and passionate in the beginning, but then she'd left, and he'd had way too much time to think. To miss her. "What's she doing? Is she ever coming out of that room? Did you make sure there were no open windows?"

Ash looked at him. "I was trying to talk her into trying on the magic wedding dress."

He felt his stomach pitch. "Sawyer won't wear Fiona's magic wedding dress."

Ash gave him a look that said he was crazy, and maybe he was. "Of course Sawyer should be married in the Callahan tradition!"

"I can't believe you dragged that thing all the way here." Struck by a sudden thought, Jace glanced wildly at the door. "You have no idea the trouble it caused our brothers. In almost every single case, that gown tried to wreck everything."

Ash gasped. "Jace! That's not true!"

"It is true." He remembered tales from their brothers with some horror. One bride hadn't seen her one true love—as she'd believed she would, according to Fiona's fairy tale—and had taken off running out the door. That brother had barely been able to get his chosen bride to give the gown a second chance.

Jace had heard other tales, too, and they all made his blood pressure skyrocket with an attack of premonition.

"What about River? The gown saved her in Montana."

"It's a trick, a dice roll. A man doesn't know if the dress is on his side. I don't need that kind of help." Jace looked at the door again, debating knocking on it and demanding that Sawyer come out. She'd been in there far too long. "Are you sure there were no windows in there she could open?"

"There may have been one," Ash said, "but Sawyer isn't the kind of woman who would ditch you in Vegas."

"She ditched me, as you say, for the past several months." His chest felt very heavy with sadness. "You have no idea what I've been through with that woman. And now you put her in a room with a diabolical magic wedding dress, and I'm supposed to—"

He glared when the door opened. Sawyer came out, wearing the same clothes she had been before. He looked at her, his breath tight.

"Is it time?" she asked.

He hesitated. "Time?"

"To do this thing."

Jace swallowed. "Sure. If you're ready."

"Are you?"

He'd been ready far longer than he'd realized, but he didn't want to seem overeager and scare her off. "Better now than never."

She didn't look certain, and he shrugged, wanting to give her as much space as possible. With the way she clearly felt about getting married, it could do no good to keep pushing her. They said you could lead a horse to water but not make it drink, and Sawyer was as untamed as the black Diablo mustangs in the canyons around Rancho Diablo.

"I am ready," she said. "As long as we agree that we'll revisit this marriage after the babies are born."

"Revisit it? I'm fine with what we're doing." He didn't like the sound of that at all. He'd heard those cold-footed-bride tales from his brothers, too—and a very merry chase some of their women had led them on.

"I'm well aware that your interest in marriage is purely because of the children, and I understand that." She looked at his sister. "Thank you for bringing the dress, Ash. I appreciate the effort you made to get it here, I really do. More than anything, I'm honored that your aunt Fiona was willing to share a favorite Callahan tradition with me." She looked back at Jace. "But I don't feel like a real Callahan bride, and I don't think I ever will."

No sooner had the words left her mouth than the small waiting area suddenly filled with Callahans and Cashs, all loud and happy, and perplexed to see Sawyer wearing a hot pink dress and not a magic wedding gown. Storm carted in a bridal bouquet for his niece, kissing her before glaring at Jace.

"It's a happy day!" Fiona exclaimed. "The last Callahan bachelor getting hitched!" She beamed with delight. "Come on, dear. Ash and I will help you change."

Jace raised a brow, watching Sawyer sputter her way out of Fiona's clutches. He smiled, seeing his family envelop his bride-to-be with their overwhelming presence. No one irritated him more than his relatives at times, but it was great to have them at his back.

The cake was delivered by two uniformed men who looked a bit seedy to Jace.

"You're putting that there?" Fiona demanded, as they

set the cake down in the foyer. "Do we look like we eat wedding cake in doorways?"

They shrugged, and Jace had an uncomfortable feeling he'd seen them before. "Aren't you going to take it out of the box?" he asked.

The men left without saying a word.

"That was odd," Sawyer said.

"Very odd." Ash went to undo the white box. "That bakery came highly recommended, and I'm going to give them a piece of my mind about their delivery service." She peeled the sides of the box down and gasped.

Instead of a plastic bride and groom there was a butcher knife, splendidly tied with satin ribbon, sticking up out of the top of the beautiful cake.

The whole thing was a disaster as far as Jace was concerned. Married hurriedly by a satin-wearing pastor who wanted them gone as fast as possible once he saw the butcher knife in the wedding cake—and wed apparently in name only to his pregnant love—Jace found it wasn't a happy-ever-after type of event.

And they'd slept in separate beds after his late-night partying family finally went to bed.

"Very sad state of affairs," he told Sawyer as they drove back toward Rancho Diablo the next day.

She didn't spare him a glance as she looked out the window. "What's a very sad state of affairs?"

"You. Me. That stupid wedding." He gulped, certain that dire consequences might lie in his future. "The whole thing was wrong."

"Wrong?"

"Not traditional." Not done right, not written in stone, the butcher knife notwithstanding.

Traditional was the way he wanted his relationship with Sawyer to be.

"Stop thinking about the cake. It was an accident, like your aunt said. The delivery drivers were new, they didn't know not to put the knife in the same box as the cake, and it somehow got stuck in it. These things happen at weddings."

"I don't think so."

"Anyway, it was delicious. You said so yourself. And the bakery gave Ash a 50 percent discount and told her that if she ever got married, they'd do a cake for her for free."

He wasn't calmed by his bride's attempt to soothe him. Jace was sure he'd seen those delivery guys somewhere, and trying to remember where nagged at him. The bakery had said they'd sent two men to deliver the cake, and the Callahans hadn't thought to ask for ID or names in the shock of the moment. "You could have at least pretended to want to wear the wedding dress Ash went to the trouble to bring you," he groused, thinking he should probably be happy Sawyer had at least said I do. That was something.

Heck, he'd wanted some enthusiasm from his bride. Perhaps even a smile. He was so out of sorts he wasn't even sure why he was complaining.

"I can't feel good about this marriage, Jace. So wearing the dress would be dishonest. I'm too aware that your family doesn't trust me, though they put on a happy face today for you."

So that's what was bugging doll face. He couldn't contradict her, either. The Chacon Callahans as a rule had never really trusted Sawyer's uncle Storm—and

Sawyer was assuming that some familial distrust was reflected on her, as well.

"We trusted you enough to hire you, let you body-guard our children."

"But when Somer and I were at Rose's father's place and fired on each other, and someone conked her father over the head, everything changed. You can't deny that."

He heard the note of sadness in Sawyer's voice. "It was a big misunderstanding. Your cousin and you probably saved Rose that night. Maybe Sheriff Carstairs, too. Hell, even my brother Galen. He's never been a fast runner, though he claims he is, and you and Somer firing at each other gave him the cover he needed to make it inside to Rose."

"I appreciate you trying to make me feel better. But I know in my heart that I was always on a probationary basis with all of you. Only Galen really trusted me. And once I became pregnant…" She glanced at him. "Jace, be honest. It had to have crossed a few of your brothers' minds that maybe I'd become pregnant as part of a plot to get inside Rancho Diablo permanently."

"No one mentioned it." He shrugged. "But you're part of the Callahan family now, and no one's sending up warning flares. In fact, you're the only one who seems bothered by the past. And anyway, we wouldn't have agreed to buy Storm's place if we hadn't decided he was on our side. We don't do business—any kind of business—with folks who are trying to kill us."

She didn't say anything else, conversation over for the moment. He hadn't convinced her that the family accepted her. Only time could solve that problem.

Maybe he could appeal to her feminine side. All the Callahan brides seemed to favor the frilly white fairy tale.

"Look at it this way. Would Ash have taken the time and the trouble to bring you the mystical treasured gown to wear down the aisle if the family didn't consider you one of us?"

Jace wished Sawyer would look at him, but she didn't, nor did she answer. He drove on, wondering if a difficult beginning could ever turn into a happy ending.

Chapter 4

"So the holy grail, as I see it," Jace said to his sister on his cell phone, as Sawyer selected some lunch offerings in a roadside café in New Mexico, "is keeping my bride out of Rancho Diablo."

"That's the family vote. There are a hundred reasons for Sawyer not to be here, and no good ones we can think of for her to be. It's just not safe. She's too good of a bargaining chip. Now that Storm has managed to break any ties Wolf was hoping to bind him with, our uncle will certainly try to get even with hers."

Jace watched his delicate wife as she chatted with the owner of the small mom-and-pop restaurant. Roadside places this size could be greasy spoons, but this one was warm and welcoming. He liked the white paint on the building and the blue shutters that seemed to welcome weary travelers. The full parking lot had been testament to the good eats inside.

"She won't like it," he told his sister.

"We all agree that's the likelihood. We hasten to warn you that Sawyer has left before, when she felt things were not optimum between you. This time, you'll have to figure out how to keep her on the road with you. Unless you can convince her to go into temporary hiding, at least until after the babies are born. We had a family council, and we vote unanimously that less of you is more. Besides, you deserve a honeymoon, brother."

He could hear his sister's giggle loud and clear. "I'll do my best."

"Then that should be good enough. Tell Sawyer hello from the Callahan clan, and congratulations again. There must be a hundred wedding gifts here that she can open when you lovebirds return."

Ash hung up, and Jace went inside to sit in a sunny, cushy booth across from his wife.

"I ordered for you."

"Thanks." He glanced around, checking the other diners. "Ash says the family sends their…" He groped for a word she'd find acceptable.

"Felicitations?"

"Exactly." A waitress put a steaming cup of coffee in front of him, and Jace waited until she was gone. "She says a few wedding gifts have arrived."

"I'll write thank-you letters when we get home."

"Yeah, about that." He rubbed the back of his neck. "Ash also says that we need to stay gone awhile longer."

Sawyer gazed over her glass of tea at him. "Reason?"

He hated to be the bearer of bad news. "Security."

"Your family's afraid I'm on the other side."

"Will you stop?" he demanded impatiently. "They're worried you're a target now that your uncle has crossed Wolf, and therefore the cartel that Wolf is in cahoots with. It's a dangerous situation for all."

Her brow furrowed. "I never thought of that."

"Yeah, well. Neither did I. I'd like to say Ash has worry overload, but considering the knife in the cake—"

"Accidental. Don't let the Callahan love of drama make you see things that weren't there."

His gaze drifted out the window. He saw a truck pass that looked a lot like the one that had been following them on the way to Vegas—and a lightning bolt hit him. The driver of the truck that had been following them had delivered the wedding cake. Maybe Jace couldn't swear to it in a court of law, but there'd been something so familiar about those men.

They'd hijacked the cake and stuck a warning in it.

His neck prickled as he glanced around the diner again, scanning each patron.

"So that's all it is? The reason your family thinks we should stay on the road? Just garden-variety Callahan worry?" Sawyer looked hopeful.

"No," he said quietly. "Ash and my brothers are right. It would be best if we stayed away from the ranch for now."

"If *I* stay away from the ranch," Sawyer said. "You aren't supposed to go back to your home because of me."

"We're together," Jace said. "A team."

"Being married isn't about being guarded, and that's what you're doing."

He shrugged. The waitress laid a piece of apple pie in front of him and a salad in front of Sawyer. She topped off his coffee, then left.

"Salad for you, pie for me?"

Sawyer arched a brow. "I've worked for the Callahans long enough to know what acts like a charm around Rancho Diablo. Nothing brings you running like Fiona's fresh-baked pies and cookies."

This was true. He eyed her salad. "And you don't have a sweet tooth, or are you eating healthy for the babies?"

She waved a fork at his pie. "Just eat, cowboy. I'll take care of myself."

"What would you say," Jace said, looking into her beautiful blue eyes, "to honeymooning in Paris?"

"I would say no, thank you. I'm going back home. A honeymoon isn't necessary." She ate her salad with apparent contentment, which was sort of funny, because he had the calorie-laden, sugar-sprinkled treat, and it tasted like paste to him. It was probably a delicious pie, but he couldn't focus on the tastiness thanks to the woman across from him.

He remembered how good Sawyer's lips felt under his, how amazing it felt to hold her. The pie just wasn't as satisfying.

"I'd take you anywhere in the world you want to go."

"I know." She looked up from her plate. "I get that. I appreciate that you're trying to keep me safe."

"You and my children."

"But you need to be working at Rancho Diablo. You don't need to be babysitting me. I'll be fine." She went back to eating. "Nothing should change because of a wedding ring."

"Everything changed." He drummed the table. "You know that Wolf and the cartel have tunnels running under the land across the canyons? We've bought the property, but there's very little we can do about the underground infrastructure that's already in place. We're pretty certain Wolf intends—or the cartel intends—to try to attack Rancho Diablo from their underground operations center."

"You think they'll eventually tunnel under Rancho Diablo? Why wouldn't they stop at the land across the canyons?"

"Because the goal is to take over the whole ranch." Jace sighed heavily. "Wolf wants the Diablos that live in the canyons. He wants the fabled silver mine, not to mention the ranch itself."

"Is it true about the silver treasure at Rancho Diablo?" she asked curiously.

He started to say, "Hell, yeah, it's true," and stopped himself.

In that moment, he saw the light of curiosity in his wife's eyes die.

But he couldn't tell her the truth.

"I shouldn't have asked," she said quickly. "I'm sorry. I forgot I'm Storm's niece, an outsider, a woman whose uncle once trusted Wolf. Uncle Storm regrets that. He's said a hundred times he wishes he'd never listened to Wolf's lies about your family. But what's done is done."

"Sawyer—"

"It's okay. Really. I'll wait for you in the truck. We need to get on the road if we're going to make it back to Rancho Diablo by nightfall."

She left, and Jace closed his eyes.

She was right on so many levels. And he didn't see any way to change that conflict between them.

Without honesty, a new marriage would have a tough time, especially when it had started as theirs had. Sawyer knew that, too.

He refused to face that ending.

* * *

As Jace drove, Sawyer sat quietly, regretting that she'd mentioned the fabled silver treasure supposedly buried somewhere at Rancho Diablo. She'd asked only because the rumor was local lore, but the moment the words were out of her mouth, she'd known she had made a mistake. It was said curiosity killed the cat. In her case, it certainly killed trust. Jace's eyes had darkened and he'd looked away, his mouth tight when she'd asked about the legend—and he hadn't said much since.

She was keeping a secret of her own, a secret that nearly guaranteed an end to their marriage if Jace ever found out. Especially if he was so sensitive about her mentioning a well-known legend in the town of Diablo.

Her uncle Storm had told her to apply at Rancho Diablo, and when she'd gotten the job, he'd asked her to keep an eye out, let him know exactly what was going on with the Callahans. She'd been a sort of double agent, she supposed, working for the Callahans but reporting to Storm, in the beginning.

It wasn't merely idle nosiness, either, not that Jace would understand if she ever admitted her past role. Storm had been approached by Wolf and given a sad story about how his land and mineral rights had been stolen by the Callahans. Storm hadn't known what to think. He'd figured it was none of his business, until he'd caught several scouts trespassing on his ranch, men who worked for Wolf. Wolf had claimed that his "scouts" were doing their job by keeping an eye on land that was rightfully his, which would be borne out by the courts soon enough.

Uncle Storm had done some horse-trading many years back with Jace's aunt Fiona, said matters had gone well enough. He trusted the Chacon Callahans, he'd claimed—except that they didn't trust him, and didn't seem to like him.

Which had made him wonder what they might be hiding. The Chacon Callahans had lived at Rancho Diablo for only the past four years or so. They'd taken over from their cousins, six Callahan boys who'd grown up at Rancho Diablo. Those Callahans had all married, and left in order to keep their families safe—as had their parents.

Her husband's parents, Carlos and Julia Chacon, had gone into hiding, and Running Bear had raised their seven children in the tribe. Jace's Callahan cousins' parents, Jeremiah and Molly, who'd built Rancho Diablo, had also gone into hiding when they'd turned in information about the cartel to federal agents. It had killed Jeremiah and Molly to leave their six boys, their friends, the wonderful Tudor-style home they'd built, Diablo itself. Molly's sister, Fiona, had come from Ireland to raise the six Callahans—as she now tried to take care of the seven Chacon Callahans.

Rancho Diablo was a tempting prize for Wolf, the one son who hadn't fit in, as Jeremiah and Carlos had. Running Bear called Wolf his bad seed, and said sometimes there was no fixing such a black-hearted individual.

There was an awful lot of money at the Callahan place, and the wealth just seemed to grow. Everything the Callahans touched turned to gold—or silver. Times were tough economically for lots of people in the country. How could one family seem to endlessly reap financial rewards, unless maybe they had cut Wolf Chacon out of his portion?

Sawyer's uncle hadn't wanted to get involved, but he'd found himself caught between a rock and a hard place. Between the Chacon Callahans and their uncle Wolf, who'd told Storm his small ranch would be safe if he turned a blind eye to the scouts who roamed his land.

He'd thought to warn the Callahans, had gone over there a few times with wedding or baby gifts, or just to chat, but they'd always seemed to flat out distrust him. He'd been a bit hurt by this, as he'd considered Fiona an honest trading partner. Obviously, times had changed with this new crop of leaner, tougher Callahans.

Yet Uncle Storm didn't trust Wolf, either, and it didn't matter that the man tried to be nice to him. He'd grown uncomfortable, and disliking the neighborly tension, had asked Sawyer to apply for work at Rancho Diablo when her last bodyguard position ended. She had, and to her surprise, was hired.

To her greater surprise, she'd found herself devotedly pursued by Jace. It was said that once you were a Callahan's woman, you were pretty much ruined for all other men, and she believed it. Jace Callahan had completely dashed her desire to even talk to another man, let alone kiss one.

When they were apart, she thought about him constantly.

When they were together, she didn't think at all. She just lived in the moment, in his arms, despite knowing very well that at the end of that silken, sexy road lay unhappiness. No way would a Callahan marry a Cash.

"I think Galen named that land across the canyons Loco Diablo," Jace said, startling her.

She blinked. "Crazy Devil? That's going to be the ranch name?"

"He figured the Callahan cousins own Rancho Diablo, and Dark Diablo in Tempest. So to keep with the naming history, he went with Loco Diablo."

"That's very organized of him."

"Yeah. Ash is roasting him about it. In her mind, she was going to win the ranch."

"Sister Wind Ranch," Sawyer said softly.

He nodded. "But Loco Diablo it is."

"Which is somehow fitting, given that the name was chosen by a Chacon Callahan."

Jace glanced over and caught the smile she hadn't hidden quickly enough.

"You laugh, but you're part of Loco Diablo now. It's where our children will grow up."

She shook her head. "Pretty sure that's not going to happen, Callahan."

"No?" He sneaked a palm over to her tummy, which felt like a pumpkin sitting in her lap. She removed his hand at once. "Where do you figure the children will live, once we get past our Uncle Wolf problem?"

Sawyer wasn't going to let herself consider a future together. "Jace, you know—and everyone knows—that Loco Diablo will never be safe. Even if they blew up the tunnels that are underneath the ranch, even if you somehow managed to run the cartel and your uncle Wolf out of your lives, it still wouldn't be secure. And don't even try to tell me that you've got Wolf on the run. He's never going to give up."

"No argument from me," Jace said cheerfully. "That's why you and I are staying on the road for now. I'm determined to keep you safe."

"I'm the bodyguard," Sawyer said with a touch of heat. "You're the cowboy. I'd be protecting you."

He laughed. "And I'll let you."

Great. He couldn't be serious about anything, least of all how important her independence was, how determined she was to keep maximum separation between them. "This isn't going to work."

"It's going to work, because there are two children counting on us to make it work. We need to choose names for them. That can be our road game until we get to Texas."

"Texas!" She glared at him. "You said you were taking me to Rancho Diablo!"

"Yeah. That was about a hundred miles ago. Now we're driving to Texas, and then on to Virginia. There are some military bases in the Tidewater. But we won't be hanging out in the officers' club or on the strip. We'll be much more undercover than that."

She shook her head. "You can take me straight back to the ranch."

"Babe, listen—"

"Don't 'babe' me. I'm not going anywhere except home. I shouldn't have married you, so don't press your luck."

He sighed, and she gazed out the window again, refusing to bend from her position. "Look, we're married. But that's it. I'll continue to make my own decisions, Jace."

"I expect you to. But eventually, we're going to have to talk about the children and what's best for them."

"So talk." He could talk all he liked, but she wasn't moving to Virginia—or anywhere else—just because he had a nervous streak.

"What about the children?"

She didn't reply, and he continued, "We can't just

call them 'the babies.' They need names. I've always liked—"

"I was thinking Jason and Ashley."

"Jason and Ashley?"

"Yes. Jason, obviously, is a variation of your name, and Ashley because I like your sister, Ashlyn."

"I approve. And my sister will be thrilled, I'm sure you know."

Secretly, Sawyer was pleased, though she didn't want to say so.

"I can't believe I'm going to be a father to a little girl and boy. It's so unreal. And wonderful."

It was hard not to soften, hearing the pride in his deep voice. She'd always loved Jace's voice, so warm and enveloping and inviting somehow, especially when he whispered to her in the dark.

She sensed those days were long gone. Nothing could be the same now that they were married, and married under spurious circumstances he'd no doubt come to regret one day. Speaking of regret, she figured she might as well put everything out in the open now. She took a deep breath.

"Jace, here's the main reason you and I have a marriage that's probably going to be in a difficult spot, even if we didn't have a few other notable issues. I know your family really never trusted mine."

"Sort of stating it too harshly," Jace said. "We didn't know what to think. Besides, we've put all that to rest with our marriage."

Sawyer knew better. "In a sense, your family's fears were well-founded. Uncle Storm did ask me to keep an eye on your family."

She turned to look at him, met his surprised gaze. "I'm sorry. I just think you should know the truth."

"We kept an eye on Storm, and will continue to. We keep an eye on everyone. No big deal."

She waved a hand. "You can't brush that off. I was working for you, and reporting to my uncle whenever I saw anything that I thought might be a problem for him."

"Why? We never had anything to do with Storm. Didn't wish him ill." Jace shrugged. "We just didn't fully trust him."

"Yet you hired me."

"We weren't worried about you."

She didn't know if she should be flattered, or insulted by the sheer arrogance of Jace thinking she wasn't a threat. "Because I'm a woman?"

"No. I wasn't worried about you because—"

"Oh, no," Sawyer interrupted, suddenly annoyed. "You weren't worried about me because you thought you'd locked me down."

He laughed. "I wouldn't have put it that way, but I would say that I feel I'm a pretty good judge of women. You never struck me as a devious sort. I could tell you liked me. Women who are hot for a guy usually have strong loyalty to him."

"Really. Yet I reported on you to Uncle Storm."

Jace shrugged again. "Probably a wise thing to do. Now that you've gotten that off your conscience, should we stop for the night? I don't want you getting too tired. My children need their rest."

She stared at him, not happy at all. "Please drive on. I don't want to spend a night with you." They'd never shared a real bed before; no sense in starting tonight. Her resolve would weaken if she got near her handsome husband and a bed, with no Callahan drama to keep them apart.

"You're having second thoughts? I'm not the date you had in mind when you spent your hard-earned money on me?"

She turned away, glanced out the window. Oh, he was every bit what she'd had in mind, and then some. She was married to the man of her dreams and the father of her children.

What more could a woman ask for from a bachelor raffle?

"You're going to have to help me get Loco Diablo away from Galen," Jace said, "or at least what should be my share of it. Now that you've proved you have a devious streak, that shouldn't be a problem at all, princess."

She turned to face him in disbelief. "You married me to get the ranch?"

He smiled. "We never claimed we were in love, sweetheart."

She was. She had been for a long time. Did he think that she'd risked her job and her reputation to sleep with him just because he was sexy and irresistible? "That's right. It was just a fling. Which proves my point. We have no business being married, but now that we are, I have no intention of letting you use me to oust your siblings from their ranch. You Callahans can work all that out."

"You forget you're a Callahan now."

She hadn't forgotten. But in her heart, she knew her husband still considered her a Cash, even if he didn't admit it.

She'd always be a Cash to him—and likely hers wasn't the family tree he'd ever hoped to graft to his.

"I'm a Callahan by name only, according to what you're saying. Everything else is just business."

"It's just business until you decide you want more," Jace said. "As I recall, you're not exactly immune to me. I'm a patient man. I'm willing to wait for you to see the light."

Outraged, Sawyer glared at him. "You're not a patient man. That's why we were married in a quickie Vegas wedding! You couldn't wait to have a reason to throw your name into the hat for the land raffle."

He smiled again. "The fact that I'm going to be a father of twins definitely gives me an edge," he said, teasing, trying to get her goat.

He was succeeding royally.

"This was a terrible idea," Sawyer said. "It's what happens when there's no plan."

He laughed once more. "It's going to work. We have no choice."

Not the tender nothings she'd always hoped to hear on her wedding day. "What a sweet sentiment."

"Kiss me and you'll get more sweetness, babe."

"No, thank you." She wished she could. She'd love to snuggle up against his chest. The problem was that his mouth got in the way, communicating his inner bad boy. Which never failed to rile her.

"After Jason and Ashley are born, you and I are going our separate ways," she said.

"You're not going to help me get my share of the land?"

"I suggest you get a good lawyer for that."

He shrugged. "We have plenty of those."

She looked at him curiously. "Have you ever tried telling Galen that you want a share of the ranch?"

"No. I prefer to do it the honest way. Marriage and babies."

He was impossible. Like all the Callahans, he had a unique thought process. And she was too tired to think through the rabbit trail that was her husband's brain. "I'm going to nap."

"Good idea. I'll still be here when you wake up."

"Lucky me." Sawyer snuggled under the blanket. "Remember—straight back to Rancho Diablo."

She closed her eyes. When she awakened, she'd be that much closer to home.

At last.

Chapter 5

Jace waited for Sawyer to wake up, hoping she'd nap awhile longer. His little wife was sweet, but she had an impressive independent streak, and when she opened her sexy blue eyes and realized they were on the road to a small town in Colorado, there was going to be serious unhappiness happening in his truck.

It wasn't the way he wanted to start his marriage.

Almost as if she sensed his unease, Sawyer opened her eyes, glancing at him. He supposed the hesitant expression on his face probably alerted her that something was going on, because she sat up, looking for a road marker, and found the Welcome to Colorado state sign instead.

She whipped around to glare at him. "What are you doing?"

"It wasn't my idea."

"It sure wasn't mine!"

"No. Running Bear's."

"Running Bear told you we should take a side trip to Colorado?"

Jace nodded. "He called while you were asleep. Asked us to stay away. Just for a few days. Apparently your uncle Storm…" Jace stopped, not wanting to go on.

"What about my uncle?"

"Your uncle is staying at his old place. He moved in there for protection."

"From what? Tell me, Jace. Don't sugarcoat it."

"Nothing exciting," he said. "Just a precaution."

"It's not a precaution," Sawyer said, "if my uncle and his wife have moved back to his old house, a place you now own because he didn't want trouble anymore. The trouble he was trying avoid was between you and Wolf. Why would he go back to where it was happening?"

Jace sighed. "Wolf's put a watch on him, and Lu got a bit spooked. It's nothing to worry about. The sheriff's got men over there, and my brothers and Ash are keeping an eye out. It's going to be fine."

"If it's going to be so fine, why are we in Colorado?"

"Running Bear is operating from an abundance of caution."

"He thinks I'll be kidnapped. It's happened before to Callahan wives."

"You could be used against your uncle," Jace stated, his tone even. "It's not going to happen, because you're my wife, and I'm going to take care of you."

"We've had this conversation," Sawyer said, "and I can take care of myself."

"You'll be housebound soon enough. It's best to take precautions."

Sawyer met his gaze. It was hard to see the distrust in her eyes, so he focused on the road and the directions he'd been given by Running Bear.

"So how long are we operating from an abundance of caution?" Sawyer asked.

"Let's call this our honeymoon. 'Abundance of caution' sounds like unfortunate terminology for newlyweds to use."

She didn't reply.

"So we'll hang out here a day. Then we'll move on to Wyoming."

"Would you care to tell me how long Running Bear advises that we should make ourselves scarce on this honeymoon of yours?"

There was so much tension in her voice. "Not sure," Jace answered. "Hopefully, things will cool down soon." He really didn't know what else to say, though he knew it wasn't a very satisfying answer.

"How long?" Sawyer demanded.

She was already ticked off. Might as well finish off the night with her ticked at him, and then hopefully, the sun would come up tomorrow with all the bad news behind them. "Until after the children are born."

She pulled her phone from her purse. "I'm calling my uncle. I want to check on him and Lu."

"Good idea."

Sawyer barely spared him a glance as she placed the call. "Uncle Storm? It's Sawyer."

Jace finally saw the turnoff that his grandfather had mentioned. He listened with half an ear as he pulled off the main road and followed a smaller, winding road up the mountain. The cabin was well hidden from the trail. Nothing fancy, but secure enough, and not easy to get to unless one had an off-road vehicle. Nobody could sneak up on them here.

He realized Sawyer had hung up. "Any news we can use?"

"Not really," she said.

He couldn't blame her for being unhappy. They were miles from home, and she thought she was stuck with a husband she didn't want.

Only she had wanted him enough to empty her piggy bank for a date. Jace let that cheer him up and give him encouragement that maybe all wasn't over between him and his delicate wife.

"Uncle Storm says he agrees with Running Bear," Sawyer said suddenly.

Jace glanced at her as he parked the truck. "Really?"

She nodded, her blue eyes worried. "I guess that's it, then."

"Look at it this way," he said. "You're getting good value for your money, huh?"

She climbed out of the truck before he could head around to open the door, shutting it with just a bit more force than necessary. He got out, met his bride on the porch of the rustic cabin.

"It's not funny, Jace."

"I wasn't joking, believe it or not. Just trying to put a positive light on things for you." He went around to the back of the cabin, as the chief had instructed, and lifted a board in the floor of the wide back porch. Two wooden chairs and a table gave the place a homey look. He supposed someone had once sat here and stared into the thick woods surrounding the house, maybe gazed at the starlit sky and felt nothing but peace.

He wasn't feeling it yet. Jace stuck his hand under the

plank and dug out a key, which was just where the chief had said it would be.

"Whose house is this?"

He patted the board back into place and stood, fitting the key into the lock and turning it. The door opened with a whiney creak, and as he stepped inside he was struck at once by the smell of flowers in the cabin. A vase full of beautiful wildflowers graced the table, welcoming weary strangers. "A friend of the chief's."

Sawyer went into the kitchen. "A good friend. The fridge is stocked."

"Nice." He went to start a fire in the fireplace. There was wood piled up at the back door, so he wouldn't have to gather his own, not for a while.

Depended on how long they were here.

"I'll get you a plate," Sawyer said.

"Thanks." There was central heat and electricity, so this house wasn't completely a rustic hideaway. For that Jace was grateful. He hadn't been sure how much roughing it they might have to do.

"Tea, beer or water? There's even a couple of sodas in here if you're inclined."

"Hot tea sounds fine." Sawyer had to be cold, too. A hot drink would warm them up. He glanced into the kitchen to check on her, suddenly struck by how beautiful she was. Her red hair caught the light from the hanging copper lamps as she filled a kettle with water.

That beautiful woman is my wife.

Holy smokes, I'm actually married.

It was the most amazing realization, and it sent warmth rushing inside him. Pride. Contentment.

He'd be lying if he didn't admit that lust hit him, too. But that part of the marriage was impossible, right?

He'd tell himself a lie: that he'd been driving too long—nearly sixteen hours—and couldn't make love even if Sawyer offered.

Yeah, I could.

He eyed the leather sofa, pretty certain that was going to be his bed for a while. Still, it wasn't his truck, which might be where he slept if he didn't stay out of the doghouse.

"What's wrong?" Sawyer asked, and he glanced up to find her staring at him.

"Nothing." But something was wrong. He had a psychic flare of warning, which didn't make sense, because they were far from danger. He went back to building a fire in the stone fireplace.

"You had the strangest look on your face."

"Probably happens more than I'd like." He held a match under the paper and kindling, and the fire slowly caught.

"Here you go." Sawyer set a red plate on the coffee table. "The tea will be ready in a moment."

He sat dutifully, eyeing the plate. She'd placed a couple slices of cheese, some crackers, a few store-bought cookies and a pile of what looked like delicious chicken salad on it. "That's a feast."

"Somebody was kind enough to save us a trip to the grocery store tonight. Or we ran someone out of their home, and like Goldilocks, we're taking full advantage."

"I don't know. Grandfather doesn't always give the game plan."

"So we're not going to wake up with someone's shotgun aimed at us?"

"I'm not promising that won't happen."

She sighed, picked up a carrot stick. "It's kind of

weird that we spent all those months sneaking around, and now we're in a cabin together with a roof over our heads."

And a bed nearby. There's got to be one in this joint. I'd like to have my wife in a bed just once.

Unfortunately, I think those days of Sawyer seducing me are long gone.

It really stinks.

"You've got that funny look on your face again," Sawyer said, "like you're in pain. Isn't the salad good?"

"It's great," he said, as if he cared about anything except Sawyer at the moment, which he didn't. He ate some chicken salad and tried not to think about how much he wanted her, failing miserably.

She gave him a long look, then put her own plate back on the coffee table. "I think I'll try to find some sheets for the beds."

Beds plural. He nodded, sighing inside. What was he, a man of steel? Being on the run with Sawyer was going to drive him mad.

All he wanted to do was take her in his arms and make love to her, the way he had many, many times before, which had been amazing and awesome, and the reason they were here together now as man and wife.

He was shocked a moment later when Sawyer returned and took his hand. He glanced up, meeting her eyes.

"The beds are made. Sheets are fresh. The rooms are really beautiful. I picked one out."

She was beautiful. Why was she holding his hand? "Guess we got lucky."

Sawyer's gaze didn't leave his. She pulled on his

hand, and he hesitated—then suddenly got smacked in the face with what was happening.

Maybe.

He didn't dare hope.

Sawyer pulled him down the hall, drawing him into a room that had a large bed with an attractive gold-and-brown comforter on it. A rocking chair and lamp and gold-painted dresser finished the decor.

But he didn't have long to assess the surroundings. Sawyer looked at him, her eyes big with what seemed like hope and invitation, and he dragged her toward the bed.

It was just like old times, with the heat and the passion and the hot desire running through him.

Yet this time would be different. There was a bed, they were married and he was going to be a father.

It was very different. "Are you sure about this?" he asked.

"I don't do things I'm not sure about."

Jace drew a deep breath. "I'm going to enjoy the hell out of every moment of this."

Sawyer smiled and he took her in his arms.

"Seems odd," she said. "There's a ceiling overhead."

"I know. But you'll still see stars. I promise you that."

Those seemed to be the words needed to trigger the sexy tigress he'd always known Sawyer to be. They pulled each other's clothes off, tossing them to the floor in abandoned piles, and only once did they stop their fevered kissing.

Suddenly, she jerked upright in the bed. "Did you hear something? It sounded like a door swinging shut."

"It was a just a shutter blowing in the wind. It's kicking up out there." Jace was half-naked and his wife's hands had been busily undoing his jeans. He didn't care if Santa was about to scoot down the chimney for a February surprise. Sawyer wanted him, and nothing else mattered.

"I'll go check it out," she said.

"Damn it." Jace got up, zipping his jeans. "You're not the bodyguard in this relationship anymore. You're a mother. You have enough to do. You get naked and be in those sheets when I return. Hell, I don't even care if you're in the sheets. Just be naked when I get back."

The sound had been nothing more than the creak and pop of an unfamiliar house, but his wife's hearing and caution were admirable. Personally, he had so much blood and desire screaming through his head that he'd probably kill any unfortunate intruder that may have crept inside the cabin.

Ash sat in front of the fireplace, warming her hands.

"What the hell are you doing here?" Jace demanded, lust fleeing like a ghost.

His sister shook her head. "I've been assigned to be your lookout. And I'm not happy about it."

"That makes two of us." He sat across from her, and she picked up the plate of food that he'd barely touched.

"Do you mind?" she asked. "I'm starved."

"Have at it." He looked at her. "How'd you get here?"

"I rode a broom," she said, put out with the whole situation. "How do you think? I drove. Grandfather gave me the meet point and here I am. I'd have been here sooner but I had a flat tire in Alamosa." She snacked on the cookies without much enthusiasm. "I always miss Fiona's cooking when I'm away from home."

"You could have gotten here later and that would have been fine," Jace said.

She looked at him, then at Sawyer as she walked into the room wearing his T-shirt and a bathrobe she'd grabbed from somewhere. "Oh. Sorry. Did I interrupt the honeymooning?"

Sawyer smiled. "I don't know if you can really call this honeymooning."

The hell they hadn't been. He'd been about to send his wife into a serious pleasure overdrive, and if that wasn't the definition of honeymoon, he didn't know what was. Jace went to the fridge and grabbed a beer to mask his grumpiness.

"The chief says he doesn't want any trouble this time," Ash said. "I'm here as an equalizer should any trouble try to rear its head."

"If you've been sent to help, does that mean this is home for a while?" Sawyer asked.

Ash shrugged, crossing her legs underneath her as she finished off her brother's plate of food. "The Feds plan to dynamite the tunnels under Sister Wind Ranch."

"Under Loco Diablo," Jace automatically said, and Ash said, "Whatever. It's going to be my ranch."

"What does Galen think about that?" Jace asked. "His ranch being dynamited?"

"Who cares what Galen thinks?" She smiled at Sawyer. "I don't pay attention to what any of my brothers think if I can help it."

"About the tunnels," Sawyer said. "If they're being dynamited, then that's going to flush out Wolf and his gang, isn't it?"

"That's the problem," Ash replied. "Wolf blames this whole situation on your uncle."

Jace watched his wife's expression turn fearful. "It'll be all right," he said quickly, but Sawyer stared at Ash.

"How could it be my uncle's fault?"

She shrugged. "Wolf let your uncle know that he blames him for the deal falling apart. If Storm had stayed put and not sold his place to us, then Wolf would have continued to have ranch land he could operate from that bordered ours. Now he's out in the open."

"What does that have to do with the tunnels?" Jace asked.

Sawyer looked at him. "Your uncle Wolf thinks I turned on my uncle to marry you."

Jace started to shake his head, then noticed his sister was nodding hers. "I don't exactly get it."

"You'll have to tell him one day," Ash said to Sawyer, who slowly nodded.

"You remember that I told you my uncle wanted me to report to him on anything suspicious your family might be doing, because he wasn't sure who the bad guys and the good guys were?"

"Yeah," Jace said, aware by the pained look on his sister's face that he wasn't going to like what he was about to hear, "but I don't care about that. You're my wife. You're having my children. Everything else is in the past."

"I told my uncle that your family was thinking about leaving the ranch one day," Sawyer said. "Especially since so many of you were married. And since Galen had bought the land across the canyons."

"Sister Wind Ranch," Ash said.

"Loco Diablo," Jace said, trying to figure out why Sawyer was so upset. "I don't see what's wrong. We *will* go home eventually. When the land and the family are safe again, we'll go back where we came from, and our cousins will return to their home."

"I told my uncle that the Callahans could return home any day," Sawyer said miserably. "I didn't mean anything by it. I just wanted to calm him down. He's been so worried for so long. Wolf has really kept him rattled. He started out so friendly, but over time began to change, got more threatening. Uncle Storm panicked, knowing that Wolf's men were close, and realizing that major trouble was coming if your family left Rancho Diablo. As far as my uncle is concerned, your family is strong, and maybe the only people capable of keeping Wolf at bay. So he sold out—to you. Wolf wanted him to sell to him," Sawyer finished. "He's furious with my uncle and promised to take revenge on him the moment his back was turned."

Jace frowned. "This is typical Wolf stuff. If I listened to every threat that came out of Uncle Wolf, I'd be deaf."

"But then the tunnels were reported to the Feds," Ash interjected, "and Wolf believes Storm ratted him out."

"How could he? Storm didn't know about the tunnels."

"He did," Sawyer said with a sigh, "because of me."

Jace felt a dawning sense of dread wash over him. "So? Wolf couldn't know that your uncle knew."

"Wolf knew," Ash said, "because your wife was wired up."

Jace stared at his wife, stunned. "Wired?"

"I thought I'd been wired by the Feds," Sawyer said miserably. "But it was Wolf's men, trying to get intel on your family."

Her pretty blue eyes welled with tears, and Jace's world turned on its head. "You ended up giving information to the enemy about your own uncle?"

"And you," Sawyer said. "About the Callahans."

"It's not possible that you're a double agent!" Jace felt his heart stop in his chest. "You were sleeping with me every chance we got."

She blushed, and he felt a twinge for embarrassing her in front of Ash. But her betrayal had sent the words rocketing out of his mouth.

"Again, I thought I'd been wired by the Feds. They told me it was to protect your family, in case another one of the Callahans was kidnapped. They said Ash was wearing a wire, too."

"You didn't ask my sister if any Feds had questioned her about the tunnels? Or wired her?" Jace demanded.

"Actually," Ash said, "I was wired. But I knew it was a trick, and I just played along to find out what I could about Wolf's operations."

"Have you lost your mind?" Jace demanded of his sister. "Do you realize the danger you put yourself in? What if Wolf had snatched you?" Anger rose inside him as he stared at the two most important women in his life. "Go outside," he said to his sister. "I have to talk to my wife."

Ash got up, slipped on her coat and went out the door. He heard a rocker scrape as she pulled a chair to the rail so she could stare into the forest. He glared at Sawyer, who tugged the blue robe around her more tightly. "I don't think I completely understand why you did what you did. But what I do understand is that you're not quite the bodyguard our family thought you were."

"Jace—"

He held up a hand. "You've endangered yourself, you've endangered my children, your uncle, my family." Jace stared at her. "I can't trust you."

"Were you ever going to trust a Cash?" she asked, her tone bitter.

Jace looked at her, wondering if the overwhelming pull he'd always felt for Sawyer had somehow clouded his mind, kept him from seeing her for what she really was. Maybe it had. He'd missed her like hell when she'd left Rancho Diablo. When she'd returned, he'd been relieved, and most of all, felt alive again.

"I don't know," he finally said. "Maybe I was too blind to see it." Perhaps what he loved most about Sawyer was that she was life on the edge, the walk on the wild side that brought amazing emotions rushing through him. "Maybe trusting you was my Achilles' heel. A weakness I brought on my own family."

He left the kitchen and went to sit outside on the front porch, away from his sister, and definitely as far away from his wife as he could get. The moon hung full overhead, and the sky promised cold, and no doubt snow by morning. A tinge of fear gripped him, and his grandfather's warning crept into his mind: one of the Chacon Callahans was the hunted one, the one who would bring danger and darkness to the family. Jace had always been so certain it wasn't him. He felt his roots deeply, both in the tribe and in his Callahan lineage.

But he had brought danger to the family by marrying Sawyer. He'd married her, for God's sake.

There'd been no choice. Not just because of the children, but because he loved her. He wouldn't admit that to a single soul, but he was in love with a woman who seemed to have different faces, different lives.

The lightning-strike tattoo on his shoulder, which all the Callahan siblings had—the sign of their bond—burned suddenly, as if he was being branded.

Jace looked up at the full moon above and wished like hell he hadn't found out who his wife really was.

He'd been sleeping with the enemy. For many long, tortured nights, he'd known his soul was hers.

He'd brought the enemy to Rancho Diablo. And made her a Callahan.

Chapter 6

"She's gone," Ash said, when he walked back inside the small cabin the next morning. His sister looked nonplussed as she snacked on some cookies and a cup of coffee.

"She isn't gone." Jace tossed his coat into a chair. He'd spent an uncomfortable night on the front porch, unaware of the time passing as he watched the snow drift down. It had piled up, maybe three inches, while he'd sat and stared at it. He'd felt dead inside, immune to cold and fear.

All he could do was play over and over in his mind how Sawyer could have betrayed him—and how he could have been too blind to recognize it. "Sawyer couldn't have left. I was sitting out front the entire night. Anyway, she's my wife. Right now, she needs me. She's pregnant with twins."

"I know." His sister brought him a mug of black coffee. "You forget she's a very well-trained bodyguard. Perhaps you even forget how skilled she is at not just protection, but evasion. It's why Kendall felt secure hiring her for the twins. Don't you remember this?"

"She must still be here, Ash. There's no place for her to go."

They were halfway up the mountain, maybe more. The road down would be a challenge, even if she'd stolen his truck.

"She took my Jeep," Ash said.

He stared at his sister, reality socking him in the face. "How in the hell did that happen?"

Ash shrugged. "I gave her my keys."

His jaw dropped. "What?"

"She wanted to go. I gave her my keys, told her how to get off the mountain without driving past your snowbound lair out there."

"You had my pregnant wife drive up to the top of this mountain and go down the other side, in this weather, without even knowing if the roads were passable at the top?" He slumped into a chair at the table, unable to look away from Ash's gamine face. She stared at him calmly.

"You can't keep her prisoner."

"I know that! She wasn't a prisoner, damn it. We had things to work out." She'd kissed him just as passionately as he'd kissed her last night, and he'd been pretty certain they were about to finally find out what making love together in a bed would be like.

And now this bombshell.

He felt wrecked.

"I'm so sorry, brother," Ash said. "I usually don't get involved in people's personal lives."

"You always get involved in everybody's personal lives," Jace said.

"What I mean is that I would never have done it, except that I can't bear for anything to be trapped. You know that." Ash stared at him. "Sawyer seemed as lost as the animals I do rescue work with. I wanted her spirit to be as free as the Diablos. You know how important that is."

He grunted, not happy.

Ash put a hand on his arm as she sat next to him. "Brother, it's bad to start off a marriage with one person feeling trapped. That's not the way you want Sawyer."

He just wanted her. He didn't really care how he got her.

Which was a problem.

"She'll come to you," Ash said.

"Runaway brides usually run for a reason."

His sister sighed. "Okay, I don't know that she'll come back for sure. But you two have a lot to build on."

"Not really."

"The children, Jace. They'll be a huge part of your lives."

He nodded. "Sharing custody with my wife isn't what I had in mind." No doubt Sawyer would want to divorce him now. Maybe even annul the marriage. Damn it, she might ask for a divorce *and* an annulment, which would stink to high heaven.

"She's just heartbroken," Ash said.

"Sawyer is heartbroken?" He got up and moved to stare out at the dawning sky.

"She knows you don't trust her."

"That's a whole other problem."

"Jace, relationships are built on mutual trust and respect."

He shook his head. "There's no reason for us to stay here. Come on. Pack your bags."

"Bags? Since when do I travel with a bag?" His sister stood, reached for her coat and backpack.

"Whose joint is this, anyway?" He glanced around one final time. It was a great place for a honeymoon—if two people wanted to be alone together. Sawyer hadn't wanted that.

"It's Grandfather's," Ash said, sounding surprised.

Jace took further stock of the cabin. "It can't be. It's too frilly."

She smiled. "Poor Grandfather. Don't you think he has a life of his own?"

Jace looked at her. "What are you trying to tell me?"

"Close your eyes."

His sister was trying his patience, but he complied.

"What do you feel?" she asked softly.

"Pissed."

"Besides that. Look beyond your own emotions."

He focused on the smell of the cabin, the feel of the hot mug in his hand, the sense of home that pervaded every corner of the small house. "A woman lives here. A happy, contented woman." He opened his eyes.

Ash smiled at him. "Yes, she does."

"Who?"

"You're older than me. You have to remember more." She slung her backpack over her shoulder. "It's time to go."

He followed his sister out, glanced behind him one last time, then locked the door. After putting the key back under the board where he had found it, he stared at the cabin a moment longer, its presence in the wooded mountain joyfully framed by the sun. Icicles hung from the eaves, and in the sky overhead, a hawk soared.

He looked at Ash. "Our parents?"

She smiled. "I don't know where our parents are. I only know I feel their spirits here."

Jace followed her to the truck and they got in. "Grandfather told you something."

"He told me that the cabin is the family's. That it's vacant right now because it always is in winter. Winter can be harsh on the mountain."

Jace drove slowly through the snow. "It's not the winter that's harsh here. It's the loneliness and solitude."

"That's right."

He was amazed by his sister's knowledge. She always seemed sort of otherworldly—had from the time she was born. "Did you even try to talk Sawyer into staying?" He'd liked to have told Sawyer about his parents. They'd never mentioned their families to each other. He had a faint memory of his mother and father; as the second eldest, he'd been old enough to remember when they'd gone.

It had been like a knife wound in his heart that hadn't eased for years. For so long he'd felt deserted, betrayed, angry. He'd known why they had to leave, but he was still angry at the people who'd made them go.

The same people for whom Sawyer had been wearing a wire. Betrayal and anger ripped through him again. "How could Sawyer do it?"

"Family is important to her."

"Damn it, I'm supposed to be her family. We've made a family together!"

"Easy, hoss," Ash said. "No one ever said our lives

were going to be easy. The path isn't straight, with magical road maps."

"I know that." He knew that only too well.

"We are all on the journey, even Sawyer."

He grunted. "You're starting to sound more like Running Bear all the time."

"I hope so," she said softly, so softly that he glanced at her curiously.

"What's wrong?"

"Nothing," Ash said. "It's just that sometimes I know I'm not as good as Sawyer is. Or even my brothers. I'm the misfit in this family."

"Ash!" Jace was completely stunned by her words. "You're not a misfit at all!"

"I'm going to sleep," she said, sticking her backpack under her head for a pillow. "Wake me when we cross the state line."

"Why the state line?"

"Because it's important to see where I've been and where I'm going."

Jace was bothered by her words, but not really certain why. He should be angry with her, yet he wasn't. In a way, she'd helped him and Sawyer. Ash was right: Sawyer's confession had changed everything. They needed time to absorb the new twists in their relationship. He still couldn't believe Sawyer had meant to harm his family. She'd won him at the ball for a reason, and it hadn't been just to tell him about the babies.

Ash was right: the path didn't point straight, with a magical road map. In fact, it was bumpy as hell and strewn with potholes.

He'd see his wife soon enough, and then they'd get everything worked out. Somehow.

* * *

"It's not going to work." Sawyer laid Ash's keys on the kitchen counter and looked at Fiona Callahan, the eccentric aunt of the Callahan clan. "Jace doesn't trust me. And he has no reason to." She took a deep breath. "Fiona, I need a place to stay, but it can't be here. Nor at my uncle's old place." She'd be too close to Jace, and she knew Running Bear wouldn't want her staying anywhere near Rancho Diablo, anyway.

Fiona shook her head. "You just let me pour you a cup of tea, Sawyer. You look exhausted. It's a long drive from Colorado. Goodness, you should have flown!"

"I wanted to drive. I like driving to clear my thoughts."

"Well," Fiona said, putting a pretty china cup with pink flowers on it in front of her and a bowl of sugar cubes next to that, "Jace is going to want you to be with him, so you might as well get used to the idea. I'd stay put until he gets back."

Sawyer picked up the delicate cup. "Fiona, I can't. You don't understand what I've done. He has a reason to feel the way he does."

"Let's let Jace decide how he feels, shall we?" The older woman slid a piece of spice cake next to Sawyer's tea. "Patience rules the day, I always say."

Patience wasn't going to help her. Sawyer was so ashamed she could hardly bear it. Everything had happened so quickly, had gotten away from her. She'd prided herself on being a competent bodyguard, and then had let herself operate from a position of weakness. Let herself be wrangled into a bad situation that could never be fixed.

"Why don't you go upstairs and take a little nap?" Fiona suggested.

"Why are *you* still here?" Sawyer asked suddenly. "If it's so dangerous at the ranch, with the Feds and the spies and the reporters crawling everywhere, why haven't your nephews made you leave?"

Fiona smiled. "When you're my age, you get to do as you please. And I cook." She tried to sound light-hearted, saw that Sawyer wasn't convinced. "I've already been kidnapped by Wolf, and he doesn't want me again. Have you forgotten I burned his last haunt down to the ground?" She looked very satisfied by that. "Life is good in my world."

"I can't wait to be at that point."

"You're closer than you think." Fiona smiled at her, then turned to put a sheet cake in the oven. "It's all about believing in your purpose."

"Maybe." Sawyer's purpose had changed. Maybe that was the problem: she'd drifted. Gotten off course.

"Wait until those babies are born. You'll have so much purpose you'll be overflowing with it. Everything will get better."

Not if her marriage wasn't going to work out. "I betrayed your family, Fiona."

"Let us decide that. Even if you did, what really happened? Isn't our house still standing? Aren't we still a family?" Fiona topped off her tea. "No one can take the important things in life away, if one knows what those treasures are."

"You're trying to make me feel better."

"And I'm succeeding. Now eat that cake. I made blue-ribbon spice cake, my dear, and there's nothing better in

February than homemade spice cake with cream cheese frosting."

Sawyer dutifully ate a bite—and to her surprise, the cake actually seemed to make her feel better. Or maybe it was Fiona, or being in the house where Jace lived. Hope rose inside her.

Maybe things could work out, after all. Maybe he wouldn't regret marrying a woman from the wrong ranch.

Maybe he would.

Chapter 7

Sawyer was in bed upstairs at Rancho Diablo, as Fiona had talked her into staying at least for the night, when she heard the measured tread of boots outside her door. She raised up, waiting to see if the man standing outside her door would knock. Her heart beat faster, waiting—then crashed a little when the footsteps went down the hall.

She lay back down to stare at the ceiling. No matter what Fiona said, the marriage was over before it had even started. Suddenly, the room felt too warm. Her conscience weighed on her terribly, and the regrets seemed overwhelming. The babies kicked inside her, unsettled by her restlessness.

She was in a beautiful home with wonderful people whose trust she wanted more than anything, a family she desperately wanted to be part of. The seven-chimneyed

Tudor house with the expansive grounds had always seemed like heaven to her, but the Callahans were the heart and soul of Rancho Diablo. There wasn't one she didn't like, and they'd treated her so well. They were the family she'd never really had—except for Uncle Storm.

She'd never be part of this family now. She'd always be an interloper.

The thing was, she'd do it all over again if it meant giving Uncle Storm the help he needed. She was no different from the Callahans, who were determined to protect their family from Wolf and his gang of dangerous cutthroats.

She sighed, trying to get comfortable, and put a hand over her swiftly growing stomach. It still felt so strange to think of Jace as her husband. She'd known eventually her house of cards was going to fall in on her—but she'd wanted him so much. Saying no had never been an option, and she didn't regret one single moment of their adventuresome lovemaking, either.

Sawyer jumped when someone knocked briskly on the door, then eased it open.

"Sawyer."

She sat up. "What?"

"I'm coming in."

Just like a Callahan, to announce and not ask. "Fine." She sat up, flipped on her bedside lamp. Her eyes went wide as she stared at the handsome man whom she'd deserted not that many hours ago. "You look terrible."

"Thanks." Closing the door, Jace sat on the foot of her bed, frowning, royally displeased.

She couldn't blame him.

"What happened?" Sawyer ran her gaze over Jace's hands, which bore a few cuts that hadn't been there last night. His dark hair was a bit wilder than usual, and his face looked drawn.

"Nothing."

"Nothing you want to talk about, you mean. Quite clearly, something happened."

He shook his head. "Long drive home."

She'd made the same drive, so that wasn't a good excuse. "Let me get you some bandages and some ointment."

"I'm fine," he snapped. "I don't need any coddling."

"Okay," she said, just as snippily, and shrugged. "Suit yourself." All she needed was a grumpy cowboy with his dark side in a twist to put the final icing on her day. It was plain he was angry, and she couldn't blame him.

But if he wanted to sit there like a big miserable lump, she was going to go to sleep. There was no point in talking to him if all he was going to do was glower at her.

"Here," Jace said, pulling a tiny white box from his sheepskin jacket and handing it to her.

"What is it?"

"The purpose of a box is to make the person receiving it open the damn thing," he said crossly.

"I don't want to." She was dying to. But she didn't want gifts. She wanted to start over, with forgiveness as the beginning point.

And lots of hot, sexy kisses.

"Then don't. It's clear no one's going to make you do anything you don't want to do."

She put the small box on the nightstand and glared at her husband. "I had to leave, and you know it as well as I do. There's no point in rehashing what I told you in Colorado, and I wish I hadn't done what I did, but I don't really know how I would have done anything differently." She took a deep breath. "Also, there's no need for you to feel like you have to protect me. I'll get my own bodyguard, Jace. What I want is…"

She stopped, and he looked at her curiously. "What?"

"Something I can't have," she finished miserably. "I don't want presents, either. I never meant for you to have to marry me, and I should have dug my heels in on that. Especially since I knew I was hiding a secret."

He nodded. "Very dishonorable of you, that secret-keeping business."

"Probably," she said hotly, "but you Callahans bring a lot of misery on yourselves. You were never nice to my uncle. What was I supposed to do?"

"I don't know," he said, sounding tired. She gazed at her big, strong husband, noting the heaviness in his eyes. He looked so sad that she ached. "I probably would have done the same thing," he said, his gaze drifting down to the Under Construction message on her T-shirt, stopping at her watermelon-shaped belly. "How do you feel?"

"I feel fine. Although I'll admit the babies are keeping me awake tonight. They're doing gymnastics."

It wasn't the babies keeping her awake, of course. It was the sexy cowboy sitting on her bed.

"That's good. They'll be big and strong." That pronouncement wiped a bit of the annoyance from his face, and Sawyer thought Jace looked plenty pleased with himself now. "Let me know if you need anything." He got up and went to the door, before turning back to face her. "It wasn't my intention to make you feel trapped."

"I know. I just spooked. And I wish our situation could have started out better." Sawyer shook her head. "I think I probably make you feel trapped."

He shrugged. "I shouldn't have taken you to Las Vegas. Or Colorado."

Was he saying he was sorry he'd married her? Icy worry flooded her. That was the last thing she wanted. "I'm glad we got married. You were right about that. For the children."

"Yeah, well, they'll have plenty of documentation. Ash has put about fifty photos of the ceremony on the website."

"Website?" Sawyer hadn't known Rancho Diablo had one.

He nodded. "Running Bear's brainstorm."

She started to ask when his grandfather had become interested in having a site for the ranch, but then realized there was no point in making Jace feel she was digging for information. "That was nice of Ash to commemorate the ceremony. Although we weren't there long enough for fifty photos. And I didn't see her with a camera that much." Sawyer had been too busy ogling Jace.

"You'd be surprised what my sister can do."

"I am sorry about everything, Jace," Sawyer said, meaning it.

"I am, too. And as much as I know this is going to be like throwing kerosene on a fire, you're going to have to leave here tomorrow."

He was right, but it felt as if a fire exploded in her heart at the thought that he was anxious for her to leave. "I know. I told Fiona I needed to go somewhere."

"Aunt Fiona says you should stay, but the situation isn't stable."

"You don't have to explain."

He leaned against the wall. "I'm not explaining. I'm

just telling you what's the safest thing for the children. And you."

Silence stretched between them for a long moment. Sawyer looked away, knowing that the days of their stolen meetings were gone forever now.

She missed that so much, missed the wild side of him, and her, and holding him in her arms.

"Jace, I want you to know that I always, always took the very best care of the Callahan children. I guarded them, and would protect them still, with my life. I adored those kids, and would have never allowed anything to happen to them."

He studied her, and she thought she saw anger and betrayal flash in his eyes. "We'll see," Jace said. "We'll see."

Then he left.

Ash knocked not thirty minutes later, whispering "Sawyer!" through the door.

"Come in, Ash." Sawyer sat up and turned the bedside lamp on again as Jace's sister slipped inside and made herself at home on the foot of the bed.

"You're not asleep," Ash observed.

"No, I'm not." She hadn't been able to sleep after Jace came to her room. Her thoughts churned restlessly. "Neither are you."

"I don't sleep much."

Ash looked perky, too pleased to be awake at nearly midnight, Sawyer thought crossly.

"Let's sneak downstairs and get a midnight snack," Ash suggested.

"Sure, why not?" Lying in this bed wasn't going to do her any good, anyway. "I assume you have something on your mind, and I might as well hear it with a brownie and some milk."

"It's sheet cake today," Ash said. She got off the bed and bounded over to the nightstand as Sawyer dressed in maternity jeans and clogs and an oversize thermal T-shirt. "What's this?" She held up the white box Jace had given her.

"I didn't open it." And she wasn't going to.

"Is it from Jace?" Ash looked at her. "Yes, I know I'm snooping, but most people can't leave a box unopened without peeking. At least I can't."

Sawyer smiled, her crankiness chased off a little by Ash's enthusiasm. "I usually can't, either. And yes, it's from your brother."

"Your husband," Ash said. "A wife should immediately open something from her husband."

Sawyer blinked. "I don't want gifts from Jace."

"Oh, pooh. Knowing my brother, it's likely those trick snakes that come flying out. Or something else equally unromantic." She sighed dramatically. "I don't know where we went wrong with him."

Sawyer looked at the box, which Ash was gently shaking next to her ear. "If you're curious, you're welcome to open it."

"I'm curious as a cat! But I never open anything that doesn't have my name on it. It's bad juju."

Sawyer laughed. "You'd open anything, most especially if it didn't have your name on it."

"Okay, that may be true. But not this box. It sounds like jewelry."

"How does jewelry sound?" Sawyer was a little shaken. She didn't want jewelry from Jace. She wanted *him*. She wanted his babies.

Most of all, she wanted his trust—and love.

"It sounds romantic," Ash said, teasing.

"Oh, for heaven's sake. It's not jewelry. When did Jace have time to shop for that? You two were on the road all day, just like I was."

"Yeah, and I got my ear gnawed off by my brother for giving you my keys." Ash looked unfazed and maybe a bit cheerful about her part in Sawyer's escape. "He was grumpier than a hungry baby all the way home."

"Sorry about that."

"Not at all," she said. "Come on, let's go hit Fiona's treasure trove of goodies. My sweet tooth is in withdrawal."

Sawyer looked at the box Ash had put back on the nightstand and seemingly forgotten. She glanced at Jace's sister, who was laughing at her.

"You might as well open it," Ash said. "Now that I've made you think about it, it's going to stay on your mind."

Sawyer tried to act as if she wasn't dying of curiosity as she picked up the box and tore off the white wrapping paper. She made short work of opening the lid, and pulled out a white jeweler's case.

"It might be jewelry," she admitted, and Ash laughed.

"It might be."

Sawyer gave her sister-in-law a curious look. "Do you know what it is?"

"I promise you I do not. He didn't stop at a store while we were on the road."

Sawyer opened the case, then gasped at the engagement ring inside. A large emerald-shaped diamond stared up at her, set in a white-gold setting, or maybe platinum. Tiny baguettes glittered on each side, catching the light like perfectly shaped pieces of ice. "It's gorgeous."

"Wow," Ash said, coming to inspect it. "I didn't know Jace had it in him."

Sawyer felt her hands shaking. All she could do was stare at the stunning ring.

"Well, try it on!" Ash prompted.

"I— Oh, all right." She was dying to. Slipping it on her finger, she was amazed that it fit, and amazed how much she didn't want to take it off.

"Dang," Ash said, "my brother's a romantic, after all."

Sawyer removed the ring and put it back in the box, which she set on her nightstand.

"What are you doing?" Ash demanded.

"I'm going to go get some of Fiona's sheet cake and milk. What you are doing?"

"What about the ring?"

"It stays in the box," Sawyer said, opening her door, "until I talk to your brother and find out exactly what this marriage is all about."

"Noble of you, but I'm too hungry to admire your nobleness. I spent many hours on the road getting my ear chewed off. Let's go do girl talk over sheet cake. We have things to discuss, if you can tear your mind off my brother for thirty minutes," Ash teased.

Sawyer's breath was still stolen by the lovely gift from Jace. She followed Ash into the hall, but couldn't help glancing toward Jace's closed door. Her cowboy had another think coming if he thought he could romance her with diamonds. He could—and it would be hard to hold out against that—but she was after the ultimate prize.

His heart.

* * *

Jace sat up when he heard his bedroom door creak open. He glanced at the military watch on his arm. Two in the morning. "Who is it?"

"Sawyer."

He felt the side of his bed sink a bit as his wife sat down next to him. He wished he could see her, but was afraid if he turned on the light, she wouldn't say whatever it was she'd come to say. "What's on your mind?"

"So much is on my mind."

He heard the hesitation in her voice. "It's understandable. A lot has happened fast."

"Yes."

He wanted everything to happen faster; he wanted her faster than it seemed he could ever get her.

So he did the only thing he could do—he scooped his wife into the bed with him. Too surprised to move, Sawyer lay still, and he wrapped his arms tightly around her.

"Ahh." Jace sighed with heartfelt satisfaction. "So this is what it feels like to hold you in a real bed."

Chapter 8

Sawyer was so stunned when Jace pulled her against him that it never occurred to her to move away from her husband or get out of the bed. It felt amazing to be back in Jace's arms again, and she wanted to lie with him like this forever. She was afraid if she left now, she would never get the courage to come back. It had taken every ounce of courage she had to slip into his room, with the full intention of telling him she couldn't accept his beautiful ring.

But that thought flew from her mind the moment Jace reached for her.

She wanted him to kiss her, make love to her.

"Babe?"

"Yes?"

"Are you okay with this?"

Sawyer closed her eyes in the darkness. "I am if you are." The guilt she'd been holding inside weighed on her, but being with him like this made her believe that maybe they could move past everything.

He rolled her toward him, gently pressed a kiss against her lips. She froze, waiting to see what he'd do next, then thought *I'm not waiting any longer* and kissed him back. Their kisses turned urgent and Sawyer felt consumed by Jace in the best kind of way. He ran a hand along her back, cupper her bottom and groaned, the way she'd heard him groan many times before.

It thrilled her, and she didn't want him to stop.

"You feel amazing," he said. "I've missed holding you." He put a hand on her stomach, tracing the fullness there. "I don't want to do anything to hurt you."

Sawyer kissed him. "You're not going to hurt me."

He pulled off her top, tossed her pants to the floor. Just like the old days—almost—he was quick to get rid of her clothes, and she dispensed with his, her hands racing to hold him.

"Wait," Jace said. "I've finally got you in a bed. I'm not rushing this." He pushed her back on the pillows, kissed his way to her breasts, teased her nipples before pressing kisses against her tummy. "I've waited so long for you," he said, parting her legs, "to be in a bed, where I can take my time, without wondering if someone's going to see us in the great outdoors."

She squeezed her eyes closed, her heart beating crazily as he stroked the inside of her thighs. He kissed her most private place, his tongue searching, and Sawyer cried out as she went over the edge into pleasure, unimaginable pleasure.

"Come here," Jace said, pulling her on top of him so that she could straddle him. "You set the pace."

She sank onto him, her body accepting him easily—gladly.

"Oh, God," Jace said with a groan, "I've missed you. I've missed *this*."

He held her close, and she sensed him trying hard not to grind his hips against her the way he wanted to.

"You're not going to hurt me," Sawyer told him.

"I'm not going to find out. We have years to get wild. Tonight, gentle is the key."

He tensed when she ground down upon him, anyway. She took pleasure in tormenting him just a bit, easing up and moving slowly while holding his eyes with hers.

"You tease," he said.

"Yes, I do."

He kissed her, holding her close. Suddenly Sawyer felt pleasure sweeping her, rising inside, eager to push her into love's mystery. She tightened up on Jace, kissing him harder, taking him with her as she began to move faster.

When the pleasure hit them, it was as if a tidal wave that had been cresting forever finally broke, leaving them helpless in each other's arms.

"Don't leave again," Jace said, ten minutes later, when she lay in his embrace, stroking his hair. "Whatever we have to do, we can work it out."

Sawyer swallowed hard as she sprawled on his chest. There was nothing she wanted more—and yet he knew as well as she did that sleeping with her had brought trouble right to his door.

She wasn't sure how to change that, either.

"Tell me what happened to your hands," Sawyer said in the night, when Jace turned her over to make love to her again.

He hesitated in the darkness, ran a rough palm gently over her breasts. "I removed someone from the premises before I came upstairs. It was no big deal."

She froze. "You got in a fight?"

"It wasn't just me. Dante, Tighe and I found someone on the grounds who didn't want to leave as quickly as we wanted them to."

Chills ran over her. "Did they hurt you?"

"Do I seem like I'm hurting?" He pushed her legs apart with his knee and kissed her. "It was no big deal."

Her breath caught when he entered her.

"Tell me if—"

"You're fine. Quit worrying." Sawyer gasped. She gave herself up to her husband, knowing he wasn't telling her everything, was holding something back.

Yet she'd kept things from him, too.

Maybe it didn't matter. She clutched his shoulders, wrapped her legs around him as he steadily, gently stroked inside her, filling her with everything she'd been missing for too long. Sawyer closed her eyes, felt passion igniting between them, and started falling into the pleasure waiting for her.

The truth was, she'd do anything to keep Jace. She'd "bought" him at auction, and she'd married him despite knowing she had a secret she should have admitted up front.

Maybe she was a terrible person—but she had her cowboy.

She surrendered, drowning in the sexy pleasure, loving the feel of Jace finding his own release inside her.

I never really thought I'd have him. I'll do whatever is necessary to keep him, she thought as he cradled her in his strong arms. Was it wrong to want him so much?

She lay against his neck, feeling his heartbeat and his slow relaxation into sleep.

I'll ask him tomorrow, she thought. *I'll ask him who they tossed off Rancho Diablo. No more holding back between us.*

Sawyer fell asleep with Jace's hand on her stomach, warming her, holding his children.

Holding her heart.

Jace rode hard toward the canyons, away from Rancho Diablo and the temptress who was still asleep in his bed. He'd wanted desperately to crawl back in and make love to her again, but at 4:00 a.m. and with chores to be done, sanity had returned.

He had a tiny problem. His wife had spied on his family, and he was going to have to explain the situation to them, in words his ham-headed brothers could understand.

"What are you going to do?" Ash asked as they pulled up near the canyons.

"What can I do? She's my wife. She's having our children." *And I'm in love with her.*

I certainly didn't make my downfall too hard on her.

"You have to forgive her for the sake of the babies," Ash said practically.

"I have forgiven her, damn it." Jace put binoculars up to his eyes, checking the activity on Galen's newly acquired land. It looked as if the Feds and reporters and various authorities were determined to turn the land inside out. In the end, it wouldn't come to anything. By now, Wolf had moved anything of strategic value out of the tunnels, relocating his operations the devil only knew where. "I'm just watching my back so a knife doesn't land in it."

He felt Ash's glance on him before she looked through her own binoculars. "I guess I can't blame you for feeling that way."

"I wouldn't care if you did blame me. It's the way I feel. I stepped in the trap, and I'll decide how it affects me. I know that Sawyer probably gave up some strategic information without meaning to. She thought she was protecting her uncle. I'm okay with that." Jace understood that family was all that mattered.

"You can't be a jerk to your wife, though. It'll be bad for her pregnancy, bad for the children. Bad for both of you."

"Thanks, Madame Buttinski, but I think I've got it handled."

"Jerk," Ash said. "I like Sawyer. I want both of you to be happy."

"I like Sawyer, too." Too damn much. Making love to her in a real bed, taking his sweet time with her, had nearly annihilated any good sense he had. "Don't worry. I've got this. Sawyer and Storm are playing on our team now." Jace was certain of that.

"Of course they are," his sister said impatiently, "now that you're married. The ties that bind and all that. Before, she had little choice. But you're her family, we're her family, and I think she needs to tell the family that Rancho Diablo comes first in her heart now."

"Confession?" He put the binoculars away. "Maybe. I'll cross that bridge when I come to it." It occurred to him that Sawyer wouldn't want to make a confession to the family. Least said, soonest mended. On the other hand, they really didn't know everything she'd revealed, and maybe Ash was right. It might be best if they cleared the air. "Shall we ride over to Galen's kingdom?"

"It bugs you that he bought the land, doesn't it?" she asked curiously.

"It bugs me as much as it bugs you."

"True," Ash agreed, "but I'm not married with kids. You are. So you actually would have been up for the new ranch."

He glanced at his sister. "I'm guessing you haven't heard from Xav Phillips lately."

Her face pinked a little, but it might have been the cold February breeze and the brisk ride here that had touched her cheeks with color.

"I haven't heard from him, no. I don't really think about Xav anymore," she said airily.

That was bad. His sister had mooned after Xav Phillips for so long Jace had begun to think she might actually manage to catch the man. But lately, he'd noticed his sister mentioning him less and less, and frequenting the canyons—where Xav had often ridden lookout duty—almost never.

It was a complete reversal for his baby sister, and he felt sorry for her. He knew too well what it felt like to love someone and not have that person return your feelings in the slightest. Or to pretend to return your feelings, while all the time crushing your heart with lies.

"You're the last Callahan," Jace told his sister. "The last free spirit in our family tree."

"I'll always be that way."

"Ash, I have no doubt that the right man will tie you down sooner rather than later. Not that I'm in a hurry to see my baby sister scooped up by a—"

"Jace, I don't want to talk about it," she interrupted,

wheeling her horse around and kicking it into a full gallop back toward Rancho Diablo.

Whoa. She was hurting bad. He felt terrible about his awkward approach at comforting her. Jace wished he could fix it for her, force Xav Phillips to love her. But just like with him and Sawyer, love played out the way it was going to. You couldn't make another person love you.

Jace thought about his parents, and wondered how they'd ever managed to find each other, fall in love, make their relationship work. Seven children, and then witness protection.

He thought about the cozy house in Colorado and felt a little peace. He, Galen, Dante, Tighe, Falcon, Sloan and Ash had done all right for themselves, thanks to the care of Running Bear and Fiona.

But it could have all turned out so much differently.

They'd been blessed. Fortunate. Watched over by angels or spirits, whatever one called the heavenly supernatural that guided them. So had their cousins, the Callahans, who now resided in Hell's Colony, Texas, until they could one day come back home.

When we've got this ranch locked down for our cousins, they can come back here, and we Chacon Callahans can go our way. Back to where we came from.

They really had no home, though. Home was where your family was.

His family was at Rancho Diablo: Sawyer and their children, Jason and Ashley. Jace smiled, thinking about his impending offspring. He'd felt them move inside Sawyer last night when he'd touched her stomach, almost afraid to make love to her. She'd urged him on, telling him it was fine. She'd whispered sweet words to him, tantalizing him, drawing him in.

The worst part was that he went into the trap so easily.

She was his family. He'd stay with her and the children no matter what.

No matter how much it hurt to know she might not be playing him straight.

Jace rode back to the ranch slowly, deep in his thoughts, until he realized Fiona was waving frantically at him from the back porch. He rode toward her, his heart catching at her worried face.

"What is it?"

"I couldn't reach you on your cell! Sawyer's having stomach pains! She didn't want anyone to tell you, but you need to get her to the hospital *now!*"

He slid off his horse and handed it over to a groom, rushing past his aunt into the house and hurrying up the stairs. "Did anybody call the doctor?"

"Yes, but I think we're past Doc Cartwright now. She needs to go straight to the hospital!" Fiona's face was pale. "Galen's looking her over."

Jace went into Sawyer's room to find his brother in full physician mode, checking her heart rate, her pulse, gently trying to keep her calm. Sawyer looked up at Jace the moment he walked in the door.

"Jace! I think the babies are trying to come. It's too early!"

"It's okay," he said, trying to soothe her. He went to sit beside her. He noted the pain on his wife's face, glanced to read his brother's.

"Let's take her in," Galen said softly, and Jace's blood turned cold. Granted, his brother was no gynecologist, but he was a skilled general practitioner of allopathic and holistic medicine. If he said a hospital was required, then something was wrong.

"I'll get the car. Don't worry, babe, it's going to be fine." Jace kissed her and then hurried down the stairs.

Fiona and Burke had already pulled the family van around. Jace gratefully nodded and hurried inside to carry his wife down.

To his surprise, Sawyer was already downstairs, being helped out of a walled-off pantry in the kitchen by Ash and Running Bear.

"What is this?" Jace demanded.

"A secret," Ash said. "A joint this large has hidden passageways, you know."

He glanced at the small elevator that had been disguised behind the wall he'd always thought held the locked and secret gun cabinet. There was no time to ask questions about this newest bit of Rancho Diablo information. Jace filed it away for later reference and scooped his wife up, carrying her to the van.

"I feel awful, Jace. My stomach hurts so badly."

Sawyer laid her head against his shoulder, and Jace's heart bled at the deep sadness and fear in her voice.

He'd brought this on her by making love to her last night. He shouldn't have; he'd known that deep in his heart. And yet, selfishly, he couldn't resist her.

He'd never been able to resist her. Which was what made him ripe for the fact he'd fallen for a woman who'd been working against his family.

That couldn't matter now. His children were in trouble. Sawyer's pale face scared the hell out of him.

He didn't know what he'd do if something happened to her. She'd become his very life.

Gently, he put Sawyer in the ranch van, and his sister

and Fiona jumped in to comfort her as he sped toward the hospital, fearful that everything he loved most might be snatched away from him by the cruel winds of fate.

Chapter 9

"Bed rest," the doctor pronounced after Sawyer had been thoroughly examined. "Absolute bed rest. I'll let you go home, because you've been stabilized for the moment with medication, but there'll be a nurse out to check on you tomorrow, and I don't want to hear that you've moved one inch from your bed. This is very serious," he told Sawyer. "I know you're used to a lot of activity, but you can consider yourself bedbound for now. It won't be forever, but it's important that we keep your babies inside you as long as we possibly can. The longer, the better," he emphasized one last time. "No stairs, no nothing. The nurse will come out and give you medication by IV if you have any further cramping."

"Thank you," Sawyer murmured, exhausted and frightened. She couldn't look at Jace's worried face again. His every thought was hidden behind a stoic expression, but she could read him every time he glanced at her.

He was afraid they'd endangered the babies.

She'd never be able to convince him that their love-making hadn't negatively affected her pregnancy. He wouldn't come near her now; that was clear in his stiff posture as he helped her slowly move to the wheelchair to be taken to the van.

Her husband had heard the doctor's warnings, and he wouldn't take any chances.

They already had too many things to regret. "Jace," she said, as he pushed her wheelchair down the hall. "The doctor said what we did last night probably didn't have anything to do with this."

He didn't say anything, just silently wheeled her to the van, which Fiona and Ash had brought around for them. The ladies hopped out to help her, and Sawyer felt silly and useless as she was assisted into the front passenger's seat.

Everything hurt more than she dared to let on. Already Jace looked as if he was ready to lash her to a bed and keep her in it, so she didn't say anything else as he closed the van door. A small tear threatened to fall from her eye, but she wouldn't allow herself to feel hurt over the sudden distance she was picking up from her husband.

She put a hand on her stomach, comforted by the doctor's words that everything would be fine as long as she rested. Didn't move.

Jace would be tied to her. He wouldn't want to let her out of his sight, which wasn't good for Rancho Diablo. As a one-time ranch employee, she knew that every person had their job and their role. Rancho Diablo had stayed out of Wolf's hands this long because all members of the family worked as a team.

She wasn't really part of the team.

But that didn't mean she wanted Jace having to stop his job to stand over her, guard her, for the rest of her pregnancy. She had every intention of keeping these babies inside her for at least the next two months.

"Jace," Sawyer said suddenly, "I'm going to stay at Uncle Storm's place. Not his town house, but his place you bought, next door to Rancho Diablo. Since he and Lu are staying there now, they can keep an eye on me. It makes sense for everybody involved."

He glanced at her. From the back of the van, there wasn't a peep. Fiona and Ash weren't going to say a word—and that was exactly why she'd brought up her request now. Jace was far less likely to deny her wishes with his sister and aunt hearing what Sawyer felt was best for herself and the babies.

And for Jace, if he only knew it.

"If that's what you want," he said, his tone remote, and she felt a dagger of sadness lacerate her heart. He'd given up easily, more easily than she'd imagined, and that was good.

The problem was, she didn't know if she could make him understand that it wasn't him she was running from this time.

Jace moved Sawyer into Storm Cash's place because that's what she wanted—not because he felt good about it. He didn't. A wife belonged with her husband, but Sawyer had made it clear more than once that she simply wasn't comfortable with him, and he supposed he couldn't blame her.

They'd been so far apart for so long that maybe there wasn't a way to bridge the gap. He knew she felt that he didn't trust her—what Callahan trusted a Cash, anyway?—and the truth was, anybody on the outside looking in would probably say Sawyer didn't deserve to be trusted.

He knew her better than she knew herself, though. She was the answer to everything he needed in his soul, and that made her good for Rancho Diablo.

"So now what?" Ash demanded when he returned to Rancho Diablo at midnight. His sister sat in the kitchen, perched on a bar stool like a fey elf, discreetly waiting up for him, probably. She pushed a cup of coffee his way and pointed to a plate of gingersnaps that were on the counter. "I advise that the two of you do *not* separate for two months, and then try to kiss and make up when the babies are born. Not that you asked my opinion. No one ever does."

He ruffled his sister's hair and sat down next to her. "Thanks for the joe."

"Don't sit down. There's a family meeting upstairs."

"Now?" He was exhausted, his mind consumed with Sawyer.

"Yep." Ash rose. "Pretty cool about the hidden passage, huh? Freaked you out a little."

He followed his giggling sister, carrying the plate of cookies and his mug with him. "If I got freaked out every time Rancho Diablo revealed one of its secrets, I'd have to go sit in the canyons and stare at cacti and mumble to myself."

"That's actually not a bad life. I wouldn't mind it," Ash said wistfully as they went upstairs. "I'm going to tell Galen tonight that he has to split Sister Wind Ranch with all of us, the big egghead."

"It's Loco Diablo, and Galen won't do it. You don't even have a family yet, and as we established, you're not ready to settle down. So you wouldn't be up for the ranch, anyway. Fiona's rules are clear."

"I'm a rule breaker. Haven't you figured that out yet?"

Ash pushed open the library door, ushering him by. The plate of cookies was promptly descended upon by his brothers. Tighe and Dante stuck their big paws in first, the latter tossing one to Galen.

"Like little piglets," Ash said with a sigh as Sloan reached to grab a few, and Falcon snagged the last. "Now that your munchies are satisfied, let business begin. Galen," Ash said. "We've got trouble around here. The place is crawling with reporters and Feds. I came across a treasure hunter the other day trespassing with one of those treasure-hunting rigs."

"Metal detector," Jace clarified.

"Not only did it detect metal," Ash said, "but this one could detect graves, hidden chambers, crypts and caves. Very sophisticated. You can imagine that I banished him from the property with all due haste." She looked around at them. "I would like to submit to all of you that we are outmanned and outgunned. We can't hold off Wolf's minions any longer. And we're a woman down."

Jace frowned. Sawyer wouldn't be on the job anytime soon, though she would excoriate him if she heard him say that. "Getting to the fact that you've recently revealed a hidden passage yourself—"

"That was Running Bear's doing," Ash said. "I didn't know about it, either. Fiona never mentioned the kitchen dumbwaiter elevator thing to me, though I'm sure she knows about it."

"What could the trespasser have been hunting?" Dante asked.

"Graves, hidden chambers, crypts and secret caves," Ash said, exasperated. "Weren't you listening, big brother?"

"What did he say he wanted, Ash?" Galen demanded. "And why didn't you tell us sooner?"

"Because." She shrugged. "We were kind of busy with the babies and all. I'm an aunt first and a trespasser-hunter second. Besides, I kept his toy, so it didn't matter to me about the grave robber or whatever he was."

Jace stared at her, as dumbfounded as his brothers.

"What do you mean, you kept his toy?" Sloan demanded.

"He was happy to give it up, considering what I told him I'd do to him if he didn't. I acquired his fancy computer that went with it, too. It's quite an amazing doohickey." She went to a cabinet in the library and pulled out the equipment.

They all gathered around, eyeing the loot with astonishment.

"Ash, you can't just take someone's stuff," Jace said. "This is nice equipment."

"Can't I?" she retorted. "I think I did. Like I said, he was happy to give it up in return for me not reporting him to the sheriff or kicking the daylights out of him."

"Ash," Jace murmured, sitting her down on a leather sofa. His brothers followed him over, and they all looked down at their tiny sister. "Ash, you're the baby. You're not supposed to be this tough," he said, feeling a bit lost.

"We kick the bad guys around, and the trespassers, and the other enemy. We want you to…"

He hesitated, and Ash glared up at her gang of brothers. "What? Comb my hair and put bows in it? Wear makeup? Heels?" She shook her head. "Sorry. I'm tougher than all of you and you know it. Without me, this team would be lost."

Someone passed around the crystal tumblers of whiskey, and Jace gladly took one. He was disturbed, but he couldn't exactly pinpoint why. Ash was being honest; she'd always been tough. Most of the Callahan women were tough.

Not this tough.

He looked to Galen for advice. His oldest brother shrugged, and judging by the others' expressions, they were all stumped by Ash.

She rolled her eyes at all of them and then looked at Galen, as well.

"Galen, I move that you split the land across the canyons among all of us. Tonight. We're no longer hostage to Fiona's challenge. I have no plans to marry, and I deserve that land just as much as anyone in this room. I know Grandfather advised you to take the land to protect us from Wolf, but I can take care of myself." She looked around at her brothers. "It's a hotbed of smugglers and thieves who want to tear this place apart. I don't have time to think about getting married. All of you have children now, but I won't be having any. So I move that the challenge is over. Done. Finished."

Jace glanced at Galen again. "She's right," he said quietly. "She deserves her piece. In fact, we all deserve a home of our own. One day the Callahans will come back here, and that will be good. But our hearts are here now," he said, thinking about Sawyer. She'd told Storm the Callahans could return any day. Why had she said that?

And did it matter? She might be next door, but his heart was with her. If he had to pitch a tent and live in Storm's garden, he'd do that to be with his family.

"Actually," Galen said, "I have news to report about that land. The Feds have discovered that it's so overrun by tunnels and smugglers that it's barely inhabitable."

"Fine," Ash said. "We'll fill in the tunnels and build an enormous amusement park. Shops and a mall. It wouldn't hurt us to have a different livelihood, and commercial real estate would suit me just fine. I'm sick to death of horses and oil wells and cows and those stupid peacocks out front. I haven't seen the Diablos in weeks, and that's very, very bad, as every single one of you know. It means we've *failed* at our mission. And that Wolf has won." She looked at Jace. "I'm sorry to dump all this on you right now. We should be throwing you a wedding party, and helping you figure out where your baby nursery is going to be. I feel sorry for you and Sawyer, but we're in a deep hole here."

Jace shrugged. "I doubt Sawyer wants anything more than going to term with the babies. We'll figure out the nursery and other details later." She wasn't even wearing the ring he'd given her. He'd hoped that the lovely ring would be a peace offering, a silent commitment to the depth of his feelings for her, but he hadn't seen it since he'd left it in her room.

"Ash is right," he continued. "They're coming. No doubt they're already here. Which means no one is safe. Wolf has outmaneuvered us. He just had more people, more resources. And maybe we never understood the blackness of our uncle's heart. But the Diablos haven't been around in a long time, and that is a very bad sign."

They all looked silently at each other.

"If we divide the land," Jace said suddenly, "it will be tough for Wolf to take it from us. Too many pieces to chase down."

"True," Galen said. "Vote?"

All hands went up. Ash grinned, triumphant. "All right, brothers," she said, standing, "we'll draw for the spaces. I'm not afraid of my stupid uncle, and I'm ready to pitch my tent there now. Tonight." She glanced around at them, and Jace thought his sister looked a little wild, a bit untamed.

"I'm not giving up on the only place I have to call home," she said. "It's been a long time since any of us had a place we could call our own. Besides the stone fire ring near the canyons, which Running Bear gave to us when we first came, we've had nothing, no stake that is ours. I will burn Uncle Wolf out before I allow him to take one square inch of what's mine."

She went out the door, and Jace and his brothers looked at each other.

"Wow," Tighe said, "little sister's got a burr under her saddle."

"It's gotten to her," Falcon said. "This job could get to anyone. We're losing, and she knows it. It's eating at her. It sucks to feel helpless."

"Damn it," Jace muttered. "We can't let Wolf get us down. There's too much at stake." He stood and addressed the room. "It's been months since we've seen the Diablos. We knew Wolf's intent was to get to them— that was why they were tunneling from Loco Diablo to here. First, to get to us from a different vantage point, and second, to take out the spirit of Rancho Diablo. The Diablos, the heart and soul of the place. Wolf knows only too well that his father's spirit—Running Bear's spirit—is in the mustangs. Without them, Grandfather will be weakened. Rancho Diablo will be seriously weakened, as well." *And we'll be lost.*

"We'll be lost," Dante said, echoing his thoughts, and Jace knew his brothers saw the situation the same way he did.

"And this bone-digging toy," Jace said, going over to study what his sister had commandeered, "tells me that we're not the only ones aware that there may be hidden caves under Rancho Diablo. Tunnels."

"Depositories," Sloan said.

"Spirits," Galen added.

"We knew that the smugglers had dug under Loco Diablo, and we knew they hadn't quite reached here, nor the canyons. Not then," Jace said. "But I never thought about hidden caves, or buried treasure here. Except for what's in the basement."

They all looked at him.

"It's secret," Galen said. "It's the Callahan buried silver treasure."

"But," Jace said, "Wolf wouldn't be sending men over here with treasure-hunting devices if he didn't think there was silver and something much more important buried somewhere under Rancho Diablo."

"Like what?" Falcon demanded.

He wasn't certain. Prickles ran over his arms, though he was warm enough in his winter clothes. He thought about the cozy house in Colorado, and the sense he'd had that there were spirits there that he recognized, happy memories he'd once known. Remembered well, deep in his heart.

"Wolf's too close," he said. "He knows something we don't know. And it has to do with the tunnels under Loco Diablo."

"Sister Wind Ranch," Ash said, sailing back into the room. "When are you lunkheads ever going to figure out that land has a feminine spirit?"

They all stared at her. She wore black from head to toe, combat fatigue style. Heavy boots, a black jacket.

"What the hell are you doing?" Jace demanded. "You look like you're about to go grave-robbing."

"I am. And you're coming with me. But first," Ash said, zipping up her jacket, "we're going to go ask your wife where her uncle hid the information we need."

Chapter 10

Sawyer didn't like being on bed rest, but she couldn't really complain because she felt so much better. The cramps were gone and the babies seemed settled. The nurse would be out early tomorrow morning to check on her. She'd had Jace place her recliner next to the window so she could keep an eye on Rancho Diablo.

And Jace, of course.

She missed the daily jolt of adrenaline that came with working at Rancho Diablo. There was always something happening, and not being part of the action was hard. On the other hand, in a couple of months she'd have two beautiful babies.

"I can lie very still for sixty days," she told herself, picking up her binoculars. She looked through them toward Rancho Diablo, watching a truck go down the long drive toward the main road.

It turned up the road that led to Storm's house. Sawyer peered more closely, not altogether surprised to see Ash and Jace get out and head toward the porch. The doorbell rang.

"Come in! It's unlocked!"

Her big husband walked in, wearing a glare—his normal expression these days.

"Why is the front door unlocked?" he demanded.

Ash looked at her sympathetically.

"Because I can't get out of this chair, and Uncle Storm and Lu went into town to fetch some groceries." Sawyer frowned at Jace. "I can't get up to answer the door, obviously."

"You shouldn't be having any visitors, and the front door should be locked. Every window and every door of this house should be locked."

"Well, it is your house," she replied, "so I guess you can make the rules." She shrugged at Jace.

"I'm not telling you what to do, babe. I'm worried about you. You know it's not safe. Unlocked doors aren't a good idea," he said patiently.

She hated it when he was patient with her, especially when she knew she was being cranky. "Hi, Ash."

"Hi, Sawyer." Ash sat down next to her. "What can I do to help?"

Sawyer sighed. "Explain to Jace that pregnant doesn't mean helpless."

Ash smiled, glanced at her brother. "Let's not try to explain things that are beyond his comprehension."

"Hey," Jace said. "I get it. I just don't like it."

Sawyer nodded. "I figured that out. So, why am I getting a family visit?"

He leaned against the wall, and she let her gaze run

over him, studying him in his worn jeans, scuffed boots, black thermal shirt and sheepskin jacket. Looking at him never failed to get her heart beating faster.

"Sawyer," Ash said, and Sawyer turned at the strangely patient tone in her sister-in-law's voice. "Did Storm give you some information about Sister Wind Ranch? That land he sold to us?"

Sawyer looked at Jace, who shrugged.

"Uncle Storm didn't say much about it, except that he wished he hadn't bought it. He was happy to get it off his hands. Said it was far too large a spread for him, and that he wished he'd never allowed Wolf to talk him into buying it."

"Why did Wolf want your uncle to buy the land we call Loco Diablo?" Jace asked.

"Wolf told my uncle that if your family bought the land, you'd basically own the county. Your power would exponentially multiply. Like a conglomerate, or a Mafia family. Wolf said he felt like he was being pushed out of the family business, which he had every right to be in, and would be in except that his father, Running Bear, didn't like him."

"So he wanted Storm to be a counterweight?" Jace asked. "Spread the power around?"

She nodded. "And Wolf offered my uncle protection if he bought it. All the bad things that were happening wouldn't happen here, to his land. Uncle didn't really know what that meant, but he said it wasn't his place to get involved in family issues. He didn't know who the bad guys were, who the good guys were. So he agreed to purchase the land from the elderly gentleman who owned it. He got a great price on the deal."

"Why would the former owner do that?" Ash demanded. "Why sell for a low price when he could have sold to any developer for more? Or to us?"

"Because your uncle Wolf told the old man he'd make his life a misery if he didn't do the deal just the way he wanted him to," Sawyer said, her gaze on Jace.

"Why didn't you tell me this before now?" he asked.

"I'm a bodyguard, not a business manager." Sawyer frowned. "Besides, Wolf is your uncle. I figured you already knew."

"Why did you come to work for us?" Jace knelt down next to her chair, put his hand on her stomach. The babies kicked as if they knew their father was holding them.

"I already told you. My uncle wasn't certain what was going on." Sawyer looked into Jace's eyes, wishing they didn't have to talk about this again. It brought up all the sore spots in their marriage, the lack of trust, the strained feelings. "He wanted me to find out what I could."

"He should have known," Ash said. "He'd done business with Fiona."

"Horse trading is a different thing, and that was many years ago. He had no great knowledge of the Chacon Callahans. Besides, Wolf was telling some pretty crazy stories about you." Sawyer shook her head. "It didn't take me long to figure out he was evil. And at that point, I knew I would do everything I could to help you."

Jace studied her, his eyes searching hers.

"I believe you," he said.

"Thank you." It meant so much to her.

"I think my uncle must have given your uncle something," Jace said. "Wolf was trying to protect his smuggling operation, and he was using your uncle to divert us by buying Loco Diablo. So when Storm bought the land, he had to have gotten something from Wolf for doing so."

Sawyer's eyes widened with surprise and dismay. "Are you suggesting my uncle accepted a bribe to do it? Beyond Wolf's promise to put his men to protecting my uncle's spread from the trouble that was occurring between you and your uncle?"

"Yes," Jace said simply. "I'm saying Storm had to have been given something of value to do what he did."

"Like what?" Sawyer demanded. "I assure you Uncle Storm's goal was getting distance from the lot of you and whatever was going on with your uncle."

Jace glanced at Ash, who seemed to understand his question. "Financial assistance," Ash murmured.

"I don't think my uncle needs money," Sawyer snapped.

Jace moved his hand to hers. "Maybe to buy Loco Diablo, he did. There were surveyors who would have needed to be bought off, plus palms to be crossed with silver at the state level, so they would look the other way at such a big land deal. Deeds to change hands. It all happened very quickly, and would have required funding."

Sawyer felt herself getting angry with Jace, and disgusted. She couldn't understand how the man could live with so much conceit. "You really think you're the only people in New Mexico who can run a spread? My uncle has always owned land. Cattle, horses, whatever. He didn't need a bribe."

"Not a bribe so much as assistance. Maybe a sort of silent partnership. An angel investor," Jace said. "You can't think of anything of value your uncle recently acquired?"

She was almost too mad to think. She glared at him,

then at Ash, who was watching her without emotion. These people were supposed to be her family! "The only thing my uncle has gotten lately is a town house in Diablo and a new wife. He sold his ranch to you, and the land you call Loco Diablo. What else do you want from him? You got everything he had," she said bitterly. "All because of the feud between you and your uncle."

"I found someone near the canyons with a metal detector, a very sophisticated setup," Ash said. "He was looking for something."

Sawyer sighed. "Okay, I'll bite. What was he looking for?"

"He said he was looking for a graveyard," Ash said. "A graveyard that was rumored to have treasure beyond imagination. I told him that was nonsense, and sent him and his two buddies on their way, of course."

"What has that got to do with my uncle?"

Jace stood, crossed to a window, looked out toward Rancho Diablo before turning to face her again. Sawyer's heart skipped a beat.

"You think my uncle knows where this graveyard is," Sawyer said. "You think Wolf told him to help him find it, and agreed to split treasure with him if he could help him get Rancho Diablo away from the Callahans. You think that's why his gang is always trespassing. And," she said, realization dawning, "that Uncle Storm sent me to work for you to find out anything I could. And of course, I romanced you as part of the grand plan."

"Not so fast," Jace said. "We're just asking if there's anything Wolf ever gave your uncle. It's a hunch, nothing more."

"I got suspicious when the man with the equipment mentioned your uncle," Ash said. "He seemed to know

Storm and Wolf pretty well, for an out-of-towner. This made me curious, so I looked the man up. Turns out he's no small-time treasure hobbyist. He's a well-known treasure seeker with a military background. In other words, he's a kind of bounty hunter. He specializes in buried treasure, and dead bodies instead of live ones."

Sawyer sucked in a breath. "You're absolutely crazy if you think my uncle sent that man to scout your property."

"He didn't," Jace said. "Wolf sent him. But you've admitted yourself that—"

"My uncle asked me to hire on at Rancho Diablo to find out what I could about your feud." Sawyer nodded. "Yes, he did. I've admitted that. But he never once mentioned anything to me about a hidden graveyard or buried treasure." She was more hurt than she could have ever imagined. Looking at Jace was too heartbreaking. Not only did he not trust her, but he thought she was part of a plot to steal his family's wealth. Sawyer put her head back against the recliner and closed her eyes. "I'm tired," she said, so drained she could barely keep her eyes open anymore. "Please leave."

Jace walked over, touched her hand. She snatched it away, not opening her eyes.

After a moment, she heard the front door open.

"I'll be back to check on you later," Jace said, but she didn't answer. The door closed, and she wiped her eyes, thankful no tears had fallen while he was around to witness them. She wouldn't let him see how much he'd hurt her. What a ridiculous thing to ask. Of course her uncle hadn't taken a bribe from Wolf! All he'd wanted was to stay out of the fracas between Wolf and the Callahans. He'd wanted protection for his land.

The worst part was how much she loved Jace. She was madly in love with him, had been for a long time. But he would never see her that way. There would always be seeds of distrust between them.

The only things holding her and Jace together now were these babies. She placed both hands around her stomach with a touch of sadness.

Babies who would grow up with a father and a mother who didn't love each other, didn't even trust each other.

Sawyer opened her eyes, gazed out toward Rancho Diablo, her heart breaking. Dusk stole over the ranch as the sun retreated, layering the seven-chimneyed house in the distance with a fairy-tale glow. How many times had she looked out on that castlelike structure, wishing she could be part of a family like the Callahans? And then when she'd gotten the job there, how fortunate she'd felt to finally be part of that world! She'd never awakened without feeling a shiver of joy that she was at Rancho Diablo, trusted with Callahan children and lives, part of an extraordinary world that was envied by everyone.

And then somehow, miraculously, a Callahan man had seemed to fall in love with her.

But the fairy tale hadn't exactly turned out the way she'd dreamed.

"I believe her," Jace said to Ash as they returned to Rancho Diablo.

"I do, too." His sister shook her head. "I'm missing a huge piece of the puzzle somehow. Storm has to know something. He must know what Wolf's true purpose is."

"Or maybe not," Jace said, struck by a sudden thought about the two men who'd followed them out to Vegas, the knife in the cake, and the two men with the treasure hunter. "Maybe Uncle Wolf sent that man with the metal detector to hunt for what he thinks is here, not what he's got. Maybe Wolf used Storm and never intended to share any treasure with him."

"Something made Storm jump and buy that land, and it wasn't the sudden desire to own twenty thousand additional acres, not at his age. Come on, Jace, what was Storm going to do with that much land? He's got a small spread and a house, some livestock. He's done well in horse trading and breeding, but he's hardly a mover and shaker."

"True." Jace ruminated on the strange turn of events, all the while trying to keep his mind off his delicate, pregnant wife, who by now was deeply unhappy with him and had every right to be. "My wife's not with me."

"You're going to have to fix that. I don't think she preferred your Sherlock Holmes approach. It was kind of meat-headed."

Jace glanced at his sister. "Thank you for your support. Especially since it was your idea."

"Indeed," Ash said. "However, I can't do everything for you. Your approach should have been more groveling. More loverlike. Sweetheart," she said, her voice cooing, as she showed her brother how to speak to a lady, "can you think of anything my mean ol' uncle might have held over your honest and courageous uncle's head? Like a map, or a plat, of—"

"I get it," Jace said, interrupting her soliloquy. "I'll have to figure out a way to dig myself out of trouble." It wouldn't be easy. Sawyer had every right to think he was the world's biggest rat.

He hated feeling like a rat when he wanted to be a conquering hero. "Damn," he muttered, "I'm ready for Wolf and his men to fall off a cliff and disappear."

"The problem is, Wolf's got the cartel breathing down his neck, I'm sure of it. They want revenge on our parents, and the Callahan parents—and Wolf wants Rancho Diablo and all its treasure."

Of which there was a lot. Running Bear and Jeremiah Callahan, and even Jace's own father and mother, Carlos and Julia, had been astute and frugal, with a vision that had built this ranch. They'd breathed Rancho Diablo to life, put their hearts and souls into every inch. With Fiona's, Burke's and Running Bear's competent overseeing, Rancho Diablo was a fine example of a successful working ranch. Join Loco Diablo to Rancho Diablo and Dark Diablo, and there was no question why Wolf would be envious.

"I wonder what happened between Running Bear and his son to get them crosswise with each other," Jace murmured. He vowed to have the best relationship he possibly could with his son and daughter. In fact, he couldn't wait to hold them in his arms.

He couldn't wait to hold Sawyer, either, but that probably wasn't going to happen anytime soon.

"Running Bear says Wolf was always different. That of his three sons, that one was a bad apple. The other two understood service and the spirit of a life bigger than themselves. They understood they were strong and blessed, and they could share those gifts with others." Ash shrugged. "Wolf, Grandfather said, was stubborn and jealous from early on. No matter how he tried to help his son, he couldn't get him to understand that the spirit inside is the real treasure. That a person can nourish their soul with good, or succumb to the darkness of negativity and envy. Wolf wanted things to be easier than they could be."

Jace grunted. "I'm going to be an excellent father to Jason and Ashley."

Ash perked up. "Ashley?"

"Yes." He grinned at her hopeful look. "That was Sawyer's choice. She wanted to name our little girl after you."

A grin split Ash's face. "I always knew I liked Sawyer!"

He laughed at his sister's change of tune. "I like her, too. I'd better go see if I can convince her that she likes me back."

"Yes, you should. You were pretty hard on her, you know," Ash said, heading inside the house. "I'm going to go tell everyone that I have a namesake. It's called bragging, and I have it coming to me."

"Ash."

She turned around at his call. "Yes?"

"Don't confront any more trespassers in the canyons by yourself."

She raised a brow. "Brother, I'm never alone."

"You were by yourself. Something could have happened." He hated to think of his little sister alone in the canyons. "You're not even supposed to be out there by yourself, as you know. Galen's orders."

"Galen is wonderful about throwing orders around, as are you." Ash blew him a kiss. "No worries, brother. Like I said, I'm never alone."

She went inside, and Jace sighed. "She doesn't listen," he muttered. "It's like talking to the wind."

He hoped Sawyer would listen better.

To Jace's dismay, Sawyer was being trundled off by an EMT when he returned to the house next door. "What the hell is going on?" he demanded, fear leaping inside him.

"Her blood pressure is high, and her vital signs worry me. She's cramping again," the visiting nurse informed him.

He knew Sally Clausen. He'd met her at some of Fiona's Books'n'Bingo soirees and charity functions. Sally was gray-haired, practical and thorough. If she'd reported her concerns to the doctor and had been told to send Sawyer to the hospital, something was dreadfully wrong.

He strode to Sawyer's side. "What can I do for you, babe?"

She was so pale, lying there on the gurney. "I don't know. The cramps came back after you left. Fortunately, Sally was scheduled to come by and check on me." Sawyer's blue eyes stared up at him. "I'm so scared, Jace."

He understood. He was terrified. "You're going to be fine. The babies are going to be fine." This was his fault, of course. He'd upset her, raised her blood pressure, when she was supposed to be resting.

What a crappy husband he was turning out to be.

"I'll ride with you."

Sawyer barely nodded. "Thank you."

He texted Ash. Follow me over to the hospital with a truck.

Instantly, his phone buzzed back. Are we having babies today? read her text.

He hoped not. The babies needed more time. He swallowed hard and followed the EMTs as they took Sawyer to the ambulance. He got in, held her hand and told himself everything was going to be just fine.

Somehow.

Chapter 11

"My poor brother!" Ash rushed into the hospital thirty minutes later, hugging Jace when she found him in the waiting room. They wouldn't allow him to go back to see his wife—not yet.

Apparently, Sawyer had told the doctor she wanted to be alone for now.

He couldn't blame her—but he was dying inside.

"I'll be all right."

Ash's eyes were wide. "It was bad juju to ask about her uncle."

"Ash, it wasn't bad juju. It's just going to be a tough pregnancy for her, I suppose. It will all work out." He hugged his sister tighter, trying to alleviate her worries.

"You don't have a nursery set up."

"This is true. If the babies come early, we'll be in a bit of a hurry to get things done. But we'll do it."

He wasn't really worried about that, though. They had enough family around with cribs and baby paraphernalia they could borrow.

The thing was, he and Sawyer didn't have a home for them and their family.

"Where will you live?" Ash asked.

"That's a question for another day." He swallowed hard, wondering how he could talk Sawyer into living with him.

Ash slumped in a chair. "I feel so guilty."

"That's not like you." He sat next to her. "No negative vibes."

"It's not doing me much good," she admitted. "I'm never having children."

He laughed out loud. "Ash, you'll have children. And no doubt they'll be the toughest kids around. They'll be born untamed, like their mother."

"I think I'd make a better aunt than a mother. And besides, my children would be plenty tame. They're not going to live like we did," she said, her voice turning a bit dreamy. "If I had children, they'd have ballet lessons."

"Even the boys?" he teased.

"If they want," she said. "And my girls will have long, silky hair that I put lots of bows in." She ran her fingers through her hair, which had grown from a short boy cut convenient for military life to a shoulder-length fall of silvery-blond strands. "And they would always have a store-bought birthday cake. Unless Fiona's around to make it. I'm no good with baking."

He listened to his sister's dreams, letting her voice soothe him, keep his mind off what was happening with Sawyer. His gut wouldn't unknot. He'd never been this scared in his life, not when he was deployed, not even when their parents had gone away.

That had been a terrible day. But just like Ash, he had dreams for his children.

He dreamed that his two babies would live in a house with their mother and father, who would never have to leave. They'd always be together, a family.

Those were his dreams.

"It had nothing to do with you, Jace." Sawyer hated the fearful look on her husband's face. After the doctor had ordered extra medication for her, she'd allowed Jace to join her. The nurse had said he was like a caged panther in the waiting room, and Sawyer had taken pity on him. "I guess I have a small frame. There's not much room. Or it's just my body's reactions. But I wasn't stressed about you and Ash asking me those questions. Irritated, but not stressed."

"Let's not talk about that anymore." He paced around the room, unable to relax. "You just rest."

She closed her eyes for a moment, too keyed up to relax. The whole incident had been so frightening.

Sawyer opened her eyes again. "I don't know that I'll be able to carry to term. Not even until April."

"I'll hire on extra help. I don't want you to lift a pinkie." Jace sat on the bed next to her and took her hand. "If you could have anything on the planet that would make your pregnancy easier and better, what would it be? I want you to have everything you need."

She looked at her husband. That was an easy answer. She wanted him. But if she said that, Jace would say she had him.

Yet she didn't, not really. And she knew that. No relationship could survive the way theirs had begun, with all the trouble that had followed their impetuous wedding.

"Whatever you want, I'll get it for you," he promised. He put a hand on her tummy, smiled when he felt the babies jostling for space. "Clearly, they're not fazed by the day's events."

"They're always active. They use my body as a trampoline."

"You're beautiful," Jace told her, sweeping her hair away from her face and kissing her lips. "I know you probably don't want me kissing you. I know you think I'm the world's biggest louse, or a traitor, or something."

"Not the world's biggest louse." She smiled, but he didn't smile back.

"We've got to have a home, babe."

She blinked. "I can't think about that right now."

"I know you can't. Let me think about it for you."

Suddenly, she liked the idea of Jace making the decisions—anybody making the decisions. It wasn't in her to be passive, but she suddenly felt so tired. Too tired even to hold him on the opposite side of the fence she tried to keep up between them. "We'll never be safe, wherever we go. It's never going to feel like a real home."

His hand tightened on hers.

"The thing is," she said softly, "we'd probably be better off with a divide-and-conquer strategy. Then the babies would be safer."

"Divide and conquer?" He sounded doubtful.

"Yes. We could have two houses, so no one can monitor the children easily. We won't keep to a steady routine that could be noticed."

"Don't think about it, Sawyer."

She looked at him. "My uncle became afraid of your

uncle, Jace. He said he threatened him. How can I not think about my children being a kidnapping threat when it's happened in your family before?"

He shook his head. "I don't know. But I'll place a bodyguard outside your room."

"Oh, I'm not scared," Sawyer said. "Not now. I'm big as a house. I couldn't be moved unless someone brings a van and a pulley."

He smiled. "I'm going to lie next to my wife and scandalize the nurses."

She wriggled over. "There really isn't much scooting I can do. I'm almost bigger than the bed."

"Bet I can find some room."

She giggled when he squeezed up next to her, put a comforting hand over her stomach. "That feels wonderful," she said, sighing.

"That's right. Just call me Wonderful Callahan. Now go to sleep. As soon as the doctor springs you, I'm taking you back to Rancho Diablo. And you're not getting out of my sight again, little fireball of a wife."

"Hardly little."

"You're sassy and fun-sized in my book. I find the extra curves enticing. In fact, it's killing me not to explore them."

He was trying to make her feel better, and for that, he was a hero. There was nothing sexy or "fun-sized" about her now, but it was sweet of him to say so.

Sawyer rested her head on Jace's shoulder and tried not to think about the fact that Wolf had called her today. Right after that awful conversation with him, she'd begun cramping. Had felt terrible. Fear such as she'd never known had sliced into her.

Wolf had told her she was going to be sorry she'd

ever worked for the Callahans, married one, was having Callahan children. He'd spent years making the Callahan parents disappear, and he could do that with her and her children, too.

Unless she told him everything she knew about the Callahans.

He'd even silkily threatened Uncle Storm and Lu, making sure she understood just how much was riding on her decision.

She shivered, and Jace held her tighter.

"What's wrong? Is it the babies?" he asked.

"It's nothing. I was cold, but now I'm not."

His arms felt good, wrapped around her. Right now she could believe that she was safe, and that her children were safe.

Just for tonight, she'd let herself cling to that dream.

Jace's world turned upside down when Sawyer insisted on being moved to a small duplex in town, conveniently located next to the main street of Diablo, not much more than a block from Sheriff Cartwright's jail and the courthouse. The other side of the duplex was rented by Storm and Lu.

Apparently, the three of them had been in cahoots. Jace sensed that a plan had been forged, one that didn't include him.

He realized he wasn't far off when his wife told him he wasn't moving in with her.

"Yes, I am," Jace said. "Where you and my children go, I am. Pretty much like your shadow."

"No, Jace." Ensconced on a pretty floral sofa Lu had ordered for her while Sawyer was at the hospital, she gave him a look that didn't seem exactly welcoming. "I need to be alone."

"Being alone is the last thing you need." He frowned and went to perch on the edge of the sofa, so he could read her eyes as she talked. He could feel her trying to put distance between them, but he was a master at putting distance between himself and things that made him uncomfortable, so he knew exactly what his little fireball was up to. "It's no good. I'm staying right here in this tiny domicile with you." He glanced around. "The four of us will be nice and cozy."

"Jace, listen to me." Sawyer took a deep breath, holding her hand against her stomach for a moment. "You need to be at the ranch. I need to be closer in town, where Sally doesn't have to drive out so far to check my vitals and give me my drip. I'm absolutely determined to do this exactly by doctor's orders, and by being here, I'm nearer to everything."

"That's fine. I'll drive in."

"I don't want you to."

He looked at his stubborn wife. "What is going on with you, beautiful?"

"Exactly what I told you. It's better for me to be in town."

He got up, looked out the window. "Are you renting this place, or did you buy it?"

"You'd have to ask Uncle Storm. He took care of everything. I just told him I wanted to live in town. He and Lu decided it was best if I had family staying with me, and this duplex keeps us close, yet with privacy, according to him."

"I'm your family," Jace said, an uncomfortable prickle teasing his senses. He couldn't say that Sawyer had ever been an enthusiastic bride—he'd practically had to drag her to Vegas—but he began to wonder if she planned on keeping him as far away from her and the babies as possible. "I'm your family, and I can care for my wife just fine. Although Lu and Storm are always welcome, I plan on taking very good care of you."

"That's nice," she said, her tone careful, "except I don't want that, Jace."

She hadn't protested his presence when she'd been at the hospital. He combed his mind for anything that might have happened between then and now, only a few days later. "Look, I know you're worried—"

"Yes, and having time to myself is the best way for me to relax." She looked at him. "I'm going to live alone."

"It's Wolf, isn't it?" Jace asked, hit by a sudden thought. "You're afraid to stay at the ranch or Storm's. If you're here in town, you think you're safer. You're practically within shouting distance of Sheriff Cartwright's office."

She looked away. "I'm a little tired. I'm going to take a nap."

She was shutting him out. He could feel her withdrawal from him so clearly. "It doesn't feel honest," he said, leaning against a wall.

Sawyer looked up at him warily. "What doesn't feel honest?"

"You trying to run me off, when you spent so many months—more than a year, if we want to get technical—chasing me." He crossed his arms, stared at his wife, a little amused. "It's dishonest."

"I'm sorry you feel that way." She sent him a glare to show him she wasn't sorry at all, but he wasn't buying any of her story.

Yet he didn't want to push her, not when she was home from the hospital after a scare. Whatever was bugging his little wife would have to wait. Jace studied her, thinking how pretty she looked in a rose-colored maternity dress, snuggled on the floral sofa with a soft white throw across her lap. She looked like a princess—even though she said she was as big as a house.

Something didn't make sense. "I'm going to go. I need to get back because I'm riding canyon tonight, but—"

"Canyon!" Sawyer stared at him. "You have canyon duty?"

He shrugged. "We all take turns doing it. All seven of us, and Xav Phillips when he's around, keep an eye on what's going on over there, especially now that the new land purchase is pretty overrun with strangers and law enforcement." Jace looked at his wife curiously. "Why?"

"It just surprises me."

"You know Wolf's been trying to get onto the ranch for a long time. We're making sure that Rancho Diablo stays secure, but it's not easy now that there are reporters and Feds everywhere. We're constantly looking to make certain that none of Wolf's people manage to sneak onto Rancho Diablo under the guise that they're with the law or reporters." He shrugged. "I wouldn't put it past them to try."

"I really wish you didn't have to do canyon duty." Sawyer looked out the window, to all appearances unperturbed. Yet he sensed she wasn't as casual as she appeared. "Maybe Ash could go with you."

"Ash is hanging out with Fiona and Burke. They wouldn't like to think that they're part of the coverage, but we all agree Fiona's always going to be a target. She's pretty much the proverbial rock in Wolf's boot."

Sawyer didn't look at him. Jace was having trouble reading her. "I'll text you later, check in on you."

"Not if you're in the canyons. You won't have cell service." She finally looked up at him. "Trade off with one of your brothers tonight, Jace."

"Why?" He was completely surprised by her request.

"The canyons are dangerous."

"No more than the rest of Rancho Diablo." He opened the front door. "I'll text you in the morning. I don't want to call in case you're asleep."

She lowered her gaze, pressed her lips together as if she wanted to say more but wouldn't allow herself. "All right," she finally said, and he nodded and went out.

When he glanced back toward the window where her floral sofa was situated, he saw her watching him. He waved, and she waved back once—then disappeared from the window.

Frowning, Jace got in the truck and drove away.

Sawyer was frantic. The last thing Jace needed to do was ride the canyon tonight. After Wolf's warning to her, she knew Jace could easily get picked off.

"This pregnancy stuff is not for the faint of heart," she muttered, reaching for her cell phone and dialing up the one person she could count on to help her.

Maybe.

Chapter 12

Thirty minutes later, Ash walked in, with Fiona at her side.

"I brought backup," Ash said. "The redoubtable aunt usually has a word of wisdom or two."

"More than two," Fiona said with asperity. "And I want to see what we've got to work with as far as a nursery is concerned." She hugged Sawyer, holding her close. "How are you, my dear? That was quite a scare you had."

Sawyer allowed herself to bathe in the Callahan kindness for a moment before stiffening her courage. "It was a scare, but I'm much better now. Thank you."

Fiona and Ash sat on chairs across from her, and Fiona placed a plate of cookies on the coffee table between them. She glanced around the room, which was bare of pictures, knickknacks and personal effects. "So what is this assistance you require? Decorating help, no doubt? You can't do much in your condition. We don't want you to move even your toes."

"It's a dilemma, really, and I need your advice."

Fiona leaned closer, her eyes bird-bright. "Advice is my favorite thing to give."

Ash laughed. "She's serious, too. So feel free to get started."

Sawyer feared that telling everything that was on her mind would cost her goodwill points with her new family, but she had to do it to keep her husband safe. And the Callahans. "I've thought long and hard about this, but there's no other way to do it than to just clear my conscience."

"Gracious," Fiona said, "this doesn't sound like you want tips on decorating a nursery in a tiny apartment." She glanced around, clearly finding the small, vintage duplex not completely to her liking. "You're making me feel like a cup of tea may be in order."

"I don't have any dishes or a teapot. Yet," Sawyer said hastily. "I'm so sorry I can't offer you anything more than a bottle of water."

Fiona sniffed. "Jace warned us as to the conditions. We came prepared. Ash, if you wouldn't mind?"

Her new sister-in-law smiled. "Sawyer, I hope you're ready for busybodying to the max."

"I don't know what you mean, niece," Fiona said. "Please bring in the housewarming gift."

Ash went out the door. Fiona looked at Sawyer. "While we're alone, I should tell you that I already know what you're going to say."

"You do?"

"Yes, I do. You don't have to do this," Fiona told her.

"You're one of us now, and nothing that came before matters."

Sawyer felt her worry melt a little in the face of such consideration. "Thank you, but I really need to get it all out of my system."

"I figured you'd feel that way. Just remember, then, that on the other side of confession lays peace. We don't judge. Unless it's Wolf. Then I myself enjoy being judgmental."

Sawyer couldn't help smiling. "You're trying to make me feel better."

"It's working, too, isn't it?" Fiona demanded with a wink.

"It actually is." Yet Sawyer still felt guilty.

Ash came inside, shopping bags hanging from her arms. "I hope you don't mind that my aunt selected the decorating colors and scheme for your new home."

"Well, Sawyer doesn't have time to do it," Fiona said, her tone practical. "She has to concentrate on staying strong for the babies."

Ash set the shopping bags in front of Sawyer. "Please feel free to keep what you like. We'll take the rest back."

Sawyer pulled out a silver teakettle, pleased. "How nice! Fiona, will you do the honors?"

"Gladly." She went into the small kitchen and set the kettle on to boil as Sawyer pulled out darling white and light blue dish towels and cloth napkins. A braided rug for the entrance, and a welcome mat for the front porch. "I didn't know how much stuff you could possibly have accumulated during the years you worked as a bodyguard, so I took the liberty of picking out a few things for a small housewarming gift," she called from the kitchen. "Every well-run, cozy home must have a teakettle and teapot, in my opinion."

"And heaven knows, her opinion runs everything," Ash whispered. "I'll take back what you don't want."

Sawyer pulled soft tan towels from a bag. "I love it all. It's starting to feel more like home."

"Have you found the teapot yet?" Fiona called. "I'm ready for it."

Sawyer reached into the final bag, pulled out a delicate white pot with pretty flowers curling around the base. "This is so sweet. You shouldn't have done so much."

"I should have if I'm going to be here watching babies. I have to have my comforts," Fiona said, taking the teapot into the kitchen. "Although I wish you hadn't moved so far away from the ranch. Still, I understand, I guess. I'll wash this up, and then tea is served. Then we can get down to business."

Ash looked at her. "Whatever you have to tell us, just know that we'll do anything to help. The most important thing is that you concentrate on your health. And my niece and nephew," she said, pleased.

"It's difficult," Sawyer admitted. "This isn't the easiest conversation I've ever had."

Fiona came back in and sat down. "Now, how can we help you?"

Sawyer swallowed. "Ash, you remember when you asked me the other day what my uncle might be hiding?"

Fiona glanced at Ash. "Ashlyn Chacon Callahan! You didn't say that to Sawyer!"

"It's okay," Sawyer said quickly. "I don't think my uncle's hiding anything, but Wolf called me."

"Wolf!" Fiona shook her head. "You hung up on him

right away, I hope! And tell Jace. He'll know what to do about Wolf."

"No, no," Sawyer said. "That's exactly what I don't want. I don't want Jace doing anything. In fact, I'm swearing you both to secrecy." The last thing she needed was the father of her children going all gonzo on the most evil men she'd ever had the bad occasion to meet. "I don't want Jace in the canyons anymore."

Ash reached for her hand, rubbed it. "You're scared. Your fingers are trembling."

"I'm not scared for me. I honestly believe I'm too huge to be a target for Wolf. It's going to take a crane to get me off this sofa. My husband is another matter. And Wolf also threatened my uncle and Lu." Sawyer sipped some tea for strength. "I want you to convince Jace not to do his job. He wouldn't be happy with me if he knew I was telling you this." Ash handed her a tissue, which she took gratefully. "Just until I have the babies."

Fiona and Ash looked at her, their eyes huge with concern.

"We can't keep Jace from his job, or the canyons. But I'll talk to Uncle Wolf," Ash said with determination.

Sawyer started. "No!"

Fiona looked at her. "Why would Wolf threaten Storm?"

"Wolf said he'll make me miserable for turning on him," Sawyer said miserably. "He knows I told you about the wire and the spying. He said I should have helped my uncle get him the information he needed. But Wolf doesn't understand that my uncle isn't his pawn. I'm not his pawn. I'm not going to do anything to hurt Jace. I'm a Callahan now."

"That's right," Ash said. "Wolf has never understood that Callahans stick together."

"This is too hard for her to deal with," Fiona said to Ash. "I'll talk to Wolf myself." She stood, a resolute figure in a turquoise-blue dress and delicate white boots. "In fact, I'll kick his mangy a—"

"No, Aunt." Ash pulled Fiona back down next to her. "All Sawyer wants us to do is keep Jace from the firing line. There'll be no butt-kicking. In fact, we're going to lie very low."

Fiona patted Sawyer's hand. "My niece is right. You just rest and don't think another thing about all this Wolf nonsense."

"Tell me the plan so I can at least enjoy it vicariously."

Ash looked at her. "You're tough, I'll grant you that. But we don't have a plan. Yet. But we will."

Sawyer leaned back. "I knew I could count on you."

"Don't let Wolf rattle you. All sound and fury, but that's it." Fiona got up. "Next time I come by, I'm bringing catalogs for you to peruse for baby decor."

"Thank you, Fiona." Sawyer managed a smile.

"In the meantime, I'm sure my brother told you not to open the door to anyone," Ash said.

"I can't even get up," Sawyer pointed out.

"That's right." Ash looked at her. "How do people get in to see you, like the nurse?"

"I've been leaving the door unlocked, since I'm lying right here." Sawyer didn't mention she'd placed a pink Taser and a can of pepper spray under her floral sofa, within easy reach. The Taser had been a housewarming gift from Lu, the pepper spray from the sheriff's wife. "Jace says the door has to be locked from now on.

But Lu and Storm are next door, and the sheriff is right around the corner—"

"Listen to my brother," Ash said. "Sometimes he actually makes sense." There were hugs all around and the two women left.

Sawyer sank against the pillow, closed her eyes and hoped they could keep Jace from canyon duty tonight. She didn't want the father of her children in danger—especially when Wolf had sounded so very definite about what he planned to do to her uncle and her husband.

Wolf had been angry. As if she'd somehow betrayed him. She couldn't figure out why he should feel betrayed. She'd never been on Team Wolf. She hated him for exactly the same reasons the Callahans did: he was determined to destroy them. She wished she was still fit, could still fight the good fight. Prove herself to Jace.

She must have dozed off, because the babies kicked inside her, waking her—and then the door blew open. She gasped and reached for the Taser.

"Jace! What are you doing here?"

She stared at her husband. He was carrying a bouquet of flowers and a box that looked as if it came from the Books'n'Bingo Society tearoom.

"I was relieved of canyon duty," he said. "Where'd you get the cute little pink equalizer?"

"I'm not supposed to tell, but Lu gave it to me. She said no woman should be without one. Who took your shift?"

He closed the door. "My sister." He raised a brow, handed over the flowers. "She said she wanted me to have a night off with my bride."

"That was nice of her," Sawyer said, feeling a bit guilty.

He leaned over and gave her a big smooch. "That flowery sofa sure looks good with you on it."

"I don't want Ash in the canyons," Sawyer said, ignoring his flattery. It was harder to ignore his strong muscles as he wrapped big hands around her stomach.

"No one tells little sister what to do." He kissed Sawyer's belly. "I hope her namesake doesn't follow that closely in her aunt's footsteps, but I'm afraid she probably will. None of the Callahan females know how to mind."

Sawyer snorted. "Thank you for the flowers. And are those snacks?"

"I was warned that it would be best if I showed up bearing gifts, although I told my sister that you'd be happy just to see me."

Sawyer raised a brow. "And I am. Hand me a cookie. Can't you send Dante or Tighe to the canyon instead of Ash?" She was trying to keep the matter light, but Wolf had really worried her.

"Everybody's got their own assignments. Ash just relieved me of mine because she didn't need to guard Fiona tonight. Fiona said she was taking Burke to a movie and that she didn't require watching, so Ash kicked me off the grid."

That wasn't the result Sawyer had wanted. She supposed she should have seen that coming, though. "I thought Ash wasn't supposed to be in the canyons alone."

"She's not, really. Galen doesn't like it. But she's earned her stripes. There's really not anything we can do about it." He looked at the Taser. "I hope you never have to use this, but I wish I'd thought of it." He kissed her hand. "More to the point, I wish my wife didn't have to be confined to bed with a Taser because my uncle's such a—"

"Not in front of the babies," Sawyer teased.

"I can watch my mouth. I'll watch yours, too," he said, kissing her, and Sawyer sighed with happiness as Jace wrapped her in his arms.

"So I heard Wolf called you," he said, and Sawyer froze.

"They weren't supposed to tell you!"

He looked at her. "Who wasn't supposed to tell me?"

"Fiona and Ash!"

He raised a brow. "Tell me what?"

She hesitated. "Who told you Wolf called me?"

"Your uncle." Jace frowned at her. "Why wouldn't you want me to know?"

"I just don't. Didn't. And don't frown at me. I've got a lot on my mind and I feel suddenly like I might be prone to tears."

He smiled. "That'd be a first. I've never seen you cry."

She sighed and leaned back, closed her eyes for a minute. "Don't tempt me. I might wail all over you, and I assure you, it won't be pretty."

"Anyway, back to Wolf," he prompted.

"I didn't want you to know because I didn't want you going all ape on his big stupid self. I'd like to keep you alive for the duration of our marriage," she snapped.

"Duration?" He rubbed her belly. "You don't have to protect me from my uncle. Although I realize it's second nature to you. I'm the man, I'll protect my family." He kissed her hand. "And I want to start protecting you by putting the wedding ring I gave you on your hand."

She looked at him. "How will it protect me?"

"It's a magic ring. Didn't I tell you?" He grinned at her, sexy as sin. "Where is it?"

"In my purse. Under the sofa ruffle, next to the Taser and the pepper spray."

"Another gift from Lu?"

"The sheriff's wife."

He grunted as he checked out her stock under the ruffle. "I'm impressed. All you need now are handcuffs and maybe a slingshot."

She sat up. "I hadn't thought of a slingshot!"

"Easy, babe. I wasn't serious." He sighed, and pulled out the ring box. "Now let's get this magic ring on you, so you can lie here and rest in a bubble of good health and happy thoughts."

She put out her finger. "Go for it."

"That easy? You've had the ring this long and suddenly you don't mind wearing it?"

"I want to make you happy," she said softly. "Anyway, I wanted to wear your ring for a long time."

"I know. You won me just for that purpose." He slipped the ring on her finger, looked at it for a minute. "You have beautiful hands. This is exactly how I imagined it would look on them."

She smiled. "That's sweet, Jace."

He kissed her. "It's true. I wanted you to have the most beautiful ring I could find, for my most beautiful bride. I didn't want you to regret breaking your piggy bank wide-open for me."

"You have a lot of ego, cowboy."

He grinned. "I know."

Just when she thought she couldn't be any happier, that maybe everything that had kept them apart was totally in the past now, the door opened with a crash.

Wolf walked in with a nasty, know-it-all grin on his face.

"Hello, nephew, Ms. Cash," he said, and Jace tensed.

"How dare you enter my home without knocking?" Sawyer demanded, incensed. "You go right back out and knock. When I say come in, then you may. Until then, you're not a welcome guest. And it's Mrs. Callahan to you, thanks."

He grinned at her, and her blood boiled. This was exactly why her and Jace's marriage was always in a state of disarray. This man was a certain, surefire disruptor.

Something had to change.

"If you don't go outside and wait to be invited to enter like a normal person," Sawyer said, "I'll call Sheriff Cartwright."

"Now, young lady," Wolf said, his voice patronizing.

God, she hated being patronized. And she hated being helpless.

She hit him with her Taser, and Wolf collapsed to the floor.

"Nice shot," Jace said.

"He looks like he's drooling a bit. Will you go make sure he doesn't drool on my new rug Fiona got me? I'll call the sheriff."

"Never mind." Jace sighed and sent a text. "The cleanup crew will be here in a minute." He went to check on his uncle, turning him faceup with his boot. "When are you ever going to learn?"

Wolf lay almost deathly still. "I didn't kill him, did I?" Sawyer asked. "I know Running Bear has rules about killing off his prodigal son."

"You didn't kill him. But that little pink version of

whoop-ass works much better than I thought it would." Jace looked at her. "What am I going to do with you?"

She just hoped her husband loved her. "I'll let you decide."

He looked out the window. "The cavalry's arrived. They must have been in town." He opened the door, and Galen and Sloan came inside.

"Hello, Sawyer," they said, like respectful school-boys, and then looked down at their uncle.

"He never learns," Sloan said.

Ash appeared in the doorway. "Toss him in the back of the truck with the rest of the trash we need to haul off."

Galen looked at Sawyer. "Are you all right?"

She nodded. "I'm fine."

"Your work? I presume my brother didn't do this," Galen said, eyeing the pink gun.

"Yes. Thanks."

Galen looked at Jace. "Can I see you outside?" he asked, as Wolf was rolled up in a tarp Ash provided. Their uncle was whisked away, as if he'd never been there.

Jace glanced at his wife. "I'll be right back. You take a nap."

He followed his brother outside. "What's up?"

They watched as Wolf was bundled into the truck bed. "This can't go on," Galen said. "Next time, you might not be here. And my understanding of the situation is that Wolf is really aggravated with the Cashs."

"He was just trying to cause trouble. He saw my truck, and came in, anyway," Jace pointed out. "My wife had issues with his mouth. She doesn't like disrespect."

"She was trying to prove she's on our side."

"I don't know," Jace said. "Maybe." He didn't think Sawyer had time enough to think through the situation. She'd merely reacted. "Anyway, she has nothing to prove. She's a Callahan."

"Ash says Sawyer's all hung up about the fact that she spied for her uncle." Galen shrugged. "I don't want her overcompensating. Wolf's dangerous. So are his compadres. Tell her."

"Tell her what?"

"Tell her everything is good, that she doesn't need to prove herself to you anymore."

"She doesn't."

"Try to understand the feelings in her heart."

Sawyer hadn't wanted to wear his ring before. Maybe Galen had a point. Jace shrugged. "I'll talk to her."

Galen slapped him on the back. "See you at the ranch later for the meeting."

He'd forgotten. He glanced back at the duplex, saw Sawyer's drawn face peering out at them. "I don't know if I can leave, Galen."

His brother nodded, got in his truck. "I understand. Sawyer might feel better if she wasn't alone tonight, anyway, considering Wolf's unexpected visit."

Jace nodded, went inside and closed the door.

"Now what happens?" Sawyer asked.

"Now you and I go back to where we were." He sat next to her for a long, sweet kiss.

"Jace, wait." She pulled back. "You can't just act like nothing happened."

"What do you mean? Nothing did happen. Not really. My uncle was being rude, you taught him a lesson."

"And you're okay with me shooting him?"

"You deserve a blue ribbon. My own Annie Oakley."

He put a hand on her stomach. "My uncle got what was coming to him."

She nodded. "Okay."

But he sensed she wasn't. Not really.

"I'm going to nap, if you don't mind."

"No problem. I'll nap with you."

"No, Jace." She shook her head. "I think I want to be alone for a while."

He hesitated. Galen had just postulated that she wouldn't want to be alone after Wolf's visit. She was basically telling him to leave.

"Are you sure?"

"I'm sure."

He had the uncomfortable feeling that they were married, but not really together. Wherever she was, that was his home, too, right? Yet Sawyer was kicking him out, like a date who'd stayed too long. "Guess I'll head over to the family meeting, then. Text me, or call me, if you need anything."

"I'll be fine. I'm just going to sleep."

He kissed her and left, not feeling good about it all. Every single woman who'd had a bad man walk into her home wouldn't want to be alone—every single woman except maybe Ash and Fiona. Jace shook his head. He glanced toward the window, but Sawyer wasn't looking out at him.

He had the uncomfortable feeling something wasn't right, but whatever it might be wasn't penetrating his thick skull. Jace started his truck and headed to Rancho Diablo.

Chapter 13

Sawyer didn't call him to come around much, and Jace had the uncomfortable feeling that his wife had separated emotionally from him in some way. For two months, he was an occasional guest at the duplex, only invited every once and again. He got used to carrying a sleeping bag for the nights his wife allowed him to stay over, which wasn't more than once a week.

Sawyer said she liked being alone, that as uncomfortable as she was with the aches and pains that kept her awake, she didn't want to keep him awake, as well. He supposed that made sense, but he'd rather be with his wife. Besides the sofa, there wasn't a stick of furniture in the house—no bed, no kitchen table, nothing. He'd offered, as had Fiona and Ash, to bring catalogs for her to choose from, but Sawyer shook her head.

She did, however, let Fiona and Ash and Lu bring

over two white cribs from the ranch, and all the baby things their hearts desired for the nursery. He wasn't sure what to think about that. Apparently Sawyer planned on staying in the little duplex, but she couldn't sleep on the floral sofa forever.

He was stuck in serious limbo.

And then in late April he got the call from Storm, of all people, that they'd taken Sawyer to the hospital. Jace was about to tear out of the meeting that was being held in the upstairs library, where his brothers and sister were arguing about what might have happened to the Diablo mustangs, which hadn't been seen in months, when Storm said, "And by the way, Sawyer says not to come until she calls you."

"What?" He'd just about had it with all the stop signs from his darling wife.

"She says she's just gone into labor. Could be hours before she has the babies. She wants you to keep working—in fact, she said she expects you to understand that you're going to have your fair share of diaper and bottle duty soon, so put your time in at the ranch now, while you can."

Jace frowned. That sounded a little better. "I'm coming, anyway."

"I thought you'd feel that way," Storm said cheerfully. "If you wouldn't mind, bring a thermos of coffee, would you? This stuff here is dreck. If we're going to be here for a long time, I think you're going to want something that resembles coffee and not sludge."

"Sure. Thanks, Storm." He hung up, and his family looked at him.

"Babies are on the way." As he said it, his chest filled with pride.

"It's time! I'm going to be an aunt again!" Ash leaped from the sofa and hugged his neck. "I'll drive you. Come on."

He stared around the room at his brothers, who grinned at him with knowing expressions.

"It's your turn," Sloan said. "You don't know it, but your life is about to change. It'll never be the same again. Enjoy these last few moments of rarified pre-daddy air, because you'll never know them again for the rest of your life. What you're about to smell is entirely different."

His brothers guffawed like asses.

"No sleep. No silence," Dante said. "No more navel gazing, which you have to admit, you've honed to a fine art."

Jace raised a brow.

Tighe leaned back on the sofa with a grin. "From now on, no such thing as life unplanned. Every moment has a schedule, a routine. You'll feel guilty if you're not at ballet lessons, church groups, or being ridden like a pony."

His brothers didn't seem to be too unhappy. Rather, they seemed like men who lived in a secret world he had yet to enter. "Anything else?"

Falcon waved a majestic hand. "We have no more secrets to offer. You're in the daddy club now. Just be sure you remember that every day that ends in *y* now starts with baby and ends with baby." He grinned, proud of his contribution.

"What a bunch of wienies," Ash said. "Are you trying to scare him to death?"

"For me it's the scrapbooking," Galen said. "The photo puzzles, the picture files. How to capture all the little moments that don't seem important to anyone else but you. Like the first time they smile at you." He grinned at Jace. "And the first giggle—there's nothing, nothing, nothing better than baby laughter. It's innocent, it's delightful, it's free. And your whole spirit goes straight up like a lightning rod. It's the gift of the Creator, allowing you another peek at true happiness."

They all stared at Galen.

"Wow," Ash said, "you almost made me want to have a baby, Galen."

Jace's throat went tight. Everything his brothers teased him about sounded awesome. He couldn't wait to meet his own children, to hold them. He was a family man, through and through. "I can't wait," he said, past the tightness.

His brothers came over and pounded his back.

"Congratulations, bro," Sloan said. "We tease, but only because we know you wanted it from the time you were a kid. Family was always your cause."

His other brothers murmured in agreement.

"Thanks," Ash said. "He says thanks. He has to go now, as he's having my niece and nephew. Goodbye, brothers. Try to achieve world peace while we're gone, okay? Find the Diablos, and other creative things. In other words, be productive."

She pulled Jace down the hall, and he let her. "Gosh, they're windbags," she said. "I love them, but holy smoke. Always have to stick their scrawny little oars in. Are you all right?"

"Yeah. I promised Storm a thermos of coffee. He says the coffee there isn't up to par."

"I'll do it. You go change, and I'll fill up some thermoses and grab some snacks. Might be a long wait. None of us have delivered in under eight hours, I don't think."

"Us?" he teased.

"We Callahans. You're having the last children of the family, Jace, unless the talking heads upstairs become more focused on babymaking. Go change those clothes. You've been riding canyon, and you don't want to insult your new babies' nostrils with eau de barn."

"Ash, you'll have children," Jace said, feeling as if he needed to comfort his sister. She had such a broken heart over Xav Phillips. But there was nothing that could be done about it. "You'll find the right man one day, and you'll have a baby."

"Go," she said, waving a thermos at him. "Today is your day. And if you stand around yakking like the rest of our brothers, we'll miss the arrival of my niece and nephew. One thing your little ones are going to always know is that their aunt Ash was right there with a catcher's mitt, waiting to teach them the ways."

He loved his sister. More than anyone, she had his back. She was tough and fearless, and he wished he was better at making the women in his life happy.

But what Ash said made sense. He, too, was going to be there, from the beginning. When they fell, when they succeeded, his children were always going to know that their father loved them.

Even if their mother wasn't in love with him.

He tore up the stairs, his mind in overdrive. He showered, so fast it couldn't be called a shower but a rinse, then jumped into fresh jeans, grabbed a clean shirt. Hauled down the stairs when Ash roared up at him that he was slower than molasses at Christmas, and that the babies were going to be going off to college before he pulled his head out. By his watch, he'd been upstairs all of eight minutes.

He hurried through the house and followed his sister

out the door. "Let me carry the picnic," he said, taking the hamper from her. "What'd you pack? Enough food for the entire hospital?"

"The nursing staff will want cookies. It's manners to share what you have with nurses and visitors. Everybody likes a party, Jace, and we want the babies spoiled by all. They've had a tough start."

"But they're not going to be eating the cookies," he said, laughing.

"You laugh, brother, but when you share your toys, other people like you."

He held the door so she could hop in the truck. Then he shoved the hamper in the back and went around to the driver's side, thinking about sharing his toys. They hadn't really had toys to speak of in the tribe, but his Callahan nieces and nephews had toys like mad, and maybe he should stop by the hospital gift shop to pick up bears....

Just then a sting in his chest stopped his thoughts. Jace felt himself falling back from the truck door he'd been about to open, and it was so very strange to be falling, not in control of himself, staring up at the sky, with Ash's wide eyes staring down at him. Jace was amazed that he couldn't feel his body. He was floating, and felt strange, like he'd never felt before, light and airy, his mind no longer full of a thousand thoughts.

The last thing he remembered was Ash's frantic screams. He wanted to tell her it was going to be all right, that he'd protect her; he always had, he always would. He'd take care of Sawyer and the babies, too, because that's what he did. He was a guard against darkness and evil, a shield for the good in the world, because

Running Bear had told him from the time he was young that he was a warrior.

But he was so tired. So he went to sleep, overtaken by exhaustion, but comforted by the thought that when he woke up he was going to tell his wife how much he loved her.

Sawyer was his whole life.

"Jace can come in now," Sawyer told her uncle and Lu. She'd had an emergency C-section, and the babies were doing well, though they were tiny. Sawyer thought Ashley and Jason were the most beautiful babies she'd ever seen, and before she fell asleep, she wanted to see the expression on Jace's face when he was introduced to his children.

He was going to be so proud.

Ash wore a funny look. "Jace will be by in a little while."

Sawyer thought he'd have been breaking down the door by now. In fact, she was amazed that Jace had waited so patiently until after she'd had the C-section to come barreling in. She hadn't wanted him to worry as she had when the doctor had told her they'd have to perform the emergency procedure. The babies had been stressed, and everything had moved awfully fast.

"Where is he?" she asked Ash.

His sister set two adorable teddy bears down in the window. "He got called to do something at the ranch. It couldn't be avoided."

Ash was acting strange. She'd been tickled and joyful when she'd seen the babies, snapping a thousand pictures—but when the newborns were whisked away to the neonatal nursery, she'd turned solemn. Sawyer thought her sister-in-law's eyes were red, as if she'd been crying.

That was impossible. Ash never cried.

"Are you all right, Ash?"

"Me? I'm fine. Good job bringing my namesake into the world."

Sawyer smiled. "It was an amazing experience. I can't wait to do it again someday."

Ash looked pained. "You should sleep now. What do they feed you around here, anyhow? I brought a hamper of goodies to Lu and Storm and the staff. You want me to sneak you something?"

She shook her head, lay back against the pillow. "No, thanks. I'll just wait for Jace to get here. I think the nurses do some special candlelight dinner thing for the mom and dad after the babies are born."

Ash hesitated. "Tonight?"

"I think the night of the birth, yes. But I'm sure it could be another night, too. I'll go home the day after tomorrow, though the babies will stay a little longer. Why?"

"No reason."

Sawyer studied Ash, checking out her pale face and her eyes, which didn't seem quite as bubbly as they had when she'd visited her at the duplex. And Ash had been a frequent visitor. Almost daily. Like a bodyguard.

They were all bodyguards and protectors, Sawyer included. Jace was, too—and he wouldn't have missed the babies' birth for anything. He would have torn a hole in the wall to get to his kids, if for no other reason than to see for himself that they were all right, that they had everything they needed. The warrior code was strong in

Jace. He was more quiet about it than some of the other brothers, and even Ash—but he was a strong defender.

And he would have been here for his children.

"Where is he?" she demanded. "And don't tell me he's doing something at the ranch, because your face is giving you away. You look like a ghost has infested your grave."

Ash burst into tears. "I can't tell you."

Alarm flooded Sawyer's bloodstream. "You'd better tell me, or I'll get out of this bed and pull your hair."

Ash blew her nose, tears brimming in her eyes. "I want to tell you, but I can't."

Sawyer made a move to get up, which hurt like hell because her stitches pulled, and Ash gasped, put her hands up in surrender.

"Get back in the damn bed! If the nurses see you moving around, they'll yell at me."

"Since when do you care who's yelling at you about what? Where's Jace?"

"In the operating room," Ash said. "He had a slight accident."

Sawyer blinked. "It's not slight if he's in the O.R." Her heart rate sped up uncomfortably.

"He's going to be fine." Ash swallowed hard, blew her nose on a tissue. "But I have to go now, Sawyer."

"If you step one foot out that door, I'm changing Ashley's name to Bessie Brunhilda Callahan—"

"You wouldn't!"

"I would. And you'll no longer be the namesake aunt," Sawyer said coldly. "Tell me everything about my husband."

Ash stalked around the room, upset. "We were on our way here. He'd just put the hamper in the truck when—"

her eyes widened as she looked at Sawyer "—when someone shot him."

Sawyer gasped. "Shot him!"

"Don't worry. The doctors wasted no time getting him into the O.R. And Galen's in there overseeing everything, and no doubt whispering the words of healing to him."

"I've got to see him!" Sawyer wished she could get out of this stupid bed. She was tired of being helpless. "Find a nurse who will wheel me to his room."

"No nurse will. There's not a one who will risk her job, so you can forget that. And don't ask me, I'm already in enough trouble." Ash was clearly miserable. "I shouldn't have even told you. Your uncle Storm told me not to. I thought that was good advice. But I'm so worried that I blabbed!" she said with a wail. "I never blab!"

Ash was so upset about her brother that she wasn't herself. Sawyer tried to stay calm despite the panic swamping her. "He'll be all right, won't he? Where'd he get shot?"

"The bullet hit a lung," Ash said, sobbing into a tissue. "I'm so sorry. I shouldn't have told you. I should have listened to your uncle." She blew her nose again, wiped her eyes, and Sawyer felt herself grow cold inside. Tight and angry. Someone had shot her husband, had tried to take away the father of her children. Whoever it was had meant business, aiming, no doubt, for his heart.

Wolf had meant to kill his nephew. Wolf, or perhaps one of his minions, had done his best to steal away what she wanted more than anything on this earth.

She'd shot Wolf with the Taser, and he'd returned the favor.

"I'm going to kill him," she muttered under her breath, and Ash straightened at her furious words.

"You'll have to beat me to it," she said softly, and Sawyer's skin crawled at her tone. "I don't care what Running Bear says. It's my life's mission to make sure my uncle never tries to hurt any of my family ever again."

Chapter 14

Jace awakened, feeling like death. He was groggy, he hurt like hell and something wasn't right with his body. It was out of focus in some strange way. And he wasn't at home. Something had happened to him. He was going to be with his babies at their births, and then he'd fallen. He remembered that much, because of the deep beauty of the sky overhead and Ash's face hovering over him, her navy eyes wide with fear. That's what was wrong—Ash was never afraid.

His sister had been terrified.

"You awake?" he heard someone ask.

He peered at the corner of the room. "Where am I?" he asked.

"In the hospital," the soothing voice replied.

He knew that voice. It spoke to his soul, reminded him of who he was. "Grandfather. What happened?"

"You were shot." Running Bear stepped closer to the bed to look down at him. "Coming from the north, where the canyons are, three scouts crossed Rancho Diablo. One of them shot you."

It made sense. "Don't worry. I've been shot before, when I was in… When I was somewhere."

"You were overseas," Running Bear murmured. "In Iraq. But the enemy here meant to kill you, too."

"Why?"

"My son is evil. There is no purpose to his desire to kill. His heart is black, and it can never be clean again. He has forgotten the old ways, his ancestors, the ancient words, loyalty to family. Everything has left him. So you must live."

Jace grunted, but it came out more like a pained groan. "Of course I'm going to live. I survived Iraq. I can survive my uncle."

His grandfather touched Jace's forehead, put a hand over his heart, and Jace felt strength flood into him.

"Energy transfer," Running Bear said. "Rest. Galen was in the O.R. with you. He spoke the healing words. You will live to fight another day."

"I'll live to fight many years." He looked up at his grandfather. "I have babies to teach the ways to. Where are my children? Where's Sawyer?"

"One floor down. You'll see her soon."

"I'll see her now." He struggled to sit up, but his grandfather pushed him gently back into the bed.

"I've got to go," Jace said. "Sawyer needs to know that I'm all right. I'm going to take care of her and protect her always."

"She knows." Running Bear's hand pressed against him. "You can't take danger to her."

Jace stared at him. "What do you mean?"

"You now walk with a shadow. It's not safe to go there."

A chill sliced into Jace. "Am I the one you spoke of, the hunted one?" he asked desperately. "The one who'll bring devastation and danger to the family?"

One of the seven Callahan siblings was the hunted one, but he'd never thought it was him. Jace had always been the family man, the one who longed for tribe, for community, for his own to hold. "Am I?" he demanded.

"I don't know," Running Bear said. "I only know the mysteries, not who puts them in motion."

"It's not me." Jace again tried to make it to the edge of the bed. "It's *not* me. And I have to be with Sawyer. She's my heart, my life, Grandfather."

"I know. But don't take danger to her door."

"How?" He looked at the chief impatiently. "Are they here? Will they try to kill me again? Even here?"

Running Bear sighed. "I do not know the answers."

"You didn't know I was going to be shot, either."

"I did not. Evil hides itself in many forms. Where my son is concerned, I do not always see." His dark eyes looked deeply sad.

He put a hand in front of Jace's face briefly. "Now sleep," he told him. "Sleep and heal. You were born a warrior. You are a shepherd to the land and your family. Sleep, and let healing chase away the evil."

Jace was about to tell his grandfather that he was sorry, he had to get to his wife and babies no matter what—but then he was overcome by weariness so profound that he fell back into the hospital bed, worn-out.

And then peace claimed him. He dreamed of the Diablos running through the canyons, wild and free. He rode a Diablo, and his children rode with him, and his heart was alive and shining with the mysticism and beauty of the spirits. Sawyer stood on a mesa far away, watching proudly. It was a dark, mystical dream, infused with wonder and breathtaking splendor, and Jace was content to watch from afar, called by the majesty, resting in the knowledge that Sawyer and his children were in good hands.

And while he watched himself riding with his children, he heard his grandfather's voice in the background, murmuring the ancient words without pause. Jace heard soft music from a flute that played the lullabies he'd heard in the tribe, as his grandfather's voice reminded him of the spirits.

He was hypnotized and calm, and safe.

For now.

Sally Clausen came to check on Sawyer, and Sawyer realized the nurse was exactly the visitor she needed. "I have to see my husband."

"You will soon," Sally said. "For now it's important that you rest. Your body's been through a lot."

"Sally, help me get to my husband," Sawyer begged. "If I leave here with anyone but a nurse, I'll get put right back in my bed. I know you can spring me. Wheel me to the nursery so I can see my children, and then slip me into my husband's room. Please."

"I can't." Sally's eyes were huge with concern. "Sawyer, I'd do anything for you, but there's a guard on your husband's door in the ICU. No one's getting in except the chief."

"Chief Running Bear?"

"Yes." The nurse nodded. "He's not really supposed

to be in there, but he's in a trance or something. No one dares disturb him, especially not since Jace is doing so much better. It was really touch and go for a while."

Sally's eyes widened further at Sawyer's gasp.

"I think I've said too much already," the nurse stated. "Look, you rest, Sawyer. You want to be strong when your husband is ready to wake up, don't you?"

"Wake up?" Sawyer glared at her. "What do you mean, wake up?"

Sally sighed. "He's in a slight coma."

"It is either a coma or it's not." Her blood roared in her ears. "You go out there and you find the chief of staff of this hospital, and you tell him that I want to see my husband. Today."

Sally backed up at Sawyer's ferocity. "I'll tell the head nurse and she'll pass the word along. But I doubt they'll let you. It's important that Jace rest. Even Ash can't get in to see him."

"Oh, Ash will find a way. Nothing keeps Ash from her brothers, trust me on that." Sawyer slumped back in the bed. "Fine. You pass my message along to the chief of staff. And I'm sorry I crabbed on you, Sally. You've been a really good friend, and I'm…"

"Just feeling at your wits' end. I know. I would be, too. Get some rest." She went out the door, her cheerful sunniness restored, and Sawyer told herself she wasn't going to have any friends left if she didn't quit snapping at everyone who came into her room. She was just so afraid for Jace! "I should have aimed for Wolf's heart with that Taser," she muttered crankily. "Maybe I could have short-circuited it since it's such a tiny, black piece of evil."

She was stunned when Running Bear walked into

the room, his dark face lined with exhaustion. "Running Bear!"

"Hello, Sawyer."

She'd never seen the chief look so tired. "There's Rancho Diablo coffee in that thermos, and cookies in the tin. Fiona brings by a truckload of stuff every day, she says to bribe the nursing staff to take good care of her Callahans. Please, help yourself. I'm pretty sure you need Fiona's sugar jump."

It was a well-known fact that the chief had a sweet tooth for Fiona's baking, not that it showed on his lean frame.

"Your babies are strong," he said.

Sawyer smiled. "Small, but very strong, according to the doctors."

"They have mighty spirits. Their bodies will grow and they will gain weight. All will be well." He munched on a cookie, his color returning a bit. "You have a strong spirit, too."

"I don't think I do," Sawyer said. "I'm so scared, I feel weak."

"Jace is fine. You will see."

She looked at the chief. "I thought he was in a coma."

"He will awaken because he lives for you."

Their marriage hadn't exactly been a bedrock of marital bliss. "I don't know if he'd agree."

"Jace is strong because of you, and you're strong because of him. That can't be broken, unless one of you chooses it."

Was that a warning or just a bland statement? "What can I do to help him? They won't let me see him."

"You will tonight. When you do, tell him what you've been wanting to tell him for a long time."

She looked at Running Bear. "I will."

"It will help him to hear the words. Tell him, too, about his children. That will give him the will to heal faster."

"I'll gladly do it, Running Bear." Time had seemed to be moving so quickly for her and Jace, and she'd never really felt comfortable falling for him. As if she'd somehow taken advantage of the Callahan family. She'd felt awkward because of why she'd hired on at Rancho Diablo—but always, always, she'd loved Jace.

"We understand loyalty in our family," Running Bear said. "Do not be afraid that you are loyal. You would not be right for Jace if you were not true to your family."

"Thank you," she murmured. "How will I see him tonight? No one will take me."

"Jace needs his family. He always has. It's from family that he draws his strength." Running Bear left the room as silently as he'd walked in, and Sawyer sank back against the pillow.

She had to devise a plot to get to her husband. Tomorrow she'd be released, so she'd be free then. She could visit the babies as she liked, too. But the sooner Jace got well, the sooner they could all be together.

Running Bear said Jace was strong because of her. If that was true, then he needed her now.

She got up, pain shooting through her abdomen.

Fiona announced herself just then in a flurry of pink, the scent of warm cinnamon surrounding her like a cloud. "Hello, Sawyer!"

Sawyer grabbed a pair of sandals she'd planned to wear home. "Hi, Fiona."

"What are you doing?" She came over to help with

the sandals so Sawyer wouldn't pull the stitches in her stomach.

"Going to see Jace."

"Oh," his aunt said mildly. "I happened to note that the nursing staff at the desk seem to be a bit preoccupied."

"You just happened to notice that?" Sawyer asked, knowing Fiona loved to meddle.

"I'm a very observant person." She shrugged. "And Running Bear told me you might need some help."

"He thinks my place is with Jace."

"Exactly! The two of you need a total restart, in my opinion. No more of this halfway-married business."

"Halfway married?"

"Indeed. The two of you don't live together. If I hadn't seen your check from the ball, and cashed it, I wouldn't have believed you were the woman who bid so hard for my nephew."

"Fiona, do you have something on your mind?" Sawyer asked, a bit startled by the unusual amount of opinions the woman was sharing.

"Is there ever a time I don't?"

She sat on the bed. "Feel free to share it. But hurry. I'm on a mission." Sawyer waited, her gaze on the tiny woman who ran Rancho Diablo.

"My nephew was shot, I believe, because Wolf is angry that Jace married you. You were supposed to be Wolf's ace in the hole, and as you know, aces are very important."

Sawyer swallowed hard against the guilt rising inside her. "He did say he'd make me regret turning on him. Those were his words."

"But you were never on his side."

"No. I wasn't."

"You must make Wolf believe you have seen the error of your ways."

Sawyer stared at the determined woman who was the backbone for Diablo. "All I care about is my husband and my children. Whatever Wolf thinks is immaterial. He can take a flying leap. And if I were he, I'd be watching my back. I believe he may have a Callahan after him who's not easily intimidated."

Fiona shook her head. "For Jace's sake, for your children's sake, you may have to appear to be more Team Wolf than Team Callahan for the time being."

"I won't do it."

"Not even if it calms Wolf down? Keeps him from sending more agents after your husband? Or your children?" Fiona looked at her curiously. "Then what's your plan?"

"My plan right now is to sneak down the hall to see my husband. When my babies are stronger and the hospital says they can be released, when my husband is well enough, I'm taking him home. We're going to be a family. And I don't care what Wolf thinks about that. I can protect my own family."

"All a very fine plan, except that you can't expect Jace to live holed up in that tiny duplex with you. He belongs at Rancho Diablo."

"It may be months before he's healed. Jace is off *your* team for now." Fiona didn't understand. Sawyer was going to do whatever she had to do to keep her family safe—and if that meant moving to the ends of the earth, that's what they'd do. "Jace already said we should go into hiding. He took me to Colorado for that purpose." She walked to the door of the hospital room. "Running

Bear specifically said at that time that we should be in hiding. I should have listened to his very wise advice. Now," she said, holding Fiona in front of her, "walk slowly past the nurses' station, but not too slowly, because you're always a whirlwind. But I can't keep up with you if you walk your normal flying-aunt gait."

"What are you going to do?"

"I'm taking a walk down the hall with my dear one-time employer," Sawyer said, "which is good, because the nurses advised me to walk a little."

"A little," Fiona said. "Not to the ICU to see your husband."

"Just walk, Fiona."

The older woman sighed. "I don't like being a part of a plot."

"You love being part of a plot. Keep that cheery smile on your face as we stroll to the nursery window so I can see my babies."

"That's better," Fiona said, perking up and not looking so worried. "We can just stand here and look at Jason and Ashley and think about planning their christenings. I'm thinking matching gowns—"

"Continuing on," Sawyer said, as they stopped in front of the nursery window. She took a deep breath at the sight of her children sleeping peacefully, watched over by nurses, and then took Fiona's arm again. "You're doing this for Jace. Keep walking, please."

Fiona sighed, pressed the elevator button. "I've done a lot over the years for my nephews and niece. Twelve nephews and one niece I have, and I don't think any of them ever involved me in a shenanigan like this."

"First time for everything. And I really appreciate you

helping me out. I'm desperate to see my husband." They stopped outside Jace's room. "Don't desert me, please."

"I should think not! Make it snappy!" Fiona glanced around the hall. "I'll have you know the Callahans put a wing on this hospital, and have flooded it with Christmas charity ball funds over the years. I'm an honorary chairman of some such. I can't be seen disobeying hospital protocols and orders. Just lay eyes on him and get out!"

The guard who was parked outside the door straightened when he saw Fiona, obviously recognizing her. Then ever so slowly, he turned his head away, a signal that he didn't see them enter Jace's room.

"Cookies for you and a bonus at Christmas. You have my thanks for keeping an eye on one of my favorite nephews. Of course, they're all my favorite, but you understand," Fiona muttered to the guard, and Sawyer hurried inside the room, stunned by the sight of her husband lying so still. She'd never seen Jace motionless like this, almost lifeless. Even when they slept together, he seemed to have one eye open for danger—or on her.

"Jace," she murmured, and his eyes opened.

He didn't speak. She crept closer to the bed.

"Jace, I'm so sorry. I know you got shot because of me." She bent close to him, kissed him on the lips. "Running Bear says I make you strong. If that's true, then just know that I'm here."

He closed his eyes. She wasn't sure he'd even heard her.

"Sawyer, come on!" Fiona said, whispering urgently into the room.

She held Jace's hand, put her head down on his shoulder. He lay on his side, probably because of the location of the shot he'd taken, and Sawyer's heart bled. "Winning you was the best thing I ever did for myself," she softly said, hoping he could hear her, "although probably not the best thing for you."

"Sawyer!" Fiona called. "You're about to be off my cookie list if you don't come on!"

"I have to go," she told her husband, kissing him again. "But you have to see our babies, Jace. They're worth every penny I paid for you," she said, meaning to be lighthearted, bring a little laughter to him in whatever dark place he was in. But she choked on the words. "From now on, it's you and me and the babies. That's our Team Callahan."

She hated to leave him. Reluctantly, she released his hand and left the room. "Thank you," she murmured to the guard, and let Fiona grab her hand to lead her away.

Fiona's eyes were wide with apprehension. "Did he say anything?"

"No." They made their way back past the nurses' station, Sawyer walking as close to Fiona as she could in order to not attract attention. Her heart was melting inside her. "I'm not sure he heard me."

Fiona made a murmur of distress. Sawyer felt suddenly weak, exhausted, and clutched the other woman's arm.

"Don't you dare fall," Fiona said sternly. "I'll never forgive you if you faint right here, when I told you this was a bad idea! You just lean on me and keep putting one foot in front of the other, young lady!"

Jace's aunt was in drill sergeant mode. Her starchiness made Sawyer smile—and keep moving. When they made it back to her room, Sawyer gratefully returned to her bed, and Fiona collapsed into a chair.

"I'm not so sure that little adventure didn't give me an attack of angina!" Fiona said dramatically, with a hand on her chest.

"Have you ever had an angina attack?" Sawyer asked, easing her sandals off with her toes and letting them fall to the floor.

"Goodness, no. Heartburn, yes." Fiona sighed. "You remind me of me when I was your age. Did I ever tell you the story of the magic wedding dress and how it came to be in my possession?"

"No." Sawyer looked at her through half-closed eyes. "I haven't had the pleasure of hearing that tale from your grand collection of fairy tales."

Fiona sniffed. "I detect a bit of irony in your voice."

"Respect, more likely."

"Glad to hear it. Because after what you just put me through, you and I are going to have a serious discussion about the fact that the magic wedding dress hasn't been aired out in quite a while."

"Why tell me?" Sawyer asked. "Ash is the one you should be spinning tales to."

"Because," Fiona said, "you're the one whose marriage requires a complete makeover, as I said before. You married Jace under false pretenses, knowing all the while you were spying on our family for your uncle." She waved a hand at Sawyer's glare. "Don't deny it. And the only way to make such a deception right is to wear the magic wedding dress and start the whole thing over. If you're sincere about loving my nephew, and I'm sure you believe that you are."

"What does that mean?" Sawyer demanded.

"Could be baby blues talking. Could be your sense of responsibility, because you don't listen to anyone. You wouldn't go into hiding, as Running Bear recommended. You wouldn't move somewhere safe. You shouldn't have visited Jace today, but you did, even though he's not supposed to have visitors."

"Running Bear told me I'd see him tonight."

"That's right." Fiona nodded. "But it wasn't for you to take into your own hands."

Sawyer sighed. "You're right."

"Of course I am." She nodded again, vigorously. "And I'm right about you getting married again—only this time, you have to do it for the correct reasons. In other words, it's high time you proved yourself as something other than a double agent who accidentally got pregnant in the line of duty."

"I most certainly didn't get pregnant on purpose," Sawyer said hotly.

"Oh, I know. And yet I believe there aren't any true accidents. Remember the night you and Somer were shooting at each other at the Carstairs place in Tempest?"

"I wouldn't have ever tried to harm my cousin! Galen hired me for that job, and I would have protected Rose and her babies with my life!" Sawyer was devastated that the Callahans might think differently.

"I know," Fiona said gently, "but the fact remains that you have some growing to do. I know you're an independent lass—that's why you remind me of myself, and my stubborn Irish roots. But we all have to change, Sawyer, do what's best, even if it's counter to our natures."

"And getting married again does that?" she asked skeptically.

"I'd wait until my nephew is himself once more to find out if he wants to marry you again."

Fear jumped inside Sawyer. "Jace wouldn't change his mind."

"No. He wouldn't want to not be married to you. He has two beautiful babies with you. But," Fiona said, her eyes focused on Sawyer, "he nearly died. Who knows?"

"Running Bear says I make Jace strong," Sawyer said, needing to believe that she was good for her husband.

"Of course you do. And you made him weak, vulnerable. You've kept him at arm's length your entire marriage. He's been sleeping in a sleeping bag, when you'd let him come around the duplex." Fiona stood. "Running Bear is right, he always is. I'd have listened to his first advice, I'd listen to his advice today, and I'd listen to the next advice he gives you, should you ever be so fortunate to be on the receiving end of his wisdom again. Now," Fiona said brightly, "I'm off to the Books'n'Bingo Society to see my friends Mavis Night, Corinne Abernathy and Nadine Waters. We're planning the Christmas ball for next year—and guess who's going to be the final Callahan on the block?"

"Ash. But that didn't go over too well last Christmas, did it? Didn't Ash have a secret bidder she hired to put in a top bid?"

Fiona gave her a wise look. "That's the rumor. But Ash says she didn't rig her own bid. No one knows the identity of the bidder who won her this past year except me. This year, I'm planning to flush that bidder out of the shadows." Fiona grinned. "It's fun chasing bidders out of the shadows. I fully anticipate this particular one will be as productive to our family as the last one was!"

She waved at Sawyer as she left. Sawyer lay back exhausted, her mind in turmoil. She needed to feed her babies, needed to think about everything she'd learned.

And she was so overwhelmed by remembering how still Jace had been in his bed that she just wanted to cry.

It was several hours before she remembered Fiona's glee about flushing bidders out of the shadows—and realized the most recent one she'd flushed out had been Sawyer herself, this past Christmas, with the full contents of her savings account.

Fiona had known all along that she was crazy about Jace. She'd also known Sawyer had a conflict of interest where her uncle was concerned. There had been a lot of beautiful women at the ball that night who were just as eager as she was to win Jace.

But Sawyer had been top bidder.

Every word Fiona had said was true. She hadn't acted like a woman who'd won the man of her dreams. Had she felt she hadn't deserved Jace, after all?

She waited until the night shift came on, and her room finally darkened by the nurse. When it sounded quiet in the hall, she slipped on her sandals, and shortly after that Running Bear came to her room, as somehow she'd known he would.

"You have seen Jace," the chief murmured.

"Yes, I have. I'm not sure he knew me, Running Bear."

He nodded. "He did. But he doubts what he knows."

Her heart nearly stopped. "Jace is going to be all right, isn't he?"

Running Bear didn't answer. "You must leave Diablo. When the hospital says you may go, you must take the children and go away."

She gasped. "Go into hiding?"

He looked at her. "Would you have him in further danger?"

"No. Of course not. Nor the children!"

"Then that is what you will do."

Sawyer hesitated. "Fiona thinks Wolf shot my husband because he felt I'd betrayed him. I was supposed to get information for him, through my uncle, apparently. And since I didn't do that, because I married a Callahan instead, this is the price I'm going to have to pay."

Running Bear's expression was inscrutable. "One never tries to discern the mind of someone who does not think with wisdom and understanding. What is known is that Wolf nearly killed Jace."

Sawyer felt herself grow weak with fear. She told herself to not give in to the gnawing panic thundering in her ears. "So you want us to go."

"You and the children. Yes."

"And Jace?"

"Only time will tell."

Running Bear left. Sawyer got back in bed and made herself close her eyes.

Pictures of Jace danced in her head, including the many times he'd made love to her, in the open, wherever, before they'd ever had a bed. Stolen moments she'd known weren't really hers to steal. He was a Callahan, the man she'd fallen for despite knowing that a Callahan would probably never marry a Cash. Couldn't marry a Cash.

She'd set her heart on the moon, and hoped somehow it would come back down to earth, wherever Jace was. She'd gone away for many months, trying to keep her head together about her feelings for him—and still, when she came back, they'd found each other.

They'd made two adorable babies.

But there was a price to pay for love that was stolen.

Chapter 15

Jace opened his eyes to find his worried sister staring at him, almost as if she was looking into his brain through his pupils. "Ash, please take yourself out of my face."

"Oh, Jace!" She flung herself against his chest, and then sat up. "God, I'm sorry! Did I hurt you?"

"No. Of course not. Don't be weird. Where am I?" He glanced around, mystified.

"You're in the hospital," she answered.

"I can see that," he said, feeling a bit crusty. "I mean, where am I? What happened?"

"You're in Diablo," Ash said carefully, as if he was a bit thick, "and you had a small incident. But now you're much better!"

She was too bright and cheerful all of a sudden, when a moment ago she'd been trying to peer inside his skull, her pixie face tight with concern. "So what was this accident?"

"You and I were on the way to the hospital to see the babies and Sawyer. Oh, they're so cute, Jace, so very precious!" His sister perked up considerably. "Little Ashley's going to be just like me when she grows up." Ash leaned close. "I can already tell she has a strong personality. Her aura is very powerful. And I think she may have the wisdom."

He sighed. "How long have I been here?"

She looked confused. "Four days. Don't you want to hear about Jason? And Sawyer?"

Jace sat up. "Yes, I do. And what I also want is out of here. Can you do that for me? Call our brothers for an extract."

Ash shook her head. "I can't do that. The doctors won't release you."

"I'm releasing myself." He went to get out of the bed, was startled by the grogginess that washed over him.

"Whoa, brother." Ash put a hand on his chest, pressing him backward. "Let's not be hasty."

"I want out."

"You don't get everything you want. Don't be a baby."

He snorted. "There's nothing wrong with me. No reason at all why I can't go home."

"You nearly died, Jace. You'll be moved out of ICU today, but I have a feeling it'll be a good few days before you're released."

"What happened?" he asked, disturbed that he couldn't remember.

"You had babies," Ash said. "You and Sawyer had two precious babies. Don't you want to hear about Jason?

Sawyer named him after you, you know. Ashley's my namesake, and—"

"Ash," he said, interrupting her, "I don't want to talk about babies."

"Your babies," she said, and he nodded.

"That's right. I don't want to hear about my babies."

"What's the matter with you?" she demanded. "The babies were practically all you talked about for the past two months."

"Yeah, well. I'm just not ready right now, is all."

Ash blinked. Got up and paced a few steps. Turned to face him. "Sawyer wants to go," she said.

"Probably a good idea."

"You mean that?"

He shrugged. "Yeah. Ash, look. I already know all this. Everything is fine. I saw it in a dream."

"Saw it in a dream? Saw what?"

"Sawyer. The babies. It's all coming back to me now. We were riding the Diablos. Sawyer wasn't—she was watching us from atop a cliff. We were all together. It's fine. I just need to get out of here."

"You and the children were riding, and Sawyer was atop a cliff watching you?" Ash asked curiously, sounding startled.

"Yes. That was the dream." He wasn't certain why his sister looked so strange. It was his dream, nothing that mattered to anyone else.

"But the Diablos haven't been around in months," she murmured.

"I know. I think Wolf's done something to them. I believe the tunnels were a way for the cartel to begin to infiltrate from Loco Diablo—"

"Sister Wind Ranch."

"—to our ranch. That was their plan, to conquer us from below. Really smart plan, too. But Wolf wants the wealth of Rancho Diablo. And the Diablos are the true wealth."

"He doesn't know that," Ash said, her voice full of passion. "Wolf doesn't understand the spirits, or the ways."

Jace considered that. His brain was foggy; every fiber of his body seemed to be drifting. Maybe it was the medication messing with him.

"None of this matters, Jace. What matters is you and Sawyer and your family."

He knew that. Deep inside him, he knew it. But he also knew that the shot that had hit him could just as easily have been intended for Sawyer—or his children. Sawyer had stunned Wolf with her Taser—and Wolf had been looking for revenge, a reminder that he called the shots. Had he ordered that Jace be killed, or just badly wounded? It didn't matter, because whatever the intention, he'd nearly died. If that same shot had been aimed at Sawyer, it might have killed her, and that would devastate him. He wasn't certain he could survive something happening to his wife. Whatever else had gone on between them, Sawyer was the only woman who could ever hold his heart.

Until she left, she wasn't safe—as Wolf's bullet had so plainly indicated.

"Tell Sawyer I want her to leave. Take the babies and go."

"Why? Because you got shot?"

He thought about the dream of riding in the canyons with his children and the Diablos, and Sawyer watching from afar. "We're not meant to be together," he said, knowing he was speaking a certain truth he'd only just realized in his soul. But the facts had been staring at him for a long time; he just hadn't wanted to acknowledge them. "Tell her what you have to, but convince her she has to leave."

"I'm not telling her that," Ash said hotly. "You tell her. Because I think you're crazy. What about my niece and nephew? You're just going to shuttle them off into hiding?"

What else could he do? "You have a better idea?"

Ash glared at him. "No, I don't!"

He heard a commotion outside his room, laughter, some chatting, a few quick whispered words, and Sawyer walked in, a breath of fresh air in his very dark world. "Hi, Ash." She came over, saw that he was awake, and smiled at him. "You're starting to look like your old self. Yesterday you looked like you'd seen better days."

He studied his beautiful wife. His heart ached when he gazed at her, he wanted so badly to hold her, kiss her. But that would just prolong the agony. "You were here yesterday?"

She nodded.

"I don't remember."

Sawyer sat on the edge of the bed. "They're going to put you in a regular room today. You're out of the woods."

"I'm going," Ash said, with another glare for him. "I don't think you're allowed to have multiple visitors, so I'm going to make myself scarce."

"You're never really scarce," Jace said, "so don't go far. I have a job for you."

"I'm not doing it!" she snapped, and disappeared.

Sawyer pushed his hair back from his forehead. "What are you two up to? You're supposed to be resting."

"Says the pot, who's calling the kettle black." He felt himself relaxing, giving in to her ministrations. He'd missed her so much. "Why aren't you in bed?"

"I just came by to see if you wanted to come with me," she teased, kissing him on the lips.

Of course he wanted to go home with her. He wanted that more than anything. "No," Jace said, "I'm not going home with you."

"Keep getting strong, cowboy, and I'll bring you home maybe this week. And then the babies. We'll be a family at last."

He grimaced.

"Are you in pain?" Sawyer asked, immediately concerned.

"No." He was in all kinds of pain, and it wasn't from the bullet they'd had to remove from his lung. His heart felt as if it was on fire. "You need to go."

"I know. But I had to see you." She ran a gentle hand along his face. "I can't wait for you to see the babies. They're amazing. And the nurses have been wonderful."

"Sawyer, you have to go into hiding. With the children."

"I know. Running Bear told me. My heart breaks, Jace. I wanted the babies to grow up with your family, the way you had in the tribe. I wanted them to get to know Fiona and Burke and their aunt and all their wonderful uncles and cousins. But I understand."

She didn't entirely understand what was coming, and he felt his heart turn to stone. "We always knew it wasn't destined to work out."

"What wasn't destined to work out?"

"Us." He shrugged. "It's probably a Cash-Callahan curse kind of thing."

"You can put whatever you're thinking out of your head, Jace Callahan. You married me, and we have two wonderful babies. You're going to be a family with us. So if that's the meds talking, then just close your mouth for now, because I'm not listening."

He wanted to smile at her fire, but the situation was far too serious. "Running Bear's words are wise."

"I agree, but he never said we couldn't be a family."

"This is the right thing to do."

"Separating our family will never be the right thing."

Jace thought Sawyer was beginning to sound doubtful, as if she was starting to think he didn't want to be with her. Somehow he had to make her believe that, to get her and the children out of danger. Sawyer wasn't afraid of anything, and that bravery kept her from recognizing the true danger she and the children were in.

"In fact, Fiona thinks we should remarry, renew our vows at Rancho Diablo." Sawyer bent down to kiss him again. He tried not to lean forward, tried not to lengthen the kiss—but it was oh, so hard, like ripping his heart out not to reach for her. "She wants the magic wedding dress to get an airing for the final Callahan bachelor."

He shook his head. "That's not going to happen."

Sawyer pulled away. "You get strong. In the meantime, I'll go take the children to a safe harbor. But I'll be waiting for you, Jace. And I know you'll come. Because if there's anything I know in my heart, it's that I may have won you, but deep inside, you always wanted it that way. No cowboy chases a woman around and makes love to her under the stars for almost two years and then lets her go. So get over whatever it is you've suddenly decided you're afraid of. Because I'm not afraid at all. I know I belong with you, and our children belong with you, too. We're Callahans."

She left with a swirl of Sawyer energy. Jace closed his eyes. Of course she was right; that was one of the things he loved about Sawyer. She was headstrong, spirit-strong and determined. She was brave and fierce, and he was proud of her. There'd never been a woman more suited for him. Sawyer felt like the other half of his whole world, the better half.

But he had to let her go.

Chapter 16

"This is all my fault," Storm said as he drove her and the children to Hell's Colony, Texas. They planned to stay with the other Callahans for a few nights before she was taken on to a safe house. It was June, and the babies were thriving. Sawyer and the babies had been staying in the duplex, and it had been a fun rodeo of learning to breast-feed and juggle baby needs, as well as heal herself.

She wouldn't have traded it for the world.

What she did wish was different was her husband. He came to help at night, but there was a distance between them now. Jace had gone back to work on the ranch before she'd wanted him to, and though he never spoke about his wound, she was pretty sure it still took a toll on him. He didn't talk much, and slept a lot when he wasn't helping her with the babies.

Jason and Ashley kept them very busy. They could be the happiest babies, but when they fussed, it was like a tornado had ripped through the duplex. Jason fussed if Ashley fussed, and vice versa. Neither of them liked to hear the other cry. The situation was made worse by the fact that Jason had colic. When it flared up at night, his cries kept both parents busy and exhausted. The house was small and close, especially with an unhappy baby, and Ashley got upset when she heard her brother wailing.

Lu said it broke her heart to listen to the babies at night. She and Storm could hear them, from the other side of the duplex. They would have needed walls a lot thicker to keep the sound from carrying.

Somehow, Jace managed to calm the babies eventually, and then the three of them slept, both infants on his chest, wrapped together like pieces of pie dough. Sawyer snapped a photo of the babies with him like that, and she treasured it.

When they did talk, it was a bit painful. Jace was pretty focused on her going to Texas, and then into hiding. He constantly made plans about it. Gradually, she'd quit fighting him, ever cognizant of Running Bear's and Fiona's words. Sawyer told herself it didn't matter anymore—ever since the night he'd gotten shot, Jace had been different around her.

Quiet.

"I should never have involved you in my worries about Wolf and the Callahans," her uncle said, breaking into her thoughts. "I was just so certain Wolf was telling me the truth. I couldn't imagine him making so much stuff up. And of course, everyone knows about the bad blood between them."

"I shouldn't have worn the wire. I think that was the

part that really bothered Jace. He never said it, but the fact that I'd been recording conversations was hard on him."

"You thought you were acting for the law enforcement agencies that were working the case."

"It doesn't matter, anyway. I should have asked him. I just didn't know him well enough then." Yet she'd known him well enough to let him make love to her every time he'd caught up to her—which was often. In the canyons, when she was supposed to be working. On a mesa… Anywhere she was, somehow he seemed to be, too. Eventually, he would appear, and she'd never told him no. She'd wanted him as much as he'd wanted her.

And now he wanted her gone.

"If he hadn't gotten shot, he wouldn't be so spooked," Storm said. "I can understand his position."

"I can, too, and that makes it even harder. He worries about the babies."

"Sure he does. He worries about you, too."

Sawyer sighed. "Jace is an excellent worrier."

"Well, they've been fighting this battle for a long time. I'm confident that no other family could have withstood Wolf and the cartel as long as the Callahans have."

"What will happen, in the end?"

"I think," Storm said heavily, "that the Callahans are outgunned and outmanned. Once the land across the canyons got overrun with smugglers and the like, I knew I'd made a bad mistake buying it from that old man. No wonder he'd been so eager to sell me his spread. I wondered why he was willing to let it go at such a rock-bottom price, but none of the preliminary information I had on that ranch showed any trouble. Who would have ever imagined that there were miles of tunnels under that place?"

"And we were sitting ducks for Wolf's plan," Sawyer said. "He got you to buy the property, and then had you send me to work at Rancho Diablo for information, while the cartel was busy tunneling underneath. The Callahans still don't know how far they've managed to get, or if the tunnels reach under the canyons to Rancho Diablo yet. The Feds say it's like a maze under there. A virtual city of catacombs."

"It creeps me out," Storm said. "I'm very happy staying in the duplex these days. But wherever you end up, Lu and I will probably follow. At least for a while. Lu says she wants to help you with the babies."

"It would mean you'd be in hiding," Sawyer said. "Uncle Storm, I can't let you give up your life and hers that way. But I love you for offering."

"Nah," Storm said. "As Lu says, we have nothing better to do. We'd rather be with family than not. But do you have any idea where you're going?"

"No. I'll find out once I'm in Hell's Colony." She was worried, fearful of being away from family. Away from Jace. He wasn't coming with her, that much was clear. He'd always said he didn't want to live the way his parents had, but she'd never thought he'd desert her and the babies.

Then again, they hadn't had much of a marriage.

She wished she could change that.

"The thing is," Storm said, "Wolf used me."

"We know he did," Sawyer replied. "He used all of us to get to the Callahans. And though I never thought I'd fall for it, I did."

"No, I think his plans ran much deeper. You remember how I told you that a long time ago I'd done some horse trading with Fiona?"

Sawyer nodded, and leaned into the backseat to check on Jason and Ashley. "I remember."

"Well, a couple of weeks before Jace got shot, Wolf came to me and mentioned he had some horses he wanted to sell. Wanted to know where the best place for horse trading was."

Sawyer frowned. "What did you tell him?"

"That I didn't know. It didn't work that way, in my experience. If a man had horses to sell, he talked to other people in the business who might know folks who were looking. But as far as I knew, there was no horse outpost or trading center where mass sales occurred around here. Maybe I'm wrong, but it just isn't the way I'd done things." A gentle rain began to fall as they crossed the Texas state line, and Storm turned on the windshield wipers. "Later, I wondered what horses Wolf was talking about. Was the cartel planning to bring horses up from Mexico to sell here?" He shrugged. "I just didn't know. I never asked, either. By then I knew the less time I spent with Wolf Chacon, the happier I was going to be."

"Horses," Sawyer murmured. "It's so weird. Everyone knows you used to breed and train horses. But Wolf could ask anyone in town where to buy or sell them."

"And where would he be keeping horses, if he was planning to buy or sell them? He has no barn, no training area. As far as I know, he and his men seem to float, live off the land."

Sawyer frowned. "I'll ask Jace if he knows. He'll probably call tonight. Maybe he'll be able to figure out exactly what Wolf was after."

"It just doesn't make sense." Storm glanced her way.

"I know he loves you, Sawyer. You two are just going through a rough patch right now."

Rough didn't begin to describe it. Yet she'd always known there was a heavy price to being a Callahan. "Thank you for taking us to Texas, Uncle Storm."

The sky turned darker as night fell. Soon it was almost pitch-black. "I'm going to need to feed the babies soon."

"I know." He pulled off the highway and headed down a deserted road.

"Where are we going?" Sawyer asked.

"Just keeping away from prying eyes."

"You think we were followed?" Fear jumped into her heart. She couldn't bear it if anything happened to the babies. "Surely we weren't!"

"I don't think so. But it pays to be careful."

He stopped the truck, switching it off.

"You don't have to stop driving." Sawyer looked at her uncle. "I can get in the backseat and feed the babies."

He let out a deep sigh. "Sawyer, I'm not taking you to Texas."

"Why? What are you talking about?"

A truck pulled up behind them.

"This is just the way it has to be. I'm sorry I couldn't tell you, but I was asked not to." He got out of the vehicle.

"Uncle Storm!"

He opened the back door, unstrapped one of the baby carriers and lifted it out.

"What are you doing?" Sawyer jumped from the truck to run around and face her uncle.

"Shh," a voice said next to her, and she whirled.

"Jace!"

"Thanks, Storm," Jace said. "Put the babies in the

back. Sawyer, do you have everything? Anything else I need to get out of the truck?"

"I have everything." She looked at him, shocked to find him there. "What's going on?"

"Get in the truck. Quickly." He shook Storm's hand. "*Vaya con Dios,* Storm. I can't thank you enough."

"No problem. Take care of my little girl." He kissed the top of Sawyer's head, pushed her toward Jace. "Mind your uncle, girl, and get in the truck. I'll see you again one day."

Sawyer hopped into the dark truck, which was exactly like the one Storm was driving. The whole transfer had taken less than sixty seconds—and the next thing she knew, Jace was behind the wheel. He gave her a long, sexy smooch and then a rascally smile, obviously pleased with himself.

"You didn't really think I was letting you go without me, did you?"

He turned the truck down the dirt road. Sawyer glanced back at her uncle, who was driving the opposite way. It looked as if someone was sitting next to him, though she could barely see in the dark. "Yes, I thought you were sending me and the babies off. I didn't know when or if I'd ever see you again." She glared at him. "Why all the secrecy? Couldn't you have given me a little hint? I've cried because of you, you ape!"

"I'm sorry about that. But we had to keep everything very quiet. Storm agreed to help me, and I couldn't endanger him. Even Lu didn't know."

Sawyer took a deep breath. "Never mind. I don't care what rabbits you pulled out of hats to make this happen."

"I have no intention of living without my family."

"You're taking us to Texas?"

"Actually, we're not going to Texas. Storm is going to Hell's Colony. He's the decoy."

"And conveniently, has a body decoy in the front seat." It was all coming together—even the quick switch on the dirt road, the duplicate trucks.

"He'll continue on to Hell's Colony, and then my cousin's going to fly him back in the family jet. By the time Wolf's men figure out we've pulled a switch, you and I and the babies will be long gone."

"Never to be seen again?" Sudden fear made Sawyer's pulse leap. It sounded so scary. "Actual hiding, like your parents? And the Callahans?"

"For now," he said grimly. "We shot Wolf. We're on his short, fast list of enemies."

"*I* shot Wolf. *You* had nothing to do with it." She thought about the past and everything she knew about the Callahans. "I'm not the only sister-in-law who shot your uncle, either. So why has he pursued us so diligently?"

"When Rhein was arrested, he spent some time being interrogated by Sheriff Cartwright. The sheriff learned that Wolf took it particularly hard about the pink Taser. He felt like we weren't taking him seriously. That a little pink toy gun wasn't a respectful way to shoot a man."

"So he would have been happier if I'd used a Sig Sauer 9 mm?"

"Apparently so."

"The egos in your family tree never cease to amaze me," Sawyer murmured. "If it helps, I'm sorry. I shouldn't have shot him, I guess, but he came into my house uninvited, and I'm never going to be the kind of girl who sits helplessly and waits to be rescued."

Jace laughed. "Fine by me. Personally, I admired your approach."

"Except that now you're going into hiding because of me."

"With you, babe. And my children. No worries."

She nodded and looked out the window. There were worries, plenty of them—but Jace was with her now, and their babies had their family.

It was worth shooting ugly old Wolf.

They ended up in a small house in Oklahoma, in a small town so far from anything, Sawyer imagined she could walk for days and not see another soul. If Wolf or his band of weirdos ever tried to find them, they'd have to go out of their way to do it. They were so far out in the country, it was a thirty minute drive for groceries. She'd have to go into "town" to get any mail—not that they got any at the post office, of course. They never would.

Jace was quiet all the time, and she could tell he was thinking about his family, and how he was walking in their footsteps, hiding out from an enemy who never seemed to rest.

There wasn't any way to change it now.

Anyway, she knew Jace hadn't been entirely forthright about why Wolf was in such a killing rage. He'd thought she'd been on his side, that she and Uncle Storm had cheated him. He felt betrayed, and was determined a price would be paid for that betrayal.

Jace rolled over in the bed next to her, reaching to hold her close to him. The babies slept on pallets in the same room. She wasn't certain what they were going to do when Jason and Ashley got a couple months older.

There were no cribs, and no reason to buy any furniture; they weren't sure how long they'd be here. Or anywhere.

For now, the road was their home. They'd be here until a signal was sent, and then they'd move on to the next safe house.

"It's okay," Jace said. "I can feel you thinking about it, but let it go, Sawyer. Nothing matters but the fact that we're safe, we're together."

She snuggled up against him, grateful that he was there, that she wasn't walking this road alone. "I'm glad you're with me."

"That's right," he murmured, nearly asleep. "Tell me I'm your Prince Charming."

"You could say that," she said, kissing him. "It's most likely true."

"I know. But it's more fun when you admit it," he murmured. "Now go to sleep, angel mama."

"If I was an angel, you wouldn't have gotten shot because of me."

"Trust me, you're an angel. It's not your fault my uncle shot me. Wolf's been trying to pick one of us off for a long time. I don't know that him shooting me was payback for the little zap you gave him." Jace kissed her hand. "I do know you're the only woman for me. Now go to sleep."

"Jace?"

"Hmm?"

"When you showed up with your truck, it really did feel like you were my Prince Charming. Fairy-tale ride-off-into-the-sunset and all that. I was so happy to see you."

"Good princes have plans. And I planned on being your Prince Charming."

She giggled, and he held her close, and for the moment, Sawyer felt like the luckiest girl in the world.

In the night, when the babies awakened for their feeding, Jace helped Sawyer diaper them, then rock them back to sleep. These were the moments she'd been missing, had been so afraid might never happen. She loved seeing her big strong husband hold Ashley and Jason.

"You're beautiful," he told her. "There's nothing more beautiful to a man than watching a woman take care of his children."

She smiled. "I was just thinking pretty much the same thing about you. I was so worried we'd never be together."

"Nothing to worry about anymore."

His mobile phone rang, and they looked at each other. "An odd hour for someone to get in touch," Sawyer said. A call at 2:00 a.m. seemed like a bad omen, but she didn't voice her worry aloud.

Jace grabbed his phone off the nightstand. "Ash? What's going on?"

Sawyer put the babies gently back onto their pallets to sleep, and laid blankets over them. She rubbed their backs as Jace went outside to talk.

He came back in, began putting on his boots.

"What's happening?" Sawyer asked fearfully.

"We're going back home."

"To Rancho Diablo? What's happened?"

Jace walked around the room a couple times, stared down at his babies. Looked at Sawyer, seeming undecided. She held her breath, waited.

"Fiona's had a heart attack." His aunt needed him,

needed all of them. "All I know is that right now, we belong at Rancho Diablo."

Family meant strength, and no one had given them more strength than Fiona.

Chapter 17

"I don't want anybody fussing over me," Fiona announced loudly to anyone within earshot, particularly medical personnel, and Jace thought his aunt had never been more stubborn.

"And I especially want to know why you're back here, when you're supposed to be *in hiding*," she said, the last two words directed at him softly, urgently. "What do you not understand about your present circumstances? It wasn't that long ago that you were in this hospital, in worse shape than me."

He sat down next to his aunt, took her hand in his. "Sawyer said family's all that matters. She said I should be here with you."

"Doesn't mean you had to bring her and the children back, too. We went through a lot of planning to get that mission just right." She sniffed. "You don't want to give me any peace in my old age? First you get shot and now you're here."

He knew he shouldn't have brought Sawyer and the babies right back into the jaws of danger. He remembered the knife in the wedding cake, and every other warning Wolf and his men had sent his way. But he couldn't leave Sawyer alone with the babies in an unfamiliar place—and Sawyer had told him if he tried to leave her, she'd follow him back in a taxi and run up such a bill on him he'd be paying for it until the next Christmas ball. Sawyer had also reminded him in no uncertain terms that she'd emptied her bank account to win him, and now that she had him, she wasn't sending him into Wolf's clutches without backup.

Which she considered herself to be.

Jace smiled at Fiona's grumbling and rubbed her hand. "So how's the ticker?"

"Better now that you're here," she said begrudgingly. "Family makes me strong. You are my greatest weakness."

"It's not a weakness," he said fondly. "We'll get you back on your feet, and then you can shoo us off again."

"I don't think it'll work," Fiona said. "Your parents stayed away. I also got my sister, Molly, and Jeremiah safely off. But my luck broke down with you, and I sense you're probably here to stay under my feet for good."

"Could be worse."

"Could be," Fiona said, closing her eyes. "Frankly, I think you took my heart with you and that's why it broke. That's probably the meds talking, though."

"The doctors say you didn't actually have a heart attack, more like a cardiac event that could have been triggered by some of your other meds. Nothing that will keep you off the ranch more than a couple of days. You're strong as an ox, Fiona."

"Stronger," she said, her voice suddenly light and tired, and Jace sat rubbing her fingers until she fell asleep.

Fiona had a point, though. Sawyer and the babies shouldn't be here. The thing was, he was pretty certain if he sent his wife and babies away, he'd end up like Fiona, with a badly broken heart.

Jace walked into the kitchen at Rancho Diablo, astonished to see his sister holding little Ashley and Galen holding Jason. "What are they doing here?" He took his daughter from Ash, who protested, then kissed her namesake on the cheek. "I thought I left my family at the duplex."

"Through the wonders of automation," Galen said, "they ended up here when their mother drove them to the ranch."

"And where is my beautiful wife?" Jace asked.

"Cleaning out the far foreman's bungalow," Ash said. "Don't worry, I sent help with her. But a woman has to put her house together the way she wants it to be, or it never feels like home, you know."

This wasn't good. Jace stared at his sister. "You don't mean the foreman's bungalow near the canyons?"

Ash nodded. "That was the one Sawyer chose. She said she liked the way the sun rose over the canyons there."

It was also closest to Wolf and the tunnels and everything bad Jace didn't want around her and his family. He handed Ashley back to her aunt. "Could you watch them for another thirty minutes? I need to speak to Sawyer."

"Sure. No problem." Ash greedily took her niece back in her arms, and Jace went out the door, jumping in his truck and speeding off to the bungalow like a madman.

He burst into the house, startling Mavis, Corinne and Nadine.

"Mercy!" Corinne exclaimed. "Do that again and we'll all end up in the hospital with Fiona!"

"Very sorry, ladies." He gave them his most apologetic smile and looked around for his wife. "Where's Sawyer?"

"She went back to the main house," Mavis said. "Didn't you pass her?"

He looked around the bungalow, amazed by how fresh and homey everything looked. "You ladies have made this place look better than it ever has."

"Oh, we just helped Sawyer put up curtains and the like," Nadine said. "She called into town for what she wanted, while you were with Fiona."

"Go see the nursery," Corinne said, her tone gleeful. "Sawyer said she'd had a long time to think about how she wanted the nursery to look, and we think it's perfect!"

He went down the hall, his heart sinking. Sawyer didn't understand—they weren't staying here. Once Fiona turned the corner, they'd go back on the road. He shouldn't have brought his wife and the children home, but he'd wanted them with him, couldn't have borne to leave them alone in a strange place where they didn't know anyone, didn't know the town.

Although he knew Sawyer well enough to believe she would have done just fine.

He walked into the nursery, his pulse hitching briefly as he saw Sawyer's dreams for their children expressed in the amazing decor. It looked like a real home, a place where children would be happy and secure in their world.

They would have nothing like this in hiding, and his heart broke a little. For the first time, he understood why his parents had chosen to leave them with Running Bear, among the tribe.

Because they'd wanted this—stability and comfort and continuity—for their children. Tears welled in his eyes as he recognized the full weight of their heartbreak.

He felt as if he stood at an intersection, with each road heading a different way, and he had to choose the right path for his family. Jace looked at the pink and blue painted signs, one reading Ashley and one Jason. He took in the plaid valances that hung over the white cribs, which had pink sheets for Ashley, blue for Jason, with knitted baby blankets to match. A portrait of black mustangs hung on the back wall, along with pictures of the babies and one of him and Sawyer. A photo of all the Chacon Callahans stood on the dresser. Each crib had a mobile with dainty stuffed animals hanging above it: puppies, kittens, giraffes and bunnies that danced when he touched them.

It was a room for babies to start out in, get their footing in life. And suddenly, he realized Sawyer had no plans on going anywhere.

She'd finally found her home.

Sawyer went into the attic at Rancho Diablo, sent by Fiona, because, as Jace's "redoubtable aunt" said, her curiosity was killing her. So Sawyer went, slowly going up the fabled staircase to find the treasured wedding gown she never thought she'd wear.

But Fiona said she'd feel better—enormously better—

if Sawyer tried it on. Sawyer had assured her that she was happily married, and there was no need for her to do so. At which point Fiona had said that only one Callahan bride hadn't tried on the wedding gown, and that was a special occasion upon which no magic was needed.

"But you," she'd told Sawyer over the phone, "could use a giant dose of magical assistance."

So here I am, Sawyer thought. *In the attic where all the magic gets stored for loading up the magic wand when necessary.*

It must be necessary if Fiona's sent me here.

She turned on the light and went to the closet, opening the door slowly. Just as Fiona had instructed, a billowy white bag hung there, the contents of which could only be the Callahan dress of dreams. Sawyer undid the zipper apprehensively, reminding herself that she was married with children, and no magic was needed.

Except that Fiona seemed to think Sawyer could use a sparkly dose of fairy dust. She opened the bag and drew out a lovely gown that seemed to shimmer as she held it against her. In the reflection from the cheval mirror, the dress glowed, inviting her to try it on.

What could it hurt? She'd be making Jace's aunt happy when she most needed to be. "Oh, for heaven's sake," Sawyer mumbled. "It's just a dress, no different than if Fiona had asked me to run down to the store and try on a pair of jeans. She's not asking that much."

So she pulled off her clothes and stepped into the dress, drawing the twinkling bodice up, sliding her arms through the lovely lace sleeves.

The gown seemed to zip itself up, encasing her in a magical whisper of fairy-tale romance.

She'd never felt so beautiful, so at peace within herself. So Callahan.

Somehow she felt all the misgivings and worries slide away, never to return.

Jace walked in, put his hands on her waist. "You look beautiful, babe, but you always are to me."

She smiled. She'd expected the vision; all the Callahan brides talked about them. Those were just tales they told each other, surely. Still, she felt Jace's warmth and the strength of his hands holding her, and was amazed by how real the vision seemed.

"As beautiful as you are right now," he said, kissing her shoulder, "I never thought you were more beautiful than when you had our children."

"Jace," she murmured, touched.

"It's true. I'd always heard motherhood made a woman glow with inner beauty, but I fell in love with you even more the day I saw you pregnant. Which was the first day you came back." He turned her and kissed her gently. Sawyer was shocked by how a vision could smell as delicious as her husband did in her arms, feel the way her husband felt when he held her. If this was a dream, she needed to wake up soon, or she was going to end up like the other Callahan brides, chattering and giggling over her own special "vision."

"The best part is we're together forever," Jace said. "I knew that when I saw the nursery at the bungalow. You're not hitting the road. You're not going into hiding."

"No," Sawyer murmured. "I belong here, just as much as you do."

He smiled, sexy and handsome. "I've waited a long time to hear you say that, babe."

"It's true. Wherever you are, that's my home. I love you, Jace."

Happiness lit his eyes, and Sawyer expected him to disappear, to evanesce with the fading light that was streaming in the windows. But he stayed strong in her arms, holding her, his touch warm and strong. And magical.

Because it was magic. And no matter how hard the road had been, no matter how hard it would be in the future, they were together.

Forever.

"Can I help you out of this gown before it disappears?" Jace asked, kissing her again. "I've heard a rumor that it vanishes when the fancy takes it."

Sawyer smiled. "I think that's just a fairy tale, a Fiona legend."

And maybe it was a legend. It didn't matter. All that mattered was that she had her Callahan.

And wasn't that the stuff of dreams?

"Disappear, husband, so I can change," she said, and Jace grinned.

"I'd offer to help, but I know you'd like to be alone to enjoy the bibbidi-bobbidi-boo awhile longer." He kissed her again and headed down the attic stairs, and Sawyer turned back to the mirror, hardly able to believe the enchanting loveliness of the fabulous wedding dress.

To her surprise, the gown suddenly tightened, warmed a bit, then felt as if it was falling away. Sawyer stared at her image in the cheval mirror, absolutely stunned when the gown evanesced and reshaped itself into an entirely new garment.

She was wearing black leggings and a bulletproof vest, with a black, long-sleeved T-shirt overtop.

And that's when she knew the fairy-tale happy ending wasn't yet hers.

Chapter 18

Reality brought Jace crashing to earth the next day when he paid a visit to Wolf. Jace didn't tell Sawyer when he left. He knew she would either send a team along or insist on coming with him herself. Probably would have ripped up the magic wedding dress and burned it in a blazing bonfire in the canyons if he'd tried to leave her behind.

After seeing his wife wearing the splendid dress, he fully intended to allow her the magical moment of which all Callahan brides dreamed. He wouldn't take that from her.

But first things first, and he had a bullet and a scarred lung to thank Wolf for—not to mention a warning to deliver, since Sawyer was absolutely determined to stay at Rancho Diablo with him and the babies. She said he was a family man, and that was what she loved most about him, and that he wouldn't be happy living out of duffel bags and backpacks. That he was more the soccer coach and ballet recital kind of dad.

He loved her all the more for knowing him as well as she did.

"Wolf Chacon!" he yelled when he got to the stone and fire ring. Many moons ago Running Bear had brought all the siblings here to meet their Callahan cousins. He'd told them this was their home now, that they would hold Rancho Diablo in their hearts. Their parents' mission had become theirs.

This was the perfect place to face his uncle. Jace figured that as soon as he'd left the ranch and ridden toward the canyons, his progress had been marked.

When his uncle appeared at the fire ring, Jace knew he'd been right.

"You want to see me?" Wolf demanded.

"Damn right I do."

"Come for another bullet, nephew?"

Jace smiled grimly. "Where are your bodyguards? The minions who put knives in wedding cakes and do all your dirty work?"

Wolf laughed. "Don't worry. They're never far away."

Jace thought about the secret passage in Rancho Diablo's kitchen he'd never known about, the missing Diablos and the silver treasure, which was supposedly hidden on the ranch. He thought about the kindness and gentleness of the people of the town of Diablo, who were always willing to help, and he thought about his family, every last one of them committed to the heartbeat of Rancho Diablo.

"You really don't understand, do you?" Jace said. "You can't ever win, Wolf. You can't possess Rancho

Diablo. It's a *spirit,* a spirit wind that can't be held by anyone."

"You've been listening to Running Bear's nonsense far too long. Trust me, land is easily held. I won't have any problem doing it."

"You will," Jace said. "You will because you don't understand the land. To you it's a thing that can be bought and sold, drained of its resources and life."

"It's called making money, son. If you hadn't fallen for Running Bear's fairy tales, you'd be making money instead of working for your cousins for nothing."

Jace frowned. "You can't understand the calling of the spirit."

"Blah, blah, blah." Wolf laughed, pulled his black cowboy hat down over his eyes. "I understand the calling of money. Cash is king. If you were a smarter man, you'd learn that lesson. And that wife of yours—"

"Tread carefully," Jace warned.

"That wife of yours is just like her uncle, always trying to do the right thing. Gets folks in trouble every time. You see, when you believe that people are inherently good, you fail to understand their dark side. Everyone has a dark side, Jace. Sawyer hasn't seen yours. But it's there. Eventually, it will trip you up."

Jace's skin chilled despite the hot sun. "And then what? You think we'll join your cause?"

Wolf shrugged. "Either that or I'll just keep picking you off, one by one. Or two by two, in your case, right? You have two little babies by that sweet bodyguard wife—"

Jace's fist slammed into Wolf's jaw so fast he didn't see it coming. Wolf lay crumpled by the fire, stunned for a moment, before he got to his feet.

"You shouldn't have done that."

Jace shrugged. "Whatever trouble you have with me, you stay away from my wife."

"Everyone has a dark side, and she's shown hers," Wolf said, rubbing his jaw. "She's fair game now."

It was too easy. Jace could kill his uncle right here, and no one could stop him. Wolf didn't think he'd do it; that's why he'd come alone. He knew quite well that Running Bear had said none of the Callahans were to harm their uncle.

But Wolf was right: Jace did have a dark side.

And killing Wolf would be so sweet.

"Where have you been?" Sawyer asked anxiously when he walked inside the bunkhouse.

"Out checking on a few things. Everything good?" He glanced at the babies, snug in the laps of Ash and of Fiona. Recently released from the hospital, Fiona moved more slowly now, and complained that they were making her sit around too much for no reason at all. Ash stayed very close to her, so close that only Burke ever really got any time with his wife without Ash hanging around.

"Everything's fine." Sawyer put on a hat and her boots while he watched her suspiciously. He looked at the tight black leggings and long-sleeved T-shirt she wore—pretty warm stuff for weather that was as hot as a pistol outside. Not to mention that she looked as if she was on her way to a raid.

"Are we supposed to be going somewhere?" Jace asked.

"You're going shopping for the grand wedding I'm throwing," Fiona said, beaming. "You realize I got up off my deathbed for your marriage, which will be the event of the year."

Sawyer glanced at him. "She's very excited about us saying our vows again."

Now that sounded better. For a moment, his wife's serious face had puzzled him; he thought he'd forgotten something important. "Shopping it is." He looked at Sawyer's clothes a bit doubtfully, thinking his wife really looked more like she was in recon mode than shopping mode. "I really don't like you to be out long. You should still be resting." He kissed both his babies on their small downy heads.

"Yes, but you don't like me to be out without you, either, so I have to wait for you to bring your muscles home. And you were gone longer than I expected," Sawyer said, glancing out the window, though he wasn't sure what she was looking for. "So now we have to hurry. The sun will go down in about an hour."

What the sun's positioning had to do with wedding preparations, he couldn't have said, but he kissed his babies again, kissed his aunt, tugged his sister's platinum ponytail and took his wife's hand to lead her out the door. "We'll be back in a bit," he told his family. "Wedding stuff should be a piece of cake."

Ash laughed. "Keep thinking that, brother."

Sawyer hurried to the truck. She hopped in and buckled her seat belt. "We're making a detour to the house you bought from my uncle."

That wasn't so strange, he supposed. Though the Callahan conglomerate now owned Storm's ranch, maybe she wanted to return for sentimental reasons. He backed up the truck. "I thought we were going to do fantasy bride stuff?"

She shook her head. "You can call this fantasy bride stuff if you want to. Just hurry. We don't have much time, because if we don't get to the stores to pick out the stuff Fiona wants us to, she'll know we didn't go. But we have a very small errand to run first."

"I guess all wisdom will be revealed to me in due time," Jace said, heading for Storm's old ranch. The place was probably thick with Feds, and cartel thugs, too, since it was practically deserted these days. He wanted no part of his family being over here until the ranch was cleaned up.

Storm had been right to move away.

Sometimes Jace thought Ash was right, and that they should dynamite the land across the canyons, cover it over with concrete and turn it into Callahan Rodeo Land, to flush out the bad guys.

"Speaking of fantasy bride stuff, you sure did look like an angel in Fiona's magic rag."

Sawyer gasped. "You can't call it that! Your aunt would be appalled if she thought you were making fun of the magic. And anyway, you aren't supposed to see me wearing the gown before the big day. I'm pretending you didn't, and that you were just my special Callahan vision."

He laughed. "It was very good luck for me. In fact, it was all I could do not to make that fairy-tale frock disappear from your goddesslike body and make princely love to you."

"Every Callahan bride has supposedly seen the man of her dreams when she's worn the gown."

"You did see me. Only it was even better, because I was there in the flesh." He reached for her hand, raised it to his lips, kissed her fingers. "You can't believe everything my aunt tells you. Most of it's wonderfully childlike, romantic tales, to get us to do what she wants us to do."

"What she believes is best for you," Sawyer amended. "Her track record is pretty amazing so far."

"I know. So what's this we're going to see?"

"Remember when Ash commandeered the treasure-hunting equipment from the trespasser?"

"Oh, yeah. I forgot all about that." Jace laughed out loud. "My sister has nerves of steel. Did the guy come wanting his equipment back?"

"No, surprisingly. And that got my curiosity up. Remember how Uncle Storm got used by Wolf to buy this ranch, so Wolf could get access to the land through him? Obviously, Wolf didn't want to buy it. He doesn't have the resources, and the land he really wants is Rancho Diablo. Which he wanted access to."

"Through your uncle's land, and this land." Jace parked the truck. "I'm with you so far."

"I was thinking about why he wanted my uncle to help him so much, and then got so mad at me when he felt I'd betrayed him. And I thought it was odd that the man from whom Ash took the equipment never made a stink about it. Plus I remembered Uncle Storm telling me that Wolf was always asking him a lot of questions about selling horses, buying horses, etc."

Jace followed his wife as she pulled the metal detector from the back of the truck. "I don't know if it's a good idea for you to have that out here. Wolf's thugs have eyes on everything."

"It's okay. I don't really care." She took off at a good clip across the ranch, carrying the equipment.

She was scaring hell out of him. A tingle hit him,

a sense of karma colliding—and suddenly, he remembered the dream he'd had in the hospital, which had seemed so much like a vision. He and Sawyer had been here—only she'd been atop a mesa, and he'd been far away, riding a Diablo. It was an impossible dream, because the Diablos hadn't been seen or heard in a long time—but a sudden premonition told Jace there was danger here. He followed Sawyer quickly, glad he was armed, wishing he had backup.

Once Sawyer reached a particular destination—he happened to know that it was near the cave Galen had been held in some months ago, but didn't want to say so to Sawyer, because with his luck, she'd decide to go spelunking—she stopped and looked toward Rancho Diablo. "It's beautiful, no matter where you stand to look at it."

He eyed the seven chimneys of the main house, rising in the distance. "It is."

"If you stood here and looked at that long enough, you might wish you lived there."

"I do live there."

She ignored his lame attempt at humor. "One day I'm going to take our babies riding on this land," Sawyer said, "and it's going to be free and safe."

He hoped she was right, yet his scalp prickled all the same. "Let me carry this thing. It's too heavy for you." He took the metal detector from her, still not sure why they needed it, but not about to interrupt his wife when she was on a mission. Everyone had a holy grail, and if this was hers, far be it from him to throw a wrench in the works. He glanced around, made certain they weren't being followed as she strode toward the canyons.

When Sawyer stopped at the edge, looking over, he gulped. "Please don't do what I think you're going to do."

"That's where the Diablos run," she whispered. "This is the yellow brick road."

"Yes, but we haven't seen them in months."

"I know." She looked across the canyons at the burned-out farmhouse, then turned back to stare at Rancho Diablo. "If you had always lived there, and looked across these canyons, you might have wished life had gone differently for you."

"Maybe, but Rancho Diablo's been built up over many years. Three, four decades?"

"And all those years, that farmer watched. And you know who else watched?"

"Wolf," Jace said.

"That's right. The man who lived in that house was a friend of Wolf's. All those years, he was a spy for him, until Wolf was ready to put his plan into action."

"How do you know all this?" Jace's heart began an uncomfortable thumping.

"Because I asked him. I looked at the property deed at the county courthouse and found the gentleman's name, and after I got out of the hospital and had time to think things through, I went and asked him everything I wanted to know. When you were shot, I knew we hadn't heard the whole story, and I knew someone else had to have pieces of it."

Jace swallowed hard. "You were supposed to be resting."

"And you were supposed to stay alive so you could be my husband," Sawyer told him. "I knew it wasn't my uncle who'd given up information. He didn't know anything. So someone had been feeding information to

Wolf. The only person who could have kept a closer eye on things than my uncle was the man who owned that land over there. And that's exactly what happened. He was quite willing to tell me everything, because Wolf reneged on his promise of land and Rancho Diablo silver."

"Still, why are we standing out here with Ash's nefariously acquired equipment?"

"Because," Sawyer said, "we both know the silver is important, but it's not the ranch's most prized possession. Life according to Running Bear states that the most important part of the ranch is the spirit. The *spirits*. And that's what your uncle simply can't get through his thick skull."

"I just love how your mind works," Jace said admiringly. "All this time I thought you were just a gorgeous face, a redhead with a body to drive me mad."

"You thought nothing of the sort."

"I swear I did."

"Good. Hang on for the ride, cowboy. I'm about to drive you really mad."

And with that, she disappeared off the side of the canyon. Jace cursed, looked over the edge, knew that the only woman he could ever love had figured out there was a stairway of rocks leading downward.

Which meant she'd been hanging around over here by herself, with no Callahan protection, because she was determined to clear her uncle's name—and hers.

She still didn't accept that she was a true Callahan.

"We're going to fix that," he muttered, checking his gun. "And somehow I don't think we're going wedding shopping today."

So he followed her.

Chapter 19

It seemed they'd walked for miles in a tunnel Sawyer had found. Jace didn't even want to think about the fact that his wife was basically charting unknown territory in a recently dug maze leading from Storm's ranch to a point unknown.

"I should send you home," Jace said. "You're taking ten years off my life."

"Shh," Sawyer said over her shoulder. She'd pulled a flashlight from a holster he hadn't realized she was wearing, and shone it in front of them. "Walls have ears, they say."

It was definitely true at Rancho Diablo, but he wasn't sure if these dirt-packed walls had any listening devices. "So when you were supposed to be home resting and taking care of our children, you were playing detective?"

"I am a bodyguard," she reminded him. "Just because

we had children doesn't mean I stopped trying to protect the family."

"Remember when we had that discussion about you being a stay-at-home mom?"

"And you volunteered to be Mr. Mom? Hold this." She handed him the flashlight, bent down to put her ear against the dirt floor.

"I don't think it's going to work," Jace said. "I can't stay at home with the kids and keep an eye on you, too."

"This is the easy part. Learning to breast-feed was much harder. Rewarding, but harder."

"What are we looking for? I sense you aren't playing underground Miss Marple just for fun. We lugged this treasure-hunting device with us for a reason."

"I'm not sure what I'm looking for. It just seemed like a good thing to have, since someone was on the property using it. For all I know, Wolf's found the fabled Callahan silver treasure." She rose, pushed on a cave wall. Something moved slightly, and he helped her push, and a crude door opened.

And there, fenced off from the canyons they so loved, were the black Diablo mustangs. A lone silver mare was enclosed in a pen, and several stallions had tried to kick their way to her. There were bloody marks along the pen walls and the fencing that blocked them from the canyons. The stallions stayed close to the mare—a trap to keep them from trying to escape. The Diablos were hidden away from the sun and the wind and the independence they loved.

"Oh, no," Sawyer murmured under her breath, and before Jace could stop her, she was in the middle of the herd, little more than her red hair visible among the black horses. He threw down the metal detector and followed her, his gun at the ready.

Suddenly, as if someone had shouted "Freedom!" the Diablos surged past him. They bolted for the wide-open spaces beyond the mouth of the tunnel as Sawyer held open a heavy wooden gate. A few stallions stayed tight to the pen of the silver mare, but after a moment, even they gave in to the desire for liberty. Soon the underground corral was empty.

"Come on!" Jace muttered to Sawyer. "As soon as those mustangs hit the canyons, Wolf's going to know we freed his stolen treasure."

"Just a minute." She approached the silver mare, which was looking patiently over the pen wall at her. "Come on, girl."

"Sawyer," Jace said, "we don't have time. We're on stolen time, in fact."

"Don't leave the metal detector behind. Ash will want her equipment back." Sawyer swung up on the silver mare and he opened the pen. "See you at home, husband."

"You're not going without me. I'm riding shotgun this time," he said, grabbing the metal detector and whistling at the cave entrance. A lone mustang stallion danced nearby, nervous, ready to run, and Jace swung up on its back. "Head for home and don't look back for any reason at all."

They shot out of the underground maze and tore across the land toward Rancho Diablo. Jace glanced behind them to see if they were being followed. *Not yet, not yet.*

He heard hooves behind him. "Go!" he yelled at Sawyer, glancing over his shoulder again. Running Bear rode a hundred lengths back, before wheeling his horse to protect their departure. Jace rode hard to cover Sawyer, praying that she'd make it at least to the perimeter of Rancho Diablo. A moment later, the sight of his five brothers and Ash galloping toward them nearly stopped his heart.

It was going to be all right.

In fact, it was going to be even better than all right.

He and Sawyer were finally home.

"Just so you know, you nearly gave me heart failure," Ash said to Jace as she stood beside him two days later at the altar. He'd chosen Ash to be his best man because she simply was—and Sawyer had agreed, saying Ash could also be her maid of honor. If anyone could handle both honorary duties, it was her sister-in-law.

Ash had spied the Diablos running in the canyons, and from her perch on the bunkhouse roof, she could see that the horses were wild with some kind of pent-up panic. She'd told her brothers that something was wrong, that the mysticism felt weak and somehow almost invisible, and they'd instantly ridden for the canyons.

Jace had never been so glad to see his family in his life. At that moment, as he'd spotted them riding to the rescue, he'd known Sawyer would make it home. With Running Bear at their back, they stood a chance.

Somehow, incredibly, Wolf's men never even put up a fight. Which was a warning in and of itself: Wolf had never suspected that they would find the underground corral that shut the Diablos away from the canyons they called home. He'd planned to sell them over the border, no doubt, which was why he'd asked Storm the questions about horse trading, and why he'd wanted Storm's ranch available to him to hide the Diablos—except that Storm had sold the ranch to the Callahans, thus dashing Wolf's hopes to make a huge fortune.

"You only think you nearly had heart failure, Ash. It

was my wife who…never mind. I can't think about it." He swallowed hard, still shocked by what Sawyer had done. She was a Callahan bride for sure.

"You definitely married the right woman." Ash giggled. "I believe of all my brothers, you won the prize. Kind of funny, isn't it, since she had to buy you at Fiona's Christmas auction just to get a date with you?"

He smiled. "I'm a fortunate man."

And it was a perfect day to marry a woman who had completely stolen his heart. Fiona and Company had decorated the ranch splendidly, with satin bows, and torches ready to be lit at nightfall, when the party would begin. White lights twinkled like stars along the corrals, where more bows topped every post. He didn't think the ranch had ever looked more magical.

But then Sawyer came down the aisle on her uncle's arm, with Storm beaming from ear to ear, and Jace's own grin felt as if it stretched a mile wild. His bride wore the magic wedding dress, which looked totally different than it had the other day. The gown was white and simple, elegant with lace sleeves and a long train, and two Callahan nieces tossed pink petals before Sawyer as she walked toward him.

He was the luckiest man in the world.

"You're beautiful," he told Sawyer when she came to stand beside him. "The magic wedding dress is perfect on you." He didn't know about Fiona's tale of magic, but his wife was so lovely, so breathtakingly sexy, that he couldn't wait to hold her in his arms as soon as possible.

She smiled. "It's more magical than you'll ever know. I have a little story to tell you one day about this dress, and how it led us to the Diablos."

"We'll have many years for you to tell me this fairy tale, and I look forward to hearing every word."

"It's my own chapter for the Callahan books. By the way, I definitely got the sexiest bridegroom on the planet. I might even say I won my sexy groom."

"You've definitely won my heart." He couldn't wait for the vows to be said, so he kissed her, feeling that special magic zip between them. "This is the happiest day of my life, besides the day our children were born," he told her softly. "I love you so much, Sawyer."

"I love you, too," Sawyer replied, and Jace knew he was the happiest man in New Mexico.

They said the vows, and Sawyer's eyes sparkled as he slipped the wedding ring on her finger. She did the same for him, and Jace thought hearing the deacon pronounce them man and wife was the moment he'd waited for all his life. Colorful paper hearts floated on the air as their friends and family celebrated. The babies were handed to them so he could hold Ashley, while Sawyer held Jason. And that's the way their wedding photos looked: one big happy family in a wonderful place called Rancho Diablo.

The sound of hooves thundering through the canyons filtered to them on the summer breeze. Jace smiled at Sawyer, the woman who'd made everything possible for him. He was finally the family man he'd always wanted to be.

And it was more magical than he could have ever imagined. It was enchanting, a miracle.

Best of all, it was family. His family.

Forever.

* * * * *

**IF YOU ENJOYED THIS BOOK
WE THINK YOU WILL ALSO LOVE**

◈ **HARLEQUIN**

**SPECIAL
EDITION**

Believe in love. Overcome obstacles. Find happiness.

Relate to finding comfort and strength in the
support of loved ones and enjoy the journey
no matter what life throws your way.

6 NEW BOOKS AVAILABLE EVERY MONTH!

Adam and Wes looked at each other and Adam felt like
Wes could see right through him.

"You don't have to," Adam said. "I just… I accidentally
promised Gus the biggest Christmas light display in the
world and, uh…"

Every time he said it out loud, it sounded more
unrealistic than the last.

Wes raised an eyebrow but said nothing. He kept
looking at Adam like there was a mystery he was trying
to solve.

"Wes!" Gus' voice sounded more distant. "Can I touch
this snake?"

"Oh god, I'm sorry," Adam said. Then the words
registered, and panic ripped through him. "Wait, snake?"

"She's not poisonous. Don't worry."

Love Harlequin romance?

DISCOVER.

Be the first to find out about promotions, news and exclusive content!

Facebook.com/HarlequinBooks

Twitter.com/HarlequinBooks

Instagram.com/HarlequinBooks

Pinterest.com/HarlequinBooks

YouTube.com/HarlequinBooks

ReaderService.com

EXPLORE.

Sign up for the Harlequin e-newsletter and download a free book from any series at **TryHarlequin.com**

CONNECT.

Join our Harlequin community to share your thoughts and connect with other romance readers!
Facebook.com/groups/HarlequinConnection

That was actually not what Adam's reaction had been in response to, but he made himself nod calmly.

"Good, good."

"Are you coming in, or…?"

"Oh, nah, I'll just wait here," Adam said extremely casually. "Don't mind me. Yep. Fresh air. I'll just… Uh-huh, here's great."

Wes smiled for the first time and it was like nothing Adam had ever seen.

His face lit with tender humor, eyes crinkling at the corners and full lips parting to reveal charmingly crooked teeth. Damn, he was beautiful.

"Wes, Wes!" Gus ran up behind him and skidded to a halt inches before she would've slammed into him. "Can I?"

"You can touch her while I get the ladder," Wes said.

Gus turned to Adam.

"Daddy, do you wanna touch the snake? She's so cool."

Adam's skin crawled.

"Nope, you go ahead."

Don't miss
The Lights on Knockbridge Lane
by Roan Parrish, available October 2021 wherever Harlequin Special Edition books and ebooks are sold.

Harlequin.com